He'd already killed once, but he couldn't believe he had done it again…

Appraising the damage to his Honda, Pike noted a spider web crack in the windshield and one busted headlight. He tried remembering what his deductible was then hoped Cynthia hadn't canceled his car insurance out of spite.

He spotted Roxy thirty yards south, squatting alongside the carcass of the dead animal. The way she huddled over the lifeless creature indicated she was a caring soul, an animal lover.

Pike never had pets. Not as a child, nor an adult. He occasionally considered getting a dog, but despite years of loyalty and unconditional love, pets always died. And Pike didn't handle death well.

Thanatophobia.

He approached Roxy and the lifeless coyote.

Twenty-five yards away, his pace slowed.

Twenty, a fist reached into his chest and ripped his heart out.

Ten, his legs wouldn't move forward.

Roxy ran to him. Her voice cracked but her words were crushing. "You killed him."

Pike couldn't pull his eyes from the *coyote.* Only it wasn't a coyote.

"You killed a kid, Pike."

Again.

To find yourself, you must be lost.

Pike Graves, a former boxer who suffers thanatophobia—fear of death—has done everything right. Degree from an Ivy League university, respectable job with a reputable newspaper, and always helping others. He wakes up one day to find himself middle-aged with nothing to show for a forgettable and unexciting existence.

He hasn't been living his life. Instead, his life has been living him.

With nothing and no one, regimented Pike sheds his skin and sets out on a cross-county pilgrimage to reconnect with a long-lost love from high school, Paige Rhodes, the one he believes is his destiny. She's his last chance at salvation.

To have a future, he must revisit his past.

Back home, his ex-girlfriend learns she's listed as beneficiary on one of his accounts. She stands to inherit a fortune if he's killed and promptly enlists the help of a past lover to hunt him down, thereby setting in motion a coast-to-coast pursuit.

As Pike tries to find himself, someone is trying to find him.

Pike learns life is not black and white but rather a gray mosaic. He uncovers truths about himself and his family. Nothing is as he remembers. Nothing is as it seems. The former boxer discovers that oftentimes the most painful blows in life are not the physical ones.

You can win…but still lose.

KUDOS for *Punching at Fog*

In *Punching at Fog* by Rob Silverman, Pike Graves suffers from thanatophobia, fear of death. Even though he has done everything right—from the right schools, to the right job, always helping others—he is now middle-aged and unhappy. He loses his job and finds out his girlfriend is unfaithful and stealing from him, and he decides to go find the one that got away. The journey is long and fraught with peril from mysterious hitchhikers to runaway teens, to deranged muggers. Through it all, unbeknownst to him, he is being chased by an assassin. Can he make to California to reconnect with his lost love, or will he die on the way? Intriguing, fascinating, and unpredictable, this one will hold your interest from the first page to the last. ~ *Taylor Jones, The Review Team of Taylor Jones & Regan Murphy*

Punching at Fog by Rob Silverman is the story of Pike Graves, a middle-aged "failure." Although Pike has a degree from an Ivy League school, a good job with a respectable newspaper, and a long-time live-in girlfriend, he is unhappy and feels as if he has accomplished nothing in his forty-seven years. Then suddenly his life is turned upside down. He loses his job and discovers that his girlfriend has not only been stealing from him, she has been unfaithful. Disgusted and infuriated, Pike packs his car and takes off for a cross-country road trip, heading to California to get back the girl that got away. It's a journey that will change his life forever. *Punching at Fog* is both fascinating and poignant. I never knew what would happen next, or what strange new character would come into play, and I found it very hard to put down. ~ *Regan Murphy, The Review Team of Taylor Jones & Regan Murphy*

ACKNOWLEDGMENTS

I've always believed life is about the journey and the people we meet along the way. This is something my protagonist, Pike Graves, learns and something I rediscovered writing *Punching at Fog*. Certain individuals cross our path for a reason, and I am indebted and grateful to all of you.

First, I'd like to thank the following for your support, friendship and taking the time to help spread the word about my previous novels, *Plain God* and *Sacrificing the Pawn*:

Georgia Goodwin Stephens, Red Bradley Lapitan, Denice Duffin, Kristy Micak, Kurt Smith, Brian Needleman, Delena Richardson, Nanette Toner, Laura Gualtieri, Gina Schreur, Cindy Traisi, and Barb Blutt.

Extra thanks to Shari Maurer who took time out of her hectic schedule and went above and beyond.

I'd especially like thank Laurie Zodkoy Fox, Brian Wright, Amy Feiner, and Janice Fish for the friendship, for always having my back, for lifting me up and for putting up with me all these years. I love you guys.

Lastly, Faith, Arwen, Lauri, Jack, and the entire staff at Black Opal Books for your help, assistance, and especially your patience. You guys rock!

PUNCHING AT FOG

Rob Silverman

A Black Opal Books Publication

GENRE: THRILLER/SUSPENSE

PUNCHING AT FOG
Copyright © 2019 by Rob Silverman
Cover Design by Rob Silverman
All cover art copyright © 2019
All Rights Reserved
Print ISBN: 9781644371275

First Publication: APRIL 2019

Published by Black Opal Books **http://www.blackopalbooks.com**

DEDICATION

My mom never stopped believing in me through all the times I battled self-doubt like all writers.

No one could tell a story like my dad. No one. I like to think I inherited some of that. I miss him every day.

This book is for them.

"For every moment of triumph, for every instance of beauty, many souls must be trampled."

~ Hunter S. Thompson

PROLOGUE

Thirty years ago:

Since his first breath, he sensed the icy grip of death clawing at his back. And tonight, it had finally come for him.

Moments after Pike Graves entered this life three weeks premature, screaming, and crying and covered in blood, a sibling followed. The fraternal brother didn't live through the night. Pike obviously had no recollection of this. His father, however, had no qualms about reminding him. Constantly.

"You lived, your brother didn't."

Haunted by a memory of something he couldn't remember.

His earliest recollection was seeing Mom in tears. Sobbing hysterically, she dissolved before his eyes, crumbling to the floor and pulling the phone from the kitchen counter where it exploded against cheap linoleum. It was the only time he saw the woman cry.

Grandma, the squat, pudgy woman who smelled funny and surreptitiously passed candy from her papery arthritic fingers into Pike's small hand, had keeled over of a heart attack in Toys R Us.

"She was buying *you* a birthday gift," Pike's father declared. Repeatedly.

Five-years-old, Pike was surrounded by somber-looking men and grief-stricken women. Dressed in black, dabbing their eyes, listening reverentially to a bespectacled man with a white collar. Amidst fierce merciless winds and a biting winter chill that penetrated to the bone, a bronze casket containing Grandpa was lowered into the earth.

Pike shifted on his father's lap, wrapped his little arms around the man's beefy neck. "Don't cry, Daddy."

At eight, he and his friends were playing stickball in a makeshift field between two tenements when Eddie Mullins went down rounding second base and began flopping around like a fish on dry land. Eddie was such a prankster. The boys ran over and laughed. Pike prodded him with the toe of his Keds. "Get up, dip-shit." This was when Pike first heard the term Grand Mal Seizure.

Now at seventeen, Death had returned.

First Saturday after graduation, he and his best friend had their dreams intact. Pike would write the great American novel and Dewayne would become a cop. But that was down the road. To-night was for browsing albums at Tower, racing kids in De-wayne's souped-up Mustang, and whistling at cute girls.

Decreasing the volume on Michael Jackson's "Dirty Diana," Dewayne announced, "Dude, we should cruise by Grizzly's."

Pike gave his buddy a pitiful look. "She's not working to-night."

"How do you know?" Dewayne considered that then asked accusatorily, "Yeah, how *do* you know?"

"It's our first weekend of freedom, man. I'm sure she's off." Leaning forward, Pike searched for a different song. "Besides, like *you* have a shot?"

"And *you* do?"

Pike busied himself with the radio. "She's not my type."

"Gimme a break!" Dewayne hooted. Pulling a pack of Marl-boro's from the dashboard, he tapped one out and flung the empty box out the window. Pushing the cigarette lighter, he expressed his disbelief. "Molly Ringwald lips, Demi Moore eyes, and Heather Locklear's bod. And she's not your type?"

Finding Van Halen's "Why Can't This Be Love" Pike leaned back. "You have no shot with Lisa Dufresne."

"No chick can resist the D-man's charm."

"You guys spent four years together in high school. She doesn't even know you exist, *D-man*."

Tramping the gas and running a yellow light, Dewayne took a drag and rolled things around in his mind. "You think I have no chance 'cause Lisa's white and I'm black?"

"I think you have no chance 'cause she's hot and you're you."

"Maybe she'd like ridin' the chocolate D-train."

Pike laughed. At a red light, he added gently, "Just don't wan-na see you get hurt."

Dewayne grumbled. "Pike Graves, always protecting every-one."

When Dewayne unexpectedly jerked the wheel right and floored it, Pike nearly ended up in his friend's lap. The Mustang tore down a side street and bottomed out, rocketing into a parking lot. Slowing to a crawl parallel to the expansive front window of Grizzly's, he asked "You see her?"

Pike scooted lower. "Jesus!"

Curling his lips, Dewayne muttered, "You're right."

"I am?"

"She doesn't know me." He parked on the mini-mart's south side. "But she knows you. You had classes together."

"Hell, no. I'm not playing Goose to your Maverick."

"Dude, just go in, see if she's there."

"She's not working. Did you see her? I didn't."

"Maybe she's in the storeroom."

"No."

"Pike, you owe me."

"For what?"

"Who got you through Berkman's Criminal Justice class? Me."

"Who let you copy off him for Palmer's English final? Me. We're even."

Dewayne ruminated. "Okay, look. You're the one with the fake ID and I need cigarettes. Go in, ask the old guy where Lisa's at."

Pike exhaled. "You're not going to drop this, are you?"

Dewayne opened his palms. "It's Lisa Dufresne."

Grabbing the proffered bills, Pike smirked. "You're a dick."

The weary fifty-something clerk lifted his large mass from the small stool and suspiciously eyed the teenager.

Offering his friendliest smile, Pike asked, "Lisa's not working tonight, right?"

"No."

"That's what I figured." He vacillated. The diligent cashier possessed a permanent scowl and intuitive eyes. Pike knew his phony ID wouldn't cut the mustard. Screw Dewayne and his cigarettes. He traipsed to the refreshment area to get a forty-four ounce Coke for himself and a sixteen-ounce for his love-struck buddy. Reaching for the lids, he garbled, "Excuse me."

"Pike?"

His brows came together. The diminutive girl with a fawnlike gaze, thriving blonde hair tapping her shoulders and a swan's neck looked vaguely familiar. "Hey…you."

"Paige."

"Right, Paige. How's it going?"

"Good, good." She stepped aside so he could reach the lids. Pike nodded his appreciation.

"You don't remember me."

Fiddling with the straws, he replied, "Sure, I do. Paige…"

"Rhodes."

"Right, Paige Rhodes."

"We had Rosen for Economics."

"Sure, right, Rosen. Of course."

She emitted a syrupy giggle. "No, we didn't."

He adored her laugh. "Okay, you got me."

Pike felt himself drifting away, swallowed by mesmerizing basset-hound indigo eyes and thin lips that curled into a guiltless radiant smile. Time stopped. The outside world irrelevant. Nothing mattered. It was a flash, an instant. But something foreign rose in his chest. Something he'd never felt before.

He'd seen Paige Rhodes around school. Sitting alone in the cafeteria, getting shouldered aside in the hallway by bigger classmates, her books clutched against her chest like a shield. Embarrassed. Female students were becoming women while she remained trapped in the body of a girl. Pike preferred more on top. And taller. And brunette. He never gave the flat-chested, short, blonde a second glance.

But unexpectedly, her physical attributes were now irrelevant. And here she was at Grizzly's, their lives intersecting as if bound together by some invisible tether.

The prolonged stare was broken by tolling bells announcing a customer's arrival. Assuming it was Dewayne, Pike rose to his tiptoes and peeked over the shelves. Nope, some other customer. When he faced forward, Paige hadn't taken her eyes off him.

"An angel just got their wings."

After a moment, he laughed. "*It's a Wonderful Life.* It does kinda sound like that."

She wavered, debating saying more.

Pike found her innocence endearing, but hey, his buddy was waiting. "See ya around sometime."

Her expression was a mixture of abandonment and rejection.

Pouting, she lowered her eyes. "You too, Pike."

Maneuvering the aisles, doing a double take at the condoms, he stood a respectable distance behind the hulking customer angling over the counter. Through the front window he spotted a late-model Chevy crammed with Paige's friends. For some reason, he was relieved not seeing any guys. Swiveling his head forward, he knew he was about to die.

Pike had only seen a firearm up close once before when a friend picked his father's gun safe. He didn't like it then, liked it less now as he stared down the foreboding barrel. The broad-shouldered customer outfitted in a dark hoodie, dark jeans and dark footwear resembled the Grim Reaper. Through a constricted throat, a name fell from Pike's trembling, parched lips. "LaMarcus King?"

The gunman's eyes enlarged like saucers.

Shit. I just IDd him.

"Who are you?"

"Pike." He managed to swallow. "Graves."

"Who the hell's Pike Graves?"

Hearing a sound, LaMarcus spun and brought the cashier into his sights. "Don't get no bright ideas fat man or you'll leave here in a box." Proficiently waggling the weapon, he ordered "Get your ass out from there."

The clerk momentarily glimpsed down. *Silent alarm? A bat?* Thinking better of it, he slinked out from behind the counter.

While LaMarcus focused on the cashier, Pike scanned the store in search of Paige. The refreshment area barren. Empty aisles. A corridor that likely led to an office and probably a rear delivery entrance. Was the rear door locked? Could Paige escape that way? Would she unintentionally trigger an alarm and send the gunman into a frenzy?

And why am I so concerned about her anyway?

When the employee was ordered to stand alongside Pike like two prisoners facing a firing squad, he knew the brief window of opportunity had closed. LaMarcus had half a foot and sixty pounds on him. Even without the gun, there was no way he could take the guy.

"How you know me, kid?"

Pike was again staring down an ominous cylinder of death. He stammered. "Laf...Lafayette High. Everyone knows LaMarcus

King. You took us to State last year." *And now you're holding up a convenience store? What the hell happened, man?*

LaMarcus weighed a heavy decision. Pike's life hanging in the balance, his destiny in the hands of a washed-out former high school running back whose dreams never materialized.

"Get outta here, kid."

Pike didn't move. Couldn't move. Not without Paige. He barely knew the girl but yet felt...*something*. How could he go on living his life if hers ended?

"I said, Go! Get the fuck out!" Spittle flew from his taut lips. He halved the distance between them and coiled his finger like a snake around the trigger. "Don't be a hero, Pike Graves."

cɔɛɔ

The stifling humidity exacerbated the queasiness in his rolling stomach. On spaghetti-like legs, he staggered along the sidewalk fronting Grizzly's, chastising himself. Just last week he went to see a movie titled *Die Hard* in which a NYC cop saves dozens of hostages from machinegun-toting terrorists in a Los Angeles skyscraper. Meanwhile, Pike couldn't save one girl from a mini-mart.

Dewayne jumped from his Mustang. "Dude, what took so long?"

Pike doubled over and vomited.

"Ah, man. That's not cool"

Pike slid the back of his hand across his mouth, unable to shake off the fear seizing his soul. In a voice that didn't sound like his own, he mumbled a name. "Paige..."

"Who?"

Crazed screaming of a desperate young man at the breaking point split the night. LaMarcus King backpedaled out of Grizzly's, shouted into the store "Don't try anything stupid," and jostled his hostage forward.

Pike completed the name in a whisper. "Paige Rhodes."

Panicked shrieks came from the gas pumps. All four doors on the Chevy opened. Paige's friends looked on, helpless and horrified.

LaMarcus brandished his hand-cannon at the cluster of girls. "Get back in the car!"

The piercing wail of sirens drew nearer. Red and blue strobe lights bathed the area in an eerie glow. Two police cruisers bulleted into the lot and screeched to an askew stop thirty yards away.

Decision time. LaMarcus could drop the weapon and turn himself in. He could make a break for it, but he'd seen enough episodes of *Cops* to know he'd never get away. Or he could stand his ground and use Paige as a bargaining chip. He chose the latter. Cocking the hammer, he placed the barrel of the firearm under her chin.

She bawled, powerless against the football player towering over her.

"Is that...LaMarcus King?" Dewayne murmured disbelievingly.

Pike didn't answer. Couldn't make a sound. He took one tentative step forward. Stopped.

Paige was on LaMarcus's right, dwarfed by the colossal All-State running back. Pike chewed his lip, narrowed his eyes. He could cover the distance in five seconds, six tops.

A yellow stain appeared on her white jeans.

Respectfully, Pike looked away. He recalled LaMarcus's warning: *Don't be a hero, Pike Graves.* He gave his friend a prolonged look.

Dewayne frowned.

And then Pike Graves ran forward.

Seconds, yet an eternity. Rapidly, yet playing out in slow motion.

Hurried footfalls had LaMarcus turn. He brought the gun around, took aim on the charging kid. Paige dived left. The girls in the lot screamed. A cop barked an order that sounded tinny and muffled.

Transforming himself into a human battering ram, Pike tucked his head into his shoulders and threw his full weight against the gargantuan chest of the gunman.

The former running back effortlessly darted left, as if avoiding a defensive lineman. But he'd lost a step since being on a gridiron.

Pike didn't tackle him directly but made enough contact to send LaMarcus stumbling backward.

The kid who'd gone from a can't-miss NFL career to robbing a convenience store in one short year lurched backward, did an awkward dance, tripped over a concrete parking bumper, and went down. Pike somersaulted across the pavement, came up, and regained his bearings.

He felt a rush, realizing Paige was safe. But the triumphant feeling was short-lived.

LaMarcus King convulsed once, twice, then stopped moving. A crimson puddle widening below his shattered skull.

A cop guardedly approached, crouched beside the body, and wistfully remarked, "Shit, it's not even a real gun."

PART I

The End

"A man who views the world the same at fifty as he did at twenty
has wasted thirty years of his life."

~ Muhammad Ali

CHAPTER 1

Present Day:

Beads of perspiration stippled his forehead. The back of his neck, clammy. His shirt stuck to his skin. Yet, he shivered. His heart ready to catapult through his chest wall as his pulse skyrocketed. Gooseflesh coated his arms. Bringing his hand level with his eyes, his fingers trembled. Pike Graves was again losing the battle to thanatophobia.

He wanted to remain in the safety of his car. But even secure with locked doors all around and windows rolled up, he felt vulnerable. An imaginary noose tightened around his neck.

Extricating himself from the conservative gray Honda, he swung his legs out and regulated his breathing.

Steeling himself, putting one foot in front of the other, Pike crested the hillside, refusing to look down.

Losing someone. That phrase made him laugh mirthlessly. Car keys got lost, a cell phone, nail clippers. Even one's innocence, something Pike was all too familiar with. But a whole person? Like they'd simply been misplaced. Like you could see them again after *losing* them.

Eyes forward, he methodically sidestepped neatly lined headstones. Many were neglected, departed souls clearly forgotten by loved ones still alive. He circumvented overturned dirt where someone had recently been…*lost*.

A hundred yards south, underbrush was getting cleared anticipating new arrivals at Mount Serenity Cemetery. *Mount Serenity*. Yet another ploy in distracting the living from rotting flesh and decomposing bodies in the earth. Reaching his destination, he used his hand as an improvised comb across his windswept mocha-colored hair. Sliding a palm over his wrinkled shirt, he glanced around, noticing a muddy pond with placidly gliding swans and ducks. His gaze inadvertently swept across hedges at his father's plot a few yards north, then quickly turned away and bowed his head.

"Hey, Mom."

The generic tombstone listed her name, approximate date of birth, and day she...passed. *Approximate* because Cora Graves was delivered by a midwife in a remote area of central Pennsylvania where recordkeeping was shoddy at best. Pike had wanted something along the lines of loving mother, devoted wife, caring sister. He would've welcomed input from his sister but as usual Stephanie wasn't around.

The engraver, however, fouled up and a cherubic angel blowing a horn was emblazoned on the headstone's upper left corner. Rather than asking it to be corrected, Pike let it go. Cora had been a Louis Armstrong fan. Maybe she'd chuckle at the irony from the great beyond.

The death certificate cited breast cancer, but Pike knew the truth. She'd simply been worn down after eighty-nine-years. And despite his mom almost becoming a nonagenarian, it still wasn't enough time. *It never is.*

Surveilling his surroundings and verifying no one was within earshot, Pike took a knee and picked out blades of grass that became mired in the *a's* in her name. "Things're good. Work's fine. Cynthia and I are doing well." He smiled. "Even the Phillies are having a good season."

Bullshit.

His job was anything but fine, his relationship with Cynthia was on thin ice, and the Phillies would be lucky to avoid a hundred losses. He could never lie to the woman when she was here, and it tugged at his heart now that she was...*resting.*

Cora's doctrine was simple: Avoid all negativity. Her optimism and zest for life was a primary reason she almost made ninety. When the oncologist mentioned chemo and radiation, she heartily agreed. "Good. I can finally get rid of these extra twenty pounds."

Pike knew the living were too caught up in their daily grind to pay respects to a loved one who'd...*expired.* It was a mind game. Movies, television, pseudo-psychiatrists, and grief counselors—whatever the hell they were—espoused tired clichés like doling out candy to children. *They're in a better place. They're no long-*

er suffering. They're still in your heart. They'll watch over you from Heaven. You'll see them again someday.

More bullshit.

One night in college, after too many beers and extremely potent weed, he and Dewayne engaged in a philosophical debate. "Technically," Pike prophesized, "we start dying the moment we're born."

Dewayne took a hit and through the sweet smell of marijuana, replied, "Dude, you're depressing the shit outta me."

Thanatophobia notwithstanding and visiting Mount Serenity for eight years, he never knew proper graveside etiquette. *How long do I stay? Five minutes? Thirty?*

His mind wandered. His girlfriend. A deadline at work. His car overdue for an oil change. The cable company raising their rates.

Time to leave.

Tapping the top of the headstone, Pike said, "Happy birthday, Mom." He turned, took one slow step forward, and nearly fell onto his ass.

"Sorry, mister."

A boy of six or seven scampered over. He clumsily hoisted up his baggy jeans and adjusted a ball cap resting crookedly atop his head.

Pike squatted and handed over the baseball that caused the misstep. "Here ya go."

The boy pounded the ball into his glove. "Thanks, mister."

Pike smiled. Whereas adults nowadays seldom expressed courtesy, encountering a polite, well-mannered young boy was a positive sign for the future. Or maybe, Pike was just becoming a crotchety old fart. "Phillies, huh?"

"Wow, how'd you know?"

Pike pointed to the cap then waved his arms. "This *is* Philadelphia."

Disappointment crossed the young freckled face. "Oh, I thought maybe you were a wizard."

"Nah, just deductive reasoning."

"De-*what*?"

Obviously I'm not a parent.

"Putting one and one together."

"Oh." The boy lobbed the ball a few feet into the air, playing catch with himself. Then he looked at the headstone. "Who's that?"

"That's my—" A short distance away a shrouded woman dressed in black was mourning someone buried close to Pike's father. The woman's attire more befitting a funeral, not visiting someone who'd...*departed.*

As if intuiting Pike's eyes, the melancholy woman painstakingly faced him. She remained stoic, gave a barely perceptible nod before returning her attention to her loved one.

"Who's Cora?"

Pike looked away from the woman he assumed was the boy's mother to the grave of his own mother. "Just someone I knew."

The boy scrunched his face, studying dates of birth and death. "I'm seven."

Pike needed to go but his legs wouldn't cooperate. Silly, but he felt uncomfortable leaving Mom alone with a stranger. "So...who's your favorite player on the Phillies?"

The kid shrugged, eyes glued to Cora's headstone. "I dunno."

"You like'm all?"

The boy nodded.

"Don't have a favorite?"

He hiked his shoulders. "Lenny, I guess."

Pike mentally inventoried the team's roster then creased his brows. "Dykstra? Lenny Dykstra?"

"I guess."

The centerfielder had a career batting average of .285, was a three-time All-Star, Silver Slugger winner in '93 and won a World Series with the Mets in '86. Pike knew this because his favorite player as a boy was also Lenny Dykstra. "You're seven?"

"Yup."

"Lenny retired long before you were born."

The kid shrugged again. "Bye." He turned on his heels and scooted to the cloaked woman who draped a protective arm around her son.

Despite something hauntingly familiar in the boy's demeanor, Pike didn't push. This was a place people came to mourn and reflect, not be pestered. He trekked down the hillside and glanced back when reaching his vehicle.

From this vantage point, it appeared as if the veiled woman was standing over his father's grave. "Must be the angle."

Lowering himself behind the wheel, he brought the car to life. At the apex of the hill, the woman matter-of-factly waved good-bye.

"Strange." He shifted into drive then slammed the brakes.

The little boy. The woman at his side. The two of them lamenting someone interred alongside Pike's father. Unless they were actually mourning Pike's father. His skin crawled. The mitt was on the kid's right hand indicating he was left-handed. *I'm left-handed.*

It was as if Pike just encountered a younger version of himself.

He threw the car into park, killed the engine, and got out.

They were...*gone.*

ℰ�ℓ�

The *Franklin Union Chronicle*, cynically referred to as "FUC" by Philadelphians, was located in a dumpy brick building in Warminster. The putrid green color gave the impression God Himself upchucked on the place.

Pike's Honda Accord bounced through the lunar landscape of a parking lot. Locking his vehicle, he bypassed the craters and traipsed through the front door where he was instantly overcome by repressive air and cigar smoke. "Hey, Jodi."

The receptionist, resembling a young Valerie Bertinelli, ignored him, continuing with her heated phone call. Engaged six months earlier, planning the wedding had aged her six years.

Out of habit, Pike checked the wire in-box for messages, though he couldn't recall the last time he received one. Turning, he clumsily stumbled over the well-polished shoe of a man seated in the waiting room. "Sorry."

The clean shaven fellow, dressed immaculately in a Hugo Boss ensemble and excessive cologne, dismissed it. His apparel screamed attorney, causing Pike to wonder who was suing the newspaper this week. Eyeing the man's impressive attire, Pike adjusted his own tie and walked away.

The work area was boxy. Dreary gray cubicles were set haphazardly giving the perception of a bustling office larger in size than it truly was. Pike's workstation was situated far away from his boss, just outside the bathrooms.

As his computer booted-up, he checked his voice-mail. Cynthia was in New York on business settling a problem with a client and wouldn't make it home until late. "There go our dinner plans," Pike sighed to no one.

Perhaps it was a remnant from when he'd been an investigative reporter, back when he had a real job with a real newspaper, but something gnawed at his gut. There'd been a time when he and Cynthia would talk and laugh and joke and text throughout the day. Those happier moments were now a transient memory.

Leaning back, he massaged his neck and measured the gray walls enveloping him. Push-pinned on one side were business cards of numerous sources he'd compiled over his career. Most he hadn't spoken to in some time, and they had probably forgotten Pike Graves. The wall facing him was chockfull of photos he'd taken during five years with Cynthia. His favorite, one taken at the Jersey shore, showed her striking a goofy pose. Cutoff jeans showcased long legs, a tank top showed what she—using self-deprecating humor—called Popeye arms. Sunblock on her speckled nose, eyes squinting below a visor, a smile reserved for only him. Fair-skinned, she never tanned well. "I always come home looking like a freakin' lobster."

Pike perused the abundant pictures: Cynthia decked out in Phillies regalia at Citizen's Bank Ballpark, Eagles gear at Lincoln Financial Field, and sporting a sophisticated gown in Atlantic City on New Year's Eve. Two others included Cynthia's daughter, Wynter, who shared her mother's blonde hair and light complexion. A recent photo showed mother and daughter mugging for the camera beside Wynter's sixteenth birthday gift, a three-year-old Mitsubishi Pike got a smoking deal on. Another photo showed Cynthia crouching beside a younger Wynter dressed as Tinkerbell, long before Pike knew them.

There were no photos of him and Cynthia together. He told himself it was because he was the one taking the pictures.

The third wall once contained reprints of his better articles, countless accolades, and snapshots with the city's most influential people. Stewart Stafford insisted they be removed.

Pike was yanked from his daydream by raucous laughter and incessant yipping of a little dog emanating from his boss's office.

Whereas most college graduates get gifts like an expensive pen, an attaché, a new phone, or maybe a car if they're lucky,

Stewart Stafford was bequeathed a business.

Myer Stafford was a legend in Pittsburgh media but to his son's credit, Stewart wanted to blaze his own trail on the opposite side of the commonwealth after graduating Penn State. Or maybe he realized he'd never measure up to his old man.

The elder Stafford purchased the *Franklin Union Chronicle* lock, stock, and barrel and handed junior a three million dollar toy.

The son promptly ran it into the ground.

Print journalism was dying, soon to slip into history along with milkmen and cops walking the beat. FUC began publication in the mid-seventies when two college buddies decided local sports coverage was lacking. The paper eventually expanded to news across the Delaware Valley.

Along came the internet, twenty-four hour news, bloggers who thought they were Woodward and Bernstein. And so began the slow demise of the print journalism.

Pike never imagined newspapers would cease to exist. Then again, he never imagined he'd end up working here of all Godforsaken places.

"Graves!"

Hoisting himself from his wobbly chair, he looked over the sea of vacant workstations. Stewart motioned, *C'mon, get in here.*

"Mr. Stafford," Pike said as way of greeting when knuckling the open door. Wrinkling his nose at the overwhelming stench of cigar smoke, he noticed a lanky effeminate man close to his boss's age seated comfortably.

"Mr. Stafford?" Stewart mocked. "I'm younger than you, Graves. You can dispense with the formalities."

"You're my boss."

Relishing the title, his chest puffed out. "Yes, yes, I am."

Stewart Stafford was an odd looking type, appearing as if he'd been assembled by a mischievous child. Brown pompadour with blond streaks, abnormally oblong face and beady eyes, a barrel-chest and stumpy legs. He wore older jeans, a dress shirt that had seen better days and sandals with white socks. The mangy Schnauzer perched in his lap, growled.

"Be nice, Bundy."

Pike often wondered if the pooch was named after Ted or Al.

Stewart mindlessly stroked Bundy's head while shuffling papers. Not meeting Pike's eyes, he asked disinterestedly, "Have a good lunch, Graves?"

"Went to see my mom."

"How is she?"

"Uh, she died."

Stewart's face shot up. "While you were at lunch?"

"No, eight years ago."

Stewart looked at the other man in his office. "Well, don't I look like a prick?"

Pike said nothing, wondering who this person was. Stepping forward, he introduced himself. "Pike Graves."

"Kurt Wiley." He reached for a Starbucks cup instead of the proffered hand.

Pike clucked his tongue and asked his boss, "What'd you need?"

"Any plans for the Fourth?" Stewart asked mechanically.

"Just gonna grill up some burgers and dogs." *Dogs.* He eyed Bundy.

"And you didn't invite me?"

Pike faltered. "I…assumed you had plans."

Stewart guffawed. "Just screwin' with ya. By the way, how's Cynthia?"

His boss had no recollection of his mother dying but knew his girlfriend's name. He didn't know what to make of that. "Fine."

Angling back, Stewart pulled on his chin. "You feeling okay, Graves?"

"Yes. Why?"

"You don't look so good."

"Oh?"

"He look okay to you?" Stewart asked his guest.

Kurt did the same chin pull. "Can't say, Beef Stew. Don't know the dude."

Beef Stew? One thing was clear. The camaraderie between his boss and this Wiley character left no doubt they shared membership in an exclusive club that Pike wasn't allowed into.

Stewart asked, "Are you growing?"

"Pardon?"

"Are. You. Growing?"

Pike went for humor. "Not since I was a teenager."

"How tall are you?"

"Five-eleven."

"Your arms look longer. Don't they look abnormally long, Kurt?"

Kurt shrugged. "No idea, Beef Stew."

Stewart refocused. "Look here, Graves, you gotta go."

"Go?"

"Home."

"Home?"

"Yes."

Pike checked his wristwatch. "I'm expecting a call from Principal Mathers about that ammo shop opening down the street from his school."

"It's not your problem."

"It's no problem. But—" Pike's chest tightened. The insight so blatant, yet he missed it. No wonder he was no longer an investigative journalist. "You're firing me?"

"If you choose to see it that way."

Pike snorted. "How would you see it?"

"Doing you a favor."

"A favor?"

"Absolutely." Stewart patted Bundy's hind quarter. The dog bounded off his lap, sniffed the cuffs of Pike's slacks, lifted a leg, and proceeded to pee.

"*Bundy!*" The two buddies cackled boisterously like schoolboys but didn't stop the dog. "Sorry, Graves, but that's pretty funny."

"Hilarious."

When the merriment subsided, Stewart wiped tears of laughter from his eyes. "Where was I?"

"You were explaining how you were doing me a favor by firing me."

"Oh, yeah, right." His boss straightened and tried acting professional. It didn't take. Puffing on the stogie, he blew smoke rings like Edward G. Robinson in some 1930s gangster movie. "Look, you're not happy here, see? You don't fit in, see? It's a different business now than when you started, see?"

"I'm forty-seven," Pike stated for some reason.

"It's a young man's game, Graves. The proof is you just looked at your watch."

"So?"

"*So*? No one wears watches anymore. Right, Kurt?"

"Right, Beef Stew."

"You're a dinosaur, a relic. Our lease is up the end of the month and the Russian landlord's tripling our rent. We'll all work from home."

"I can work from home."

"That's not you. You can't change the way you're wired."

Pike closed his eyes and ran down what bills were due. He and Cynthia would be okay. More than okay. But that wasn't the point.

"You should be grateful, Graves."

"Grateful, right."

Stewart tried a different tact. "This job's beneath you. You went from the *Inquirer* to FUC. No one would be happy. You deserve better. You'll thank me in the long run."

Kurt Wiley interjected, "You worked at the *Inquirer*?"

Pike nodded.

Wiley sneered. "Were you the one who broke the story about aliens landing on the White House lawn?"

"The *Philadelphia Inquirer*, not the *National Enquirer*."

"Oh."

Stewart came out from his desk and draped an arm around Pike's shoulders like they were best buds. "I like you, Graves, so I decided to have your health insurance and benefits remain intact until the end of the month. You can pick up your final check from Jodi on your way out."

Mind clouded, Pike asked, "Why'd you ask if I had plans for the Fourth if you were firing me?"

Stewart balked like it was the stupidest question ever. "Because I'm a nice guy."

Like a young child steered through a crowded department store by a parent, Pike was handed over to two security guards who normally patrolled the strip mall.

"These men," Stewart explained, "will verify you don't take any company property. You've got five minutes to gather your things and leave." He handed over an empty box.

Pike was tailed as he crossed the expanse four minutes later. Bundy barked from under a chair as he sidled by.

In the lobby, Stewart Stafford enthusiastically greeted the guy in the Hugo Boss outfit, first with a strong handshake, then a man-hug. "Glad to have you aboard," Stewart said breaking the embrace. "Welcome to the *Franklin Union Chronicle*." Pivoting, he turned beet-red seeing Pike. "Crap. I thought you already left, Graves."

Pike sized up the man hired to replace him, then told his former boss, "To answer your question from before, yes, you *are* a prick."

Jodi, the Valerie Bertinelli look-alike, despondently handed over an envelope containing his final check. "Just take it one day at a time."

Pike was shepherded through the front door and into the sweltering humidity of Philadelphia in July. He instinctively looked back one final time. Jodi waved at him through the window. Lately, everyone was waving good-bye.

CHAPTER 2

Pike was in a fog the entire drive home. It wasn't being terminated that gnawed at his gut, nor being told by *Beef Stew* of all people that he wasn't good enough. The loss of income was immaterial. Since the staff at the *Franklin Union Chronicle* primarily worked from home, he wouldn't miss rapport with colleagues he seldom saw. Instead, it was having nowhere to go tomorrow.

Pulling curbside, he studied the three-story American Colonial he shared with Cynthia and her daughter. It was one of the bigger homes on one of the larger parcels of land in unincorporated Buckingham an hour north of Philadelphia.

When Cynthia first moved in she was awestruck by the size and elegance. A far cry from decrepit apartments she was accustomed to, she referred to this as *Buckingham* Palace.

Opening the front door, he broke into a trot to answer the phone. Cynthia teased him about keeping a landline but Pike didn't like change. "Hello?" he said at the kitchen counter.

"This is Ms. Jenkins. Is Cynthia Grimm available?"

Pike looked around before remembering she was in New York City. "No. Can I ask what it's regarding?"

"I'm calling from Liberty Financial about one of her accounts. Is there a better time to reach her?"

Pike knitted his brows. He knew nothing of her having an account with them, much less more than one. *Accounts?* "Are you sure you have the right Cynthia Grimm?"

After verifying her social security number and date of birth and with curiosity spiking, he lied. "I'm her husband."

After hearing a few keystrokes, he was told, "I'm sorry, Mr. Grimm, but I don't show your name listed anywhere."

Pike jotted down her contact info, hung up, and impulsively called out, "Cyn?" He was answered by silence.

In the den, he powered up his PC situated atop a mahogany desk that had been his father's, then trudged upstairs. Slipping into a pair of washed out jeans and a frayed Flyers T-shirt, Pike returned. Four new emails: one soliciting discount Viagra, one offering penile enlargements, one asking if he'd been inflicted with mesothelioma, and one from a girl in Africa pleading for five thousand dollars to save her dying father. He accessed Facebook, quickly scrolling through the newsfeed. Everyone happy, everyone eager about the upcoming Fourth, everyone enjoying life.

Thumping from above redirected his thoughts. He attributed it to the old house creaking. But when he heard it again, then a third time, he tensed. Never home in mid-afternoon had he stumbled upon a burglary?

Just last week an elderly couple two blocks over had been soundly beaten when a home invasion turned ugly. Removing a Louisville Slugger from the coat closet, he clenched the balustrade at the base of the stairs. His heart pounded ascending to the second floor.

Many times Cynthia suggested they buy a gun. Pike, suffering from thanatophobia, refused.

He triangulated the origin of the sound as Wynter's room. Placing his ear against her closed bedroom door, he fortified his grip on the bat. He moved his right hand to the doorknob, surprised how damp his palm was. Hearing a scream, he barged in.

Wynter's face was buried in a pillow, her backside in the air. The rhythmic thumping he'd heard was the headboard banging the wall, synchronized with each thrust from the man behind her.

Pike froze. A disturbing childhood memory came back with the potency of a mallet. He promptly shoved the painful recall back into the dark recesses of his mind where it belonged.

The guy with Wynter looked left. "Hey, man, you want seconds?"

Wynter faced Pike. "What the—ow—hell are you—ow—doing? Get out!"

⌘

Pike strategically placed himself to catch the guy on his way out.

Forty minutes later, merrily skipping down the stairs, he zipped his fly reaching the landing and grinned brashly. "Your daughter's a freak."

"She's not my daughter."

The guy shrugged. "Don't matter. She's a freak anyway."

Pike advanced on the man twice Wynter's age then arched a brow. "You're her boss. Brock, right?"

"So?"

Wynter scurried down the stairs and gave Pike a look. Unabashed, perhaps showing off, she stood on her tiptoes and shoved her tongue down Brock's throat. After a brief make out session, Wynter escorted her boss out.

When she returned, Pike was waiting. "We should talk."

"If you weren't home, you wouldn't have known." Like it was Pike's fault. "You think this is the first time he fucked me while you and my mother are at work?" She disdainfully shook her head.

Pike didn't have kids. He couldn't. And he never knew how to relate on their level because his own childhood, for all intents and purposes, ended outside Grizzly's.

The only thing he thought to say was, "My mom and dad worked a lot too."

"Well, you're not my dad."

She shoots, she scores.

Wynter entered his personal space. "Did you like the view?"

Pike furrowed his brows.

"You didn't turn away quickly. I saw the way you looked at me."

He closed his eyes.

"It's all good. We're not related so, ya know, if the urge ever strikes, my door's open."

"How old is he anyway?"

"Brock?"

"Who do you think I'm talking about?" Pike snapped, only now considering there could be others.

"I dunno. Old. Like thirty-five. But it's not my fault his wife doesn't put out."

"He's married?"

"Oh. My. God. Newsflash, married people cheat. Duh!"

"Don't you think he's using you?"

She rolled her eyes, a trait she picked up from her mom. Smelling of sex, she whispered, "You ever think maybe I'm using him?"

Pike watched her sashay upstairs. The slamming door shook the home to its foundation.

The bizarre encounter at the cemetery, losing his job, discovering accounts in his girlfriend's name he knew nothing about and now catching Wynter in bed with her boss sent Pike's mind reeling. Needing to reach Cynthia, he tried her cell.

She didn't answer.

∽∾∽

Each election cycle politicians tossed around catchphrases like "gentrification" and 'urban renewal.' Except when it came to this particular neighborhood in the shadow of downtown. Even Philadelphia's most forward-thinking city planners knew the area was beyond hope.

Some residents were lucky enough to flee, their former homes now inhabited by squatters or falling under the control of drug dealers who conducted business behind graffiti-covered plywood. Those too destitute to escape survived behind barred windows listening to the nightly rat-tat-tat of gunfire and rotors of police helicopters. If the power went out, PECO wouldn't make repairs without a police escort, forcing homeowners to hunker down until sunup.

Cynthia Grimm parked her Dodge Charger by the fire hydrant. No worries about a ticket since cops avoided this war zone at all costs. The aroma of barbequing burgers and popping firecrackers in preparation for the holiday filled the stagnant air. Verifying the contents of her purse, she crossed the dead lawn.

A comatose black man lay sprawled at the bottom of a wraparound porch after injecting who-knows-what into his bloodstream. A white man—a boy, really—eyed Cynthia while twirling a switchblade. A shirtless Hispanic, whose scrawny chest was covered in ink, swaggered over. "Well, well, what we got here?"

"Dragon around?"

"What's it worth to ya?"

She asked again, "Dragon around?"

Rather than answering, his eyes roamed her lithe figure. Denim skirt, navy blouse, and tan sandals, she stood five-eight, a good four inches taller. "Have some pity and show me your titties." He began lifting her shirt.

Without skipping a beat, Cynthia bent back two of his fingers. His whimpering drowned out any potential snapping sound. "Gonna tell me if Dragon's here?"

"Let go, bitch."

She did.

Examining his hand and flexing his fingers, he said, "It's been a while, okay. I just came out."

"Of the closet?"

"Prison." Undeterred, he moved closer and breathed, "manslaughter."

Unimpressed, she started moving around him.

He blocked her path.

Cynthia's hand shot to his crotch and through baggy jeans squeezed his testicles. "Don't make me ask again. Dragon?"

Doubled-over and in a voice two octaves higher, he indicated the house. "In there!"

The late-afternoon sun was incapable of penetrating the disconsolate interior of the ramshackle dwelling. Cynthia identified the smell that was part cat-urine and part-painter's toolshed, as meth. An orange shag carpet that hadn't been in style since the Bee-Gees topped the charts was tattered and threadbare, exposing a cement slab. Furniture—if you could call it that—was a hodgepodge of frayed sofas, ragged chairs, and tables with legs missing. Fist-sized holes in the drywall were everywhere. Three framed pictures hung crooked: A black and white of Bob Marley toking a joint, an autopsy photo of Kurt Cobain, and the Mona Lisa on a chaise lounge engaged in a threesome.

The scattered occupants, like the furnishings, had long surpassed their usefulness. Twisted lifeless forms, barely conscious and in varying stages of drug-induced stupors, were oblivious to the leggy blonde.

Cynthia entered what had been an eat-in kitchen. Hoses and pipes denoted where appliances used to be. The kitchen table was a wicker patio set. A lone occupant, crushed and unmindful, snorted a line of coke, jerked his head up, and pinched the tip of his nose. He squinted at the woman, trying to place her.

"Dragon."

Recognizing the hoarse voice he always found sexy, he blinked clarity into his eyes and offered a crooked smile. "Pull up a chair, Cyn. Make yourself at home."

She calculated him from the threshold. Bobby Dragovich had gone by "Dragon" since before they'd met. They were the same age—thirty-seven—but he appeared to be knocking on the door of fifty. Alcohol had ballooned his weight to the two-eighty range. His disheveled red-brown hair, more unkempt than usual, hadn't been washed in weeks. He had untrimmed muttonchops and an unruly soul patch that she thought never looked good on white guys. Pronounced dark circles under his eyes and hollowed cheeks, his body odor wafted across the room. Flabs of fat slung from his shamrock-colored tank top. She wanted to say "Look how far you've fallen" but Bobby Dragovich had been a bottom feeder from the start.

She crossed the run-down kitchen and pulled out a chair but elected to remain standing when noticing a wet spot on the seat cushion. "Lose your job again?"

Dragon jeered. "I didn't *lose* it. Dude was an asshole."

"Anything else lined up?"

"I'll find something."

"Right. I can see you're hard at work pounding the pavement."

"Get off my ass, Cyn! It just happened."

"When?"

"I dunno. What's today?"

"Wednesday."

Dragon curled his mouth. "Few days ago...I guess."

She removed a tissue from her purse. "Your nose is bleeding."

He brushed her fingers when accepting the Kleenex, wiped away blood and snot, then returned it.

"Uh, no. You can keep it. Are there any body shops in Philly that *haven't* fired you?"

"I'll get something." Eyes glazed, he gauged his surroundings as if suddenly waking in an alien world. "There any beer in the fridge?"

"There's not even a fridge."

"Ah, snap." He cried out, "Hey, which one of you fuckheads took the fridge?"

Cynthia took a deep breath. "We need to talk."

"Not that again."

"Not what?"

"I just lost my job, okay? I'll catch up on Wynter's child support once I get back on my feet, all right?" Dragon slid his hand across his nose. "Good, no blood. I just need time, a'ight?"

"I've been hearing that since she was three. She's almost seventeen."

"Seventeen?" Dragon looked off into a memory. A beat later, he gave Cynthia a sideways glance. "If you ain't here about kid support, you want me to hook you up? We got good shit."

"I've grown up, Dragon."

A knowing expression crossed his face. "If it ain't kid support and it ain't to score, there's only one thing left." Unsteadily, he stood and began unzipping his fly.

"Don't flatter yourself."

"Then what?" He sat down.

Removing a Glock from her purse she set it on the table between them. "I want you to kill Pike."

Dragon gave the weapon a cursory glance before reacquainting himself with its heft and feel. He hadn't held a firearm in a while. It was like reconnecting with an old friend. After a moment, he searched her eyes.

"Problem?" she asked.

"Once he's out of the way, you and me can get back together?"

She waved her arms like Vanna White. "So I can live in this lap of luxury?"

"Then why?"

"Same as it's always about. Money." She leaned forward, palms down on the table, and lowered her voice to a conspiratorial tone. "Lots of money."

"How much we talking?"

We. She knew she had him. "Between stocks, bonds, savings, treasury notes, certificates of dep—"

Dragon's head was about to explode. "How *much*?"

"Two hundred seventy five thousand."

His jaw dropped. "I get two hundred seventy five grand to off that asshole? I just fell in love with you again."

"No, dork. I'm joint on all those accounts."

Dragon raised his fingers and pretended to toke. "Joint?"

Cynthia rolled her eyes. "Joint, meaning two names are on the accounts. That money is as much mine as his."

"Can't he just like, I dunno, take your name off?"

"I've got that covered."

"So why not just take his money and leave with Wynter?" He paused. "And me."

"That's the appetizer. I'm after the whole enchilada."

Dragon's forehead creased.

Despite the soiled chair, she sat on the edge and continued whispering. "I'm the benny on one account."

"Who the fuck's Benny?"

"Beneficiary. Meaning if he, let's say, hypothetically of course, dies or, I don't know, gets killed, I get *everything*."

"How much?"

"A lot."

He eased aside the mirror from where he'd snorted two lines and shook off the effects of the cocaine. "How much?"

"One point four million."

Dragon whistled. "You shittin' me?"

"Nope. Your cut is ten percent."

Dragon's face contorted as he worked out a complicated math problem. "Fourteen thousand? I just hit the freakin' mother lode."

His stupidity had always been charming. "No, one hundred forty thousand."

"You sure?"

"Positive."

"You askin' me 'cause I was in the army?"

"Yeah, for four days until they dishonorably discharged you."

Dragon threw his finger at her. "Hey, that king shit sergeant had it comin' to him. Who does he think he is waking me up at five every morning?"

Cynthia couldn't help but smile. Dragon was so simple, so uncomplicated, almost a Peter Pan innocence. It was why she fell in love with him. Briefly. In some ways he came off as a badass, in other ways he fell far short. Years earlier, he personified his tough guy image and got a tattoo. However, the artist was an amateur, and the dragon on Dragon's arm came out resembling an iguana.

"Where'd you get the piece?"

"It's hot. Can't be traced to me or you." She paused. "You in?"

Before he could answer, a muffled sound emanated from her

purse. Cynthia pulled her phone and shook her head. "It's him. *Again.*" She let it go to voice-mail and repeated the one-point-four million dollar question. "You in?"

"If I say yes, we gonna be square on the child support?"

"Yes."

"Then I'm in."

The air seemed different. Everything seemed different. She'd crossed the point of no return. The plan she'd kicked around for a while was now in motion. Initially, Pike was her knight in shining armor. If it wasn't for their happenstance meeting, she'd likely be living in this dump alongside Dragon. Pike saved her. Like he tried to save everyone. He was her hero, like he tried to be to everyone. The self-righteous ass.

Cynthia flailed through adulthood. Switching jobs regularly, lengthy periods of drug use, countless long weekends in an alcoholic fog, taking lovers with reckless abandon. She was lucky to be alive, damn lucky. But she could never sever ties with Bobby Dragovich. He was a tumor she couldn't remove. Her comfort food. Dragon would always be there for her.

The antithesis to him was Pike Graves. He was the type of guy she yearned for during moments of quiet introspection when her mind wasn't dulled. He was ten years older but that didn't matter in the bedroom. Mature and motivated, sensitive and sensible. Everything Dragon was not. Dragon was Wynter's biological father but Pike was the one involved in her life. And despite the girl being a handful, Pike strove to be a positive influence.

Nevertheless, Cynthia was a party girl who missed the party lights. She'd heard about those upstanding suburban housewives who routinely attended PTA meetings, baked cookies to support the local soccer team, and attended church religiously. Then, when no one was around, they'd cry in loneliness, sip from a bottle of bourbon concealed in the back of the kitchen pantry, and seduce the horny sixteen-year-old kid down the street. Anything to offset the mundane reality they'd found themselves trapped in. Screw that. That wasn't Cynthia Grimm.

Pike had served his purpose. A means to an end. And this was the end.

"I'll be in touch." She stood.

"Hey." No longer unstable, he came to her. "Where'd Pike get that much money?"

"His dad. The guy owned several upscale watch stores in different malls."

Dragon laughed.

"What's funny?"

"Watches. Now he's the one outta time."

Cynthia smiled.

"When you want me doin' this?" he asked.

"Sooner the better."

CHAPTER 3

Pike woke the following morning and impulsively reached over. No Cynthia.

Mouth curled, he checked his cell. No texts. No voice mails.

Getting out of the California king, he stretched, lumbered downstairs, and groggily made his way toward the Keurig when he spotted a hastily scribbled note. Cynthia apparently came home late, decided to sleep on the sofa so she wouldn't disturb him, and rose early because she had to "put out fires at work." The note was signed *C* but her customary x's and o's had been omitted.

Putting out fires? She was an account manager for an ad agency in Center City, not a firefighter. What could be so urgent on July Fourth? Waiting for the Keurig, Pike dialed her number. When it again went to voicemail, he opted to leave a message. "Yo, Cyn, it's me. Just wanna make sure we're still on for tonight. I'd like to get there in time for batting practice." He was about to press *end* before remembering, "Love ya."

Pike had his customary two cups of coffee while perusing the *Inquirer*. Like keeping a landline, Cynthia chided him about that also. "We're the only ones on the block who still get the paper."

"I like newsprint on my hands," he had replied.

"You're *so* old-fashioned."

He concluded his regimen by shaving, showering, and preparing for the day, despite having nothing on the agenda other than tonight's Phillies-Cubs game. After checking his email and purposely avoiding Facebook where everyone boasted about how perfect their lives were, he popped a movie into the DVD player and reclined in his La-Z-Boy. Twenty minutes into the film Wynter appeared. "What ya watchin'?"

She wore painted-on miniscule pink shorts that scarcely covered her rear and a push-up bra beneath a snug cerise shirt. Pike found the outfit demeaning, especially worn by a sixteen-year-old. Or perhaps Cynthia was correct. *Maybe I am old-fashioned.*

With Wynter's reprimand about lingering in her doorway fresh in his mind, he quickly redirected his eyes to the film. "True Grit."

She watched a moment. "That's not Jeff Bridges."

"This is the original with John Wayne."

"Who?"

Yep, definitely old. "It's a good film."

"What's with you and all the old movies? Anything from *this* century you like?"

"Sure." Pike thought about it but drew a blank.

Wynter chuckled. "See what I mean."

"Things were purer back then. Good guys, bad guys. Simple."

"Life's not so simple."

From the mouths of children. He paused the film, situated his elbows on his knees, and searched for the right words. "Listen, about last night—"

"Don't worry, I won't tell Mom."

Pike grimaced. "*You* won't?"

"About watching me and Brock."

"No, not—that," he spluttered. "I'm talking about—"

"It's all good. I know you and Mom don't screw anymore so, hey, whatever creams your Twinkie."

Sidetracked, Pike asked, "How do you know we don't...ya know?"

Wynter rolled her eyes, a younger version of Cynthia. "It's obvious. I can see it."

He laughed uneasily. "You *can*?"

"Nah, but it's noticeable once she told me."

Pike blanched. "Your mom told you we're not *having sex*." The last two words barely audible.

Wynter looked at him like viewing an unwanted dog at the pound. "You're sweet."

Pike vacillated. The relationship between him and Cynthia seemed to be on life support recently. Wondering if she was considering pulling the plug and now hearing mother and daughter discussed personal things, he asked, "What else has she told you?"

Ignoring the question, she remembered, "Some woman called for Mom while you were showering."

Pike hearkened back to yesterday's conversation. "Ms. Jenkins from Liberty Financial?"

"Didn't say." Wynter checked her phone. "Gotta go."

Pike sprang off the couch and met her at the door, mindful of keeping physical distance between them. "Is she happy?"

"Mom's never happy."

He chewed his lips.

"Look," Wynter sighed. "You've known her five years but I've known her longer. And better. Mom always wants what's next, what's new. She's like one of those peeps who buys the latest phone with all the new gadgets and stuff and, then a week later, wants the newer phone with newer gadgets and newer stuff."

Pike considered that.

"Want some advice?"

"Sure."

"Be spontaneous. Mom doesn't do predictable."

"And that'll make her happy?"

"For a while."

ღღღ

Since it was America's birthday, Pike decided a John Wayne marathon was apropos. He piggybacked *True Grit* with *The Shootist*. The latter, the Duke's final film, was a saga about a gunslinger dying of cancer who decides to go out in the proverbial blaze of glory rather than succumbing to a painful end. Pike often wondered what he'd do if facing the same ultimatum.

He was twenty minutes into *The Searchers* when he heard Cynthia's car. Meeting her at the door, he moved in for a kiss.

She wiggled away. "Hang on, I gotta pee."

After disappearing upstairs for fifteen long minutes, she returned. Pike hadn't heard the toilet flush.

"Wanna share a Sam Adams," she asked, looking in the fridge. "Last one."

"Nah, I'm good." Indicating the table, he asked, "Got a sec?"

"Uh oh. Nothing good ever comes from a kitchen table discussion." She sat cross-legged on the chair. "What's crack-a-lackin'?"

After exchanging small talk about her day which was "crazy hectic" and his which was "sitting on my ass doing nothing," he breathed deep. "It's about Wynter."

Bzzzt.

"Wait, wait." Pulling her phone from her jeans pocket, she blushed reading the text, then speedily tapped out a reply.

"Who's that?"

"Just someone from work." A hearty swig, then she asked, "So, Wynter?"

"I caught her with someone yesterday afternoon."

She frowned. "Who?"

"Brock."

"Who's Brock?"

"Her boss."

Cynthia curled her mouth. "He's kinda cute."

Pike bristled. "The guy's her boss. And in his thirties. *And* married."

"I guess his wife isn't putting out."

Cynthia had always been a joker. Once at dinner, using the guise of needing to use the restroom, she informed the hostess it was Pike's birthday. During dessert, a dozen waiters and waitresses serenaded him and presented him with a cupcake and a candle. The comical part was Pike's birthday was four months away. "Don't you think that's inappropriate?"

"She's sixteen. We all do crazy things at sixteen."

"Cyn, he's *married*!"

Another long swig, the cool amber liquid comforting on a steamy afternoon. "How'd you know they were having sex?"

"I heard them," he replied flatly.

"Yesterday?"

"Around three-thirty."

"Why were you home at three-thirty?"

He cringed. "That's the other thing I wanted to discuss. I, um, got let go."

She barked, "They shit-canned you?"

Ouch. "Yeah. But they gave me my final check and my benefits remain intact through the end of the month. Don't worry, I'll find something."

It was the same thing Dragon had said. "So now *I* have to support all of us?"

Pike's brows shot up. Cynthia had been unemployed three times totaling ten months since they first got together but he never threw that up in her face.

She cried, "What about Orlando?"

He'd forgotten their vacation the first week of August. "We'll have to see about that."

"But you promised!"

Pike looked at her. Her uncomplicated outlook, childish in some ways, was a trait he generally liked. Now, however, it was irritating.

He was out of work and needed her to act like an adult. "Wynter's probably too old for Disneyworld anyway."

"I'm talking about *me!* I've never seen Epcot."

Pike opened his palms like a homeless man seeking a handout. "It's not like I purposely got fired."

"You have plenty of money."

"I wouldn't be able to have fun knowing I'm between jobs."

"That's your problem."

The air around him was asphyxiating. "Cyn, look—"

"Whoa, hang on." She rifled through her pocket again and giggled when reading another text. Typing out a lengthy response, she placed it screen-down on the table. The fleeting smile vanished as quickly as it appeared. "What?"

"Who's that?"

"Told ya, someone from work."

"Again?"

She snorted. "Yes, I *still* have my job."

"Who?"

"Alex."

"Alex? I don't remember you mentioning his name before."

She gave him an abject eye roll and shifted the spotlight away from herself. "You've got money. One freakin vacay to Orlando won't break us."

"That's not the point."

"It *is* the point!" She vehemently jumped to her feet, the chair toppling behind her and crashing to the floor. Angrily pacing, she made her argument. "You're so predictable. Live a little. Be spontaneous. Have you ever, *ever*, just done something spur of the moment? Just go with your heart and not your head. Just *once!*"

He offered a meager laugh. "This is different."

Glowering, she challenged him. "Why?"

"Christ, Cyn, I lost my damn job!"

"Fine. I'll go alone."

"Huh?"

"I'll go myself. Just cause *you* can't afford to go doesn't mean I hafta stay home."

"I thought we were a team."

"I thought so too."

"Orlando's not going anywhere. We'll go in the fall." Going for humor, he pointed out, "You really wanna visit the only place in the world more humid in summer than Philly?"

She lifted her phone and dropped it into her purse out of sight. "I'm not dealing with this today."

Pike hustled over. "What about tonight's game? We have tickets."

"We have tickets to Orlando too but that doesn't matter, does it?"

෬෧෬

One hour became two. Two became three. And as the game moved into the eighth inning, Pike found himself unconcerned with the outcome. Turning off the TV, he went to the window and again peered through the verticals.

No Cynthia.

He admitted her earlier comment had been spot-on. Money was of no concern. Pike didn't need a job. Today, tomorrow, ever. But the monetary peace-of-mind he enjoyed was due to his father's hard work, not his. And deep in his gut he was wracked with guilt knowing his financial security was the result of someone else's labor. The fact his sister Stephanie received nothing from Mom and Dad added to that guilt.

In his home-office, he powered up his desktop to verify account balances.

Access denied. Pike rekeyed his password.

Access denied.

Concern creeping into his soul, he peeled a post-it note affixed to the back of the monitor and meticulously reentered the password a third time.

You have exceeded the maximum number of attempts to access your account.

Scooping up his cell and keying in the required information, he was surprised when someone answered. Verifying the same info he'd already entered, plus his address, social security number, date of birth, mother's maiden name, place of employment, favorite pet, blood type, who he voted for in the last election and age he lost his virginity, the customer service rep finally asked, "How can I help you, Mr. Grades?"

"Graves."

"I beg your apology. Mr. Grapes."

Pike let it go. "I didn't expect anyone to be working tonight."

"We're here twenty-four-seven."

"I mean being a holiday and all."

"Holiday?"

"July Fourth."

Silence, then a chuckle. "I don't know about that, Mr. Grapes, I'm in Mumbai."

After explaining his reason for calling, "Biff" from Mumbai reset the password. Pike returned to his computer and entered it carefully.

Access denied.

"Shit." Leaning back he kneaded his neck which was glazed in perspiration. His hands hovered above the keyboard like a surgeon about to make an opening incision. He tried Wynter1221. Her birthday was the first day of winter.

Access denied. With the specter of having to again call his buddy Biff, Pike tried Cyn0420. Cynthia's birthday was April twentieth, same day as Hitler.

Access granted.

Ninety minutes later, Pike's world had collapsed.

೮෨೮෨

Using Cyn0420, Pike accessed various accounts spread amongst several institutions. He'd always been good with money. Cynthia was not. She'd filed bankruptcy twice before turning thirty, constantly got collection calls when they first moved in together and, for a while, had a garnishment on her wages. Pike, always endeavoring to help others, decided to educate his girlfriend about finances. The fact no one had ever taken the time to explain things hurt his heart. As she wrote checks and paid bills, he'd watch over her shoulder like a parent observing their child doing homework. Once satisfied, he walked away and never looked back.

"Idiot!" he screamed into the silence. He had no one to blame but himself.

A year ago the sum total of their liquid assets—his assets, or technically his father's—totaled $275,000. Now it was down to just over $39,000. Credit card balances—something Pike never carried—were at $32,500. Scanning the previous eight months of checking statements, he noticed a disturbing trend. The day after his paycheck went in via direct deposit, Cynthia withdrew the funds. He also realized she'd stopped depositing her own paycheck into their joint account, apparently stockpiling her earnings elsewhere. Based on yesterday's conversation with the woman from Liberty Financial, whose name he couldn't recall, that's likely where Cynthia was hiding her money.

We don't have sex but she screwed me anyway.

Unable to sit, Pike was on his feet pacing aimlessly. Anger. Fury. Sadness. Heartbreak. Betrayal. He didn't know what to feel. He went to grab a beer from the fridge. Cynthia had taken the last one. He patted his pockets for cigarettes that hadn't been there since college. His fists clenched and unclenched. Walls tapered around him. He felt entombed in a coffin and buried alive.

Thanatophobia.

Fireworks erupted outside. As neighbors celebrated the birth of a nation, Pike was facing the death of his relationship.

How long had she been doing this? When did she start? And why? Where'd the money go? Cynthia hadn't traded her Dodge for a Lamborghini, hadn't replaced her T-shirts with elegant gowns, hadn't switched out *Dogs Playing Poker* with a Rembrandt.

"Fuck!" he shouted. "Fuck, fuck, fuck."

Fists on the table, he focused on ATM withdrawals. One establishment showed up repeatedly. Opening a second browser, he Googled the location for Cherry's Bar.

Pike yanked his keys from the key rack. Pulse hammering in his neck, he practically ripped the front door from its hinges then leapt back startled.

"Dragon?"

CHAPTER 4

Bobby Dragovich was a pebble in Pike's shoe. Despite Cynthia hearing it from friends and the limited family members she interacted with, she refused to purge Dragon from her life. "We can't move into the future," Pike implored during one of their infamous kitchen table discussions, "unless you cut out the past."

She'd be better for days, sometimes weeks, even months. But Dragon always resurfaced.

"Dammit, Cyn," he would cry out, exasperated. "Why do you allow him to have an invisible hold over you?"

"Look who's talking."

Pike was back on his heels. "What's—what's that mean? Who're you talking about?"

"You know *exactly* who I'm talking about!"

He never brought it up again.

Filling the doorway, Dragon had cleaned himself up. Well, as much as he ever does. The stench of working in body shops oozed through his pores. A dark shirt extended below his waist. "Where's Cyn?"

"She's not here."

"Oh?"

Pike threw his chin forward. "I was just on my way out."

Dragon deliberated then crossed the threshold.

"Hey!" Pike warned, unintentionally retreating. His voice cracking like a prepubescent boy.

Dragon eyed the surroundings then moved his hand toward the rear of his jeans as if about to pull something concealed.

"Dad?"

Dragon blinked. "Hey…Wynter." The hand reappeared from out of sight, beckoning his daughter forward.

Wynter warily bounded down the stairs. Alarmed at the impromptu visit, she embraced him nevertheless. "What're you do-ing here?"

Pike theatrically sighed and checked his watch.

Dragon, thrown off, acted like a deer-in-the-headlights. "I was…uh wonderin' if…ah, you wanted to watch fireworks."

"*Now*?" Wynter cried. "It's kinda late. And I've got a date. Hey, that rhymes."

Assuming it was her married boss, Pike remained tightlipped. Dragon was here. He was her real father. *Let's see if he acts like it.*

Dragon told his daughter "Maybe some other time." He gave Wynter a transitory hug then made a gun with his hand and told Pike, "Catch up with ya later."

Exiting, he became swallowed by darkness.

☙❧

The colony of New Hope was less than a mile top to bottom and boasted a population of twenty-five hundred. Tonight, how-ever, it was Times Square on New Year's Eve. As the hour grew late and fireworks died off, New Hope came alive. Tourists and locals alike flocked to revel in the bustling entertainment of clubs, restaurants, antique shops, art galleries, and a river walk that trailed the Delaware Canal.

New Hope was also home to Cherry's Bar.

The drive took thirty minutes. Finding a parking space took fifteen. But Pike's fury had not lessened. He scolded himself for trusting Cynthia, for believing Cynthia, for loving Cynthia.

Fuckin' moron.

Pike missed his parents—his mom anyway—every day but was glad they weren't here to see their son played for a fool.

After handing over twenty to park, he wandered the crammed sidewalks overflowing with carousers. Street performers dressed as Ben Franklin, Abe Lincoln and for some reason, Mr. T., posed for photos. Uncle Sam, on stilts and standing nine feet tall, bel-lowed exuberantly, "Welcome to New Hope."

After what I learned tonight, I have no hope.

Cherry's Bar was intended to conjure up the ambiance of an old-style British pub. To Pike, however, the name "Cherry" didn't come to mind when thinking of merry olde England.

Hand shaking, he reached for the brass handle. A deep breath, then another, he steeled himself and went in.

Smaller than expected. To his left, a paneled room reminiscent of a VFW hall showcased spinning strobe lights in a disco-like setting. A woman doing karaoke was butchering Melissa Etheridge's "All American Girl." To his right, a man in a Brando-esque leather jacket lifted a pack of Marlboro's from the tray of a vending machine. He sized up Pike then offered a bizarre smile.

Pike ignored the man and swept the interior. A U-shaped bar where harried bartenders struggled keeping up with the frantic pace. All the stools were occupied, the tables lining the periphery also filled with barflies.

Cynthia sat on the last stool on the right.

Pike's heart skipped a beat. Over the cacophony of intoxicated partiers and the crooner in the adjacent room, her laughter rose above everyone and everything. A person with a Marine-style buzz cut, their back to Pike, leaned close to her.

Alex from work? Alex who texted numerous times?

Pike observed from the doorway, unable to recall the last time Cynthia looked so happy. It hurt like hell.

She laughed uproariously, tilted her head back, and guzzled from a bottle of Bud.

She hates Bud. Funny how the mind works.

Cynthia went wide-eyed spotting Pike.

He'd been made, the element of surprise gone. Eyes tight with rage, adrenalin coursing through his blood like a raging fire, his hands impulsively fisted as he stepped forward.

A disturbing memory shot to the front of his mind. Grizzly's. LaMarcus King lying dead. A crimson patch spreading below his fractured skull. The last time Pike acted impulsively things hadn't turned out well. His feet stayed rooted in place.

Without breaking eye contact, Cynthia whispered to the person she was with then slyly pointed with the bottle and lowered her head in shame. The friend turned and looked in Pike's direction.

He was simultaneously relieved while feeling like a dope for overreacting. True, Cynthia was far from being off the hook.

She needed to explain where she'd spent all that money. And why. But at least she wasn't cheating on him. The person beside Cynthia was female.

"I have to go out back to smoke," said the guy dressed like Brando. "Wanna join me?"

Investigative journalism, Pike's forte, was akin to being a detective. You had to put the pieces together, compile facts, build a case, and follow the evidence wherever it leads. No wonder he'd been, as Cynthia scathingly said, *shit canned.*

The facts were plainly apparent, yet he missed all the signs.

Men sat with men.

Women sat with women.

His girlfriend was in a gay bar.

I gotta get the hell outta here. Pivoting, he turned toward the exit, bounced off a biker dude rushing in, and landed on his butt.

Customers laughed.

Mortified and red-faced, Pike saw a hand appear to help him up. Long fingers, nail polish. It was a biker *chick.*

"Pike, wait!" Cynthia called across the din.

Righting himself, Pike scurried away like a scared rabbit.

இல

The streets were clogged with pedestrians. Pike threaded faceless forms, incoherently shouldering many aside. "Watch where you're going!" someone shouted.

"Pike, stop!"

He sprinted into the alleyway that had been converted into a parking lot and looked around in vain to locate his car. *Wrong damn lot.*

"Pike, wait. Please." Cynthia wore a navy blue T-shirt emblazoned with a US flag, snug jeans, and crocs. All new.

I wonder if I paid for that without knowing. Blonde hair done up, makeup highlighting her teal eyes. Dressed for a date. Wearing different clothes than when she'd stormed out earlier, she apparently stored part of her wardrobe elsewhere.

Beyond her shoulder, the woman she'd been with hung far enough away to allow them privacy.

"Who the hell are you?" Pike growled.

The woman said nothing.

Cynthia grabbed Pike's biceps. "Look at me. Pike, look at—"

"How could you?" he said wrenching free.

"How could I what?"

"Steal from me? I trusted you. I opened my heart to you. I opened my home to you and your daughter."

Void of regret, she claimed evenly, "I'm not happy."

"Why didn't you tell me? We could've talked it through and worked things out."

"You can't change, Pike. You're not wired that way."

He was incredulous. She'd drained their funds—primarily his father's—of almost $300,000 that had been bequeathed to him. She'd run up over $32,000 in credit card debt. And was now acting like her unhappiness gave her license to steal. "So this is *my* fault?" he snapped.

She bobbed her head in a yes-no way.

"Un-fucking-believable."

"Look, I tried. I thought you were the one. You're a good guy and all but...well, I got bored."

"Bored?" he barked. "*Bored?* We were building a life together. A future. Why lie to me?"

"I didn't lie. I just kept things from you."

"Ah, much better." He smirked. "Am I supposed to ask, Cyn, are you stealing from me? Cyn, are you cheating on me? Cyn, are you running up our credit cards?"

"How 'bout, Cyn, are you happy?"

Pike became stock-still. "I thought we were adults. I assumed you'd tell me if something was bothering you."

She stepped closer and held his face. Her touch repulsed him. Her fingers like insects crawling on his skin. Jerking away, he inadvertently backhanded her.

"Omigod, omigod. You fuckin' hit me."

"I didn't...You...it was an accident."

The other woman sprang forward. Wearing a frilly purple top and form-fitting white pants, she was a good six inches shorter than Pike but wasted no time getting in his face.

Jamming her finger against his sternum, she said, "Back off." Her stern tone belied her frame. To Cynthia, "You okay?"

"He hit me, Alex. Didja see? He hit me."

Pike's eyes enlarged. "You? *You're* Alex?"

"Alexandra."

He snuffled. "Sure didn't see that comin'."

Alex said, "Of course you didn't. That's the point. You don't see the obvious."

Cynthia hiked one shoulder. "Man? Woman? What's the difference?"

"There is a difference, okay."

Alex curled her mouth. "So…you'd be okay if she was sleeping with a guy but you're not if it's a woman?"

Pike knew she had a point. Infidelity was infidelity. Still, this was…surreal. A direct affront to his manhood. If Cynthia had been seeing a guy, Pike could resort to the age-old desire for revenge. A woman made things different. He changed course. "How long, Cyn? How long have you been cheating?" He couldn't believe they were having this conversation.

"A while."

"And with *her*?" He threw his hand at Alex.

"What's wrong with me?" Alex exclaimed.

Cynthia said, "She gets me. She understands me."

Alex lopped her arm around Cynthia's waist. A unified front. Two against one.

"So *she's* the reason you're stealing from me?"

"Stealing from you?" Cynthia countered angrily. "*You* put my name on those accounts. *You* added me onto those credit cards. But now it's only yours? I see how you think. I'll never be equal." She paused exaggeratedly. "Just because you can't have kids, Pike, doesn't give you the right to treat me like one."

"Does she fuck you as good as me?"

Cynthia rolled her eyes. "Now who's acting like a child?"

"Does she?" Pike shouted, noticing a bystander who increased her pace, jumped into her car, and sped away.

"Actually, she does."

Grinning in pride, Alex raised a finger like a schoolgirl. "Can I say something?"

"No!" roared Pike then asked, "What about Wynter?"

"What about her?"

"She's your daughter.

"Yes, *my* daughter. You have nothing to do with her."

Alex did the finger thing again. "Excuse me."

"*What*?" yelled Pike.

"You honestly don't get it, do you?"

He narrowed his eyes. "What don't I get, *Alexandra*? Why don't you enlighten me? You've known me all of three minutes so I welcome your insight."

He hammily folded his arms across his chest.

"You're upset because she found someone else. You're angry about her supposedly stealing from you."

"No 'supposedly' about it."

"I haven't heard you say you love her."

"Of course I do." His face turned back and forth between his girlfriend and *her* girlfriend, seeking affirmation from anyone. "You know I do."

Cynthia pursed her lips. "Do I?"

"Yes. You should, anyway."

Alex again. "I'm just saying—"

He raised his hand like a traffic cop. "Look, just shut your mouth. This doesn't involve you."

Noticing his hands had balled into fists, Alex asked rhetorically, "You think a man's never hit me before?"

Pike looked down as if his hands weren't his own. He unclenched and asked Cynthia gently, "When did you stop caring about me?"

Equally tender. "Been a while."

"Did you love me?"

"Of course."

It didn't sound convincing. "But not anymore?"

"No, not anymore." She breathed deep and took his hands in hers. Pike didn't pull away. He was too crushed, too shattered. "We're two good people who just aren't good together. I tried, I gave it a shot." She shrugged. "Like when you order a Coke and the waitress says 'Is Pepsi okay?' It's not that I stopped loving you. I just found someone I loved more."

"Uh huh."

Cynthia continued. "Alex is fun, exciting, spontaneous. You're not. Nothing personal, but that's not you. I'm a fly-by-the-seat-of-my-pants girl. You like structure and routine. When was the last time you did something crazy, something spur of the moment? Just without thinking and throwing all caution to the wind?"

Pike wanted to let her have it with both barrels, to refute her and win the argument. But in his heart, he knew the truth. For the first time since high school, he knew the truth. Adulthood had been an act, a sham. "You're right."

"Huh?" Cynthia brows wrinkled. She looked at Alex for confirmation that she'd heard correctly. Then to Pike, "I am?"

He nodded. "I've never done anything spontaneous. Until now." Pike was smiling as he walked away with a bounce in his step. An imaginary weight lifted from his shoulders.

CHAPTER 5

The detective exited the Thirty-Ninth District of the Northwest Division of the Philadelphia Police Department and scowled at the mugginess. Slackening his tie, he crossed the street, entered the diner, and was promptly greeted by someone channeling their inner Tom Hanks from *Castaway*.

"Wilson!"

Dewayne Wilson approached. "Yo, Pike." He indicated a different table granting unobstructed sightlines of all ingress and egress points as well as an unimpeded view of the customers. Once a cop, always a cop. "Friggin' humidity," he bellyached when sitting.

Seeing Dewayne, Pike faced a harsh reality. His parents were gone, the relationship with his sister was non-existent, the fraternal brother born minutes after he was didn't survive the night. There were aunts, uncles, and cousins...somewhere. And now, after what transpired last night with Cynthia, Pike realized his childhood friend was all he had left. Almost. "What's good?"

"Nothing. But the a/c works."

"My treat," Pike announced.

"On my salary, I won't argue."

The waitress materialized, lowered an Iced Tea in front of Dewayne, and held his shoulder in a familiar way. "The usual?"

"Sure, Claire. Thanks."

"For you, sir?"

The usual. Claire. Iced Tea at the ready. Clearly, Dewayne was a regular. "Coke. And whatever he's having."

"Two Meatball Hoagies comin' up."

"Have a good Fourth?" Dewayne asked after Claire left.

"Memorable."

After emptying six sugar packets into his beverage, Dewayne noticed Pike staring at him. "I don't wanna hear it."

Waving his arm like a clairvoyant, Pike said, "I see...diabetes in your future."

Dewayne histrionically downed half the drink and smacked his lips pleasurably. "I'm a Philly cop. I doubt it'll be sugar that kills me."

"Noticed you limping. You all right?"

Sixteen years on the force, first as a beat cop, then rising through the ranks to homicide detective. Dewayne Wilson chased hundreds of perps down hundreds of dark alleys, engaged in immeasurable clashes with addicts hyped on all types of illegal substances, totaled two cruisers, and had been shot at more times than soldiers in Afghanistan. But playing hoops in the driveway with his brother, he stumbled over a raised sprinkler head, went down hard, and obliterated his meniscus. "What're you, my mother?"

He smiled. "How're the kids?"

Dewayne's face lit up like a full moon on a dark night. He retrieved his phone, tapped a few icons, and handed it over. "Janai's fourteen and Little Dewayne is eight. Crazy, huh?"

Heart dropping viewing the kids, Pike commented "Little Dewayne's not so little anymore." He handed the phone back.

"Life goes too fast, my friend."

Pike agreed.

"Lisa and I will hit twenty-three in September."

"Twenty-three?"

"Years. Twenty-three years."

Pike deflated. Twenty-three years. Like the blink of an eye. "I guess she does like riding the chocolate D-train after all."

Dewayne shot daggers at him. "Dude, that's my wife you're talking about."

Hands up, Pike said, "You don't remember? That night we went to Grizzly's to see if Lisa was working. You were all shy. Imagine that? *You,* shy? Anyway, you mentioned about her riding the chocolate D-train."

Dewayne grimaced. "I never said that."

"Yeah, you did."

"I don't remember."

Pike realized—and not for the first time—that he was living too much in the past. Ironic, since the past is what brought him here today.

The waitress lowered their meals, her eyes lingered on Dewayne an extra moment, then sidled away having forgotten Pike's Coke.

"You should come by. Lisa asks about you and the kids miss their Uncle Pike."

"Just busy." His eyes drifted to the window where a couple around his age ambled arm-in-arm down the street.

"How's Cynthia?"

Watching the happy couple walk away, he remarked "It's done."

Dewayne deliberated his friend the way he did a potential suspect in the interrogation room. He remained quiet, allowing information to spill forth.

Instead, Pike threw it back. "You don't seem surprised."

"Truth?"

"Sure."

Dewayne came off relieved to unload a heavy burden. "Cyn's fun and bubbly, a total contrast to you." He leaned forward and playfully smacked his pal in the shoulder. "She's like Chicago. Great place to visit but you don't wanna live there. Just never saw the connection. Always seemed forced."

"On her part?"

"Yours too." Dewayne sipped his iced tea. An obvious stall. "My job requires me to see through people. And what I see in you is…well, you seem distracted, not fully committed." His eyes dropped. "Gonna finish those fries?"

"Help yourself."

Dewayne extended his brawny hand and shoveled a mound onto his plate, immediately dousing them in five tons of salt before soaking them under a sea of ketchup. "My advice? Take some time, dude. Find whatever you're looking for. Seek and ye shall find. Matthew, Seven: Seven."

"Actually that's why I'm here. To seek." He withdrew a folded paper from his wallet and handed it over.

Dewayne wiped grease from his big hands then furrowed his brows. His eyes darted back and forth between the note and his friend of thirty years. "You can't be serious."

"Dead serious."

 споро

Pike looked around one last time.

Returning from New Hope last night, he hit a Wawa on the way home, picked up a six-pack of Sam Adams and sat at his desktop drinking until the remaining balance in his accounts became blurry. Calling an all-night locksmith he was told an after-hours service call would run two hundred. But the guy was honest and advised Pike, "Even if I change the locks, your girlfriend still is allowed to get her stuff." Apparently possession was not nine-tenths of the law. The home was a rental and, despite Pike writing the check each month, Cynthia had just as much legal right as he did.

When was the last time you did something crazy, something spur of the moment? Just without thinking and throwing all caution to the wind?

Cynthia was right. He hated to admit it but dammit, her cutting accusation was true. His entire life he'd played by everyone else's rules and did what he was supposed to. Studying hard, he got into Villanova and earned a BA in Journalism. Shortly after graduating, he landed an entry level position with the *Philadelphia Inquirer.* Drive and dedication, something inherited from his father, elevated him to the position of investigative reporter. Awards, accolades, rubbing shoulders with political bigwigs. Always doing what was right. Always. Hell, he even risked his life to save a girl he barely knew.

And now, at forty-seven years old, what the hell did he have to show for it?

An icy home with a cold woman who lied, cheated, stole, and probably never loved him in the first place. No job. No paycheck. No family. One lone friend who Pike relied on mostly for convenience.

The mantra his father lived by exploded from the recesses of his mind. Laughing sardonically, Pike looked up to heaven and doffed an imaginary cap. "You were right, Dad."

What tugged at his heartstrings was Wynter. The teenager was definitely an ordeal. Rebellious, moody, promiscuous. Okay, a typical sixteen-year-old. But with parents like Cynthia and Dragon, Pike was pleased she wasn't worse. He'd endeavored to be a positive influence in the girl's life and walk that fine line between parental figure and friend.

Only time would tell. Unable to conceive children, Pike knew all you could do is plant the seeds and hope they grow.

Contesting the credit card debt wasn't feasible. Due to his own shortsightedness—or perhaps, blinded by what he thought was love—he'd added her name onto his accounts thereby opening himself up to a shit storm of trouble. It was his fault and now he'd have to the pay the piper. And pay Citi. And Wachovia. And Chase. And Meridian.

He still had assets totaling $1.4 million, the result of his father's hard work. At least Cynthia wasn't joint on that account.

With fire in the belly, he knew he needed to be…well, impulsive, not disciplined. If he started overthinking, he'd reconsider. Moving quickly, Pike loaded his Honda in under forty minutes.

For once, he was happy Cynthia didn't come home and that Wynter was away, likely with her married boss.

"Crap, almost forgot."

In the spacious bedroom closet, he moved aside boxes containing his life: numerous articles that had been picked up by AP, praise from past bosses, a photo with Dan Rather, boxing gloves that had cracked and disintegrated with time. On his haunches, he slipped his fingers into a trivial gap where the carpet stopped half an inch from the wall. Despite being alone, he guardedly looked over his shoulder then peeled back the rug and blindly rifled around for the partition. Twisting his face, he pried the loose wooden slat a few inches before probing for the item.

A smile crossed his face when touching a black felt box the size of a pack of cigarettes. Respectfully blowing off the dust, just clutching the box warned his heart. For a moment, just a moment, everything was right in the world. He'd kept it hidden from Cynthia and from other girlfriends for thirty years, dating back to the summer after graduating Lafayette High. An item purchased from a jewelry store.

Returning everything where it had been, he slipped the item into his pocket and exited the house.

Headlights swept the driveway.

"Hey!" Dewayne got out and gave Pike his cop stare.

"Wilson!" The customary *Castaway* greeting. "I thought you'd text me the info."

"I wanted to come over and talk about…this." Forehead more creased than usual, he appeared agitated.

Pike waited.

Dewayne leaned against the driver's side door, intentionally preventing Pike from getting behind the wheel, and flapped an envelope. "You could've found this on your own. Why'd you ask me?"

"You're in law enforcement. Figured your info would be more accurate than what I'd find online."

"Bullshit."

Pike didn't rebuff.

Dewayne studied him for a beat. "You think this is the answer?"

"Yes."

"*You*? Pike Graves spontaneous?"

"Me spontaneous."

"What're you hoping to find?"

Pike hiked his shoulders. He didn't know.

"It's me."

Pike articulated the first thought that came to mind. "Completion."

A sideways glance, he said, "Go on."

"Completing something I started but never finished. Following through."

Dewayne grinned small. "When you boxed, your follow-through sucked. That's why you didn't last."

"People change."

Dewayne exhibited the envelope. "And you think Paige Rhodes is the answer?"

"She looked back."

"What's that mean, 'she looked back'?"

"Nothing. Never mind."

"Maybe she's married."

Pike's stomach dropped. "Is she?"

"No," his friend replied after a theatrical pause. "But that's not the point."

"She still out west?"

Dewayne nodded. "North of San Francisco, place called Mill Valley. Why not just call her? Email her. Jeez, Pike, you're a journalist, a wordsmith. If anyone can explain it, you can."

"I...wouldn't even know how to start or what to say." Pike wiped something from his eye and looked away. Chin quivering, he breathed, "I'm...lost."

"Who isn't?"

Staring at his pal, Pike said, "You're not."

"*Really?*"

Pike rolled his eyes then scolded himself. Cynthia was the eye-roll master. "You've got the girl you've been crazy about since high school. The girl I've been crazy about is on the other side of the country. You've been at your job sixteen years. I just got fired. You have two wonderful kids. Me?" He shrugged.

"You're an idiot."

"Thanks. Love ya too."

"I do have all those things. But trust me, we're all lost."

Pike swallowed.

Dewayne clasped his shoulder and bore a laser-like gaze into his friend's soul. "Go after her. You won't rest until you do." He paused. "Honestly, I'm envious of you for following your dreams."

Touched, Pike said, "Thanks."

"But remember one thing."

"Yeah?"

"Sometimes you can win and still lose."

Pike waved it away like a pesky fly.

"How long's it been?"

"Eight years. Not since she flew back for Mom's funeral."

"But you didn't keep in touch?'

"No, Dewayne, I didn't."

"Why not?"

"I just…shit, I don't know. I was thirty-nine. Now I'm forty-seven. Big difference."

"And Stephanie?"

"Yeah?"

"Why are you hoping to reconnect with your sister now?"

Pike didn't answer. "She still in Vegas?"

"Yes. And who's this third name on the list you gave me? Virgil Holland."

"Did you find him?"

"Yes, I found him," snapped Dewayne. "But that doesn't answer my question."

Pike ripped the envelope away. "Something else that needs completion." He looked at the addresses: Arizona, Nevada, California. Neighboring states.

Maybe my luck is changing.

Dewayne broke the obstreperous silence. "You won't be coming back, will ya?"

"Are you speaking as a detective, Detective?"

"No, as your friend."

Pike clucked his tongue. "I'm not sure."

Dewayne came off the car and embraced his lifelong friend in a tight hug. "Nah, you won't be."

When the embrace broke, Pike started to say something but Dewayne cut him off. "I know you're a movie buff, but this is real life. 'Happy endings are Hollywood bullshit."

෪෨෪

Too keyed up, sleep never came. The bedside clock glowed two forty seven when subdued footsteps trudged up the stairs. Pike grew rigid, anticipating an unwanted confrontation with Cynthia. Amidst a stifled giggle, footfalls padded in the direction of Wynter's bedroom. Her door closed and minutes later, cries of passion emanated down the hallway. Wynter and some guy. And some other guy.

Just after four in the morning, Pike surrendered. He wanted to say farewell to Wynter but she was likely fast asleep sandwiched between two lovers. In a perfect world, he'd leave her with some helpful advice. But Pike knew the world was anything but perfect.

The morning air was unseasonably nippy. Thunderheads were rolling in from the west. There was a storm on the horizon. Streaks of white hot lightening stabbed the night.

Reaching the main thoroughfare, he only now realized he never bothered looking at his home one final time before driving off to an uncertain future. Freud would have a field day with that.

At the entrance to the Penn Turnpike, there was only one lane open at this early hour. Pike took the ticket from the guy in the booth. "Thanks," he said robotically.

"Good luck," the man said. "Have a safe journey."

Pike arched a brow at the strange comment.

Accelerating down the onramp, he noticed a hitchhiker cloaked in shadow. Dark clothes and barely discernible in the moonless twilight. The only distinct article of clothing was a white straw hat with a green band.

Pike chuckled when reading the creative cardboard sign.

Pacific Time Zone.

"Pretty vague."

He moved into the left lane and embarked on his pilgrimage. Behind him the tentacles of a new day as carroty orange bands fractured the blackness. Ahead of him, the darkness refused to yield to the light.

Pike accelerated and headed into the coming storm.

PART II

Starting Over

"One of the joys of travel is visiting new towns
and meeting new people."

~ Genghis Khan

CHAPTER 6

Whereas most would be daunted by the tedium of a cross-country drive, Pike welcomed the unending asphalt ribbon. A plane would get him out west in five hours, not five days. But travelling by car gave him ample time to formulate a plan.

First stop, Phoenix. It was doubtful Virgil Holland remembered him but he would never forget Holland. And what he did. After settling that score, Pike would head north to Vegas for…what? His sister Stephanie would be as stunned by his arrival as Holland. And lastly, his journey would culminate with Paige in northern California.

Though he was loathe to give Cynthia credit, she was onto something regarding his regimented existence. Always disciplined and orderly, his new outlook of spontaneity was liberating. He was reborn, shedding his skin and allowing a new Pike Graves to emerge. A resurrection of sorts.

Reaching the outskirts of Zanesville, OH, Pike's hunger pangs kicked in. He'd fill his own tank then his Honda's.

A pungent aroma of fuel coated Barney's Travel Stop. Semi-trailers sat at islands like dinosaurs being fed. Inside, weary motorists took a breather after battling a deluge that blanketed the Ohio/Pennsylvania border.

Pike casually perused aisles and aisles of snacks, ball caps, bumper stickers, automotive supplies, puzzle books, and DVD's. On an endcap hung a discounted T-shirt declaring "I'd rather push an American car than drive a foreign car." *Welcome to the Rust Belt.* Bypassing Hardee's, Roy Rogers, and Subway, he selected the diner.

After he seated himself, a plump waitress skulked over. Her gruff voice and yellowed fingernails left no doubt she was a lifetime smoker. Perfunctorily pouring water from a pitcher, getting as much on the table as in his glass, she recited, "Today's special's a Chili Cheese Dog, side 'a slaw, chick peas, cornbread, and your choice 'a chocolate ice cream or a cookie." Incessant gum chewing like Morse code.

"I'll have a BLT, fries, and a Coke. Thanks." He politely drew her attention to the spill. Like Houdini, she whipped a rag from between her ample bosom, sopped up the water, and returned the rag to her cleavage.

As she waddled away, Pike searched for a rating from the health district.

Long-haul truckers clustered on one side of the restaurant, families opposite. A wall-mounted TV was muted. The banner across the anchorman's chest claimed *Tennessee Minning Disaster*. The misspelled word had Pike wondering how he lost his job while someone at a major cable network kept theirs.

The waitress reappeared; brusquely lowered his meal, packets of ketchup and mustard, and the check all in one fluid motion; and walked away.

Guess I didn't want dessert.

The only person seated alone on the family side of the diner, Pike, not wanting to stand out, lifted a discarded newspaper from an adjacent table for companionship: A ferry capsized off the coast of Laos killing seventy-three on board, a twister leveled a mobile home park in Oklahoma, the President was holding a campaign rally even though Election Day was seventeen-months away, a video of a disgruntled fast food employee urinating into a fry grill had gone viral and a Kardashian posted a picture of her ass on Instagram. It wasn't until finishing lunch that Pike realized the newspaper was three weeks old. *Some things never change.*

"Stop being a bitch!"

Four booths away was a broad-shouldered man just this side of forty in a green tank top and arms covered in ink. Buzz-cut blond hair and Nordic features, his body was taut, his neck as a red as tenderized meat. The woman at his side appeared beaten down. Or just beaten.

She glared at the guy, wavered a moment, then angled forward and overtly glugged the vanilla shake.

"I said, no!" Belligerently, he snatched the glass away and moved it beyond her reach. "I ain't havin' the guys at the plant givin' me shit bout you gettin' fat."

She bowed her head. Crying? Praying? Either way, it hit close to home for Pike. Too close.

"Move it! We gotta hit the road." When she didn't react quickly enough, he pitched his bulky torso against her, knocking her from the booth and onto all fours like a dog.

Pike looked around. Patrons did a poor job of busying themselves, pretending not to notice. No one wanted to get involved.

Using the table for support, the young woman hoisted herself up and defiantly moved her hand toward the shake. The man's blinding swiftness contradicted his girth. A hostile sweep of his thick forearm sent the mug flying where it crashed against a nearby wall and shattered into a million shards of glass. Not one person reacted.

"Somethin' you wanna say?" Lips tight, Nordic-man bore his gaze into Pike. The booths between them a demilitarized zone.

Pike dithered. He matched the guy's glare, then eyed the beleaguered woman. The fear and helplessness in her lifeless eyes caused a painful memory to explode like a starburst.

Stephanie.

The words LaMarcus King spoke all those years ago that fateful night in Grizzly's came back: *Don't be a hero, Pike Graves.*

The moment passed.

The man scoffed. "Yeah, I didn't think so." Uncoiling from the booth, he put his hand in a proprietary manner on the small of the woman's back. "Move your fat ass."

Nursing his Coke, Pike feigned interest in a TV commercial touting the return of the McRib. He straightened unused silverware and fixated on a Pace Arrow motorhome being filled at the gas pumps outside. Allowing enough time to pass, he lifted the check and approached the register.

Nordic-man was going off on the cashier about the service. Avoiding confrontation, Pike trudged to the men's room.

After taking care of business, he started exiting but was met with broad shoulders filling the doorway.

Nordic-man, beer-gut and all, outweighed Pike by forty or fifty pounds. Contemptuously scanning him, he hissed. "Got a problem, mac?"

Pike shook his head.

"What?"

"No, I don't have a problem."

"I don't like the way you were lookin' at my girl."

Pike said nothing, hoping the bully wouldn't hear his thumping heart.

He stepped closer. "Or were you looking at me?"

Lowering his eyes, Pike tried evading him. "I wasn't looking at anyone."

Nordic-man now a human blockade. "You *were* looking at me, weren't ya? You one of them faggots takin' over my country?"

"No."

The palm against Pike's chest knocked him back. Blindly flailing, he found the basin and managed not to fall down.

"You was either lookin' at her or lookin' at me. Which is it, pretty boy? You a pervert or a faggot?"

"I'm nobody."

"Ain't that the truth." He laughed and melodramatically stepped aside. As Pike passed him, a powerful shove between the shoulder blades sent him stumbling into a rack of roadmaps and brochures of things to see and do in Zanesville.

Trudging to the register, the ground moved in waves beneath his feet. Knees weak, stomach churning.

The cashier moved in slow motion. "You okay?" she whispered without looking at him.

"Yeah, why?"

Her eyes swept the lobby. "Everyone heard. But even if you are an f-a-g-g-o-t, that was inappropriate."

Pike didn't answer.

Handing over his credit card, she presented an over-the-top toothy smile. "Don't forget to come back and see us."

"Oh, of course."

Determined strides. Not running, but not walking casually either.

Don't be a hero, Pike Graves.

He had once played hero outside Grizzly's. And despite the passage of decades and the life-altering path he found himself on after that auspicious night, he still was unsure if he did the right thing. Since then, Pike flew under the radar. Or tried to. Kowtowing too often and swallowing his pride, he'd become a human piñata for the likes of Cynthia Grimm and Dragon and Wynter and Stewart Stafford and many others along the way.

Not anymore.

Pike Graves was reborn. Impulsive, spontaneous, tired of being irrelevant. The weakling who got sand kicked in his face at the beach on the back of those comics Pike read as a kid was done looking the other way. Turning on his heels, he marched toward the store and leapfrogged three wooden steps.

"Don't." Slouching shamefacedly on a bench and an iPod in her hand, she looked at Pike over the top of her rose-colored sunglasses. "Please, don't."

"You okay?"

She smiled wretchedly. "Wonderful."

"Ya know, you *can* get out. I'm sure there are shelters in town for battered women."

She smirked.

"I know it's not my business but you seem like a smart, young woman. You deserve better."

"Yeah, right."

"Everyone deserves—"

The blow to his kidneys had Pike lurching forward. Somehow he avoided doing a face plant onto the sidewalk.

"Hey, faggot, I told you to stay away from my girl."

Pike tasted the BLT in the back of his throat. A prolonged glance at the girl, he threw up his palms in submission. "I'm sorry."

"That's better," sneered Nordic-Man.

But he was only beginning. "I'm sorry you're such an asshole. I'm sorry you need to make yourself feel bigger by making others feel smaller. I'm sorry your parents never told you how to treat a woman. I'm—"

As expected, the guy came at him with a loping right cross. Pike effortlessly dodged the predictable move and delivered a blistering one-two combination into the guy's expansive gut.

Nordic-Man blinked in surprise at the wiry man's agility. Snorting like a bull, he charged forward.

Pike feinted left, danced right to the man's weaker side, and released a potent hook into his solar plexus.

Nordic-man was already winded. "You—son-of-a—bitch!"

It was like riding a bike. Second-nature. Innate. Watch the shoulders, not the eyes. When the shoulder flexed, Pike knew the guy was coming with a left this time. He slanted back, easily eluding the predictable punch. Moving quickly, Pike grabbed the guy's wrist and jerked it up behind the back of his neck.

The bully dropped to his knees, sniveling. "Don't break my wrist. I'll lose my job if I can't work."

Pike knew what it was like to be terminated, but before he could release the guy on his own motorists and truckers who'd encircled them stopped recording with their phones and like a boxing referee separated the brawling combatants.

Now that Nordic-Man was restrained by four men equal in size, he reasserted his machismo and cursed Pike while getting shepherded inside. The crowd dispersed as if this was a daily occurrence in Zanesville.

A smile crossed Pike's face. It was invigorating standing up for someone who couldn't stand up for themselves. Speaking of...

"Where'd she go?" he mumbled.

Turning in all directions, he realized the young woman had slipped away during the altercation.

Pike had heard stories about battered women who stayed in abusive relationships because it was all they knew.

He'd said his piece and, like with Wynter, all he could do was plant a seed and hope it grew.

Ten miles down the road, still amped up by the adrenaline rush, he slipped a Warren Zevon CD into his console and casually glanced at the rearview.

Two eyes stared back at him.

ↄ∕ᵔↄ∕ᵔ

The Dodge Charger jumped the curb and sideswiped the garbage can, causing it to spin like a top and ejecting detritus across the lawn. The vehicle stopped half a foot shy from the garage door.

Cynthia spilled out. Victorious for getting home without a DUI, she staggered her way to the front door. Going through her keys twice before finding the right one, she struggled inserting the key into the lock.

"Honey, I'm home," she hooted.

Tottering, she used the wall for support and made her way to the bathroom. After relieving herself, she kicked off her shoes, hastily removed her top, and sighed pleasantly when collapsing into the La-Z-Boy. "I love you recliner." The combination of mixing drinks with nachos was wreaking havoc. "Nacho cheese. Nacho cheese. That's not yo cheese." Laughing so hard, she felt food rising. "Uh, oh." Before finding the lever to sit forward, Cynthia spewed on herself. Chunks of vomit coated her chest and bra. "That's freakin' cool." She laughed and laid her head back.

"Ms. Grimm?"

Her eyes shot open. Cotton mouthed and dried spittle on her chin, she glanced toward the blinds. "What…time is it?"

"Just after eight."

"At night?"

"The morning. You musta fallen asleep."

Gathering her senses, she squinted at the man standing over her. "Brock, right?"

"Yes' ma'am."

She giggled. *Ma'am.* So what if the guy was married and banging her underage daughter. At least he was respectable to her. Noticing the sustained gander at her bra, she joked, "I don't know where Wynter got her boobs from either."

"Um, I should get going."

Cynthia, loitering between a hangover and drunkenness, tittered. "Going…going…gone."

The front door closed.

"Mom!"

Cynthia opened her eyes. "Hey."

Frantically, Wynter looked around, yanked a throw blanket from the sofa, and handed it over.

"Thanks." Cynthia wiped crust from eyes.

"No. *There!*" Keeping her distance, she pointed at regurgitated orange chunks spread across her mother's upper body. "Oh my God, did Brock see you like *this*?"

"I dunno." She eased the recliner forward. "What time is it?"

"Almost eleven. You passed out drunk."

"Eleven?" She started to stand. "I gotta get to work."

Wynter held her in place. "It's Saturday."

"Oh? Oh, good. I can go out drinking again tonight." Assisted to her feet, Cynthia chortled over her shoulder. "I just puked on Pike's chair. Or piked on puke's chair. Where is he anyway?"

"Gone."

"Of course he is. Looking for a job on the weekend. So noble."

"No," Wynter said. "I mean gone, left, took off."

Cynthia's brows wrinkled.

Wynter nodded. "Suitcases, car, lotsa clothes. All gone."

"Why would he do that?"

Wynter rolled her eyes. "Gee, Mom, I wonder."

Willing away the hangover, Cynthia hustled upstairs to the bedroom to confirm her daughter's claim. Gaps on his side of the closet. Boxes rearranged. Spotting a slice of carpet peeled back, a frown crossed her face before altering into a wicked laugh. "You dumb bastard. You think I didn't know."

Cynthia didn't smoke except after sex. And while drinking. And after a meal. Sometimes driving to work. But never inside the home. Pike was so self-righteous, so self-important, that she was banished to the backyard like some mangy mongrel.

Now Pike had taken off, damn him. And for two hours, she chain smoked while learning what that devious SOB had done.

When he added her onto his accounts, she incorrectly assumed it was as a joint account holder, believing she had equal access. Now she discovered she was merely an authorized user. She could use his credit cards and access his accounts but, as an authorized user, she could make no changes.

Pike had closed the credit cards.

Pike had removed her name from all of the liquid accounts.

Pike had tied her hands financially.

"That two-faced lying fucker!"

Signing in online, she accessed her accounts with Liberty Financial. Months ago, she began draining funds from their checking account into one in her name only, an account Pike knew nothing about. She never touched those funds. Instead, she stockpiled. While increasing the balance in her secret stash, she depleted Pike's. She had four thousand dollars to her name and one lone credit card with a measly five hundred dollar limit.

"Shit!"

Cynthia was shrewd enough to realize that as an authorized user she wasn't legally responsible for the debt, even if she accrued it. Pike was primary. Pike was responsible.

She did learn, however, that he hadn't closed his main account, the inheritance from his parents. That still stood at $1.4

million. The credit card linked to that account remained open as well. As far as Cynthia knew that was the only open credit card he still had. Her name, however, had never been added. She couldn't close that account, nor could she make any changes.

However...

After sending Wynter to the corner Wawa to pick up cigarettes, she made a call and paced nervously until he answered.

"Yeah?" grunted the man.

"Dragon, change of plans."

CHAPTER 7

Hope I didn't scare you."

"No, not at all," Pike replied. "First time I crapped in my pants since I was two."

Emitting a sugary laugh, she climbed over the seat. Pike tilted left to give her space. After buckling up, she remarked, "That was pretty kick-ass what you did back there."

Pike said nothing.

"I was sure you'd get walloped. He's lots bigger than you."

"Bigger doesn't mean you can fight."

She assessed him. "That's what you do, you're a fighter?"

"Used to be."

"UFC or MMA?"

He cringed. "That's brawling. I was a pugilist."

"A *what*?"

"A boxer. Well, kind of."

The girl burst out giggling then sheepishly covered her mouth. "Sorry. You don't look like a boxer."

He waggled his head. "It was a long time ago."

"Were you any good?" Already displaying a certain level of comfort, she opened the glove box.

Pike tensed. The item he removed from beneath the floorboard in the bedroom closet was in there. "What're you looking for?"

"Any snacks?"

"Nope."

"So, were you any good?"

"Boxing? No."

The girl made an *O* face. "Oh, man. I'm hella sorry." She extended a hand. Long fingers, chipped pink polish. "Roxy."

"*Roxy*?"

"I know, right? Sounds like I belong on a stripper pole."

Looking right, his eyes lingered an extra tick. At Barney's

Travel Stop his focus had been the behemoth and not the girl at her side. Roxy had flourishing raven hair hanging loosely around bare sienna shoulders. Black eyes, wide and knowing, her ethnicity hard to place. A pretty girl with pretty features, she wasn't rail thin and would never walk a runway in Paris. But there was a pleasantness about her, an innocence. Feigned toughness that safeguarded vulnerability. Confident, yet unsure. Outgoing, yet shy. "Yeah, it kinda does."

"My real name's Rosie Axl Ledesma. Rosie for my grandma, Axl for some guy in a band called Guns-n-Roses from way back when."

Way back when. Pike winced.

"Usually when someone tells you their name, they respond with their own."

"Sorry. Pike."

"Just Pike? That's it? Like Oprah or Beyoncé?"

"Pike Graves."

Roxy slapped her legs. "And I thought *my* name was bad-ass. How'd you get a name like that anyway?"

"Long story."

Roxy laughed again, something she seemingly did often. She was worlds apart from the timid frightened girl back at Zanesville. Perhaps, like Pike, she also was enjoying newfound freedom. "What's so funny?" he asked.

"'Long story.' Why is everything with guys always *long*?"

His lips turned up.

She held her hands six inches apart. "Is it this long?"

Pike blushed.

She moved her hands farther apart. "This long?"

"Jeez."

"Oh, I bet it's *this* long." Her hands now several feet apart.

"That's about right."

Now they both laughed.

"You gonna tell me how you got a name like Pike, Pike?"

Mouth curled, he inhaled. "Mom couldn't think of a name and Dad was…well, never around as usual. Months went by and they couldn't come up with anything. Any who, Mom goes into labor and Dad was M-I-A. She called her brother, my Uncle Ken, to take her to the hospital but they didn't make it." He shrugged. "Mom delivered me on the Penn Turnpike. Turn*pike*. Pike."

"Told ya it wasn't *that* long. Brothers, sisters?"

Pike swallowed. "Just, uh…one. A sister."

"You hesitated. You sure?"

"Yep."

"Name?"

"Stephanie. What's with the questions? Are you a reporter?"

"Nah."

"What do you do?"

Roxy watched the Ohio countryside roll by. "Nothing now. I waitressed a bit. Even worked a while as a telemarketer. If you're interested in a three-day-two-night stay in Cozumel, I'm your girl. How about you, *Pikeronies*?"

"Pikeronies, huh? Actually *I'm* a reporter. Well, used to be."

"No way."

"Way."

"You mean, like, for *TMZ*?"

Pike cringed. "God, no. Print journalism."

Her thin eyebrows shot up. "You mean, like a newspaper? People still read those?"

"Not enough." So immersed in the friendly banter, he hadn't noticed his reduced speed. Tramping the gas to make up the time, he asked, "How about you…*Roxyeronies*. Siblings?"

"One sister but we don't talk."

"I know the feeling. What about your parents?"

"Dad? Who cares? Having a family was Mom's thing but she died and he was stuck with a couple daughters he never wanted in the first place." Roxy stopped abruptly, losing herself in the billboards advertising businesses at the next exit. "Last I heard he was working on an oil rig in the Gulf of Mexico after dumping me and my sister at our Uncle Ronald's."

Pike couldn't turn off his reporter instincts. "And Uncle Ronald didn't like kids."

"Au contraire, Pikemeister," Roxy wailed hammily. "He *loved* kids. He *loved* watching me shower, *loved* ogling my ass when I cooked his meals and cleaned his house, and really *loved* jerking off while I slept."

Pike held his forehead. "Christ, I'm sorry."

"It is what it is."

He assumed the coast-to-coast journey would be solitary. That he'd have plenty of time to come up with a plan. The easygoing camaraderie he already enjoyed with his new passenger was comforting.

Moving into the left lane, Pike passed a Mayflower van.

"That's how I met Jonah."

He threw a thumb over his shoulder. "The guy back there?"

Folding her legs beneath her, either for a long drive or a long story, Roxy explained. "Jonah Elliott. I was on Craig's List one night—"

"Ah."

"Yeah, no kidding. Him and a buddy were starting up a moving company and needed someone to answer their phones and stuff. The business never got off the ground but that's how we met."

"He's a lot older than you," Pike commented unnecessarily.

Roxy looked away, clearly not wanting to go there.

A moment of silence before changing topics. "You have a boyfriend?" Recalling Cynthia and her lesbian lover, he amended his question. "Or, ya know, anyone?"

She shook her head. Clearly something else she didn't want to discuss.

Trying a different subject, he asked, "So, uh, how'd you get in my car?"

"Are you sorry I did?"

"No, just…curious."

"Honda's are easy peasy to get into."

"They are?"

"A ten-year-old can do it."

He met her eyes then perused her clothes. Rose-colored glasses hung from the collar of a form fitting white tank top showing firm breasts and bicycle shorts exposing athletic calves. Pink toenail polish matched her fingernails and a small stud in her right nostril. "How old are you anyway?"

"Twenty-one."

"In school?"

"Uh, no."

Pike's antediluvian thinking had surfaced. *School. Boyfriend.* Then again, he'd charted his path in life and look where that got him. "Where'd you want me to drop you?"

She hiked one shoulder. "How far are you going?"

"Far."

"Like Dayton?"

"Like San Francisco."

Her brows skyrocketed. "As in California?"

"That's the one."

"And what's in San Francisco?"

He smiled forlornly. "My second chance."

Roxy scrunched her face so tightly her eyes disappeared. She analyzed his profile then asked, "Who is she?"

Pike half-smiled. "Who said it's a she?"

"Dude," Roxy professed, "I was a mystic in a previous life."

He laughed. "Really?"

"I think I was a sorceress. I have a sense about people."

"This could be interesting." Pike shifted. "Okay, tell me about me."

Roxy closed her eyes and turned her hands palms-up as if seeking spiritual guidance. Shallow breathing became almost nonexistent. Pike split his time between watching her and the interstate. He was beginning to think she nodded off when her eyes opened. She gripped his shoulder with a firmness he didn't expect.

"I see you...searching. You're...lost. And hope to find an answer in California."

"Okay." He played along. "What else?"

"You seek...redemption."

His lips pursed.

"I'm intuiting that you're...unemployed. And unattached." She brought herself out of the self-induced trance. "Recently unattached, correct?"

Pike nodded once.

"Recently unemployed, too?"

"I *did* tell you that!" He was happy to at least shoot one hole in her supposed proficiency.

She again closed her eyes and returned to channeling the universe. "Weird," she murmured a moment later.

"What?"

"I see...neon lights. Lotsa neon lights. But they don't really have neon in California, do they?"

"Not really." *But they do in Las Vegas.*

Disappointed, she sighed. "Maybe I'm losing my touch."

Feeling marginally violated, he asked, "So how far are you going?"

"All the way."

"Huh?"

"Last I heard my sister's up in Seattle. I'll go with you to Cali then hop a Greyhound up to Washington."

"But—"

"Hey." She squeezed his knee. "It'll be fun. And my psychic powers tell me you're in need of some serious fun, Pike Graves."

e⁄ɔe⁄ɔ

Pike had noticed billboards promoting a shopping mall just off I-70 as they approached Indianapolis. Since Roxy would be riding shotgun for the short-term, she'd need a change of clothes and personal items.

Discomfited, she stated softly, "I only have, like, fifty in cash and my credit card is almost maxed."

"It's okay, I got it."

On Pike's list of dreaded activities, shopping was right alongside root canals and afternoons at the DMV. Yet, Roxy's reaction made the intolerable hell enjoyable. A Target in Indiana but she acted like it was an upscale boutique on Rodeo Drive. Exuberant, thrilled, animated. He didn't need to be a self-proclaimed mystic to deduce she was seldom treated well. It tugged at his heart.

Checking out, she thanked him and winked. "I'll make it up to you."

e⁄ɔe⁄ɔ

He wanted to find a hotel but Roxy claimed she was "famished." At a nearby Red Robin, he ordered a cheeseburger, fries, and a Coke.

"And for your daughter?" the waiter asked.

"Oh, she's not—" Pike was kicked under the table.

She went with a triple bacon cheeseburger, bottomless fries, a side of mac and cheese, and a large vanilla shake. After the waiter left, she said, "The shake's okay, right?"

"I'm not Jonah. Get what you want."

She showed that gushy smile and leaned forward to pat his cheek. "You're *definitely* not."

Dinner finished, the sun was slipping beyond fertile farm-lands. Pike hoped locating a suitable hotel would be quick but the late hour combined with it being Saturday of a holiday weekend resulted in a two-hour quest. Roxy waited in the car while Pike went in and out checking availability. One motel had a room. Single bed only. He kept looking.

After endless searching and with the pull of sleepiness grow-ing stronger, they came upon a place far off the interstate. Inferi-or, substandard, and catering to a specific clientele, the marquis announced *rooms available, XXX movies* and a double-entendre boasting *the customer always comes first.*

Roxy giggled reading the name. "Hoosier Daddy Inn?"

"Clever, huh?"

"Ya know," she said thoughtfully, "I remember this place."

Pike shot her a look.

"I'm kidding, I'm kidding."

When Pike entered the fetid lobby, the clerk didn't get up from his stool. Reaching the counter, he realized why. The guy was pintsized. His nametag ironically read *Larry Little*. "I'd like a room."

Repositioning a stogie to the opposite side of his mouth, Larry Little squinted through the front window then evaluated Pike skeptically. "You think you can keep up with a stallion like her."

Pike flinched then echoed the waiter's sentiment from earlier. "She's my daughter."

Larry Little's laughter morphed into a hacking cough. After nearly expelling a lung, he stated, "Yeah, sure. And Mila Kunis is at home waitin' to sit on my face."

"How much?"

The elfin man considered Pike. "Look, buddy boy, I don't care what people do here. They give me money, I give 'em a key. But I don't condone no pedal files."

"Pedophiles."

"That's what I said, pedal files." He again leaned left to gauge Roxy then shrieked "Sonofabitch!" as he disappeared from sight, sliding off his stool and dropping three feet to the floor.

"You okay?" Pike asked, suppressing laughter.

The guy shook off his nosedive and frisked himself. "Where's my flippin' cigar?" Climbing back onto the stool, he asked suspi-ciously, "How old is she anyway?"

"Twenty-one." Pike retrieved his wallet, making sure Larry Little saw green. "How much?"

"A hun'red."

He started counting out bills.

"An' sixty. A hun'red sixty."

☙❧

As Pike fiddled with the keycard, the door to the neighboring room opened with a flourish. An obese sixty-something staggered out wearing only boxers and holding an ice bucket. A broken-down woman in her mid-forties, failing to look decades younger and wearing a face with smeared makeup, emerged seconds later. Slipping her hand into his underpants, she cooed. "Hurry back. I already miss Mr. Wiggles." Facing left, she winked at Pike and blew Roxy a kiss before backpedaling into the room.

Mr. Wiggles's owner regarded Roxy for an uncomfortable few seconds before nodding his approval at Pike. "Way to go, man."

Entering the motel room, they were instantly overcome by the reek of cigarette smoke embedded in the walls. Twin beds, circular table with only one chair, green shag pockmarked with indescribable stains, an outdated nineteen-inch RCA and ceiling tiles swelling from water damage. Even the local thrift store had better furniture.

"Ooh, boy," Roxy groaned.

"Not exactly the Ritz-Carlton."

"More like the Shits-Carlton."

"We can look for someplace else," Pike offered.

"We're both exhausted. One night won't kill us."

Despite the A/C rattling all night, headboards thumping against the common wall, and sirens piercing the darkness, Pike's mind was firing on all pistons. He couldn't wait to get up, get out, and get back on the road. If everything worked according to plan, they'd reach Kansas City tomorrow, maybe even a little beyond.

However, Pike knew things in his life seldom worked out as intended.

CHAPTER 8

The following morning, after showering and feverishly scrubbing away one night at the *Hoosier Daddy Inn,* they were on the road by eight a.m. Traffic at the end of the holiday weekend was unexpectedly light allowing Pike to make good time. The flat gray ribbon was hypnotic in its unchanging appearance crossing effortless plains and level countryside extending in every direction. Relaxed conversation between him and Roxy made the dreariness of the interminable drive pleasant.

Indiana.

Illinois.

Missouri.

Grateful for the companionship, Pike reveled in the stress-free back and forth that flowed naturally. Cynthia would sporadically chastise him for being moody, introverted, and withdrawn. Once again, there was validity in her accusation. He tended to keep things internalized. Trust in others never came easy.

Nevertheless, the comfort with Roxy after only twenty-four-hours surprised him. They shared a bond, a connection. Then Pike reminded himself:

Paige.

When leaving home, he'd tossed CDs into a backpack, intending music to be his co-pilot. But when Roxy announced "I'm gonna catch some shut-eye," he found listening to tunes unappealing, inexplicably missing chatting with her.

Paige.

With his left hand atop the wheel and no cars in sight, Pike contorted his body and unwisely rummaged through the backpack. He found *Double Fantasy*, the last album John Lennon recorded. The opening song was a catchy tune with a 1950s beat titled "Starting Over." Fitting, since Pike was starting over.

Stephanie, seven years older, had been instrumental in forming his musical taste. Their mom, Cora, claimed she was too busy raising two kids to have time for music. And their father, Sam? Pike had no idea what, if any, music he liked. His old man was so engrossed running his damn business, Pike knew very little about his dad.

What Pike found satirical about the assassination of the former Beatle was a man who spent his life preaching love and peace getting gunned down, shot in the back by a deranged man stepping out of the shadows. Pike shuddered then as he did now, realizing no one ever thought to consider what dangers lurked just over their shoulder. .

"I'm just sitting here watchin' the wheels go 'round and 'round," he was crooning twenty minutes later when Roxy jerked up with a start. "What the *hell*?" she yelped. "Was that you singing?"

He fake-coughed, cleared his throat, and decreased the volume. "No."

"Oh, em gee, I thought a cat was getting skinned alive." She scrunched her face and increased the volume. "Who's *that*?"

"John Lennon."

She listened. "That's not John Legend."

"Lennon, not Legend. Though he kinda was."

Roxy thoughtfully curled her lips. "Lennon, Lennon, wasn't he in some band or somethin'?"

He groaned. "Yeah, or somethin'."

Roxy unbuckled her seat belt, leaned over, and looked through Pike's CDs. She wore a frilly black dress that ended at her knees with a shawl and brown cowboy boots. The breeze from the partially open window caused the dress to rise to mid-thigh.

Paige.

Pike swiftly looked away, commenting matter-of-factly, "You're dressed like Stevie Nicks."

"Who's he?"

Pike moaned. "God help me."

Digging around, she asked, "Isn't Stevie Nicks that blind black dude?"

"No," he lamented. "That's Stevie Wonder."

A moment later, Roxy held two CDs side by side. "Look. *Ratt* and *Poison*. Rat poison."

"Cute."

"Admit it, *Pikesters*, you like me giving you a hard time."

He smiled.

"Any Luke Bryan or Reba?"

"Nope."

Disappointed at finding nothing she was familiar with, Roxy buckled up. "Tell me about her."

Pike contrived confusion. "Stevie Nicks?"

"No."

"Who?"

She shrugged. "Your call. The one in your past or the one in your future."

He repositioned himself. "How 'bout you go back to teasing me about my music?"

"Do you like being teased?"

Pike harrumphed. Roxy mastered that fine line between purity and wickedness, between innocence and naughtiness. She threw out ambiguous remarks then waited to see what reaction she'd get. He deflected. "You're a psychic, you should know."

"Not all the time," she countered. "So spill it, *Pikemeister*."

He was inherently reluctant to open his heart, especially to someone he barely knew. Roxy Ledesma was a stranger. And younger. But being female, he welcomed a woman's opinion. And as a journalist, he knew there were two sides to every story. Pike took a deep breath and began.

Initially, details about Cynthia trickled but soon his mouth was dry from excessive talking. Roxy, fully riveted, listened fixedly, and rarely interrupted. When finished, he asked, "Thoughts?"

"What a bitch."

Pike cracked up. "She has her good points."

She recoiled as if swallowing something tart. "Dude, *really*? She's a bitch. She's not part of your life any more. You don't need to defend her."

"I'm not defending her," Pike maintained before realizing he was, in fact, defending her.

"Why'd you stay with her so long?"

"I loved her." Met with a thunderous silence, he saw Roxy arch a brow. "I did."

"Or was it the *idea* of her?"

Pinching the bridge of his nose, he watched an SUV pass: Husband, wife, kids. *Family*. Justifying his actions, he expounded. "I felt bad for Wynter. Cyn's not mom material and Wynter's father's a waste case. I wanted to be a positive influence."

"Why? Who cares?"

Pike's gesture said *it's obvious*. "She's just a kid."

"So? That's not your concern."

"How can I just walk away?"

Roxy snorted. "You did walk away!"

"No...not really. I mean...from Cyn, not Wynter. Don't twist my words."

Roxy countered simplistically, "You can't be everyone's hero."

LaMarcus King at Grizzly's. Now, Roxy. "Look...you just...you're not forty-seven."

"Whoa."

"The world's different to a twenty-one-year-old kid."

"Oh? So now I'm just a *kid*?"

"No—"

"Don't get all pissy with me."

"I'm not!"

"I wasn't a kid before but now I am because I disagree with you?"

"Dammit, Roxy, I don't mean it that way. Don't parse my words."

Arms folded across her chest, she became one with the barren knolls of western Missouri.

After five tense minutes, Pike apologized.

Her response was to lean away and wipe a tear from her eye.

With the car restrictive, it registered. Roxy, like Wynter, never had a positive influence in her life. Roxy, like Wynter, was unwanted and regarded as an inconvenience, an encumbrance. Unlike Wynter, however, Roxy hadn't been offered a way out and a way up. Reaching over, he gave her hand a reassuring squeeze. The tingling sensation caught him by surprise. "I'm a jerk."

Roxy didn't pull free. "We agree on something." With raven hair whipping around her pretty face, she said tenderly, "You're a good man, Pike Graves. But sometimes someone can be too good. I just don't understand why you didn't throw in the towel sooner."

He shrugged.

"Cynthia didn't deserve you. She never appreciated you."

"I know."

"However…"

He laughed. "Here it comes."

"Look," Roxy began prudently, "I'm not defending her, okay? I'm not saying what she did—the stealing, the cheating, the toying with your emotions—is warranted. But…maybe she saw through you."

Facing forward, eyes squinted. "Continue."

"You sure?"

Pike wavered then braced himself. "Hit me."

She faced his profile and took a deep breath. "You were with this chick five years, right? You opened your heart, your home, and naively, your financial accounts. Dummy!"

"True."

Roxy removed a clip from her purse to put her hair up. Or perhaps so he could see her eyes. "But you did haul ass pretty fast."

"Our relationship was based on lies. Lies and fraud. It was over. It was obvious she wanted out. Relationships need to be a two-way street."

"I'm not questioning you for leaving Cyn. I think you should've years ago. Walking away is one thing, but packing up your life to drive cross country for some other chick? C'mon now, Pikesters. If you decided to get out so quick, how dedicated were you in the first place?"

Pike chewed his lip.

"We see that. We sense that."

He went for humor. "You mean clairvoyants?"

"I mean women."

He kicked that around.

"And besides, serves you right for getting involved with someone named S-I-N. Sin."

He laughed.

They rode on in silence, allowing the weight of the candid exchange to settle. Feeling enough time had passed, she asked, "How about the other one?"

"Paige."

"Okay, Paige. What is it about her?"

An electric charge coursed through his blood. Transitioning

from the gloom of Cyn to the luster of Paige caused a flutter in his chest. He couldn't find the words. How did one define destiny, define fate? He searched for the proper explanation but what came from his mouth was "Shit!"

Roxy straightened and fearfully looked forward. The thunderous banging beneath the hood sounded ominous.

The steering wheel shimmied in Pike's grip. The dashboard lit up like a Christmas tree. Signs and symbols—some blinking, some solid—taunting him. Automotive hieroglyphics.

He wrestled with the vehicle, trying to gain control over an untamable fifteen hundred pound animal that defied him. Knocking. Lurching. Slowing, slowing…

The ear-piercing horn from a speeding semi-trailer bore down on his Honda like a predator about to swallow prey. Roxy screamed.

The alert trucker veered left, barely avoiding crushing the car and cutting its occupants in half. The hauler stood on his horn for another half mile. Combatting the unresponsive car, Pike pulled to the shoulder, the left rear fender extending a few feet onto the interstate.

"What happened?"

He didn't answer. The car sputtered and coughed and choked before taking its final breath.

Dead.

Pushing his tongue against his cheek, he gaged the landscape. Never-ending wheat fields stretching as far as the eye could see. What appeared to be an abandoned granary at least four miles away. No signs of civilization, of life. Abandoned outbuildings dotting the fertile landscape. Pike glanced the rear view, estimating it'd been at least twenty miles since passing any town. Ahead lay an unremitting trail of gray asphalt. The only thing he could make out was an overpass in the distance, a good three miles ahead. But the off-ramp only led to more desolation and more uninhabited open spaces.

He showed his phone to Roxy. *No service.* Anxiously she checked her own. The abysmal expression on her face confirmed the same. "Pike," she faltered like a frightened little girl in the woods, "What happened?"

He shook his head in defeat. "Punching at fog."

CHAPTER 9

A teamster hauling pigs to slaughter had spotted the disabled vehicle. Pulling over and using the alliance of fellow-truckers, he coordinated help via his CB.

An hour later, a tow truck was on the shoulder two car lengths ahead and slowly reversing. To Pike, the rear hitch and horizontal bar resembled a crucifix. The sun slipping below the horizon had Pike making an eye-visor with his hands. The fiery red bands of sunset made it seem like the guy was stepping through the gates of Hell.

Pike's congenial greeting went ignored, the tow-truck driver focusing exclusively on the broken vehicle like analyzing a work of art. "What happened?"

His tone sounded abrasive. "No idea. Everything was fine. Then suddenly the engine thumped and the wheel locked."

"The steering wheel or the tires?"

"Um, the steering wheel…I guess."

The man had disheveled blond hair, beady eyes, and a ruddy complexion atop a tree trunk neck. Blue workman's shirt tucked into body-hugging blue jeans embedded with oil stains. His rotund frame didn't warrant wearing snug clothes. Severely scuffed black boots, he stood around six-four. A patch over his breast read Emmett.

"Pop the hood."

"Sure." Pike obeyed the command then met him at the front. "See anything?"

"How long you been drivin' for?"

"I left Philly yesterday."

Emmett scowled like Pike possessed a single digit IQ. "Straight through?"

Pike lived by the mantra there are two kinds of people you never annoy: Food servers and auto mechanics. "Oh, no. Left Indianapolis this morning."

Emmett grunted. "These Jap cars ain't designed to be pushed hard. Their entire little island is like three hun'red miles top to bottom."

"It's a good car. Never had something like this happen before."

"Ever push it this much before?"

"No."

Emmett nodded smugly. *Case closed.* He pulled a wire here, checked some hoses there. "Any smoke from the engine?"

Pike curled his mouth. "I didn't notice." Stepping back, he asked through the open window, "Roxy, you notice any smoke?"

She got out of the car. "Nope."

Emmett untwisted from under the hood and slid his thumbs through his belt loops. He inspected Roxy the same way he inspected the disabled car. Another work of art. "Emmett." He extended a burly paw.

"Roxy." She glanced at Pike as if seeking approval before taking the tendered hand.

Emmett held on too long for Pike's comfort.

"Roxy, huh?" Emmett's crooked smile displayed a slice of chewing tobacco ensnared between two incisors. "Not from 'round these parts, are ya?"

"Zanesville, Ohio."

The mechanic arched a questioning brow and pitched his shoulder. "*He* said Philly."

Roxy faltered. "Zanesville originally. But uh, yes, Philly."

"Traveling together?"

"Yeah."

Reduced to role of observer, Pike tapped the fender redirecting Emmett's attention. "See anything wrong?"

Eyes glued to Roxy, he inhaled. "Everything looks good to me. Very good." Hoisting up his already tight jeans, he claimed, "Don't see many a' your types 'round here."

"Oh?"

"Everyone 'ere has blonde hair and blue eyes. Barbie types. Where you from?"

"Like I said, Zanesville."

"I mean your heritage."

"Oh." Apprehensive, she laughed and slyly took a step toward

Pike. Emmett *unintentionally* blocked her. "Dad's Hispanic, Mom's Filipina."

Emmett nodded his approval. "Good combination."

"Thanks...I think."

Maybe it was Pike's imagination. Maybe it was his innate suspicion of people. Maybe he was just feeling old. Watching twenty-one-year-old Roxy interact with this Emmett character made him feel like a protective father watching his daughter from the front porch after returning home from a date.

A short time later, Emmett meticulously moved in slow-motion, coupling the Honda to his tow truck. His crude attempt to impress Roxy with his infinite wisdom of hooking a car to a hitch fell short. During the process, Pike took the felt box from the glove compartment and slipped it into his pocket. Task complete, Emmett rubbed his hands together and declared to Pike, "I'll come back for ya."

"*What*?"

"No room in the cab for three people."

"I'm sure we can squeeze in."

Eyes roaming Roxy but addressing Pike, he said, "It should take about two hours."

The temperature was around ninety, the humidity about the same. Yet, Roxy hugged herself as if freezing. She cast helpless eyes at Pike.

Pike avowed, "We can fit."

Emmett discharged a wad of tobacco juice that barely missed Pike's shoe. "It's against ICC regs to have two passengers in my cab."

Pike pulled his wallet. "And how much would a ticket run you?"

"Four."

Cash diminishing quicker than he liked, Pike withdrew four bills. "Okay. Two hundred now and two more when we get to town."

Emmett yanked all four bills from his hand. "How 'bout four now and a hun'red later for a tip. I done come out pretty far on a Sunday night."

Once again Pike was reacting, not acting. His car was already on the lift and he was surrounded by farms and cow shit in every direction.

He bit his lip with such intensity he drew a drop of his own blood. "Fine."

೮৲ა৲ა

As a young boy, Pike's favorite film had been *The Wizard of Oz*. Now standing in the lobby of the Ruby Slipper motel on the fringes of Kansas City, he snickered at the parallels between himself and the scarecrow, tin man and cowardly lion. Cynthia played with his heart and he hadn't thought with his brain before finding the courage to leave.

"Can I help you?"

Discarding the similarities, Pike crossly marched to the front desk. His foul mood stemmed from the drive into town. Roxy had been squeezed between himself and Emmett. The driver insisted she keep her legs spread so he could access the floor-mounted gearshift. Roxy cringed each and every time his greasy knuckles glided across her knee. Pike was thankful they didn't wind up in a ditch since Emmett spent more time gawking her legs than keeping his eyes on the road. However, being beholden, Pike held his tongue.

The front desk clerk, who resembled disgraced actor Kevin Spacey, presented an over-the-top smile. "Good evening, sir. Welcome to the Ruby Slipper. Will you be staying with us this evening?"

Pike cocked his head toward the photos lining the wall. "No, I just stopped in to look at the fuckin' Scarecrow.

The Spacey doppelganger leaned closer. "I'll take that as a fuckin' yes?"

Pike shook his head. "Sorry. It's been a long day."

Emmett had mentioned there was a tractor convention in town, the Royals were hosting the rival Cardinals, and lodging within walking distance to his shop was limited. He suggested The Ruby Slipper because his cousin worked here and could get Pike a killer rate. His stomach dropped when a perfunctory look under the hood resulted in Emmett proclaiming, "It's gonna take some time."

"How much time?"

"Three days, maybe four. My parts guy is backlogged from the Fourth."

As always Pike was marching to someone else's drum. He wasn't living his life, his life was living him.

After handing over his credit card, the front desk clerk asked, "Two people, two beds, correct?"

"Yep."

"The name of the other guest?"

"Roxy Ledesma."

The clerk scrutinized the girl perusing travel brochures. "And she is?"

"Told ya. Roxy Ledesma."

"Your daughter?"

Although he'd heard this several times, the assumption never sat well. "Just a friend."

The clerk regarded her a bit longer then winked. "Good for you, sir."

"Your cousin Emmett thinks it may take three or four days to fix my car."

"He's good. If it can be fixed, he's the one."

If?

"I'll bill your Visa for four nights."

"If we check out sooner, you'll credit me back, right?"

"Why, certainly."

ɞɷɛɷ

"Karma's a bitch!" Cynthia shouted in exhilaration after closing her laptop.

She loved Pike at one point. Probably. Maybe just loved what he could do for her. Mature, grounded, financially responsible. Everything Dragon was not. But Pike was also infuriatingly predictable. That is, until he up and left. Getting blindsided by his hasty departure truly pissed her off. Especially since she planned to leave him. Cynthia didn't give a damn about losing him. She just didn't like *losing*.

Especially to him. To Pike fucking Graves.

She'd been preparing by siphoning funds to her secret stash. Sure, some may view what she did as fraudulent, maybe even deceitful.

She viewed her actions as daring and forward-thinking. If he was gullible enough to trust her with his money, whose fault was that?

Pike fucking Graves, that's who.

Going online to verify the sneaky rat had done nothing else devious, and pleased he'd forgotten to remove her name as beneficiary on the account with $1.4 million, she accessed the credit card linked to that same account. Opening a second browser, she charted his spending.

Gas stations westbound I-70, a diner in Zanesville, a Target, and a Red Robin in Indianapolis. The food charges seemed excessive for one person. And then the motherlode. A charge for over three hundred dollars, clearly for multiple nights, at some place called the Ruby Slipper Motel.

Pike may have been the investigative reporter but Cynthia was the detective. Granted, her heart left a year into the relationship whereas holier-than-thou Pike-fucking-Graves insisted that he was, to use his words, "fully vested." *Fully vested?* Who the hell talks like that?

He had a sister in Vegas but based on the route he was taking, Cynthia knew precisely where Mr. High-and-Mighty was headed.

California.

Paige Rhodes.

The one he never got over. The one he never stopped loving.

Knowing it's wise to know your competition, she once asked, "Do you have pictures of her?"

Pike had no trouble locating the Lafayette High School yearbook, remembering exactly what page Paige's photo was on as well as easily finding a shoebox containing numerous keepsakes from their time together.

This Paige chick wouldn't turn any heads. Thin, small boobs, droopy eyes.

What resonated was not *her* looks but rather the look on Pike's face as he reflected on his past. Happy, forlorn, sorrow.

Love.

Or at least what Cynthia assumed was love. She'd never had a man—or woman for that matter—look at her the way Pike looked at photographs of his old girlfriend.

Karma!

The chiming doorbell yanked her back from her musing. With a spring in her step, she bounced to the front door, ignoring the passionate screams from Wynter bopping her boss upstairs.

"Took you long enough," Cynthia said by way of greeting.

"Whatever." Dragon replied.

"Pack your stuff. I got you a plane ticket to Kansas City."

He made a face like passing a kidney stone. "Why?"

"Pike's there." Stepping outside, she closed the door behind her. "Go, Dragon. Go finish this."

CHAPTER 10

Pike was tearing down the interstate. Grain silos and infinite cornfields passing in a blur. A becalming sensation filled his spirit now that his car was humming like a fine-tuned machine. And although he knew he was dreaming, he willed himself not to wake.

He glanced right.

No Roxy.

Emptiness rose in his chest.

Through a fog on the horizon he could make out the orange trusses of the Golden Gate Bridge. But no matter how hard he stepped on the gas, he wasn't getting closer. The city beyond his grasp, Paige just out of reach. The speedometer passed eighty, ninety, a hundred. But yet, the world-famous bridge faded. Another glance right. Stevie Wonder was in the passenger's seat humming a Fleetwood Mac tune.

"Pike." The voice, remote but welcoming. "I'm scared," Roxy whispered.

He opened his eyes and looked down.

Her transcendent black eyes revealed carnal hunger as she slipped her generous lips around him.

"Roxy?" His stomach tightened, his thoughts jumbled. It was wrong yet felt right.

"It's okay, Pike."

A moment later, she asked dejectedly, "Don't you like me?"

"Of course."

"Then why aren't you hard?"

"I…"

"If it helps, you can call me Paige." Repositioning herself, she straddled him and slipped his growing firmness inside.

He released an outbreath and began guiding her hips. "Oh, Roxy."

Emitting a gasp, she threw her head back, her face disappearing behind a veil of dark hair. "Pike…"

"Roxy…"

"Pike…"

"Roxy…"

"Pike, wake up."

He lurched with such force he tumbled out of the armchair he'd been sleeping in all night.

"It's only me," she laughed.

Beaded in sweat, he winced.

"You okay? You're blushing."

"I'm…fine."

Dropping to her haunches, she smiled. "You dreamin' about me?"

Maybe she was psychic, after all.

∽∂∽

They were a few minutes into breakfast at an adjoining IHOP when Roxy commented, "You seem distant."

The dream. Pike couldn't meet her eyes. "Just thinking."

"About Paige?"

He lied. "Yeah."

"Tell me about her."

Without effort, a smile crossed his face. "Where do I start?"

"How'd you meet?"

"Lafayette High."

"Ah, high school sweethearts."

"Nah, not really. We had some classes together but I never really noticed her. It all started the first weekend after graduation."

"Oh? Like you ran into her, fireworks erupted, and your life was never the same?"

"That's one way of putting it." He beamed at the memory. "Dewayne, my best friend, had a crush on a girl named Lisa who worked in a convenience store but he wanted me to be his wingman. So I went in to see if she was there. She wasn't. But that's when I ran into Paige."

"And?" Roxy asked after a prolonged lull.

Pike pursed his lips. "That's when…as you said, my life was never the same."

Roxy released her sugary laugh. "Like you both reached for the Twizzlers, hands touched, sparks flew, time stopped, and you both realized you were soul mates?"

"Not exactly."

Picking up on the change in mood, she asked perceptively, "What happened?"

The memory of that critical moment exploded like artillery fire. Back then, he'd regurgitated the same graphic details to detectives, lawyers, reporters, and friends who wanted to know "What was it like killing someone?" Now, years later, discussing the events at Grizzly's was like picking at a scab that would never heal.

LaMarcus King was a local sports hero destined to make the NFL. But it was Pike who became infamous for ending LaMarcus's life. Journalists hounded Pike. His father would curse them, slam the door in their faces, scream from the window how their news vans were causing gridlock, and implore them to stop traipsing through his wife's azaleas. Pike spent many nights lying in bed, tortured by guilt, wondering how much of the stress he caused ultimately contributed to his father's first heart attack that same summer.

Following the incident at Grizzly's, Cora became a nervous wreck every time her seventeen-year-old ventured out into the cold, cruel world. She repeatedly justified things. "Better LaMarcus King dead than you, honey."

Shredded by survivor's guilt, he looked at her. "Why, Mom? Why is it better?"

She had no answer, choosing instead to extol his bravery for protecting "that Paige girl" while claiming how "proud" she was.

His father, however, would stare at Pike from across the room. The distance between them becoming an ever-broadening gorge no bridge could cross. Sam Graves recurrently voiced his displeasure, scolding his son for "getting involved."

For months, Pike tossed and turned every night, not only due to the haunting memories, but because of the shouting matches behind his parent's closed bedroom door.

"He's a good boy," Mom cried. "He did the right thing."

"Good Lord, woman!" Dad shouted back. "He can't fight everyone's battles. He can't be everyone's hero. He shouldn't have even gone there with that black boy."

"We didn't raise him and Stephanie to shy away from confrontation, Sam."

"We also didn't raise them to stick their necks out for strangers, *Cora*."

Pike never had a strong bond with his father in the first place and this was the final nail in the coffin. Not only had Sam written off his son for "reckless actions" but what followed sent the family's finances into a freefall.

Knowing Sam Graves was a moderately successful businessman, the King family saw dollar signs and sued for personal damages and wrongful death. This suit coincided with local police interrogating Pike and initially charging him with involuntary manslaughter. Pike was eventually found innocent on all counts. But the financial damage was done.

The family's nest egg eaten up by lawyers, Pike's workaholic father now had to spend even more time selling timepieces. Or maybe that was an excuse to stay away from home, avoiding quarrels with his wife, and dealing with an irrational teenage son. Stephanie, twenty-four at the time and living at home after losing her job, couldn't handle the constant bickering and moved in with her former high school biology teacher who recently divorced.

The family dissolved.

The fall of the house of Graves.

And all stemming from Pike making a snap decision, something he still second-guessed to this very day. He'd lived seventeen years prior to that night, another thirty since. Yet, his entire existence was shaped from an episode that played out in under five minutes.

The media circus and ongoing investigation prevented Pike from enrolling in college for two years until things died down. In the interim he worked menial jobs and handed his paycheck to his father in an attempt to assuage his own culpability.

Pike ultimately graduated from Villanova at twenty-four and when he interviewed for an entry level position at the *Philadelphia Inquirer* he was hired on the spot. It wasn't the BA in Journalism from a respected university, nor was it his unimpressive resume or mediocre grades. Instead it was his notoriety. Everyone knew Pike Graves. The newspaper jumped at the chance for name recognition. *Take a life, get a job. The Lord truly does work in mysterious ways.*

"So how'd you and Paige hook up?" Roxy now asked, hanging on every word.

His response was to smile.

"Why're you looking at me like that?"

"Thanks."

"Thanks?"

"You ask about Paige because you want to know. When Cynthia asked, she was sizing up the competition."

"I'm not Cyn. So…Paige?"

After years of keeping everything suppressed, it was refreshing to bare his soul and not have every word dissected and picked apart.

He'd once read that strangers who face death together will forever share a bond outsiders can't comprehend. And due to one chance encounter at Grizzly's he and Paige Rhodes would be connected for eternity.

Their paths crossed in the law offices of Geoffrey Ballard, the Graves' family attorney. The lawyer needed Paige to be a strong witness for his client. Pike knew his future and his freedom hung in the balance. But just seeing Paige in the attorney's impressive surroundings soothed his anxieties. Everything would work out. His life would be okay as long as Paige was part of it.

Insomnia became a nightly occurrence awaiting trial. Pike would crawl into bed mentally drained. But the instant his head hit the pillow, his mind began clicking on all cylinders. He'd get out of bed and drive around, sometimes for an hour, other times until daybreak. He'd sit in the empty stands and stare at the lonely football field where LaMarcus King of the Lafayette Pilgrims had set school records. Other times, he'd park in the shadows across from Grizzly's and watch those with a sense of the macabre point to the spot where LaMarcus died. Most evenings he parked outside Paige's home.

He longed to see her. But how could he explain himself? Only a stalker sits outside a girl's house until sunrise. He never saw her leave, come home, or even look out her window.

Then he did.

It was dawn when Pike returned from an all-night vigil outside her house. A refurbished VW Bug sat partially obscured by a neighbor's hedgerow. Pulling alongside, he rolled down the window. "Hey, Paige, feel like getting coffee?"

Unlike Pike, she couldn't delay college. She'd been awarded a tennis scholarship to Ohio State and would lose it if she didn't start that September. Pike hadn't even known she played tennis, much less gifted enough to warrant a scholarship.

After she enrolled at Ohio State, they spoke on the phone, primarily discussing the pending litigation. That soon transformed into more personal exchanges. Weekly calls became nightly calls. Letters were exchanged. Sappy romantic cards mailed back and forth. He sent her some of his writing. She reciprocated with snapshots in her little tennis outfit.

She came home for Thanksgivings and Christmases, three-day weekends, and eventually regular weekends. Initially Paige spent the bulk of time with her large family and squeezed in Pike when she could. That changed and it was her family who got squeezed in.

Pike kissed away her tears when her grandmother died. She held him close as he cried like a baby outside his father's hospital room after Sam fell to the floor at work, clutching his chest. And they clung to each other as if together they could ward off the cruel memories that troubled them both.

Pike and Paige against the world.

Every free moment was spent together. He went to bed thinking of her. He woke in the morning thinking of her. Weekends in Atlantic City, New York and the Jersey Shore where they made love in the ocean. She called their partnership a "team." Pike called it "fate."

Returning home after graduating, Paige suggested they live together. Pike resisted. Money was tight. How could they afford it? He knew, based on hours and hours of running numbers, they'd get by but he wanted more. He didn't want to survive, he wanted to thrive. Paige didn't deserve to struggle. Plus, as often as they made love, nothing was foolproof. If she became pregnant, then what? It wasn't until later Pike learned of his low sperm count. Conceiving a child was impossible. Paige, disappointed about living separate, moved in with two girlfriends from work while Pike lived in the basement of Dewayne's cousin.

Their love blossomed. It was, after all, fate.

If only…

If only Pike would've listened to his heart and not his wallet, Paige never would have been living with co-workers, never would've met one of their uncles who had tickets to the US Open, never would've driven to New York, never would've met a tennis instructor from California whose brother worked at Pepperdine University, and never would've known about a teaching position at a university on the opposite side of the country.

"It's a great opportunity, honey," she ruefully explained one chilly morning, wrapped around him like a security blanket.

Pike was glad he was facing away so she didn't see tears clouding his eyes.

"Don't you understand?"

"Sure."

"It's a once in a lifetime chance."

Once in a lifetime. "I know."

And so she moved to California. Might as well have been Mongolia.

"Why didn't you go with her?" Roxy asked.

Pike didn't know. He'd been asking himself that for decades.

"When was the last time you saw her?"

"Eight years," he answered immediately. "She flew back for my mom's funeral." He paused, only now realizing breakfast hadn't been touched. Smiling at the memory, he muttered, "She looked back."

Roxy frowned. "What do you mean? Who looked back? Paige?"

"Nothin.' Never mind."

Rubbing her chin, she analyzed him. "You loved her."

He didn't need to verbalize his answer. It was written in his eyes.

"You never stopped loving her."

"I tried but...I couldn't."

"Paige Rhodes, the one that got away."

"Yep."

"And now you want to reverse a mistake you made all those years ago."

He shoveled watery eggs around his plate.

"This is your second chance, Pike."

"I know."

Roxy's eyes misted. "You gotta get her back, Pike. You can't lose her again."

The waitress appeared and lowered the bill. Needing to kill

time while Emmett repaired his car, Pike asked "Is there anything to do around here?"

She rattled off several things, none of which piqued his interest, until saying, "Every Monday night the Palace Theater shows a classic film."

Pike's eyes widened. "Oh?"

"This week is that old movie with the guy from *Rain Man*."

"I haven't seen *Rain Man* in forever," Roxy howled.

"No honey," the waitress said. "Not that one, the...*The Graduate*, that's it."

"Never've seen it." Roxy turned to Pike. "You?"

"Great film."

"Can we go?" she pleaded.

"Sure, why not."

Animated, she clapped. "Cool. It'll be like a date."

The waitress lifted Roxy's plate. "I'm sure you and your father will enjoy it."

ᥱᔓᥱᔓ

The Palace Theater was listed on the National Register of Historic Places. Enclosed in a glass case outside was a movie poster of the film that was shown opening night back in 1938: *You Can't Take it With You* starring Jimmy Stewart and Lionel Barrymore. Surrounding the poster were time-yellowed photos from the spectacle. Men dressed in fedoras and tuxedos, women with long-forgotten hair styles and flapper hats. The moviegoers varied in age but all were equally ecstatic for the momentous grand opening.

Pike shivered. Perhaps it was the name of the feature. Or maybe the awareness all these happy smiling souls were likely now dead.

Thanatophobia.

"You okay?" Roxy asked. "You're sweating."

He shook it off.

The interior held the musty air of a museum. The considerable lobby was designed to resemble the Roman Coliseum including statues, water fountains, and marble pillars. A grand staircase leading to a balcony had been roped off. The seats were old and didn't recline. At show time, an impressive red curtain with tassels would be manually pulled open. The place screamed bygone area but concession prices were in line with the twenty-first century.

A wizened old codger who sat in the trifling ticket booth also served as vendor and usher, escorting Pike and Roxy to their seats. Wearing a top hat and tails, Roxy commented after he walked off, "He looks like that Monopoly dude."

They both laughed.

As if it was the most natural thing in the world, Roxy leaned against Pike and held his hand. Pike didn't pull away. With the exception of an elderly couple in the front row they had the place to themselves.

Mr. Monopoly stood center stage and asked for everyone to "simmer down" even though none of the four occupants were 'simmering.' With a voice belying his age, he spoke in an imperious tone reminiscent of Charlton Heston coming down from Mt. Sinai in *The Ten Commandments*.

"Directed by Mike Nichols, *The Graduate* is a 1967 film starring Dustin Hoffman, Katherine Ross, and Anne Bancroft. With a budget of three million, the film surpassed one hundred million at the box office. AFI places it at number seventeen on their Top One Hundred films of all time. Thank you and enjoy the show."

He waited. When the older couple began applauding, Pike and Roxy followed suit. Mr. Monopoly bowed and exited stage right.

In the film, Hoffman plays Ben Braddock, a recent college graduate who is unsure what to do with his life. He gets seduced by a married woman, Mrs. Robinson, and an affair ensues. Braddock acquiesces to his parent's demands and goes on a date with Elaine, the daughter of the woman he'd been sleeping with. Ben and Elaine fall in love but she quickly learns her new beau had been having sex with her mother. At the end of the movie, Ben learns Elaine is set to get married in northern California. She is exchanging her vows when he enters the church. Chaos ensues. Elaine decides to leave the groom at the altar and chooses Ben. As the two of them hop a city bus, their broad smiles ever-so-slowly alter into an expression of uncertainty about their future with the awareness of what they did.

"Like it?" Pike asked when the houselights came up.

"Wow."

"That a good wow or bad wow?"

Roxy summarized. "So this Ben guy throws away everything he knows and impulsively goes after the woman he loves in northern California." She locked on Pike. "Just like you."

It was a reality punch in the gut.

CHAPTER 11

Emmett Snell was halfway through pissing before he realized the seat was down. "Screw it," he slurred and finished. Staggering out of the stall, he checked his reflection in the water stained mirror. "You're one suave sumbitch." He turned right then left. "And handsome too."

When Harvey Snell's arthritis became too debilitating to continue working on cars, he turned his fledgling shop over to his nephews Emmett and Evan. He hoped the boys could put aside their differences and work together.

It didn't happen.

Evan, three years older, quickly tired of Emmett's drinking, drugs, and unprofessionalism. When a squabble turned physical and he swung a tire iron at Emmett's skull, he knew he'd reached his breaking point. "You're gonna fail, you ass hat."

"Fail, huh?" Emmett now said to the mirror. His shop was flourishing while Evan worked part-time at a shitty quick lube place. "Who's the ass hat now?"

Emmett knew he was good with his hands. What he didn't know was he had a head for numbers. Overcharging customers—ten bucks here, twenty there—he kept it low enough to not throw up red flags while turning a nice little profit. He could now afford seats on the finish line at the Kansas Speedway, add to his collection of Dale Earnhardt memorabilia, drink imported beer and, best of all, pay for hookers with junk in their trunk. Sir Mix-a-Lot wasn't the only one who loved big butts.

Occasionally, good fortune became great fortune. He lived for the days when some sorry schmuck, especially those out-of-towners from big cities back east, passed through and had a car problem. They'd be so happy getting their car fixed, they never once considered they were getting gouged. As Emmett once prophesized to a black chick with big tits after she dismounted him, "There's a difference between gettin' screwed and gettin' fucked."

"Not to me there ain't," she responded and nearly suffocated him between her gigantic 44DDDs.

Quick online research revealed this new chump would be perfect. Pike Graves was from Philadelphia, had been a newspaper guy years ago, and was listed on a Villanova alumni website. Respectable career, good school. Yep, this Graves fella was loaded. Emmett would teach this city slicker about getting screwed.

Or was it fucked?

He'd hold the car hostage for five days, maybe even through next weekend. He'd weave some tale about onboard computers, Jap cars, out-of-stock parts. All that crap. Then Graves, like they always do, would pay the ransom to get his vehicle freed from captivity. Emmett figured four thousand was about right.

He balled up some tissues, put them down the front of his pants, exited the restroom crotch-first, and made sure the barmaid resembling Danica Patrick noticed him.

On the way to his condo, he decided to swing by the shop and check in on his prisoner. He fumbled with the keys, opened the office door, and stumbled to the service bays.

His eyes widened. Graves's car was missing. Four thousand dollars, gone. Emmett knew he was fucked.

Or was it screwed?

In such a state of panic, he didn't react quickly enough to shallow breathing behind his back.

※※※

Pike never slept well in strange beds and tonight was no exception. The mattress conformed to his frame, the pillow, like a feathery catcher's mitt, swaddled his head. But he remained restless.

Turning left, a sliver of ambient streetlight cut a swath across Roxy in the adjacent bed. Facing away, her nightshirt had risen, exposing black bikini-cut panties.

Recalling last night's vivid dream, Pike swallowed, got out of bed, and covered her with the blanket. The knock on the door was like a sonic boom in the stillness.

Roxy stared up at Pike. "Why are you standing over me?"

"I'm not," he whispered. "You're dreaming."

"Okay," she dazedly mumbled and went back to sleep.

Whew. Pike threaded the darkness and peeked through the eyehole. He saw no one. "Damn kids." That comment, combined with the inability to sleep through the night without peeing, had him grumbling, "I'm getting old." He took one step toward the bathroom.

Three loud knocks.

Pike nearly threw himself against the eyehole hoping to catch the little bastard. He saw only the room across the hall.

He was still peering through, seeing nothing, when another knock came out of thin air. Cursing, Pike angrily fidgeted with the chain and deadbolt and yanked the door open.

There was no one there.

Peering up and down the corridor in both directions, he saw nobody. Cursing under his breath, he was closing the door when noticing a manila envelope on the ground. Curling his lips, he squatted, undid the clasp, and emptied the contents into his hand.

Along with his car keys was an invoice and a note apparently written by Emmett. Pike's car was parked out front. The problem was only a loose wire. No charge. Pike's chin dropped. "Nice knowing there's still honest people in the world."

∽∾∽

Lying in bed anticipating sunrise, he theatrically stretched and yawned then updated Roxy the instant she stirred.

"So we can get back on the road?" she asked.

"We sure can."

Granted, Pike was on his own schedule, but he was chomping at the bit to get out west. Grinning ear to ear as he checked out, Pike barreled out of the parking lot and hauled-ass toward the interstate. Reaching the onramp to I-70, he pressed down on the gas. The car purred.

And that's when Pike saw him.

The first time was leaving Philadelphia. The hitchhiker stood alongside the entrance ramp to the Penn Turnpike. Nondescript clothes, a straw hat, and holding a sign reading a very generic destination.

Pacific Time Zone.

Now the same hitchhiker—or one dressed similarly—held a sign with a slightly less generic destination.

West Coast.

Their eyes locked for a flash.

Passing him, Pike glimpsed the rear view mirror where he watched the guy with the straw hat methodically turn his head. He grew smaller in Pike's wake but it appeared as if the hitchhiker was waving to him.

The same nonspecific gesture as the veiled woman standing over his father's grave.

Part III

Forgive Me, Father

"Living is easy with eyes closed.
Misunderstanding all you see."

~ John Lennon

CHAPTER 12

After waiting four hundred miles, Pike wasted no time once they crossed into Colorado. "I don't think we're in Kansas anymore."

"I *love* that film," Roxy said when the laughter subsided.

"I hate those flying monkeys."

"*Everyone* hates those flying monkeys. Speaking of, have you heard from Cynthia, the wicked witch of the East?"

Pike chuckled. "No, why would I?"

"You think she cares that you left?"

"I'm sure she's moved on. In some ways, she moved on before I left."

Paying homage to the state they entered, she said, "You're a good man, Pike's Peak."

He grinned but remained silent.

"You don't like hearing praise, do you?"

Pike fiddled with the radio.

"It's all good. I have low self-esteem too."

His brows rose. True, he never accepted praise easily but that didn't mean he had low self-esteem. Interesting how others perceived him.

"Was it your dad?"

His brows rose higher. "Was *what* my dad?"

"The reason you lack confidence?"

"I didn't say I lacked confidence."

Her gaze wandered to the grassy plains. "It's crazy how our parents do things or say things to us as kids that stay with us into adulthood."

Pike glanced at her inquisitively.

"My mom screwed up my life."

"I don't think she died on purpose, Roxy."

"I know. But she dies and next thing I know I'm with Jonah and my sister's in Portland."

Pike passed a Chrysler. "I thought you said Seattle."

"Huh?"

"You said your sister was in Seattle."

"Right, by way of Portland." She looked at him. "Your father didn't screw you up?"

"He couldn't. He was never around."

"Ah, one of those overachiever types."

"Definitely."

"What was he like?"

He again was touched by Roxy's authenticity. It was a welcome departure from Cynthia that someone was making an effort to know him. *And why am I always comparing her to Cynthia?* "He owned watch stores all over Philly. Work, work, work, twenty-four-seven. His job was his life, his co-workers were his family. Mom, Stephanie and me took a backseat to everything and everyone."

"You sound bitter," Roxy declared.

"Not bitter." He hiked his shoulders in a what-*can-I-do-about-it-* way. "Just…well, yeah, okay, bitter."

"I'm sure he worked hard so you and your sister would have a good life."

"He did, but look where it got us. He's gone, Mom's gone, and my sister and I don't talk. I don't know any of my extended family 'cause Dad was always too busy working the holidays for us to get together."

"Yep, big time bitter."

Pike said nothing.

"Was it a heart attack? Did he, as they say, work himself to an early grave?" She air-quoted the last two words.

Pike chewed his lips. "He had three heart attacks but that's not what…ended his life."

"What then?"

"Long story."

"Long road."

He adjusted the seat belt that suddenly felt tight against his heart. This was something he only shared once with Dewayne and that was only after too many shots of Jack Daniels. Never with Stephanie, never with Cynthia, not even with Paige. And his mom refused to discuss it. Yet, here he was, baring his soul to someone he'd known four days. "Salt."

Roxy frowned. "*Salt?*"

"Yup."

"Not pepper?"

Eyes forward, it was easier confessing to the sprawling horizon than facing someone. "Mom loved the holidays and insisted we spend them together. We were the personification of a dysfunctional family but she was a saint and tried time and time again to keep us close. It never worked 'cause none of us cared. Dad's job took priority. Steph was always off somewhere trying to *find herself.* Me? I was focusing on my career."

"Like your dad."

Pike flinched at the stinging yet valid analogy. Disregarding it, he continued. "Thanksgiving, Mom and Steph leave at three in the morning to go up to New York for the parade. They did it a few times when we were kids and Mom, as usual, was hoping to relive the past. She suggested Dad and I watch Football. So...we sat there in silence on opposite ends of the sofa. Might as well have been opposite ends of the planet. He goes into the kitchen to make himself a scrambled egg sandwich, comes back, and sits in his favorite chair. Mind you, this is two months after his third heart attack. And he douses the sandwich in salt. I don't mean a little, Roxy. I'm talking covering the whole damn thing. Three months after a heart attack!" Pike shook his head.

"Uh huh."

"I said something like, 'Hey, Dad, have some eggs with your salt.' No big deal, right?"

"Right."

"He goes off. He was on his fourth Michelob already. Dad..." His throat closed.

Roxy said softly, "If you don't want to talk, it's okay."

A few deep breaths before continuing. "He had no qualms telling everyone else how to live. Me, Stephanie, Mom, friends. Employees even. But the all-knowing Sam Graves? No, sir. Don't you *dare* travel down that road with him. Two sets of rules. One for him, one for everyone else." Pike blinked away a tear. "Things exploded."

"Because of salt," Roxy remarked.

"I was stuck. Mom and Steph took my car up to New York."

"Couldn't leave if you wanted to."

"And, oh, how I wanted to." A deep breath, he explained. "I go out to the backyard, waiting for them to get home so I can get the hell out of there. Screw Thanksgiving. Dad stays inside with his game and his salt and his beer. It was four minutes past noon. I remember the *exact* time. Four minutes past noon. He staggers outside. Can hardly stand 'cause he's shitfaced. And he's blatantly dangling his car keys in my face, telling me he's going to get more beer. Challenging me to stop him."

Roxy gave his knee a reassuring squeeze.

Pike tried dislodging the nightmare. No luck. "Typical Sam Graves, just *waiting* for me to tell him not go to or to take the keys from him. So...so damn ostentatious."

"I'm sorry."

"I didn't stop him. I just sat there. Didn't say a word. Then he walks away, goes into the garage, and gets behind the wheel."

"Ah, jeez," Roxy exhaled. "I once lost a friend driving drunk."

"He didn't die that way."

She creased her brows in confusion, then awareness. "Oh, no! He killed someone else?"

"The son of a bitch never left the garage."

"Huh?"

"Turned on the ignition, ran a hose from the tailpipe into the car, and sat there. Carbon monoxide poisoning. Sat there committing suicide while I'm in the backyard totally oblivious. I'm cursing my father under my breath as he's dying twenty feet from me."

Roxy was speechless.

"No note, no goodbye, no nothing. He just...checked out."

"And *you* found him?"

"No. Mom did when they got back. I remember her running through the house. I can...I can still hear her crying out his name. 'Sam! Sam!' Turning on all the lights looking for him. Calling his friends. I still hear the scream when she found him."

"Oh, God."

"She didn't cry. Didn't shed one tear. I was *still* sitting on my ass out back when she came at me and started slapping my chest. 'How could you? How could you just sit here while your father killed himself?'"

"She didn't mean it."

"Yeah," Pike breathed.

"She was just angry."

"Right."

"It wasn't your fault."

Pike said nothing.

Roxy searched for the right words but there weren't any.

Gazing west into the dipping sun, dwindling light was slicing peculiar angular outlines through the Rockies. She wasn't religious or spiritual. But as she beheld the breathtaking majestic summits with snow-capped peaks, she questioned how God could create something so beautiful while, at the same time, causing such pain.

CHAPTER 13

Did losing time in Kansas City put you behind schedule?"

"Not really on a schedule."

"When's Paige expecting you?"

"She's not."

Roxy laughed humorlessly. "Huh?"

"She doesn't know I'm coming."

"How do you know she'll be home?"

"I don't."

"How do you know she's not married?"

Pike elaborated. "My friend, Dewayne, the guy I told you about before, is a cop back home. He utilized back channels. She's not married."

"And she has no idea you're coming?"

"None."

"Pretty spontaneous on your part."

An image of Cynthia ricocheted across his mind. "That's me. Spontaneous Pike Graves."

Roxy mulled that over. Spontaneous? Yes. Illogical? Absolutely. But, in a way, romantic as hell. *I hope one day I find someone willing to go to such extremes.*

Since leaving Kansas City, Pike had been kicking around something. The frank discussion about his father's suicide along with the placating scenery hadn't allowed him the opportunity. He treasured Roxy's camaraderie, definitely felt a connection. And that's what made this taste vile on his lips. "When we hit Denver, I'll take you to the airport."

Her jaw dropped.

"I'm not going straight to California. I'm hitting Phoenix first, then Vegas."

"Your sister's in Vegas, right?"

"Yes."

"Who's in Phoenix?"

"Someone I have to see."

Roxy chuckled. "Another old girlfriend?"

"No."

Pulling her phone, fingers moving in a blur. Tapping, touching, sliding. "It's less mileage if you go to Vegas before Phoenix."

"I have to...resolve something before I see Stephanie. The airfare's on me. You can be in Seattle in two hours."

"Nope."

Facing right, Pike arched a brow.

"It's not open for discussion, Pike-o-rama."

He grinned. *Pike-o-Rama.* "Roxy, look—"

"Not happenin. It's like kicking me out of a theater twenty minutes before the movie ends. I want to see how things play out between you and Paige."

"I'll write you a letter."

"Oh, em, gee. No one writes letters anymore."

"You know what I mean."

"I'm not on a schedule either."

Pike moaned in defeat. "I won't win, will I?"

"Not a chance, Pike's Peak." She removed her shoes, placed her bare feet on window. "Phoenix, here we come."

❧❦❧

Cynthia Grimm was in a fantastic place.

Three weeks ago she learned Janice Haas planned to retire at Christmas. "That position would be a perfect fit for you," her boss told her.

Morty O'Day, what a guy. The dude had to be pushing a hundred but was doing everything to hold back time. He went from Mortimer to Morty, like that would make a difference. He traded in his Buick for a Corvette and bragged to everyone how much he was bench-pressing at the gym. Now there was a "position" that would be a "perfect fit." In addition to his rebirth, he'd started using double-entendre.

Cynthia wasn't a flirt. But, hey, if shorter skirts showcasing long legs or slacks accentuating her backside got her one rung higher on the corporate ladder, why not? *Men.* No wonder she switched teams. *Maybe if I wiggle my ass, prehistoric Morty will convince archaic Janice to retire sooner. Then I can get that corner office with the killer view by Labor Day.*

With Pike soon to be out of the picture thanks to Dragon, and verifying she was still beneficiary on the $1.4 million, she didn't actually need the promotion and eighteen percent pay raise. It was about ego.

She'd persuaded a couple high school kids from the neighborhood to move Pike's crap into a storage unit. Offer them a pizza, buy some beer, and drop hints she'd give them a blowjob for their time and they'll do anything. *Boys.*

She considered donating Pike's worldly possessions to one of those places that helped retards or old farts who lost limbs in some war somewhere. But she decided to hold off. Let the tards and the gimps fend for themselves.

Indeed, Cynthia was in a fantastic place.

"Ms. Grimm?"

As always, her secretary, Gavin Sugars, was dressed immaculately. Waxed eyebrows, manicured nails, and textbook posture, he flaunted his homosexuality. Cynthia already decided that as soon as she got Janice's corner office she'd get rid of the little flamer. She had no problems with blacks—or African-Americans as they wanted to be called. She even knew a few Mexicans—or Hispanics, or whatever *they* wanted to be called. But homos? No way. She'd shitcan the little fruit and replace him with that cute Filipina chick from accounting with the narrow waist. Sure, Cynthia was gay…or bi maybe. But that was different. The thought of one dude shoving his pork roll into another dude's pooper was cringe-worthy. "Yes?"

"There's a Mr. Dragovich on line three."

"Thanks, Gayvin." *Gayvin.* She loved referring to the little sausage jockey that way. Overflowing with anticipation, she lifted the handset. "Good news, Dragon?"

"Uh, no."

Her voice turned sullen. "What went wrong?"

"I got into KC and checked in to the Ruby Slipper Motel two rooms down from him. But then, well, ya know…"

"No, Dragon," she snapped. "I don't know."

"I fell asleep."

"You fell asleep?"

"Yeah."

She envisioned him shrugging.

"He checked out in the morning."

Cynthia swiveled, facing away from her office door, and whispered. "He left?"

"Yup."

She cogitated while signing online. "He didn't see you, did he?"

"No!" A pause. "Not really, I guess."

"What the hell does that mean?"

"You sitting down?"

"What does that mean, 'Not really, I guess'?"

"Are you?"

"Am I what, Dragon?"

"Sitting down?"

"Christ. Yes, I'm sitting down."

He paused dramatically. "He's got some girl with him."

"*What*? Who?"

"I dunno. She looked young. Yummy too."

That explained the restaurant charges that seemed excessive for one person. "You recognize her?"

"Nah."

Cynthia was irate. "I can't believe he's cheating on me. Who does he think he is?"

Dragon snorted. If she cheated, there was a reason. When someone cheated on her, she was the victim. He loved her, always would. But man, she could be a few sandwiches short of a picnic.

"Gimme a sec." She put Dragon on hold to get serenaded by Jim Croce. Old Morty was such a fan, two Croce songs played on an endless loop: "Bad, Bad Leroy Brown" and "Time in a Bottle." In a staff meeting, Cynthia once remarked, "I always dug 'Cat's in the Cradle.'"

Evelyn Willard scoffed. "That's Harry Chapin, not Jim Croce."

"They're not the same guy?"

Evelyn shuddered.

Yeah, I'll fire her too.

Cynthia positioned several browsers side-by-side and pulled on her chin. "Pike, Pike, Pike, what're you up to?"

Within five minutes, she pieced together the puzzle. She assumed he was heading to San Francisco for that Paige chick he never got over. Now it appeared the sneaky bastard had other plans. Accessing his credit card transactions, she uncovered a charge from a fast food joint in Lawrence, KS, followed a short time later by a gas station charge in Topeka. Westbound on I-70. If he was going to northern California I-80, not I-70, would be the obvious choice. But he would've headed north from Kansas City. I-70 ended in central Utah at I-15. And I-15 ran south to—

She took Dragon off hold. "Hey."

He was singing about a custom Continental and an El Dorado, too.

"Dragon!"

"Oh, sorry."

"I need you in Vegas."

"Vegas, baby!"

"This is business, not pleasure. I want you waiting for Pike when he gets there."

"Where? Isn't Vegas kinda big?"

"I'll get you his sister's address."

CHAPTER 14

After checking into a mid-level hotel west of Denver, Pike and Roxy walked across the street for dinner. The Sub Pub was rated four-stars on Yelp. After they were seated, Roxy announced, "Hafta find the little girl's room. Back in a jiff."

Pike nursed an ice water and took in his surroundings. Preppy types huddled close. Energetic, brash, enjoying life. And all younger.

Minutes later, Roxy reappeared but was stopped twice by two different college-aged males. One apparently offering to buy a drink, the other indicating an empty chair at a rambunctious table. She politely declined while shooting Pike a glance. *What can I do?*

An unsettling thought infiltrated his mind. Roxy was, as his father used to say about Ann-Margaret, "a head-turner." Stunning, exotic. But wearing skintight jeans that drew attention to strong athletic legs and an aqua-colored shirt that accentuated full breasts, Pike was disturbed seeing others fawning over her.

And he wasn't sure why it bothered him.

She was twenty-one. She could be his daughter. And that disturbed him for an entirely different reason.

"Shove over," she said upon returning.

He hesitated, surprised she wanted to sit beside him rather than opposite.

Pike felt an electrical charge as their hips pushed against each other. He slid over a few inches. She did also. "I thought of something."

"In there?"

"I frequently have flashes of brilliance sittin' on the potty." Roxy pulled her phone and pointed out that if they got on the road by dawn and made great time they could reach Phoenix late tomorrow night. "Look."

Nuzzling close like a couple sharing a secret, she tucked stray strands of raven hair behind her ear. To get a better view, Pike draped his arm along the back of the booth.

She looked at his arm behind her and smiled coquettishly.

I'm getting closer to the phone, not you. But the words didn't come. Google maps showed thin lines, wide lines, orange triangles denoting road construction, green splotches signifying forests, brown symbolizing deserts and blue indicating bodies of water.

But pressed against Roxy, the scent of her hair, the warmth of her body, the curve of her hip and the fragranced body wash that clung to her even after sitting in a car all day, Pike's thoughts wandered.

Only one thing jumped off the map, something that stood apart from everything else as if calling to him. A small town in northern Arizona.

Page.

"We'll be getting in late," she was saying. "If we book a room now, we can go straight to the hotel when we arrive."

"Makes sense."

As she tapped away, he observed sapphire nail polish he hadn't noticed before.

"Whereabouts do you want to stay?"

Having never set foot in Phoenix, Pike wasn't sure. He was going for one reason only: To exorcise his demons and settle an old score with Virgil Holland. He had the guy's address and there was a good probability things would turn ugly. If that happened he'd need to flee quickly. "Something close to a highway."

It took the entire meal until she located a suitable hotel. "Camel Back Lodge in Mesa. Look okay?"

"Sure."

"Cool beans. Just need your credit card."

Pike wavered.

"I'm not Cyn. Hand it over."

Blushing, he apologized and retrieved his wallet. Roxy didn't move as he leaned against her.

While she booked the room through Trivago, Pike wondered when, if ever, he'd be able to trust. The instant Roxy finished, he signaled for his credit card.

"We should probably reserve something in Vegas also."

Pike relented. "Okay."

Finding a vacancy was tougher than Phoenix. It took some time before she announced "The Hard Rock has rooms."

"No!"

His adamant refusal caught her off-guard.

"That's where my sister works."

"Oh." A few minutes later, she said, "There's a place off the Strip called Sam's Town that has vacancies."

Pike laughed. Sam's Town. Sam Graves. Choosing between a hotel/casino bearing his father's first name or a place where his sister worked. *Punching at Fog.* They decided on Sam's Town.

❧

"Whenever you're ready." The waitress, dressed in a Broncos jersey and wearing eye-black even though it was baseball season, lowered the check.

Roxy put her hand up. "I got it."

"Oh? Okay, thanks."

"No problem, Pikes Peak." Rifling through her purse, she pulled a credit card and handed it over.

The server scrutinized the card, Roxy, the card again. "I'll need to see ID."

It was a flash, a split-second. But Pike sensed a change. For the first time all meal, she slanted away, preventing him from seeing the contents of her purse.

"Hmm, this is weird."

"What is?" he asked.

"I can't find my ID." She rummaged quicker. "Do you really need it?" she asked the waitress.

"Yes."

Pike pulled his wallet. "I got it."

Roxy shook her head, a bit excessively it seemed. "That's really weird," she repeated.

Weird. "Sure is."

❧

Roxy knew the reason she couldn't sleep. She knew what she

needed. She wasn't sure, however, if she should actually follow through.

An hour in bed, maybe two. Kicking off the sheets, tossing, turning, overtly grumbling, rearranging pillows. Nothing mattered.

Pike was dead to the world.

She remembered Erin Lorenzo, a classmate who bragged about weekend trysts with their Spanish teacher, a married guy pushing forty. She remembered catching Nikki Langston going down on their boss in the break room at the telemarketing firm thinking everyone had left for the night. There had to be thirty-five years between *them*.

Roxy peered through the shadows at Pike in the neighboring bed, wondering *What's wrong with me?*

Getting up, she plodded to the bathroom and turned on the light after closing the door. She didn't want to wake him.

Or did she?

An adorable baby. A cute kid. A pretty young woman. She'd heard it her whole life. From friends. And from Jonah, though he had to say those things. Studying her reflection in the mirror, she didn't see it.

Nose too big, thighs too thick, and hips too wide. Nine people could compliment her but she'd only remember the tenth who put her down.

Joey Rowland was the star pitcher on the high school baseball team as well as president of the debate club. The *Zanesville Times Recorder* lauded his "stellar performance and everyman realism" as juror number eight, the role made famous by Henry Fonda, in the school's adaptation of *12 Angry Men*. Roxy memorized the exact wording from the article because it was the centerpiece of her Joey Rowland scrapbook. And he was the centerpiece of her world.

Joey Rowland, the most flawless male specimen she'd ever seen.

When hearing through the grapevine he and his girlfriend had split, Roxy knew it was time to ratchet things up.

She hated oysters but when Joey suggested it, she immediately agreed. She wasn't a Vin Diesel fan but when he wanted to see the latest *Fast and Furious* movie, she jumped at the chance. Exiting the theater, he proclaimed superciliously, "I could sure use a blowjob tonight." Roxy was on her knees twenty minutes later. He insisted sex was better without a condom. She concurred. He told her he wanted to have sex with her in public and two nights later she was bent over a park bench. He claimed he yearned for a threesome and that weekend Roxy found herself in a motel room with Joey and a woman she'd never met.

He announced he dabbled in bondage. "I like being submissive," she lied.

Returning home the following morning, bruised, humiliated, and mortified, she fanatically showered then checked her e-mail.

The subject line read "Whore." Clicking on the attachment, Roxy's tears came hard and fast. Her entire night reduced to a toy for his perverted depravity and twisted fetishes had not only been secretly filmed but sent to three dozen mutual friends.

Turning now, she killed the bathroom light and calculated Pike across the obscurity. He was an okay looking guy, handsomer than some, not as handsome as others. Roxy was at a point in life where she was learning physical appearance wasn't everything. Pike Graves was definitely no Joey Rowland.

He was a good man with a good heart.

But he was also vulnerable. And no matter how much he tried hiding it, lonely.

Yes, his relationship with that Cynthia chick was over. Yes, he was hoping to rekindle something with that Paige woman. But at this moment, he was unattached.

She'd flirted at dinner, deliberately burrowing close after freshening up in the ladies room. She winked at him, threw her head back when laughing and displayed innocent vulnerability in her fawnlike eyes. She was so into it, she screwed up by accidentally offering to pay for dinner. In hindsight, it was obvious the waitress would ask for ID. *Duh.*

Still, Pike wasn't interested.

Or was he just pretending?

A few deep breaths, she steeled herself, crossed the dim room, and got into his bed.

Spooning Pike, she timidly placed her hand on his bicep. He didn't respond. She began walking her fingers up and down his arm. He didn't stir. Moving furtively, she positioned his hand between her legs. Pike roused slightly. She glided his hand inside her panties, using his fingers to stimulate herself. Slow at first, then quicker. Exhaling pleasurably, she moaned moving his fingers deeper inside.

"Roxy?" Pike was wide-eyed and alert. Realizing where his hand was, he pulled back as if touching something grotesque "What're you doing?" This time, he knew, was no dream. The expression on her face was unidentifiable. He'd never seen this incarnation of Roxy.

Sadness enveloped her hearing the pity when he said her name. Aroused? Not even close. He was disappointed. Feeling sorry for her. Roxy had no idea what to say so she did what felt natural and followed her hunger, moving her hand toward his crotch.

"Roxy?" Not passionate, but not stopping her.

Her hands began kneading him, stroking him. He was hardening and growing warm. Roxy was equally turned on. Her body acting on its own. He opened his mouth. To whisper her name? To tell her to stop? She didn't wait. She climbed on top and kissed him on the lips. Passionately. Aggressively.

Recoiling, Pike bayed. "What the hell are you doing?"

The blood drained from her face. Her hips stopped grinding. The flames of passion fully doused. That's when the awareness shocked her like a million volts of electricity. She was taking advantage of Pike the way she'd been taken advantage of. She'd become Joey Rowland. "My God!" She sprang off the bed with blinding speed.

Pike reached for her as if trying to save someone who'd fallen overboard and was drowning. "Roxy."

"Mygodmygodmygod."

"Roxy, wait!"

She didn't. Darting across the room, avoiding his outstretched arm, she jumped into her clothes, slid her feet into her sandals, fought with the suddenly complex deadbolt and chain, and finally escaped, scampering into the night. Ignoring his pleas to come back, she kept running. Maybe if she ran hard enough she could run away from what she'd become.

A block away she realized she'd left her phone in the room. She'd give anything to locate one of those old phone booths that allegedly used to be on every street corner.

A cashier at an all-night convenience store wouldn't let her use the phone without purchasing something. Her wallet was also back at the hotel. Despite leaning forward and offering him a peek at her cleavage, the guy didn't relent.

Outside, a customer was filling her car. Roxy sprinted over, and panting hard, got the woman's attention. Red-headed, she wore cowboy boots, a Stetson, Wranglers, and a leather vest over a white top with a string tie. Roxy, the country music aficionado, felt marginally relieved by the stranger's striking resemblance to Reba.

"Hey, hun, you okay?"

"Yeah, yes. I was wondering if maybe I could use your cell." Roxy made a phone with her hands as if the woman wouldn't understand.

"Sure, hun." The Reba-lookalike handed it over and, in a concerned tone, noted, "Lookin' kinda frazzled. You need a ride somewhere?"

"Nah, thanks." She stepped a few paces away for privacy. "I'll stand right here."

"Take your time."

Roxy wavered. Was this the right thing to do? What reaction would she get? Was getting into Pike's car the biggest mistake of her life? At a crossroads and crippled by indecision. She looked at *Reba* as if she had the answer.

Endeavoring to regulate her breathing and bring down her soaring heartrate, she entered the number.

A sleepy voice answered after four endless rings. "Yeah?"

Unable to find the words, Roxy remained silent.

"*What?*" Anger replaced sleepiness.

"It's me," she whispered.

"Who's me?"

She closed her eyes. "Roxy."

"Where are you?" Clipped, abrasive.

"I dunno exactly."

"What the fuck's that mean?"

Roxy blinked away a tear. How could she do this to Pike? But she couldn't turn back now. "Outside of Denver."

"*Colorado?*"

"Yep."

"So?" Waiting for more.

God help me. Why, why, why? "Las Vegas. Sam's Town. Three days." And she hung up.

CHAPTER 15

"Mommy, don't go."

"Son, I have to."

"Please take me."

"Oh, honey, I would if I could. But this is an important night for your father."

Pike, nine years old, couldn't find the fortitude to let go of his mom. "I'll be good. I promise. *Please.*"

"You're always good." She lovingly tousled her son's brown hair. "But this is for adults only."

"C'mon, Cora, We have to *go.*"

Pike peeked around her waist. His dad, the timepiece guru of Philadelphia, irritably pointed to his wristwatch. Reinforcing his hold, he begged. "Mommy, I'll be quiet. You won't even know I'm there."

Dropping to her haunches, she met her son's disconsolate, lonely eyes. "We'll be home late but your sister's here."

Stephanie sidled over and clasped her brother's shoulder. Trying to act motherly at sixteen and failing miserably. "I'll take you to Mickey D's and get you one of those sundaes you like. Sound good, kiddo?"

Pike looked up. "With nuts?"

"Why not, you're a nut?"

"And you're a doofus." He laughed. His sister laughed. Mommy too.

But not his dad. "Good Lord, woman. Come. On!"

Pike remained unenthused. Siblings argue, siblings fight. But Stephanie became a different person when their parents weren't around. A person he didn't particularly care for.

Cora turned her boy and pointed. "Look."

The Christmas tree filled one entire corner of the living room. The multi-colored lights refracted off the ornaments. The sweet bouquet of pine hung in the air. An endless array of wrapped presents in a sea of red and green calling to him. Garland draped along the mantel.

"I'll tell you what, honey."

"God Almighty, Cora!"

"In a minute, Sam!"

Pike's father snorted. "I'll go warm up the goddamn car. You've got two minutes. Two." He turned on his heels and stormed into the December chill.

Cora had long since numbed herself to her husband's brusque attitude. Profanity in private was one thing. Taking the lord's name in vain, in front of the children and this close to the Christmas tree was offensive. "Be good for your sister, don't cause any problems. And maybe…"

"Maybe what, maybe what?"

"Maybe…if you're not naughty, Santa will let you open a present early."

Stephanie shook her head. *Santa.*

"Really, Mommy, really?"

"Let's see what I can work out with Santa."

"Promise?" Pike jumped in place.

"It's up to you. Will you be good?"

"Yes, yes, yes. I love you, Mommy."

"Love you too."

Pike threw himself at the presents and rattled each one next to his ear, deciding which would be opened first.

Cora gave her daughter instructions.

"We'll be fine, Mom. Have fun."

Cora Graves smiled woefully then gave a tell-tale expression as she headed toward the door. She looked like she was on her way to an operating room for a life-threatening surgery, not a Christmas party thrown by Sam Graves for his employees.

Stephanie added, "At least *try* to have a good time."

જ્જ્

The Hot Fudge Sundae—with nuts—was only the beginning. Stephanie, going against Mom's wishes, splurged and bought Pike a chocolate shake. Back home, they wrestled in the living room. Pike channeled his inner Bruno Sammartino to Stephanie's

Fabulous Moolah. But when the doorbell rang the *other* Stephanie materialized.

"Now, listen." She squatted, trying but again failing to act maternal. "I took you to Mickey D's like I said. I let you jump off the sofa even though you're not supposed to. We played in the house, even though Mom would get angry, right?"

Pike bowed his head and vehemently chewed his lip. It was how he dealt with stress. Some children sucked their thumb for too many years. Others had bedwetting issues. His coping mechanism was grinding on his own lips. Occasionally, with such intensity, he drew his own blood. His mom had taken him to a battery of child psychiatrists. After numerous sessions with so-called experts the answer was the same. "He'll outgrow it."

Pike remembered Dad griping, "That was sure money well spent."

Stephanie now reminded him. "I've been nice, right?"

"Yeah," he muttered.

"So this stays between us? You don't tell Mom and Dad about *this*." She threw her thumb at the front door. "And I'll tell them you were a good boy. Santa will be happy." She extended a finger. "Pinkie promise?"

"'Kay."

"Good." Stephanie patted his head like a puppy then cinched her Jordache jeans like she was Brooke Shields, sashayed across the room, and opened the front door. "Hey, Ponch."

Like *he* was Erik Estrada from *CHiPS*.

Ponch was older than Stephanie. "He's in *college*," Pike once overheard her confide to a friend on the phone. "He's such a great kisser. And *so* big."

Pike didn't like the guy. Nor did he like his sister when the guy came around. He and Stephanie battled for their parent's attention but for the most part, though he'd never admit it, his sister was pretty cool. Not Fonzie-cool but cool. However, when Ponch showed up, she transformed into someone else, some*thing* else.

Pike was sandwiched between them watching a TV show with jokes he didn't understand. Stephanie and Ponch did everything possible to make him feel unwanted and in the way. They held hands atop the back of the couch, just behind his head. They ignored him completely. Stephanie continually asked, "Tired yet?"

"No."

Pike wasn't stupid. He was clearly unwelcome in his own home. An annoyance. A burden. "I'm going upstairs to play Pong."

"Good!" Stephanie and Ponch elatedly cried in unison.

In his room he sat on a beanbag chair, pushed the necessary buttons on a hand-me-down black and white thirteen-inch Zenith and brought the game to life. Gray backdrop, white lines, one circle going back and forth. Pike was center court at, as he called it, Wimpleton.

He and Stephanie used to play for hours and hours, but now his sister was downstairs with someone else. Pike had been replaced.

Angrily, he turned off the stupid game and dug through the treasure chest looking for a comic book. He decided on Spider-Man and although he'd read this one a million times, it was his favorite. He was at the best part, the scene where Spidey and Dr. Octopus are fighting in the warehouse with flames everywhere, when his bedroom door opened.

"Hey, little man."

Pike peered over the top of the comic. "You're supposed to knock." He quickly returned his attention to the world of superheroes.

Ponch theatrically knocked three times. *Like now he was Tony Orlando.* "Happy?" He laughed loudly. Pike hated his laugh. "Watcha readin' little man?"

He showed Ponch the cover.

"*Spider-Man*, huh? I was into *Batman* when I was your age."

"*Batman* sucks."

Ponch entered the room without being invited. Young Pike knew that was impolite. When he lowered himself on the bed, Pike felt...uncomfortable. He also didn't like the way Ponch smelled. It was the same way Daddy did just before he broke things and used bad words.

Ponch swigged from a Pabst Blue Ribbon. "Isn't it your bed time?"

Pike glanced at the nightstand clock. For his birthday last summer, his father had given him a watch, but he lost it while bike riding. Sam Graves pitched a fit. The same man who was surrounded by watches of all types refused to give his son another until he proved he could be responsible. "It's only half past ten."

Ponch bent sideways and squinted down the hall toward Stephanie's bedroom, the room where Pike occasionally heard stuff going on between them. "Christmas is coming."

"Duh!"

Ponch took a substantial swig then showed Pike the bottle. "Wanna try?"

"I'm nine."

"So? That's almost like a man, little man."

"I'm not supposed to. That's for grown-ups."

"Don't you wanna be a grown-up?"

Pike chewed his lip. "I dunno."

"Yes or no?"

"Yeah, I guess I do."

When Ponch leaned nearer, Pike withered. "If you wanna be an adult, then you should know the truth."

"What truth?"

"There is no Santa Claus."

His little body trembled. "Wha...*what*?"

"Welcome to adulthood."

"Yes, there is!"

"Nope."

"Is too, is too!"

"It's your parents. They give you the gifts."

"Not true."

"You ever seen Santa?"

Pike's chin quivered. Through tears, he sought refuge from the comic book's cover. Spider-Man and Dr. Octopus battling in an inferno on a rooftop high above the city. How silly it all now seemed. He flung the comic book across his bedroom, sending Spider-Man into his Chewbacca poster.

The innocence of childhood gone forever.

cɔɛɔ

He woke in near-total darkness. A wedge of ambient light from downstairs caused bizarre corkscrew patterns snaking across his bedroom. Inching closer, closer...

Palming somnolent eyes, Pike noticed his nightstand alarm clock had been knocked askew. He had no recollection of doing it. When he was younger, he was such a fidgety sleeper, arms flailing and legs kicking as if fighting invisible monsters, Mom resorted to putting a rail around his bed. He felt imprisoned. But time passed, the monsters went away, and the bars were removed. He knew if he told her about the clock, he'd be sentenced to more pseudo-imprisonment.

Getting to his feet, he felt…strange. Mouth dry, mind foggy, legs wobbly. Ponch wasn't around but his alcoholic smell lingered. Licking his lips, Pike winced. Dried blood. He'd been chewing during his sleep. Something else he wouldn't tell Mommy about. Wearing his underpants and a Dr. J T-shirt, he sleepily shambled down the hall. His parent's open bedroom door indicated they still hadn't returned home. Stephanie's door was also open. No sign of her either.

Pike went to the bathroom, pleased the nightlight was still on. After relieving himself, he washed his hands. The curtain of sleep not pulled back, he shuffled down the carpeted stairs to get some juice. Three steps from the bottom he stopped dead in his tracks. Paralyzed.

A week ago he and his sister had their worst fight ever. He felt bad. He didn't mean to. It was an accident. But he really had to pee and so he threw open the door without knocking. Stephanie screamed. Taking a bath, her right hand was between her legs.

Furious. Humiliated. Mortified. Pike didn't comprehend. She told him she hated him. She told him she wished she didn't have a brother. She told him he should've died instead of the fraternal brother they never knew. Pike bawled.

Recalling her fury at being seen in the tub, he now chose to say nothing when again seeing her naked. But she wasn't in the tub. She was on the living room floor. Ponch was naked too.

Folding himself into a little ball, he wanted to run away, run back upstairs. But his legs wouldn't move. His tiny hands gripped the bannister and he peered out like watching through prison bars.

Had they been dressed it would've looked like they were wrestling, much the way he and Stephanie had hours earlier. This time, however, his sister wasn't laughing.

On her hands and knees, his sister looked puny and helpless. Ponch, behind her and twice his size, shoving his hips forward like Pike once saw old clips of that Elvis guy doing. He initially chuckled when Stephanie got spanked on her bottom. The smile quickly evaporated. Not spanked, hit. *Hard.* She whimpered in pain, either resulting from the heavy hand smacking her backside or from the malicious way Ponch kept thrusting his pelvis against her.

Stephanie's scream was muffled when Ponch covered her mouth. His other hand began pulling her hair with such hostility Pike thought her neck might snap. She was then flung onto her back like a ragdoll. Brutally, pugnaciously, Ponch shoved her legs apart. The slap to her face clearly stung. Pike painstakingly rose to his feet, but what could he do? Ponch was *way* bigger.

"Tell me you're a bitch," Ponch gritted.

She started to say something but apparently it wasn't quick enough.

"Tell me!" He slapped her face so hard her head hinged left. And across the shadowy expanse, she met the eyes of her nine-year-old brother.

Lights swept across the living room. Tires crunching snow. Mommy and Daddy were home.

If he hadn't felt so confused and powerless, Pike would've laughed at the way Ponch and Stephanie jumped up, accidentally bumping heads, frantically searched for their discarded clothes, and hurriedly dressed.

Amidst the pandemonium, Pike retreated to the top of the landing but continued listening. Harried footfalls across the kitchen. A window opened, followed by a grunt as Ponch launched himself into the backyard and fled.

The front door opened.

"Hey, Daddy, Mom. How was your night?" Stephanie sounded like she'd just completed a marathon.

"Lovely," Mom answered, though her tone indicated otherwise. "Pike cause any problems?"

Pike heard the closet door open as Mom hung up her fur coat, wondering why she only asked if *he* caused problems.

"He was fine," Stephanie responded. When the front door slammed a moment later, she asked, "Have fun, Daddy?"

Sam grunted. He, too, removed his coat then crossed the living room to the whiskey cabinet. Unexpectedly, he pulled up short and inspected his surroundings. The room, the furniture, his daughter's face. He inhaled twice like a bloodhound, then asked accusatorily, "Something you need to tell me, young lady?"

"No, Daddy, nothing."

Eyes tapering, he scrutinized his sixteen-year-old daughter with all-knowing omnipotent eyes. "You didn't have that Virgil Holland boy over, did you?"

Stephanie laughed. "Daddy, please. Give me *some* credit. You told me you didn't want me seeing him anymore."

"Mm hmm."

Pike ran. Down the hall. Across his bedroom. A swan dive onto his bed, he buried his face into his pillow so no one would hear him crying. He *was* nine after all. He was a grown-up. There was no Santa. Grown-ups don't cry. He'd been crippled by fear, doubt, and confusion. Every morning his father went to work, Pike was instructed, "You're the man of the house."

But what kind of man becomes paralyzed by the inability to act. He didn't know what he would've done. Or could've done. But he didn't even have the courage to try. He was no hero. Ponch, whose real name was apparently Virgil Holland, had a good ten years on Pike and was lots bigger. *He's in college.*

But one day Pike would be bigger. One day their paths would cross. One day he'd make Virgil Holland pay.

CHAPTER 16

Good choice." It was midnight when Pike pulled beneath the canopy of the Camel Back Lodge.

"Thanks."

Although the ski lodge décor was out of place for Arizona, the hotel appeared recently refurbished and accommodating. Then again, after eight hundred miles and sixteen hours behind the wheel, a cot at the Salvation Army would be accommodating.

The last part of the drive, Pike thought of an ex-girlfriend, Allie Madril. They got along well, shared similar interests, and had the same style of humor. However, their relationship eventually lost that new car smell. They started doing what Pike called 'The tongue-tied two-step.' Conversation stunted, dialogue forced. Today, driving from Denver to Phoenix, he and Roxy engaged in their own tongue-tied two-step.

She slept the first two hours out of town. When she woke the song and dance began.

"I'm so embarrassed," she said ashamed.

"It's okay."

"I wasn't thinking."

"I've done that myself."

"I don't know what came over me."

"It's fine."

"I'm not like that, Pike."

"I know."

"I just felt lonely."

"No worries."

"I'm sorry."

"It's okay."

She went back to sleep.

Entering the hotel room, they each went to their respective corners. Roxy feigning interest in generic pencil drawings as if visiting the Louvre while Pike mindlessly toyed with the TV. Despite the drivel of the idiot box and the humming of the air conditioning, silence hung in the air like a guillotine. Pike broke it. "I think I'll take a shower. I'm kinda stiff."

The old Roxy would've made a wisecrack about him being "stiff" and followed up with her patented sugary laugh. Now, she replied with a vapid nod. "I'm gonna turn in. I'm exhausted."

"Sure." Pike looked around. "G'night."

"Night."

In the bathroom, Pike turned on the water, undressed, and with her failed seduction attempt fresh on his mind, locked the door. He was beginning not to trust Roxy. Or perhaps, he couldn't trust himself.

ℰᐓℰᐓ

Roxy was already dressed and sitting on her bed when Pike woke the following morning. "Did it wake you?" she asked, referring to the barely audible TV.

"Nope." It was one of those shows where broken down homes are resurrected into something new and vibrant. Pike envied the shoddy old house.

Without looking at him, Roxy claimed, "There's a Burger King and a Taco Time within walking distance."

"You ate already?"

"Yep."

Hoping to ease the tension, he asked, "Get one of your customary early morning shakes?"

"Just coffee."

More proof the Roxy he'd grown to know and—like—was fading away. "Uh, okay."

She nodded once then cast a guarded glance at the door as if expecting someone.

ℰᐓℰᐓ

Scottsdale was once referred to as 'The desert version of Miami's South Beach.' One of the more upscale communities in the valley of the sun, it had been home to the likes of Steven Spielberg, Barry Goldwater, Stevie Nicks—not Wonder—Muhammad Ali, Meadowlark Lemon.

Virgil Holland.

The Holland house was a striking single-story Spanish villa situated atop a small rise that allowed the homeowner to look down on his neighbors. Cacti stood proud and prominent in the front yard. Working against Pike was the home's location on a cul-de-sac. To surveil the residence, he'd need to repeatedly drive-by and risk detection. He gambled but two passes made it impossible to ascertain much other than a white Range Rover and a red sports car parked on a circular cobblestone driveway.

Bastard sure has done well.

Pike pulled curbside a few houses away and killed the engine. The street was serene, the lone sound coming from chirping cicadas. A bunny scurried happily down the lane before tunneling into a cluster of rocks.

Pike thought of Dewayne. His best friend had been kind enough to hand over Holland's address without wanting particulars. Now observing from across the street, his car amateurishly semi-obscured by a trifling utility box, he regretted not asking his friend how to avoid boredom during a stakeout.

He'd heard the old adage about dry heat but after twenty minutes he felt like a TV dinner in the oven. Pike was wiping perspiration from the nape of his neck when the Range Rover descended the driveway with a male behind the wheel. And headed in Pike's direction.

He had to think fast. The combination of bug splatter on the windshield and grill along with out-of-state plates was a red flag. He got out and exchanged glances between a house and an imaginary piece of paper in his hand. Just some guy looking for the right address. He turned his back to the street as the white vehicle passed. When Holland disappeared around the corner, Pike jumped behind the wheel of his Honda and pursued the man he'd kept in the crosshairs for nearly four decades.

⁂

Thursday morning rush hour had ended and the light traffic made it harder to tail his prey. When the Range Rover stopped at a red light, Pike had no option other than pulling behind.

The awareness smashed his chest like a ton of bricks. *Stupid.* Pike never considered it until this very moment.

The driveway.

Two vehicles.

Virgil Holland was married.

Even more unsettling were the stickers on opposite sides of the rear bumper. *My daughter and my money go to Arizona State University* on one side, *Proud parent of a United States Marine* on the other.

The son of a bitch has a family.

It underscored an agonizing distinction. Virgil Holland: wife, kids, beautiful home, fancy car. Pike Graves: no wife, no kids, technically no home and a six-year old Honda with pigeon shit on the hood.

Virgil Holland had moved on with his life while Pike Graves remained buried in the past.

The light turned green. Holland drove forward. Pike noticed a decal in the bottom corner of the tinted window. A depiction of a forsaken Christ, head bowed, Crown of Thorns on His head. *He died for my sins.*

"Sins," Pike spat. Remembering the way Holland forced himself on Stephanie, he mumbled, "You sure got plenty of those." And stepped on the gas.

ఇఇఇ

Fifteen minutes later, Holland drove into a shopping center and, charmed as he was, found a spot directly in front of Barnes and Noble. Pike parked two aisles over. Holland emerged from his vehicle, peering around.

Cautious? Nervous?

He was thinner than his Ponch days. Hair like steel wool, poised gait, bronzed skin, and shoulders held high, he gave the manifestation of a well-respected elder statesman. White polo, white tennis shorts, white sneakers, white socks. He even drove a white vehicle. *White. Pure.* Pike snickered at the irony.

Holland entered the book store and within minutes Pike was roasting. He was about to get out and hopefully find a breeze in this Godforsaken desert when his target exited the store holding giftwrapped presents like he'd been Christmas shopping in July.

Christmas.

There is no Santa Claus.

Having an epiphany, Pike pulled his phone and began taking pictures.

Holland good-naturedly held the door for a woman and her four children who casually sauntered through, then exchanged a cordial greeting with a young man ambling along the sidewalk before assisting a young mother cram a cumbersome stroller into the back of a Mini-Cooper.

"Saint Virgil," Pike snorted as a blunt awareness hurtled across his brain.

Stephanie. Sixteen. In her home where she should feel safe. Where everyone should feel safe. Sexually assaulted on the floor. Violated, manhandled, degraded. Mere feet from a Christmas tree. She spent years trying to find peace. Moving home, moving out again. Boyfriend to boyfriend, job to job. Pike knew her life-long quest to find herself and never-ending pursuit for tranquility stemmed from that one moment in time, a moment when Pike couldn't do a damn thing but watch.

It may have taken nearly forty years but today, Pike would avenge his sister.

ࢳࢴࢳ

He shadowed Holland beyond the city limits to Apache Junction. The area wasn't renewed and glitzy like other parts of Phoenix. It looked and felt, in a word, tired. Homes were timeworn and sagging under the cruel heat. Older cars baked in the sun. Paper cups and water bottles lined the gutter. Palm trees, once stately, now withered. Streets were potholed and pitted.

Pike followed Holland down a narrow road where foreclosed homes equaled occupied homes. Half a block down, Holland parked and exited the Range Rover. Holding the gift-wrapped books, he pulled an attaché from the rear hatch and marched self-assuredly toward a wind-swept ranch-style residence.

Pike parked on the driveway of a vacant home that afforded an unobstructed vantage point of the home his quarry entered. He again snapped pictures of Holland strolling along the curved walkway.

Bearing gifts, Holland knocked, stepped back, and rocked superciliously on the balls of his feet.

A gaunt blonde female materialized in the doorframe. Navy

blue tank top and frayed jean shorts, her hair up in a clip and small round-framed wire glasses on her nose. An academic type. Also young. Early twenties, Pike estimated.

Her hands went to her face, embarrassed by her casual appearance. She took Holland in her arms. When he handed over the presents, she embraced him a second time. And much longer. She then stepped back, welcoming him into her home.

The SOB is cheating on his wife.

Pike had him. Virgil Holland had destroyed his family. Now he'd do the same.

∽∾∽

While Holland spent time with a woman half his age, Pike played with his phone, trying to adjust the resolution on the photos he'd taken without ruining their clarity. He received an incoming text from Roxy who had stayed behind in the motel to watch Netflix. Pike was thankful for her decision. What he needed to do, he needed to do alone.

Happy 1 week anniversary tomorrow Pike-a-doodle-dandy. Perhaps the old Roxy was back. He smiled, but only briefly. No distractions. Retribution was his mission.

He was fine-tuning the pixilation when a woman's laughter broke the silence. Lifting his gaze, he watched Holland depart the residence, still clutching his briefcase but sans presents. Pike checked his watch. Twenty-five minutes. *Nothin' like a quickie.* Holland moved to his car, waved goodbye, and drove off.

Pike had proof of infidelity but he wanted more. He wanted to destroy the guy. Bringing the car to life, Pike continued tailing.

Thirty minutes later, Virgil Holland—husband, father, pillar of the community—promenaded into Bottom's Up, a seedy topless bar abutting abandoned railroad tracks. Pike, like paparazzi cowering behind hedges, snapped more pictures. He resisted the urge to go in and take a few more of the pompous ass getting a lap dance. Pike had him dead to rights. It was time for a little chat with Mrs. Holland.

∽∾∽

You're a good man.

He'd heard it his entire life. Family, friends, co-workers. Even from Cynthia as they were separating and from Stewart Stafford as he was firing him. The conundrum Pike faced approaching the Holland home had his stomach roiling.

He'd longed for this moment since childhood. But now Pike was unsure how to proceed. Virgil Holland had ruined Stephanie and left Pike laced with guilt for decades. And now, he'd finally even the score.

But he wondered if a *good man* do such a thing? Sauntering toward the front door of the home, his resolve waned.

His thoughts reverted to the utter humiliation in Stephanie's helpless eyes. His feeling of paralysis, unable to save his sister. Does that give him license to wreck this man's life?

Hell yes.

The grinding to his immediate left caused him to jump. The garage door was rolling up. Pike froze. More proof he wasn't wired to be impulsive. He turned tail and hid behind the AC unit on the home's north side.

The red sports car squealed away. The lone occupant, likely Virgil's wife, had blonde hair just like his fuck-buddy in Apache Junction.

His mind spun. When would Mrs. Holland return? Would Virgil come back before his wife? Time was passing. He had to think fast. He had to act fast.

Brazenly, Pike bolted from his concealed position, hustled toward the lowering garage door, and pitched out his leg to break the sensor beam. The door roared to an immediate halt before reversing and rolling up.

Pike went in.

※※※

Through the garage, a laundry room, and then a door leading to the kitchen.

Appliances were immense and futuristic. The stove, twelve burners in total, was better suited for a five-star restaurant. The microwave had more buttons than Mission Control.

"Hello?" he tentatively called out. The home's exterior was upper-middle-class but the inside had likely been the work of an interior decorator. Open, airy Southwest motif. Leather sofas.

Matching love seats. A knockoff of Da Vinci's The Last Supper. Recliners befitting a Saudi oil sheik. A mammoth TV—no, correction, small movie screen—bolted on the living room wall, a second one in a family room.

Pike's breath caught. His emotions tangled. First, anger. A man like Virgil Holland had no right to amass such riches while Pike, who'd done everything right—or tried to—struggled.

Anger turned to anxiety.

Only now he realized he'd committed a crime. Trespassing.

Was it simple curiosity? A few weeks ago he'd read online about a pop star he'd never heard of selling their Malibu mansion for twenty million. He couldn't help but scroll through the pictures. How often does one get to see inside a life of affluence most only dream about? Maybe that's why Pike intruded. A glimpse into Virgil Holland's world.

Despite breaking the law, he wasn't ready to leave.

Pike Graves had lived two lives: Pre-Grizzly's and Post-Grizzly's. The latter filled with guilt mincing his soul. Guilt for taking the life of a local sports hero. Guilt for erasing much of his family's finances. Guilt for likely contributing to his father's first heart attack. The courts found him innocent and chose not to punish him. So Pike punished himself.

He started boxing—if you could call it that. He became a sparring partner.

The pummeling, the beatings, the thrashing, the barrage of bone jarring jabs to his head, his face, his jaw, his belly. Maybe if he stood there long enough the guilt and remorse and accountability would be beaten out of him. Self-flagellation.

Enough.

He suffered enough. He needed to get away from Holland's opulence. It was depressing as hell. He'd find a way to get the pictures to Mrs. Holland.

Man, he'd give anything to be a fly on the wall when she'd learn her dedicated, loving husband was visiting titty bars after banging a girl their daughter's age.

He'd locate a Kinko's, upload the pictures onto a jump boost, and then like a spy in a cold war thriller, leave the evidence in a place Virgil's wife was sure to find it. Perhaps he could find out where she worked. Maybe email her the lurid photos. For once in his life, Pike Graves had plenty of options.

For once, he could act and not react.

Crossing the lavish home, he reached for doorknob to leave.

It was already turning. Someone was coming in.

అల్లి

Virgil Holland had a fruitful day. He'd risen early, swam laps in his Olympic-sized pool, and Skyped with his daughter who was taking summer courses. Despite ASU being only ten miles away, Lucy insisted living on campus to "relish the college experience." Of course, Virgil acquiesced. Only the best for his little girl. With Lucy in college and Louis proudly serving in Afghanistan, he and his wife started every day as empty nesters enjoying a healthy, hearty breakfast.

This morning, however, Gail seemed out of sorts. She detested flying, especially a Red Eye. With all the trouble in the world, a week in Paris of all places exacerbated her Aviophobia. Hopefully, her physician would refill the Prozac. Maybe throw in some Ambien as well. Anything to help deal with fear of flying.

Unlike his wife, Virgil was eager to return to France. It'd been two years. Far too long. He had no worries about flying or being injured in some terrorist attack because he knew he was blessed.

While Gail ran errands in preparation of tonight's departure out of Sky Harbor, he decided to visit Megan in Apache Junction then spend time with Nicolette at Bottoms Up. Tasks completed, he returned home. First thing, as always, was going to his internal sound system. Scrolling his infinite choices, he settled on Wagner's Flight of the Valkyries.

With the energetic powerful tune wafting from hidden speakers throughout his villa, he marched to the kitchen and began brewing Chamomile Tea.

"Long time, no see."

Virgil spun, inadvertently knocking two trinkets to the floor where they shattered. Facing a man cloaked in shadows at the Cherrywood dining table, he stammered, "H—how—did you get in?"

Pike remained silent.

Virgil narrowed his eyes. "Who are you?"

"No one."

His heart pumped faster. The trespasser's demeanor was placid, his voice level. He slyly glanced over his shoulder.

"Looking for this?" Pike eased forward a knife holder containing cutlery that he removed from the kitchen.

Virgil backpedaled and showed his palms. "Look, if you want money, I'll give you money. I have lots—"

"I'm sure you do."

"Name your price. All I ask is don't hurt my family."

"Can't hurt the family now, can we?" Uncoiling slowly, Pike gradually emerged from the darkness.

Eyes glued on the intruder, Virgil retreated cautiously, his hand feeling its way behind his back. "Please, I...beg you. If you have an account in the Cayman's, I can wire the funds within an hour."

Pike guffawed. Only a man of his standing would think of offshore accounts. "I don't want your money."

"Then...what?"

He stopped. *What* do *I want?* "To see you. To look at you."

Eyes narrowed, face contorted like trying to see through impenetrable fog, Virgil muttered, "Do I know you?"

Pike's heart pounded in his ears. His stomach clenched. Adrenalin, like a narcotic, coursed through his bloodstream. All those years, all those sleepless nights, all that guilt. The moment was at hand.

And he wasn't sure what to do.

The tea kettle whistled.

Virgil cocked his head. "Can I get that?"

Pike nodded once.

He fearfully turned his back to the burglar.

"Breathe, Virgil," Pike cautioned. "I'd hate for you to have a heart attack."

"You know my name?"

"I know—"

He moved quicker than anticipated. Pike hit the floor, narrowly avoiding scalding water that erupted like a geyser from the tea kettle hurled at him. Lifting his head, he saw Virgil yank open the door to the garage. Beyond that the street where he could cry for help.

Pike tried standing but his foot found no purchase on the damp tile. He dropped to a knee. Forty years waiting and it was turning to shit in mere seconds.

Punching at Fog. Pike ran through the door and dove like a wide receiver going for a pass. He knocked Virgil to the ground. Both men went down hard.

"Stop! No!" Virgil sounded like a little girl.

Stop! No! The same words Stephanie bawled on the living room floor.

The powerful elbow into his ribcage knocked Pike aside. Virgil jumped upright. The guy in tennis whites held his briefcase in a two-handed grip and, like returning a serve at Center Court, swung the metal case at Pike and impacted the side of his skull. His brain rattled, Pike collapsed against a pegboard. Leaf rakes, pruning saw, border spade, gloves and various gardening tools—and Pike—came crashing down.

Rumbling in his head.

No, not in his head. All around him. The garage door was rising. Virgil anxiously hopped in place waiting for a wide enough gap to escape through. Squatting, he screamed through the broadening opening. "Help! Somebody help me!"

Pike was in the ring again. Another time, another life. Unlike then, however, he wouldn't stand there and take the hits. Discounting the thundering in his brain, he rose to his feet, wilted slightly.

The door opened.

Virgil was free.

Pike flew forward, drove his forearm between Virgil's shoulder blades. Both men grunted as they hit the driveway. Pike, again on top, stifled Virgil's screams by covering his mouth and slamming a knee into the man's kidneys. "Enough!" Pike gritted, nervously scanning neighboring houses.

Writhing, Virgil bit down on Pike's fingers.

Pike yowled. He had to shut the guy up. And quick. Grabbing a handful of once perfectly coiffed steel wool hair, he slammed his head into the concrete.

Virgil stopped moving.

എ�😊ൊ

The booming on the door jarred Roxy. She skulked to the peephole and lowered her voice in an attempt to sound menacing. "Who's there?"

"It's me. Open up."

The voice sounded familiar yet different. "Pikemeister, that you?"

"Roxy, open up!"

"What's the password?"

"Roxy, please. Open the damn door."

"Nuh uh. Not until you tell me the password."

"Roxy!"

"Okay, okay." A second later, she turned white. "Whoa, what happened to you?"

"We're leaving."

"Now?"

"Yes! Now!" Frenzied and panicked, he tossed their suitcases onto the bed. "C'mon," he clipped, now facing her. "We gotta go!"

"Is that blood on you shirt?"

Collecting their belongings, he feverishly started packing.

Grabbing his face, she forced him to meet her eyes. "Pike, my God, what *happened*?"

"I think I killed Virgil Holland."

CHAPTER 17

Every street looked alike. Every building, business complex and landmark, identical. Everything constricting around him. The A/C blasted full force but was futile against the sweat oozing through his skin.

Killing the A/C, Pike listened. No sound from the trunk. Good? Bad? He didn't know. Four blocks later he barreled up an entrance ramp. The Superstition Freeway. No idea where it would lead him. He moved into the left lane. Accelerated.

Roxy shook beside him.

Unable to find comforting words, Pike reached for her knee. She pulled away.

A short time later reaching the only area of Phoenix he was familiar with, he exited at Apache Junction on the city's easternmost edge.

For the first time since checking out, Roxy found the courage to speak. "Where're we going?"

"Someplace remote."

He turned down a rutted, long-forgotten road that had been built with the intention of leading to new homes. But the economic downturn hit and all that remained were wooden, skeletal frames.

The pavement ended two miles later. Pike pushed on for another six before reaching a cliff with a steep drop-off. He got out, angrily looked up and cursed the merciless sun. Or maybe God.

Standing at the edge of the abyss, Pike would've laughed had the situation been different. The gorge resembled something Wile E. Coyote drops into perched atop an Acme rocket.

But he doubted he'd ever laugh again.

Roxy remained beside the car, far away from the man she no longer recognized, sizing up the barren wasteland extending miles in every direction.

With light steps and a heavy heart, Pike traipsed to his Honda, placed his palms on the trunk, closed his eyes, and, despite cursing God moments ago, now silently prayed. He'd spent decades wishing harm to Virgil Holland. Now he hoped the man was alive. A deep breath, a second one, a third. Pike popped the trunk to meet his fate.

Virgil's body was curled like a fetus, face hidden under the crook of his arm. His chest not rising.

Shit. Terror gripping his soul, Pike tapped a motionless leg. "Hey."

No reaction.

Louder. "Hey!"

No response.

Oh, God. Imagine the irony if the guy survived having his skull slammed into concrete only to die from dehydration.

Punching at fog indeed.

Unexpected convulsing had Pike hopping back.

Seeing the man who attacked him in his home and realizing he was in the trunk of a car, Virgil began comically clawing his way through to the back seat like a desperate animal.

"Give me your hand."

Virgil slapped it away and shouted for help.

"No one's around for miles." Pike's voice cold like death.

"Please, I'm sorry. I'm sorry for whatever I did. Please don't kill me."

"Your hand."

Virgil yielded and was heaved from the trunk. Gazing around, he felt as if he was on some distant alien planet. While sweeping the uninhabited desolate landscape, he spotted a dark-haired woman. She offered a small wave as if to say *we mean you no harm.*

He faced his trespasser/kidnapper/abductor. Executioner? It became clear why he'd been driven to such a secluded area. This is where he'd be killed. Despite his weakened state, Virgil took off running. Crying out, he was answered only by his own echo rebounding off canyon walls. Sprinting and screaming uncontrollably, he tripped and nearly sent himself over the lip of the cliff into a bottomless chasm.

Pike advanced on his enemy. The same Virgil Holland who'd been larger than life to a small boy when raping Stephanie, the same Virgil Holland who haunted Pike's dreams, the same Virgil Holland who was successful and pompous and haughty, was on his knees begging for mercy. "Don't kill me."

Pike wanted to vomit.

"Whatever I did, I'm sorry. If I could undo whatever it was, I would. I'm actually a good person."

Moments ago Pike doubted he'd ever smile, but now, hearing this pathetic weasel claim to be a good person, he laughed boisterously. "Really?"

"Yes, yes."

From twenty yards away, Roxy called, "Um, hey, Pike."

He flinched.

Virgil squinted at the memory. "Pike?"

Pike locked on him with an unfeeling stare.

"You're what's-her-name's brother?"

What's-her-name. Like she was one of many. Like all his victims ran together. "Stephanie."

"Right, yeah. Stephanie Gray."

"Graves."

"Yeah, right." Surprisingly, Holland calmed as if being thrown into a trunk and taken against his will to the middle of the desert wasn't as perilous if you knew the person. He held a level hand to his hip. "You used to be this tall."

"This isn't a reunion, you prick."

Roxy again. "Pike, c'mere."

"Just a *second*!"

"I am a good man," Virgil reaffirmed.

"Sure."

"We all make mistakes, Pike."

Pike. Like they were old buddies reconnecting.

"Pike!"

He ignored her. "Married now, coupla' kids."

Virgil, wondering how he knew, tried joking his way into Pike's good graces. "Two kids but only one wife."

"One wife," Pike mimicked. "But you drive to Apache Junction to fuck someone."

Eyes bulged. "How...do you know about Megan?"

"And when that's not enough, *Virg*, you go to a topless bar."

"Nicolette." A sideways glance, he whispered, "You followed me."

Pike answered with a knowing glare.

"It's not what you think."

"Pike! Get over here!"

"No, I'm sure it's not."

"Honest to God, it's not."

"Dammit, Pike! *Now!*"

Pike pointed at Holland like he was a dog. "Stay." He petulantly paraded to the Honda's trunk. Roxy had opened the briefcase and perused its contents. Things had been so harried and chaotic fleeing Holland's home, he didn't remember taking it.

The attaché was crammed with books which explained the extra heft when Holland slammed it against Pike's head. Roxy held up one of the books. Pike looked at it, then at her.

She shrugged.

Pike rifled through the briefcase.

"They're all the same," she stated feebly.

Bewilderment crossed his face, confusion filled his very essence. Rage and fury became helplessness and puzzlement.

"Maybe he's a salesman?" she half-heartedly suggested.

Pike yanked out two hardbacks with black covers and gold lettering and sauntered away. Presenting them to Holland like a prosecutor questioning a defendant on the stand, he asked, "What is this?"

"What's it look like?"

"It looks like The Old Testament."

Virgil nodded.

"So, what, you're a God-fearing man by day and an adulterer by night? You're this century's Jim Bakker?"

He was genuinely offended. "I'm no such thing."

Pike reminded him. "Megan. Nicolette."

"Oh?" He laughed. He actually laughed.

"You think this is funny?"

"I can see why you'd think that." The tables had turned. Holland had taken control. Pike, as usual, was reacting.

Roxy, now alongside Pike, asked, "Are you like…one of those religious nuts?"

"Hardly. I'm affiliated with The Church of The Holy Redeemer."

"The church of the…" Roxy tried echoing but her words tailed off.

He offered a hand. "Reverend Holland at your service."

Pike closed his eyes. "And Megan and Nicolette?"

"Megan's little boy was recently diagnosed with Autism. Nicolette's mom with ovarian cancer. They asked me to pray with them."

Pike aimlessly wandered away and dropped to his haunches, massaging his pulsating temples. A consoling squeeze of the shoulder, followed by Reverend Holland saying, "I forgive you, my son."

CHAPTER 18

It was after nine p.m. by the time they were en route for Vegas. After taking Virgil home, they had an early dinner rather than braving rush hour traffic. Pike wasn't hungry but three Sam Adams sure hit the spot. It also allowed him to decompress.

Judicious Pike Graves mutated into impulsive Pike Graves. And so far, not one damn thing had gone according to plan. First stop on the *Righting Past Wrongs Tour* was settling an old score with Holland. Strike one. He hoped Stephanie and Paige wouldn't be strikes two and three.

"You think he was telling the truth?" Roxy asked an hour north of town.

"About not calling the cops or about forgiving me?"

"About being a reverend."

"Yeah, I do."

"And what about not calling the cops and forgiving you?"

Pike had no answer.

"Were you seriously thinking of killing him?"

Despite the sun setting hours ago the temperature remained in triple digits. Pike was living in hell. Literally.

"Were you?"

"Was I what?"

"Really planning to kill him?"

"Yes."

Roxy gave him a look.

Pike already had blood on his hands. He'd been around death his entire life. He'd *caused* enough death in his life. "No, I wouldn't have killed him," he amended. "I just, I guess, wanted to see him, to say something to him."

"And now you feel, like…vindicated or whatever?"

"Not one damn bit."

Pellets of rain began thrashing his car. Gentle finger-tapping rapidly transformed into pounding fists. Reducing his speed on the twisting road, he turned on the windshield wipers. *Punching at Fog.*

"What?"

"Huh?"

"You keep saying that. 'Punching at Fog.'"

He didn't realize he'd articulated his thoughts. An intake of breath, a slow exhalation. "Something my dad used to say."

"What's it mean?"

He turned the wipers higher and drove head-on into the deluge. His midsize shook and battled the elements. Sunbaked water bottles, fast-food wrappers, and other debris pirouetted across the road. A miniature dust devil materialized in the lifeless desert to his left. Gripping the wheel, Pike explained best he could. "Punching at fog means there are things in life we have no control over. That we try and try but get nowhere. There's an old adage that goes 'man makes plans and God laughs.' It's kinda like that. You do what's right, yet all the forces in the universe are aligning against you. Picture it. Picture punching at fog? You'd get nowhere. You'd accomplish nothing. You have no control over things out of your control."

Roxy ruminated. The two-lane road narrowed as they approached the quiet town of Wickenburg.

"Like you, Pikeronies?"

He pointed to himself.

"You did what's right. Went to college, yet you're unemployed. Tried making things work with Cyn but she ends up stabbing you in the back. You wanted to avenge what Holland did to your sister but that didn't work out either."

"Yep," he ceded her point before throwing it back. "Or like you."

Now she pointed to herself.

"I'm sure you had plans, dreams, goals. Then, your mom dies, your life gets turned upside down, you wind up with that guy…uh, Jonah, right? Yeah, Jonah. You lose touch with your sister and she winds up in Seattle."

"Spokane."

"You said Seattle."

"No, Spokane."

Pike frowned. "Didn't we have this conversation once?"

"You're right. My bad. Seattle."

He glanced right but she refused to meet his eye. Instead, she screamed.

Pike's head swiveled forward. He processed everything in nanoseconds. To his left, a jagged rock face bordered the highway. To his right, a guardrail safeguarding motorists from a drop-off of interminable height. His knuckles whitened. He jerked the wheel right and headed toward the guardrail.

Roxy was pitched left. The friction of the seat belt across her neck broke skin.

The centrifugal force threw him against the door. His foot slipped off the brake. His hand slipped from the steering wheel. The Honda spun like an amusement park ride. The tires finding no traction on slick pavement.

The world rotated.

Pike again had reacted too slowly.

Collision. The animal in the road Roxy noticed, the reason she screamed, crashed against the hood, the windshield, then disappeared.

Pike heard Roxy scream. Or was it himself?

When everything stopped spinning, he reached over. "You okay? You hurt?"

Ghostly white and chest heaving, she inched open her eyes.

"Hey, you okay?" He held her knee. This time she didn't pull away.

"I...don't know."

"Just take deep breaths."

"What *was* that?"

Pike straightened, grimaced in response to a seizing pain along his lower back, and checked the rear view. "Coyote probably." Heartrate returning to normal, he was thankful no one was behind them or heading southbound. It could've been much, much worse. When he tried pulling to the shoulder, the engine revved but the Honda didn't move.

"Not again," Roxy lamented.

During the hellacious spin, he'd accidentally knocked the car into neutral. Shaking his head, he shifted into drive, pulled over, and got out. His equilibrium out of whack, he relied on his car for support.

With the motor rumbling loudly, he hoped this wouldn't be a

repeat of what happened before. To a Philadelphian, Kansas City was small. Wickenburg was a frontier settlement.

Approximately a mile north were the fringes of the tiny hamlet. He saw bright klieg lights from a car dealership, now closed due to the late hour. On the opposite side of the bend was the illuminated sign for a Shell station and just beyond that, Burger King. Strangely, they appeared to be closed also. Wickenburg was no bustling metropolis. The sign welcoming motorists announced the population around sixty-three hundred. However, this artery was the primary road connecting Phoenix and Las Vegas. It was one of the few places a sleepy driver could fuel up, stretch their legs, or down some coffee.

Pike checked his wristwatch. Nine-nineteen. He lifted it to his ear. Still ticking. Gas stations and fast food joints who survived solely on travelers shouldn't be closed this early.

Moving to the double yellow line and chewing his lip, he looked both directions. Highway 93 was crammed between darkened canyons and uninhabited landscape. No northbound traffic. No southbound traffic. It was like he and Roxy were the last two people alive after some cataclysmic event. Oddly, the downpour had stopped as quickly as it began.

Appraising the damage to his Honda, Pike noted a spider web crack in the windshield and one busted headlight. He tried remembering what his deductible was then hoped Cynthia hadn't canceled his car insurance out of spite.

He spotted Roxy thirty yards south, squatting alongside the carcass of the dead animal. The way she huddled over the lifeless creature indicated she was a caring soul, an animal lover.

Pike never had pets. Not as a child, nor an adult. He occasionally considered getting a dog, but despite years of loyalty and unconditional love, pets always died. And Pike didn't handle death well.

Thanatophobia.

He approached Roxy and the lifeless coyote.

Twenty-five yards away, his pace slowed.

Twenty, a fist reached into his chest and ripped his heart out.

Ten, his legs wouldn't move forward.

Roxy ran to him. Her voice cracked but her words were crushing. "You killed him."

Pike couldn't pull his eyes from the *coyote.*

Only it wasn't a coyote.

"You killed a kid, Pike."

Again.

She held up a student ID. "Freddy Marquez, fifteen."

Thoughts like machinegun fire bulleted across his mind.

If only he and Roxy would have left Phoenix before eating dinner or not even come to Phoenix in the first place or not gotten sidetracked in Kansas City or missed one red light or made one green light or eaten one meal quicker or slower or...or...or...

Destiny. Fate. An infinite number of possibilities, every star in the universe against him in order for Pike Graves to just happen to be driving down a highway three thousand miles from home at the exact moment in time a kid crossed in front of him.

If it wasn't for Cynthia and her games Pike would still be in Philly and this kid, this Freddy Marquez, would still be alive. And how ill-advised and reckless the whole journey now seemed. If it wasn't for Dewayne insisting on going to Grizzly's, LaMarcus King would still be alive too. If it wasn't for Roxy asking him...whatever she asked...Pike's attention wouldn't have been diverted, especially in such miserable road conditions, this kid would still be alive.

What did she ask? What were they discussing? Then he remembered.

He was explaining punching at fog.

How ironic. How fucking ironic.

Pike paced in a circle before acknowledging his anger was misdirected. It wasn't Cynthia's fault, Dewayne's fault, or Roxy's fault. This was all on him. He pulled his cell. "I'm turning myself in."

"*What?*" Roxy ripped the phone away. "No!"

Unable to think coherently, he waved a flaccid arm toward the unmoving...object, opened his palms in surrender as if sacrificing himself. His eyes misted over. "Give me my phone, Roxy."

She held his face in her comforting hands. Her voice determined, her eyes unyielding. "Hear me out."

"Please, Roxy, lemme call the cops."

"This time it's different."

"Why?"

"The story you told me about Grizzly's and all that. You got off. They found you innocent, right?"

He nodded.

"You were local. Look where we are now. Look around. We're in the middle of nowhere. And you're some guy from out of town. Your last name doesn't mean anything here. You don't have your father's connections and his reputation to bail you out this time."

Pike peeked toward the corpse. "You sure he's…"

"Yes. Listen to me. You were found innocent last time. And rightly so. You think that will happen again?"

"I'll plead my case. It was dark, the road was slick. They can check skid marks. They'll know I tried to stop."

"You drank. At dinner."

"Just one."

"No, three. Three." She held up corresponding fingers. "I can smell the alcohol on your breath."

"Look, whatever it is, it is." He hiked his shoulders in defeat and lost himself in Roxy's enthralling black eyes. She seemed taller. Or maybe he was slumping under the weight of the situation.

"Goddammit, Pike. I touched him."

He frowned.

She again displayed the student ID. "My DNA's on his clothes."

"I'll tell them—"

"What about Paige?"

"What about her?"

"You gave up *everything* to be with her. You spent the first half of your life kicking yourself for losing her. You wanna spend the second half kicking yourself for losing her *again*? You wanna rot in a jail cell the rest of your days playing what-if?"

He closed his eyes.

"Open your eyes. Open your…look around. No witnesses. No one saw." She pivoted like Julie Andrews on a hillside then was in his face. "No cars coming south. No cars going north. It's like this is your chance."

"My chance?" Pike scoffed.

"Yes. You were going to kill Virgil Holland."

"No, I wasn't."

"You were thinking of it. Then you find out he's a reverend, a man of the cloth, or whatever. And you let him live. Maybe, I dunno, maybe God's giving you an out."

"An out!" His laugh was incredulous. "Christ, Roxy, I just killed a kid. You think God's up there saying, 'Hey, Pike, I know you took a life but it's okay, buddy. I'll hold up traffic so you can get away with vehicular manslaughter. Jesus, Roxy, be reasonable."

"Then explain why no cars have come in either direction for ten minutes.

"I can't," he admitted.

"Then let's go."

In a trance, Pike felt himself turned, felt himself guided to the car, felt Roxy strap him in as if he was a helpless child. "I can drive." His voice low, his mind in a fog.

"That's debatable." She winked.

As if suspended in some altered state between reality and fantasy, Pike watched her get behind the wheel. She presented a sweet yet sad smile, patted his knee, adjusted the seat to accommodate her smaller frame, and drove away from the body in the road.

Looking through the rear windshield, Pike watched fifteen-year-old Freddy Marquez get smaller and smaller until it vanished completely as if taken by the night.

He was disoriented as they slowly passed closed businesses of Wickenburg, Arizona. Pike suddenly felt very tired, wanting to sleep. Forever. His eyes started lowering.

Then his entire body twitched.

"*What?*" Roxy wailed.

"Impossible."

"What is?"

The Burger King was closed so surely the inadequate lighting must've played tricks on what he saw. It had to be his imagination.

The first time was at the entrance to the Penn Turnpike holding a sign reading a very generic *Pacific Time Zone*. A similarly dressed hitchhiker—because it certainly couldn't be the same one—the morning they left Kansas City, holding a sign that said *West Coast*. Now, masked in obscurity, a guy with a straw hat pulled low and unremarkable forgettable attire, sat at a table outside the closed fast-food joint, a sign resting against his leg.

California.

"You okay, Pike? You look like you've seen a ghost."

"I'm not sure."

Roxy chuckled. "Don't know if you're okay or don't know if you've seen a ghost."

Again. "I'm not sure."

PART IV

Cyn City

"You know the sad thing about betrayal?
It never comes from an enemy."

~ Sam "Ace" Rothstein (Robert DeNiro) *Casino*

CHAPTER 19

I t's me."

"Dragon?"

"Did I wake ya?"

Rubbing crust from eyes, Cynthia squinted at her alarm clock. "Four in the morning? No, of course not." A pause. "Where're you?"

"Vegas, baby! Sin City."

Tracking Pike's credit card transactions, she discovered he'd booked a room at a place called Sam's Town and immediately got Dragon a room at the same hotel. In the background she heard the cacophony of chiming bells and hooting gamblers. Everyone making a fortune. If Dragon pulled this off she'd make a fortune, too.

"Guess what?" he asked.

"No idea."

"C'mon, don't be a killjoy."

"What?"

"Guess who I see?"

Cyn sighed. *I should be handling this myself.* "Wayne Newton?"

"*Who*?"

"I don't know, Dragon. Who do—"

"Pike freakin' Graves."

Cynthia bolted up in bed.

"Everything okay?" Alexandra asked drowsily beside her.

"Fine, baby, just go back to sleep." Amped up, Cynthia sprang out of bed and shrugged herself into terrycloth robe. Stealing a glance at Alex's nude body irradiated by moonlight slithering through the curtain, she shuffled out of the bedroom. "He's there? Already?"

"Yes, siree."

"Are you drunk?"

"No, siree."

Yes you are. "What's he doing? Wait, he hasn't seen you, right?"

"Of course he hasn't seen me," Dragon snapped. "I have a talent for this hitman shit."

She balked, hoping no one overheard. "So?"

"So what?"

"So what's he doing?"

"Let me recon my HVT. That's high value target, by the way."

She rolled her eyes.

"I'm surveilling my HVT from a concealed surreptitious position behind a slut machine." He cackled. "See what I did there? *Slut* machine."

Good Lord, I've recruited Beavis.

"HVT's at a bar lookin' pathetic and—wait! He's got that chick with him."

"The one from before?" Picturing Dragon doing a piss poor job of moving from his 'concealed surreptitious position,' she warned "Don't let him see you."

"That's a big ten-four, good buddy."

Covert spy to trucker. "You're mixing your metaphors. Is it her?"

"That's affirmative, base."

She groaned.

"I gotta give that old fart some credit. She's h-o-double-t."

Cynthia's blood boiled. Sanctimonious Pike Graves giving her crap for cheating while he wastes no time finding someone who's h-o-double-t. "What does she look like?"

"Why do you care?"

"Just curious."

"Yeah, sure."

After hearing Dragon's description she drew a blank.

"Shit!"

"What?" Cynthia heard hurried footsteps. "Dragon, *what*?"

"Pike and Miss Hottie left the bar. I think he saw me."

"Dammit." Cynthia hustled downstairs and booted up her laptop to book her own flight to Vegas. What the hell was she thinking recruiting Dragon?

"I'm secure now. I slipped away under the cover of darkness."

She shook her head. "Don't screw this up, Dragon."

"You can count on me." Then in a softer tone. "Cyn?"

"Yeah?"

"Maybe when this is over me and you can leave the country together. I was thinkin' Hawaii."

Bobby Dragovich, so simple, so unworldly. "Sure."

"Is that a yes, you and me?"

"I have someone."

Dragon hesitated. "Oh, Wynter? Sure, bring her too."

"I was referring to Alex."

"Well, I was thinking, ya know, just us two like the good ol' days."

"We didn't have good ol days."

"Hey, Cyn?"

She sighed again. "Yes?"

"I—uh, I—never stopped loving you, ya know."

A smile crossed her face. "I know."

"And it's not only 'cause you were great at givin' head."

Cynthia rolled her eyes. "Just keep me abreast of what he does." She immediately regretted her choice of words.

"A breast?" He chuckled.

Beavis.

"Agent Sixty-Nine will now RTB. That means return to base. Dragon going dark. Out."

A bad feeling rose from the pit of her stomach. Her monetary future at stake and in the hands of a guy going dark and returning to base. *God help me.*

"Hey."

Startled, Cyn said, "Didn't know you were up."

Her daughter, wearing a baseball jersey that stopped mid-thigh, took a bottle of water from the fridge and sat at the kitchen table opposite her mom. Throwing her chin at the cell, she asked, "That Pike?"

"No, it was Dragon."

Wynter's face contorted. "Why are you talking to *him*?"

"*Him* is your father."

"*Him* is an asshole."

"Not if he does what he's supposed to."

"What's that mean?"

"Never mind."

"Have you heard from Pike?"

"No, thank God."

"I wonder where he is. I hope he's okay."

"I'm sure he is. Everything's always okay for Pike Graves."

"He's been gone a while. Maybe we should call the cops."

"No!" Cynthia barked.

Wynter recoiled.

Cynthia walked it back. "He's history." *Or will be if Dragon does his job.* "What do I always tell you? Never look back."

"You've never told me that."

"Well, I've been meaning to."

"I kinda miss Pike."

Cynthia said nothing.

"He's a good guy."

Cynthia rolled her eyes.

A moment later, Wynter said, "G'night," and went upstairs.

"G'night, *Mom*," Cynthia mumbled under her breath, unable to recall the last time her daughter called her "Mom." Hearing the bedroom door close, she wondered if Wynter was alone. The remark about Pike being a "good guy" shocked her. Pike, a good guy? Cynthia neighed. It underscored the fact that Wynter didn't know the real Pike. Or, disconcerting as it may be, Cynthia didn't know her daughter.

Come to think of it she knew nothing about her daughter. How was she doing in school? What did she want to do with her life? Was she happy? Then her thoughts reverted to Alex and those textbook curves and skin as soft as a feather calling to her like a lighthouse to a weary seafarer. Discarding all thoughts of her daughter, she hustled back to bed.

℘℘℘

"What'll you have?"

"Sam Adams for me," Pike faced Roxy. "You?"

She nodded tiredly. "Make it two."

"ID."

Pike bent forward to get wallet.

"Not you," the bartender said. "Her."

Pike grew hot. Maybe the barman who spent every waking hour in a tanning bed and had a face pulled so tight it looked painful to speak was just doing his job. Maybe the guy was just busting Pike's balls. Maybe Pike was just pissed off with himself.

"I can't find it," Roxy moaned after ransacking her purse. "Just give me a Mountain Dew instead."

"ID."

"For a Mountain Dew?" Pike clipped.

The bartender ignored his tone. "Can't sit at a bar unless you have proof you're twenty one. I can get you one, sir, but your…friend can't sit here."

"This is bullshit!" Pike bellicosely jumped up. "C'mon, Roxy, let's go." Then his eyes went wide.

"Something wrong?"

Pike blinked, thinking he saw someone familiar. "Guess not," he shrugged. "I'm gonna hang out down here."

Comprehending he wanted to be alone, Roxy nodded. "See you upstairs." She walked off without saying a word.

As Pike watched her wander the maze of poker machines and Blackjack tables, his thoughts jumbled. He regretted not sticking to his guns. He should've dropped her off at the airport in Denver and bought her that ticket to see her sister in Seattle.

Not Spokane, not Portland. Seattle. Was the emotional and physical exhaustion draining him of all reason? Despite leaving Cynthia behind, she'd be with him forever. Just like Virgil Holland. Cynthia had played him for a fool and destroyed his ability to trust. It wasn't fair to pass suspicion onto Roxy.

But still…

The chirping, chiming, whistling, buzzing and ringing that encircled him was overpowering. Dashing from the casino, he hoped fresh air would subdue his growing misgivings about Roxy. Outside, he cursed under his breath. One in the morning and still a hundred degrees.

LaMarcus King. Cynthia Grimm. Virgil Holland. Now Freddy Marquez. Four individuals who, in one way or another, would remain with him until his dying day.

He hearkened back to eavesdropping a quarrel between his parents after grandma keeled over in Toys R Us. Mom claimed Pike was too young to attend the funeral. His father insisted otherwise. "We can't shield the lad. Death's a part of life. He needs to accept it."

"I don't know, Sam."

"I *do* know, Cora."

Mom, too grief-stricken to argue, relented. Dad got his way. Like always.

Falteringly, Pike was guided through the funeral home, his mom's hand between his shoulders, steering him like a rudder. Through tears flowing down her face, she warned her child, "It's going to look like Grandma's sleeping, honey."

When Pike rose to his tiptoes and peeped into the casket, he knew his mother lied to him. Grandma didn't look asleep. She looked cold and artificial. She looked like an empty shell. She looked dead.

The same as LaMarcus King in the Grizzly's parking lot.

The same as Freddy Marquez on the interstate.

Thanatophobia.

Pike suffered fear of death, thanatophobia, as long as he could remember. Maybe it all started with his father insisting he needed to accept mortality at a young age. *Thanks, Dad.*

Granted, he could partially mitigate the onus over LaMarcus King because he saved Paige Rhodes in the process. Nevertheless it sliced through his soul. Even entering the ring with the hope that the regret and sadness would get punched out of him, did nothing to lessen the sorrow and ease the pain.

He now stepped behind a new Malibu that was one lucky pull away from being won and, in privacy, pulled his phone.

"Directory assistance, can I help you?"

"Wickenburg, Arizona. Marquez family."

"Please hold for the number."

Just like that he could confess. Let the chips fall where they may. A sardonic axiom considering he was in Las Vegas. Sure, Roxy's DNA was on Freddy's body but Pike was the one driving. Pike was the one not paying attention. Pike was the one who turned a fifteen-year-old boy into roadkill.

He considered reaching out to Dewayne. His best friend was a cop and would have better insight if the courts truly showed leniency when a fugitive turned himself in or if that was all spin.

What about Paige? Roxy's rhetorical question was poignant. Pike would rot in prison until he was an old man, wondering if this whole expedition had been a grave mistake.

He put the phone away, deciding to see this through to the end.

Moving from unrelenting heat to a frosty casino, Pike sensed in his gut that eventually things would even out. Life, the universe, the invisible ethereal force that guides us all, always finds a way to maintain order and balance. If Pike Graves was destined to pay a penance for killing Freddy Marquez, the cosmos would see to it that he did.

CHAPTER 20

P ike always imagined Vegas as a place for lost individuals to find themselves. Waking Saturday morning, his theory was confirmed. Roxy, who'd been sullen since her failed seduction, was again bubbly. He initially rejected her desire to play tourist but she persisted. "C'mon, Pikies, how often are we going to be here?'

He was glad he capitulated. Definitely better than moping around all weekend. After breakfast in the hotel coffee shop, they wandered to the casino lounge. *One World,* comprised of two Jamaican's, one Hispanic, three African-Americans, a Samoan, and a transvestite lead-singer with a British accent performed cringe-worthy versions of "Word Up," "The Macarena," and a song Pike didn't know.

"'Perfect Illusion' by Lady Gaga," Roxy clarified.

"Oh."

She insisted on visiting The Venetian, Excalibur, and Bellagio. Halfway through the second casino, Pike found them to be indistinguishable once inside. Strolling side by side, she took unending selfies, some with Pike's head on her shoulder, others striking goofy poses and making duckfaces.

Saturday passed quickly and Pike was grateful for the distraction. But what happened yesterday with Freddy Marquez and what was to come with Stephanie and Paige was never far from his thoughts. Twice, when Roxy excused herself to use the rest room, he deliberated calling the Marquez family in Wickenburg but decided against it. For now.

The abundant walking combined with oppressive July heat left them bushed by nightfall. Ignoring the lure of casino lights, they turned in early and slept peacefully.

Sunday, Roxy insisted they have lunch at Wahlburgers, a burger joint owned by Donnie and Mark Wahlberg. She was saddened neither of the famous brothers were present, but her disappointment was offset by two vanilla shakes. More wandering up and down the Strip and traipsing through casinos once again left Pike sapped. They were back at Sam's Town heading toward the elevators when Roxy animatedly jumped up and down. A chick flick she'd wanted to see was showing in the hotel's theater. Pike again relented.

Silent Summer starred Gwyneth Paltrow as a Hollywood starlet who, tired of fame and fortune, decides to ditch her career and start a new life as a cowgirl on the Texas plains. Initially, Pike thought the idea of starting over would appeal to him. However, his interest waned after twenty minutes. When Paltrow's character stopped her red Jaguar for gas in a trifling New Mexico town, the attendant was none other than Casey Affleck. A malfunctioning gas pump exploded while Affleck was using a squeegee. The impact flung him sailing through the air into an old pickup truck. His spine was snapped. In addition to being paralyzed from the neck down, he lost three fingers and hearing in both ears. Paltrow's character was left disfigured and, sure enough, blind. In the end, the maimed sightless Hollywood artiste and the paralyzed hearing-impaired gas pumper with seven fingers fall in love and move to Rome where the former starlet pops out perfectly healthy triplets.

"Oh, my God," Roxy sobbed as the credits rolled. "That was the greatest movie *ever.*"

"I sure won't forget it anytime soon."

"Thanks for a fun date." Roxy kissed him on the cheek.

Pike smiled.

Back in their room, the only piece of furniture he noticed were the beds. Palpable awkwardness hung in the air.

Thanks for a fun date.

Roxy, clairvoyant or not, sensed it. "This is kinda weird."

Pike stood stationary at the brink as she moved deeper. The combination of his vivid dream with her disastrous seduction was forefront in his mind. But after today's "date" and what they shared over the past week, there was undoubtedly a bond.

When Roxy came to him presenting a smile capable of lighting up The Strip and spellbinding eyes that could swallow him whole, he tensed with uncertainty.

She locked on him. "I'll never forget you." The kiss she planted on his lips was simple and unremarkable. And strange.

Pike laughed awkwardly. "Sounds like you're saying good-bye."

"No. But you're seeing Stephanie tomorrow, then Paige a few days later. And I'll be heading off to…Seattle. That's why I'm saying I won't ever forget you. Don't overthink."

"Okay." But the little voice inside his head told him the end was near.

ↄↄↄ

More surprising than Pike sleeping until almost noon was Roxy still slumbering in the neighboring bed. "Mornin'."

She didn't stir.

Pike sluggishly got out, stretched his muscles, and lumbered toward the bathroom. An involuntary double-take at her purse before proceeding to shower.

As the hot water stabbed his body, he realized he'd forgotten to lock the door. Only a few days removed from Roxy's calamitous seduction, he hurried up.

The combination of working as an investigative journalist and Cynthia destroying his ability to trust, a disquieting thought niggled in his spirit.

He hated himself for entertaining such a ridiculous idea.

On the other hand, curiosity got the better of him. Was he onto something or was it simple paranoia?

Exiting the bathroom through a fog of steam and wrapped in only a towel, he called out "Roxy?"

No response.

A second time garnered no different response.

Chewing his lip, Pike weighed a heavy decision. He felt violated when Cynthia had gone behind his back. Now he was about to do the same.

"You awake?"

Nothing. Skulking to the bureau, ears perked and glancing over his shoulder, he furtively searched her purse.

Within seconds he located her "lost" ID. Roxy began moving. He yanked his hand out as if he'd reached into a flame.

Dressing in a rust-colored Polo, tan khaki's, and Nike's, he left to get breakfast, unaware Roxy had been awake in bed the whole time.

e৲১e৲১

Stepping from the casino into stifling midday heat, he made a call.

"Hard Rock Hotel."

"Stephanie Graves, please."

Drumming on keys followed by a woman with a squeaky voice informing him, "We have no guest registered with that name, sir."

"She works there. HR."

"Is this about a job?"

"No, I'm…an old acquaintance."

"If you know her direct extension, I can put you through."

"I don't. Sorry."

"I can't transfer you without that."

"Thanks anyway." Two more attempts accomplished nothing.

In the coffee shop, he downed a rubbery omelet, tepid coffee, and cold bacon. By the time he paid the bill his stomach was already churning, either due to breakfast, anxiety over his impending encounter with his estranged sister or confusion regarding Roxy's claim to have misplaced her ID.

Exiting the elevator, he withdrew his keycard and strolled down the corridor. At their room, he became stock-still. The door was wide-open. Hesitantly, he peeked in. "Roxy?"

A hulking figure emerged from out of sight.

Pike blinked. "You?"

"Son of a bitch!" A massive fist filled Pike's vision. He ducked, his collarbone taking the brunt of the violent blow. Knocked backward, he stumbled across the hallway, falling clumsily against the wall.

Roxy screamed, "Jonah, no!"

Too astonished, Pike didn't have time to mount a defense. Meekly putting his arms out, he muttered something along the lines of "Wait, hang on," but the vicious jab to his stomach cut off the plea. The rubbery omelet rose in his throat.

Roxy threw herself into the fray, frantically trying to restrain Jonah.

"*Policia!*" shouted a housekeeper cowering behind a cart down the hall.

"Hold on," Pike implored.

"Jonah! No! Stop!"

"*Policia, policia.*"

"Wait."

"You motherfucker!"

When the guy who'd verbally and likely physically abused Roxy in Zanesville shoved her aside, Pike saw his opening. He scooted around Jonah's blindside, seized his right wrist and brought his arm up behind his back. Locking Jonah's neck in the crook of his forearm, Pike moved his mouth to the guy's ear so there'd be no misunderstanding. "Easy, big boy."

Jonah kept squirming, grunting like an animal. But Pike squeezed his neck tighter. "Relax or you'll pass out."

"I'm…her…father."

Pike's eyes found Roxy. She hung her head. "Her…her *father*?"

"I oughta have your ass arrested," Jonah seethed.

The shock to his system caused Pike to release him altogether. Jonah turned, stood ramrod straight, and cracked his neck in a futile attempt to reassert his manhood. "You should be thankful I didn't call the FBI when she told me you were bringing here. Here. To Vegas. To *fucking* Vegas."

"*You* called him?" Pike asked Roxy.

She went into the room, sat on the edge of the bed, buried her face in her hands, and sobbed like a child.

A child?

Jonah's reference to the FBI.

The waitress in Denver.

Front desk clerks.

The bartender downstairs.

Her claim to have lost her ID.

Everything in Pike's life was upside-down and inside-out. His voice trembled as he fearfully asked Jonah, "How old is she?"

"Seventeen."

Fuck me.

"You took my daughter, an underage girl, across state lines." Jonah's neck reddened. "I oughta rip your fucking heart out."

"I think it already has been."

∽∾∽

"You probably have lotsa questions."

Roxy's comment came an hour later. Security had already come and gone, realizing there was no damage to the hotel and doubting Pike's claim that he mistook Jonah for a burglar. However, they reminded him in no uncertain terms, check-out time was high noon, and he needed to be off the property, never to return. Jonah grudgingly heeded his daughter's request for ten minutes with Pike.

"Eleven and I call the Feds."

Pike and Roxy sat on their own bed, each with elbows on their knees, an unseen wall between them.

"I guess I want to know why."

"Why what?" Roxy stared at an imaginary spot on the carpet.

"Why you lied."

"About?"

"Your age, for starters."

She listlessly raised her eyes. "Didn't you have doubts?"

Pike raked his hair. In hindsight it was obvious, but he chose to disregard it, chalking it up to paranoia stemming from Cynthia.

He repressed all doubts, refusing to consider he was getting lied to yet again. "Yeah, I had doubts," he confessed.

"Why didn't you just ask me?"

He shrugged. "Maybe...I didn't want to know. Maybe I didn't want to think were using me."

"I wasn't *using* you, Pike."

"No? What would you call it?"

She anxiously twirled a strand of her raven hair. "Fun. Excitement. You came along at the right time."

"Yep, you used me. And you lied. Why?"

"I didn't lie. If you would've asked, I would've come clean."

Pike snorted. Her rationale sounded so...juvenile.

"If I told you I was seventeen, you would've turned around and taken me back."

"Hell yes."

Her justification sounded like an attorney merely going through the motion of addressing the jury when everyone knows the defendant is guilty as sin. "My life is boring with a capital B. Jonah—"

"You mean Dad."

"Jonah's my stepdad. My real dad died when I was young and Mom was pregnant with my sister. Jonah was there for her. No, he wasn't a good husband or a good father. But my mom was twenty-two with two little kids and only working part-time. Jonah was a helping hand. But when Mom…" Her words trailed off and she blinked away a tear.

Pike wanted to console her, pat her knee like he'd done a hundred times over the past week. But he repelled the urge. She was a minor.

Roxy shook off the sorrow. "After Mom died, Jonah found himself with kids he never wanted in the first place. So he sends my sister Kelly to live with our uncle."

"Uncle Ronald, the guy who masturbated while you slept?"

"I made that part up. There is no Uncle Ronald. Kelly lives in Boston with Uncle Gerald. We talk all the time on Snapchat."

Pike massaged his pulsating temples. "So the story about your sister in Seattle—not Portland, not Spokane—but Seattle was bullshit? The line about your real dad working an oil rig in the Gulf of Mexico was bullshit?"

Roxy hung her head and talked to Pike's shoes. It was easier than seeing the displeasure in his eyes. "Think back to when I told you all that."

It took a moment. I-70. A road sign for a service station at the next exit. A Gulf station. *Gulf.* Gulf of Mexico. There was a Starbucks at the same exit. Starbucks is headquartered in Seattle. '*My sister's in Seattle.*' Also at the same exit was a McDonalds. Ronald McDonald. *Uncle Ronald.* Pike remembered passing a Mayflower moving van when Roxy claimed she answered an ad on Craigslist. '*He and a buddy were starting up a moving business.*' Reaching back even farther, Pike recalled Jonah's comment that, at the time, seemed innocuous but now made sense. '*You was either lookin' at her or lookin' at me. Which is it pretty boy? You a pervert or you a faggot?*'

Of course Jonah would think that. Only a pervert would express interest in an underage girl. It was all so blatant now. So fucking blatant. All Pike could do was doff an imaginary cap. The investigative journalist got played by the source.

"Is Ledesma your real last name?"

Roxy nodded. "Jonah's, too. Elliott's his middle name. Jonah Elliott Ledesma."

Pike shook his head in disgust. "That still doesn't explain all of this."

"Vegas?"

"No, this ongoing week of deceptions."

Her lips curled. "Like I said, my life is boring."

"Right, right, capital B."

Swallowing, she dabbed another tear. "I'm seventeen but I feel seventy. I live in Zanesville, Ohio. *Zanesville.* After I graduate next May, I can work in a factory or I can work in a factory. Oh, wait. I know. I can always work in a factory."

"So leave. Find yourself."

"Like you're doing?"

Pike's brows went up. "Well, yeah."

"You're the exception, Pikeronies."

Pikeronoies. He smiled small.

"Two months from now, I'll be a high school senior. I've spent my whole life doing for others. Changing my younger sister's diaper. Helping her with homework. I was acting like a parent at nine years old. Cooking and cleaning 'cause Jonah hurt his back and couldn't. I was balancing the family checkbook by age eleven. By thirteen I was old. So I wanted more. I wanted excitement. I knew once I graduate I'd be trapped. You were…well, my last chance to have fun." She paused, went for humor. "And it sure hasn't been dull."

"So I'm a diversion? An escape?" His words were sharp but his tone rang of empathy. Was it so bad? Was wanting to break free from reality so wrong? Who amongst us hasn't thought of escaping from our mundane lives, even for a short while?

In that way he and Roxy were alike. Maybe that explained the bond between them. Only difference was Roxy was doing as a teenager what Pike was doing at forty-seven.

She came off the bed and dropped to her knees before him. "Pike," she whispered.

Seventeen.

A high school kid.

A minor.

He jumped up. "Was trying to seduce me for fun too? Seducing someone your father's age."

"No."

He brayed. "So you care about me?"

"Yes."

He was stunned.

Roxy said, "And you care about me too. Admit it."

Rather than answering, he said, "What made you call Jonah?"

"Every vacation has to end. It was time to go home and return to reality."

Pike felt betrayed. Used and cast-off. The crazy part was he actually understood where she was coming from. Pike had once been seventeen also.

She stood and reached for him before thinking better of it and sliding her hands into her back pockets. "Will I break out again someday? Maybe. I want to live a little before turning into everyone else I know. I'm going to fall into a routine of predictability and be too comfortable to risk changing my life. Everyone gets to a point where they become too afraid to gamble what they know." She paused. "Except you."

Pike narrowed his eyes.

"Do me a favor?"

He waited.

"Make things right with Paige. It's like you're fighting for all of us who never took a chance." She rose to her tiptoes, kissed his cheek. "There's a little of Pike Graves in all of us."

CHAPTER 21

Unlike casinos he'd visited with Roxy, the Hard Rock was unique. Under different circumstances, Pike would've enjoyed perusing the endless collection of guitars, drum sets and wardrobes worn by rock legends. But he wasn't here for pleasure.

A front desk clerk advised him no one was allowed up to HR without an appointment. Assuming Stephanie worked until five p.m., he now did have time to check out the memorabilia. He browsed the gift shops, ate a leisurely lunch, and at four forty-five made his way to the second level of the indoor parking structure reserved for employees. At the end of a gangway leading to a bank of elevators stood a twenty-something with a shaved head leaning against the wall. Pike offered a cordial nod.

"Waitin' to pick someone up."

Pike couldn't tell if it was a question or a statement. "Me too."

"My baby momma gets a DUI and now I gotta come alla way down from Summerlin to pick up her sorry ass."

Not knowing where Summerlin was, he simply nodded.

Fifteen minutes later, employees were filtering out in clusters of threes and fours. Casino employees still in their uniforms strolled by Pike with nary a glance. One employee, unescorted, clutched her purse tighter when noticing him.

Pike unintentionally was taking a looksee at the cocktail waitresses strutting by. Blondes, brunettes, an older looking red head, small chested, ample bosomed, short and tall. All types, all ethnicities.

"Hello?"

He turned. "Yes?"

"Oh my God! *Pike*?"

"Stephanie?"

He cherished being swathed in her loving embrace like a day

hadn't passed. After breaking the hug, they looked at each other. It served as a painful reminder how fractured their relationship had become. He didn't recognize the older redhead was his sister.

Stephanie's questions came rapidly. "What're you doing here? Why didn't you call? I didn't know you were in town. Are you staying here at the hotel? I could've gotten you a discount. How many years has it been?"

"Too many." Like many siblings, their relationship was strained. As kids, they'd argue over silly things. As a teenager Stephanie avoided tension at home by spending time with friends, mostly male. She was a self-proclaimed nomad. Job to job, apartment to apartment, lover to lover, she never stayed put. Her quest for inner peace extended into adulthood. Months became years, and she and Pike, focusing on their own lives, lost touch.

A sore point for him was her refusal to fly home for Mom's funeral. Even Paige flew in but not Stephanie.

But now, face to face, all those quarrels seemed petty. Stephanie was his sister. Stephanie was blood. And that awareness brought tranquility he hadn't felt in a long, long time.

"Oh my, are you tearing up?" she giggled.

Surprised at the emotional pull, he laughed it off. "I guess I am." It was gratifying feeling true love and not be judged, something he was unaccustomed to. Indicating her outfit, he said, "I thought you worked in HR."

"I do. But the big wigs decided we were too isolated and wanted us spending one week every three months doing the jobs we recruit for."

"And you chose cocktails?"

Her coquettish smile hadn't changed. It never would. She pirouetted. "Not bad for some broad in her fifties."

Pike's jaw dropped. Yes, he was forty-seven and yes, his sister was older but...*fifties*? "Wow."

"Wow? That's it?"

He faltered. "No, you look great."

And she did. A natural blonde, she'd tried auburn, black, and even purple for a time. Now it was a cheerful red, short and wavy. There was a hint of crow's feet around her eyes and her legs were chunkier than he remembered. But her spellbinding green eyes and gentle features remained breathtaking. The low-cut top had him wondering if she'd gotten implants.

"You look good," she said, studying him. "Tired, but good."

"Thanks."

"So," she wondered, "What're you doing in my neck of the cactus? The *Inquirer* fly you out to cover the big fight?"

He hadn't worked at the *Inquirer* in six years and never at the sports desk. It underscored the disconnect between them. "What, I can't come to Vegas to see my sister?"

Like a switch being flipped, she went from happiness to worry. "Are you sick?"

"Sick?"

"Dying?"

Pike laughed. "No. Just wanted to see you. Is that so bad?"

"Okay." Rolling that around, she then asked, "Still in Philly?"

"Yep."

"Same house?"

"Different one."

Another prolonged pause. "Wife, girlfriend, both?" She winked.

"Actually, neither."

"Any nieces or nephews I should know about? Am I Aunt Stephanie?"

It highlighted the earlier awareness. His sister apparently forgot he was unable to conceive. Or maybe he never felt close enough to impart something so personal. They shared blood, but little else.

There was much more than just twenty-five-hundred miles between them.

A man about sixty materialized beside Stephanie and put his hand on the small of her back. Too much cologne and a leer that made him look like a politician about to ask for a donation, he wore a sophisticated Brooks Brothers suit. Pike knew it was Brooks Brothers because at one time he owned seven.

Eying Pike distrustfully, he asked Stephanie, "Who's this young man?"

"This is Pike. Pike, Chet. He's my boss."

Chet offered a hand. "Pleasure."

Pike accepted the proffered hand.

"Pike's my brother."

"Oh." Chet's forceful grip eased. "Staying here in the hotel?"

"Nope."

He seemed hurt. "Why not? If Stephanie would've asked, I could've comped you."

"Just passing through."

"I see." Chet shot a glance between them. "Good meeting you. And Stephanie?"

"Mm hmm?"

"Cocktails?" He appraised her like a gemologist would a diamond. "Stunning as always."

"Thanks."

"Well, kids, don't stay out late." Chet winked at Pike, two guys sharing a secret.

"What's *his* story?" Pike asked with Chet gone.

"Don't worry about it."

The body language between Stephanie and her boss convinced Pike they shared more than a work relationship.

Looping her arm around his waist, she announced, "Let's get outta here."

ↄↄↄ

The Grateful Bread sandwich shop was popular, as evidenced by the line of customers waiting to get in. Ignoring the grumbling and mumbled profanities, Stephanie guided Pike to the front of the line, introduced her brother to the hostess and requested "the best table."

"Why's this one so special?" Pike asked once seated.

Stephanie pointed to the casino floor. "See that glass case beside the Madonna slot machine? In between the scarf Janis wore at Woodstock and the tank top Freddie Mercury wore at Live-Aid is Jim Morrison's belt when The Doors appeared on the Ed Sullivan Show.

"It's like working in a museum."

"It's way cool. I love my job."

The waitress, who perhaps because of the hotel's theme, bore a striking resemblance to Sheryl Crow, greeted Stephanie warmly. Pike underwent a new round of introductions.

"I'm starved," Stephanie said. "Can I order for both of us?"

Pike winked. "If it makes you happy."

They all laughed at the mention of one of Crow's biggest hits.

Stephanie ordered "The usual."

Sheryl, keeping up the act, said, "A change, a change would do you good."

They laughed again.

After the server left, Stephanie said, "You promise you're not dying?"

"Technically, we're all dying."

She studied him. "Oh, that's right. Than...than..."

"Thanatophobia."

"Right. Remember what Daddy used to say?"

"I've tried blocking him out as much as possible."

Stephanie arched a brow. "He said 'Dead people can't hurt you. The living ones still can.'"

Pike smiled ruefully. "I'd forgotten that."

"You've forgotten a lot."

He pursed his lips.

"If you're not dying, why'd you come?"

Pike toyed with the salt shaker. "Just needed a break."

"When'd you fly in?"

"I didn't."

"You *drove*?" she screeched.

"Yep. More time to think."

"About seeing me?"

"Well...yeah. I wasn't sure how things would play out."

"Why?"

"Admit it, Steph. We weren't close as kids and we're not as adults."

"So? We're still family."

"You sound like Mom."

Stephanie took on an inexplicable demeanor. "Ah, yes. Mom."

Sheryl Crow lowered their meals and quoted another song title. However, sensing tangible awkwardness, she promptly hurried away.

"The past is past," Stephanie said, salting her meal. "Yesterday doesn't matter. It's called history for a reason."

"I'm on my way to see Paige Rhodes." Just like that. No lead-in, no warm up. Pike blurted it out, possibly to rebuff her claim that yesterday didn't matter. "She's in a place called Mill Valley, up by San Francisco."

After biting into the chicken sandwich Stephanie asked, "So you've stayed in touch?"

"Not really."

"She looking forward to seeing you?"

"No."

Despite the passage of years, she could read her brother like a novel. "She doesn't know you're coming, does she?"

"Nope."

Stephanie gave him a look. "You're just going to show up on her front door?"

"Yes."

"And what, you expect her to run away with you?"

Pike smiled.

"My God, you're silly."

"It worked for Ben Braddock."

"Who?"

"Dustin Hoffman in *The Graduate*."

"Uh, hello? Movie, not real life."

"Life intimates art."

Stephanie's mouth opened, exposing partially masticated fries.

"What?" Pike cried.

"My borderline OCD brother acting spontaneously? I guess people really can change."

"Crazy, huh?"

"Very." She wasn't smiling.

"You think I'm wrong?"

"I think you're impractical."

"Because?"

"If Paige would've showed up on *your* doorstep out of the blue, would you give up everything and run away with her?"

"In a heartbeat."

Her face contorted in astonishment. "Just 'cause you don't have a life doesn't mean she doesn't."

Pike chewed his lip.

"Still doing the lip thing? Guess you never outgrew that."

He stopped.

"Maybe she's married. Maybe she's got a family."

"She doesn't."

The pity-look intensified. "You pay twenty-nine, ninety-five for one of those sites, stalkers dot com?"

Pike laughed humorlessly.

"I just don't wanna see you hurt, Pike. No matter what, you're my brother."

"I was hoping you'd be more supportive."

"I prefer being honest."

"No, you're being judgmental. Like Dad."

"Ah, still blaming him for every problem in your life?"

"Dammit, Steph! I'm not."

She leaned forward, snarling. "I work here. Lower your voice."

Pike noticed a few customers casting cagy glances their way, others obvious in their attempt not to.

The former sparring partner retreated to his corner. This wasn't going the way he intended. He'd hoped bygones would be bygones. But thirty minutes into their reunion, they were already digging up family skeletons.

Stephanie navigated things to less turbulent waters. "You seeing anyone now?"

"I was."

"Was?"

"Cynthia. But we split."

"Sorry to hear."

"Don't be. How about you?"

"I have a guy."

Pike's brows knitted. Not a boyfriend, not a man, not dating someone. *I have a guy.* He waited for more. It didn't come.

Stephanie threw the spotlight back on him. "Where're you working?"

"I'm between jobs right now."

Again, the open mouth. This time it was partially masticated chicken.

"What?"

She crumpled a napkin, sipped her beverage, rearranged her food.

"Steph, what?"

"It's funny."

"Funny that I'm not working?"

"No."

"Then what?"

"Never mind."

"Tell me."

"I'm not traveling down that road with you."

"What road?" he asked. "If we plan to build something, we need to clear the air."

"I didn't know there was a plan, Pike. I figured we'd talk, catch up, and then drift apart like always. I thought this was a one and done."

"Is that what you want? Hi, how are you, bye, see you again in ten years?"

"No," Stephanie replied remorsefully. "We spent two-thirds of our life as strangers. Maybe the last third we can be friends."

Pike had doubts but smiled nonetheless. "I'd like that."

"Me, too," she said, though she clearly harbored the same reservations. "I do find it funny though."

"Go on."

Stephanie deliberated. "You sure you want to hear?"

Pike was back in the ring, that instant when he knew he'd get pummeled but could do nothing but stand there and take the punches knowing it would hurt. "Sure."

"You have no job. You have no one in your life. Yet, just like *that*—" She snapped her fingers. "—you have the freedom to drive from one end of the country to the other to chase a girl you were sweet on back in high school. All because of our father."

He stared at her.

"Daddy worked hard and made money, lots of money. Lots of money that all went to you. And *now*? Now you have the audacity to talk shit about him? If it wasn't for his sacrifices, you wouldn't be embarking on some half-baked scheme like a spoiled rich kid."

Rather than justifying his actions—though he wasn't sure how—Pike went on offense. The sparring partner hitting back. "Maybe you should've been home more, Steph. Maybe you should've flown in when Mom died." He looked around verifying no one was eavesdropping and angled closer. "Don't blame me because I got the inheritance. I was there, you weren't."

"I was there. I saw enough."

"Really?"

"Yes, really, Mr. Self-Important Snob." Her elbows slammed the table causing silverware to bounce. "You were a kid. You were young."

"Now you're blaming me for being a kid?"

Exasperated, "Of course not!"

"Maybe I wanted my father's love instead of his money. Maybe I would've liked tossing a football around in the backyard or just have a catch or…hell, *anything.* Is that too much to ask? You're right, he did sacrifice. He sacrificed his children. The only memory I have of him is when I look at my bank statements. Fuck him."

"No, Pike, fuck you."

He leaned back and belligerently shoved away his plate. His appetite gone.

Stephanie brayed. "Sacrifice. What do you know about that?"

Pike began chewing his lips again.

This time she didn't stop him. "Maybe there was a reason he worked so much. Maybe there was a reason he didn't want to be home."

"Screw that! He worked his ass off because he liked working his ass off. We weren't his family, his employees were. We weren't his kids, we were a nuisance. Mom wasn't his wife, she was his cook and maid and housekeeper. Remember what he used to say, Steph? Remember? 'Cora, the old ball and chain.' Nice, huh? Mom ought to be sainted for putting up with him all those years."

"Yeah, just keep thinking that, little bother."

He glowered. "What's that mean?"

"Nothing."

"No! You said something. Back it up."

"Forget it, okay? Never mind. Like I said ten minutes ago history belongs in the past."

"So you don't think Mom was a saint for putting up with him?"

"I think she was flawed like the rest of us."

"Not like Dad. That self-righteous ass cornered the market on flaws."

"Ask yourself something."

"Yeah, what?"

"You're not a kid. You live in the real world. Ask yourself why Daddy buried himself in his work. Ask yourself why he never was home." She lowered her voice but not her anger. "Ask why he reached his breaking point, said fuck it, and killed himself."

"He didn't want to be home."

"Praise Jesus! And why not?"

Pike hoisted his shoulders like the answer was obvious. "He loved working."

"Remember Mom and her Valium?"

The abrupt shift caught him off-guard. "Can you blame her? She was married to Sam Graves."

Stephanie lifted her backside, bent forward, and whispered, "She took Valium. A lot. More than she should have."

Pike laughed in her face. "You're saying Mom was a junkie? Nice, Steph."

"More than was allowed by the insurance."

He frowned.

"Remember how she constantly talked so glowingly about Dr. Grassley? How handsome he was, how educated he was, how he had beautiful hands?"

"So?"

"How do you think Daddy felt hearing that? He was blue-collar through and through. He had working man's hands. He had a tenth grade education. He didn't go to some Ivy League school like Dr. Grassley." Pausing, she added, "Or like you."

"So Dad's precious little ego gets wounded and that gives him the okay to treat everyone like crap?"

"How do you think Mom got all those Valium?"

"I—I have no—how would I know?"

Stephanie shook her head contemptuously, irritated she had to simplify things. "I saw them."

"Who?"

"Mom and Dr. Grassley."

Pike scrunched his face.

"In bed."

He burst out laughing. "You're saying Mom, *our* Mom, slept with her physician?"

Stephanie responded with a knowing stare.

"Good Christ, that's preposterous."

"Why?"

"That's our mother you're talking about."

"Oh," she howled histrionically. "That's right. Back then no suburban housewives ever cheated. No one ever committed adultery in Happyville, USA."

"I'm sure it happened but...c'mon."

Seeing a glass case beyond Pike's shoulders filled with Sgt. Pepper's artifacts, the girl who was a John Lennon fan said, "Living is easy with eyes closed."

Pike met his sister's hardened gaze. "Even if she did—and I'm not saying she did—but even if she did, look who she was married to. Dad talked down to her. He never appreciated her. She probably wanted to feel loved."

"For two years?"

"Huh?"

"Two years it went on."

"You're saying Mom had an affair—an *affair* with Dr. Grassley for two years? Get a grip."

"Remember that big hutch cabinet in the dining room? Top left drawer in the back under Grandma's silverware is where she hid his love letters."

"This is ludicrous."

"She sleeps with him. He writes scripts for Valium." Stephanie shrugged. "But along the way, sex turned into love."

"That's ridic—gimme a break. And, okay, okay, all right, then how did she keep this *supposed* two-year affair secret from Dad?"

"She didn't. He knew."

Pike melodramatically lifted her glass. "You sure this is iced tea you're drinking?"

"*She* wanted a divorce. Daddy said no. Daddy stayed in the marriage for the kids. For *us*."

Pike's chest felt hollow.

"Two sides to every story, my darling brother. Things aren't always how we see them or how we remember them." She took a deep breath. "Daddy worked all the time not because he loved his job but because he loved us. Who cares if he didn't toss a football around the backyard? He was home every night, wasn't he? He made sure we never went to bed hungry and that we had new shoes when we needed them, didn't he? He stayed with a woman who didn't love *him*, who openly cheated, and in turn, felt like less of a man because of it. He may have taken his own life, but Mom might as well have pulled the trigger herself."

"It was carbon monoxide," Pike weakly countered.

"I'm being metaphorical."

Eyes misting, Pike looked around The Grateful Bread. Couples and families all laughing, joking, cavorting. Was it for show?

A charade? Just like his childhood had been? Everything he knew—or thought he knew—not real. He started sliding out of the booth. He needed to escape, to run. To run and keep running. But he had nowhere to go.

Stephanie reached over and held him in place. "You're staying with me tonight." She signaled for the check and, moments later, draped a protective arm around her kid brother and guided him away.

CHAPTER 22

Pike was unmindful of the passing neighborhoods. The one-two combination of learning his mother bartered with her body for drugs on the heels of discovering he'd traveled two thousand miles with an underage female left him dead inside. Maybe his sister was right. Maybe history did belong in the past.

Should Paige remain in the past too?

Stephanie, unable to distract him with idle banter, kicked herself the entire drive. She'd had a lifetime to deal with family secrets but hit her brother with it all at once.

Ten miles west of The Strip, older homes were situated on large parcels of land, a major departure from the cookie-cutter jobs stretching across the valley. Stephanie's neighborhood carried an old-world charm. Quaint is how Cora Graves would've described it.

Mom.

Stephanie stopped at the lip of her driveway. "Damn."

"What now?" Pike bellyached.

Sadness crossed her face. "Don't judge me, but I'm kinda seeing someone."

"Right. You have a guy."

"Karl's nice but, well, ya know, he's not *the one*. We're friends with benefits."

She was an adult and had her own life. "That's fine," he stated, but his tone conveyed the opposite.

"He's a nice guy, sweet, *very* cute. But, ya know, he's not *the one*."

"Yeah, you said that."

"I just didn't want you judging me. I know you're old-fashioned."

"Okay."

Stephanie's crestfallen countenance left no doubt she wasn't happy about what her life had become. Like Pike, she too once wanted the family-kids-house-white-picket-fence-mini-van. Also like Pike, it didn't happen. "Karl's a good guy. But, well…"

"I know, he's not *the one*."

Within seconds of parking on the pitted driveway, a barefoot shirtless man wearing tattered jeans and chugging a beer, appeared. "Hey, sugarlips."

Sugarlips?

"Hey, sparky."

Sparky?

The man skedaddled over and smacked Stephanie on her ass. Only now noticing Pike, he asked "Who's this dude? He here for another threesome?"

Pike's eyes widened.

Stephanie slapped his chest. "Stop being such a kidder." To Pike, "He's just kidding."

Pike nodded.

"This is my brother, Pike. He just got in from Philly. Pike, this is Karl."

Karl engaged him in an intricate handshake. Two fingers were cut off at the knuckle. The remaining eight had grime under the fingernails. A scar on the left shoulder Pike knew to be from a gunshot. Disheveled blond hair, sunken eyes, and a lightning bolt tattoo on his left bicep, his voice carried a tinge of a Tennessee accent. "Where those cheesesteaks come from?"

It took Pike a moment. "Right. Philly."

"Lots of history there."

In more ways than one. "True."

"History ain't my thing, dude."

Considering what Pike learned about his family, maybe history shouldn't be his thing either.

It was Stephanie's house, but Karl made himself at home. While she changed out of her cocktail uniform, he pulled two beers from the fridge. "Want?"

"Nah, I'm okay."

"Good, two for me."

Karl collapsed onto a sectional, stretched-out his legs, rested his bare feet atop a table, pointed the remote at the TV like a gun, and arrowed up the volume. Pike dawdled in the hallway before lowering himself onto a raggedy love seat. Whereas he had no interest watching two burly, bald-headed Neanderthals pummeling the tar out of each other in a cage, Karl was fully captivated.

"Your sister's a badass chick."

Pike remained silent.

"Kinky and freaky but definitely badass."

Pike heard himself ask, "You love her?"

Karl managed to turn away from the cavemen and smirked. "Sure, dude."

Pike held his tongue, looked wistfully toward the hallway for Stephanie, then broke the stunted silence. "How'd you two meet?"

Again transfixed with the primal battle, he remarked, "She blew her fuses."

"Huh?"

"Her master cylinder went ape-shit over the two-twenty and nearly blacked out the whole neighborhood."

Sparky. The bolt tattoo. "Oh, you're an electrician?"

Karl grinned. "She's really something."

Pike held his tongue.

"Total badass."

"You boys getting to know each other?" Stephanie entered the room wearing an oversized Vegas Golden Knights jersey with a French guy's name across the shoulders. Her hair flatter, makeup washed away, and barefoot like Karl, she dithered where to sit.

Karl patted the cushion beside him. Stephanie obeyed.

"Beer?" he asked without looking at her.

She took it, sipped, handed it back.

"Hockey?" Pike asked.

Forgetting what she was wearing, she looked down at the jersey. "Yep."

"Not the Flyers?"

Stephanie angled her head left. "It's Sparky's shirt."

"Oh." *Sparky again.* Sweeping the area, sadness crept into his heart. No sign of her childhood. No photos of herself, her brother, or their parents. As if she just materialized in the desert one day. Her comment about history belonging buried in the past was clearly the mantra she lived by.

It soon became apparent that Pike, like that night years ago with Stephanie and Virgil Holland, was again in the way. Despite politely smiling and trying to engage Karl in conversation for two hours, he felt superfluous. Pike sensed Stephanie wouldn't have opened her home if she remembered Karl was here.

As the hour grew late, Karl became more intoxicated and therefore, more touchy-feely. Stephanie blushed, half-heartedly nudging him aside. Pike pretended not to notice. When Karl overdramatically yawned, Stephanie asked her brother, "You getting sleepy, Pike?"

He stifled a laugh. All these years later and nothing had changed. *You getting sleepy?* She'd wanted to be alone with Virgil. Now, she wanted to be alone with Karl. Decades may have passed but Pike was still in the way. "Yeah, I am."

Relief crossed Karl's face.

As he helped her make up the bed in the extra room, Stephanie looked ashamed. "Karl *is* a nice guy."

"As long you're happy."

She didn't respond.

ꜩꜩ

Tell me you're a bitch.

Pike sprang up. Shadows surrounding him, he wiped perspiration from his brow. The hairs on the back of his neck, damp. Maybe it was the recent confrontation with Virgil. Perhaps reconnecting with his sister was the reason. But this was the first time in a long time the memory haunted his dream in such vivid imagery.

Regulating his breathing, he got out of bed and, like a sightless man in unfamiliar surroundings, felt his way out of the guest bedroom and down the hall to the bathroom. A Garfield clock showed it was a little after midnight. He'd slept less than an hour, yet felt alert. He could reach San Francisco by noon if he left now, but if he hoped to rekindle a relationship with his sister, absconding like a thief in the night would quash that.

Splashing cold water on his face, Pike returned to bed, the floor creaking beneath his weight.

"Tell me you're a bitch!"

"I'm a...oh...God!"

"Say it! Say you're a bitch." Followed by what sounded like a slap.

Pike pivoted on his heels, took one hasty step. And stopped.

A scream of release from Karl.

A throaty wail from Stephanie.

A distressingly painful awareness punched Pike in his gut. What he thought had been a dream was real.

His sainted mother was anything but sainted. His maligned father, target of Pike's lifelong scorn, was the real victim. And now, hearing the hot-blooded cries from behind Stephanie's door, he became cognizant of the most biting insight of all: His beloved sister took pleasure from rough sex.

And probably always had. Virgil had not raped her but rather given her what she wanted.

Pike ran down the hall, slapped at the light switch, and wildly threw his things into a suitcase. Packed in under a minute, he darted through the house. His outstretched arm reached for the front door.

"Pike?"

Shoulders slouching, he couldn't face his sister.

"Where're you going? Wait, lemme throw something on."

He didn't wait. Furiously, he jiggled with the deadbolt and chain which seemed as befuddling as a Rubik's Cube. Finally figuring it out, he practically ripped the door from its hinges, leapt three steps, and sprinted to his car.

Stephanie's car. His was at the hotel.

Dammit.

She ran after him in a partially unbuttoned workman's shirt, *Karl* sewn on the breast pocket, and furry Garfield slippers. Her clear-cut fondness for the cynical cat was more proof he didn't know his sister. And apparently, never had.

At her Mercedes, she asked, "What're you doing? It's the middle of the night."

"Leaving."

"Not with my car you're not." The smile that hadn't changed since childhood got no reaction from Pike. Then, she realized. "Oh, you heard?"

"Yeah, I did."

"You promised you wouldn't judge me."

"I'm—never mind."

"We're not kids, we're adults. We all have things we like."

Pike's throat went dry. Feeling lost, feeling confused, he turned and, perhaps subconsciously, wound up facing west. Toward California. "I need to go."

"Some women like short guys, some women like nerdy guys, some like bald guys. I have a black friend who only dates white guys."

"And some enjoy humiliating sex?"

"Yes." She sounded proud.

Pike drew in his lips. "Three days ago I was in Phoenix."

Stephanie's brows furrowed. "So?"

"I had a reunion with Virgil Holland."

Her chin dropped. "Wow, haven't thought of him in years."

"I've never *stopped* thinking of him."

"So you *do* remember?"

"How can I forget?" Pike said.

The look on her face was peculiar, strange. What she did next left him stunned. Like a woman possessed, she began slamming her fists against the hood of her car. The shrill alarm punctured the stillness. Her frantic screams ripped through the silent night.

Pike, baffled by the unexpected outburst, was speechless. The porch light came on.

Karl, buck naked, pointed the fob and silenced the alarm. "What's going on, Sugarlips?"

"I'm fine, Karl. Just—go back inside. Please."

He rushed down the stairs with squared shoulders. "What—"

Stephanie turned her rage on him. "I said get the hell inside!"

He winked at Pike. "Told ya she's a badass."

With Karl gone, Pike tenderly held her shoulder. "It's okay."

Meeting her brother's eyes, Stephanie's fury turned into a flood of tears. Unrestrained sobbing. She threw herself against him, almost knocking them both to the ground. Her legs withered. Pike held her up, supporting her. Her nails, like claws on his back. "I'm sorry, Pike. I'm so...damned sorry."

He patted her back. "It's fine."

They clung to each other for a timeless few moments. Finally, Stephanie broke away and again apologized.

Pike comforted her. "You have nothing to be sorry for."

"I'm sorry I wasn't there."

"Okay."

"I was the big sister. I should've protected you."

"It's—fine," Pike lukewarmly responded.

"I'll never forgive myself."

"Like you said, history is dead."

"I'm sorry what he did to you."

His face twisted. "To me?"

Stephanie looked off into the pitch black night.

"What he did to *me*?"

She nodded.

"We are talking about Virgil Holland, right, Steph?"

"Yes. And I've hated myself every day."

Pike pushed aside his own bewilderment. "I was the brother. I should've protected *you*."

"You were nine."

"I know."

"I'll never ever, *ever* forgive myself."

Gripping her shoulder, he emitted a hesitant chuckle. "Steph, what…what're you talking about?"

"I thought you remembered."

"I do." He frowned. "Don't I?"

"I don't think you do."

"God knows I've tried to forget but I can't."

"Tell me," Stephanie said. "Tell me what you remember."

He took a deep breath. "Mom and Dad went to a holiday party. Christmas Party as they were called back then. It was late. I got up to use the bathroom and heard sounds from downstairs. I went down and—I saw."

"Saw what?"

Awkwardly, Pike shifted. "Saw him taking advantage of you. Forcing himself on you." Glancing at her house and based on what he'd overheard, he now knew it had been consensual all those years. *We all have things we like.* "I heard him—Virgil— calling you names and slapping you and…disgracing you."

"That wasn't Virgil."

Pike's stomach plummeted. "Yes. Virgil Holland."

She remained stoic.

"What, Steph? I remember. Trust me, I remember. Virgil Holland." His lips quivered. "Right?"

She lovingly held her brother's face. "No, Pike."

"*No?*"

She somberly shook her head and looked up as if seeking strength from a higher power. Instead, all she saw was a plane on final approach to McCarran Airport. "That was Erik Casella."

"*Wha*t? Who…who the hell is Erik Casella?"

"You don't remember?"

Pike opened his palms but couldn't talk.

"I took you to McDonalds. You wanted a Sundae. We wrestled around when we got home. I remember you going to your room and later, seeing you peering out from the railing on the stairs like you were in prison while I was on the floor." She closed her eyes. "But it was Erik Casella who came over that night, not Virgil Holland."

"No, that's imp—you're wrong."

"How many guys you think I've slept with?" She paused, before walking it back with self-deprecating humor, "Okay, don't answer that."

"Ponch."

"What?"

"Ponch, like the guy in that show, *CHiPs*. I remember Virgil going by Ponch."

"No, Pike. That was Erik Casella. *Erik*. Like Erik Estrada."

Pike gave her a sideways glance. "But he recognized me."

"Who?"

"Virgil. He lives up in Phoenix."

"Down. Phoenix is south."

"Wherever the hell it is. He recognized me. Not at first but he knew who I was."

"I'm sure he did."

"But if—if that wasn't him that night, how would he know me?"

"I dated Virgil *before* Erik."

Raking his hair, the former reporter tried creating a timeline. "You dated Erik *after* Virgil?"

"Yes."

"Right after?"

"Pretty much."

It was over a hundred damn degrees, yet Pike was chilled. "Suddenly everything I know, or thought I knew isn't true."

Stephanie, relieved to see she hadn't damaged her car when channeling her inner Ronda Rousey, hoisted herself onto the hood. "Mom and Dad always spent their anniversary down the shore, remember?"

"Yeah."

"One weekend, I invited Virgil over."

"Okay."

"After we had sex, I woke up at…oh hell, two in the morning. I thought he had left. I got out of bed to go downstairs and watch MTV. I saw your bedroom door open."

Pike's throat was as dry as the desert enveloping him.

"He was in your room."

"Virgil? In my room?"

Now Stephanie was unable to utter a sound.

"And?"

She waved her palms like trying to dry her hands. "It's not important. Never mind. Forget I brought this up. I'll take you to your car. Go get Paige." She came off the hood and turned, but was held in place by her brother's influential grip.

"Tell me, Steph."

"Virgil was in bed with you."

"In…" His words faded away.

"He was touching you. And making you touch him."

"Was I sleeping?"

"No."

"So why don't I remember this?"

Stephanie shrugged. "Self-preservation."

"What was I doing?" Pike asking something about himself he had no memory of.

"You were sitting up, back against the wall. You—" Stephanie was choking on tears, on guilt, on shame.

"I what?"

She shut her eyes firmly, a little child hoping if she closed them tight enough the monster would disappear. But this monster never would. "You had his penis in one hand and your Spiderman comic book in the other."

"Virgil?"

Stephanie nodded.

"In my room?"

Another nod.

"So…Virgil….*Virgil* sexually assaulted *me*?"

Her tortured expression confirmed it. "That's why I stopped dating him."

"And Erik Casella? You're saying he's the one who…hurt you?"

A corroborating nod. "You remember Erik?"

"Apparently not."

"Erik was, as Dad used to say, a bad seed. Always in trouble with the law and I'm not talking petty stuff. He was suspended at thirteen for bringing a knife to school, expelled at fourteen when he brought a gun. Remember Mrs. Sachs?"

"No."

Stephanie wrinkled her brows. "That's right. She retired by the time you were a freshman. She was this tiny frail Math teacher that Erik beat the shit out of one day in the school parking lot. His father sent him to one of those military schools and when he got out, he beat the shit out of his father."

Pike felt nauseous. "And *this* is the guy you dated?"

Stephanie shamefully hiked a shoulder.

"Why?"

"I actually called him that night, the night of Dad's party."

"*What?*" Pike cried incredulously.

"To hurt myself." Swallowing, she continued. "I thought I could…I don't know, offset the guilt. I wanted to punish myself for not protecting you from Virgil."

"That's absurd."

"Is it?"

"Of course."

Stephanie clucked her tongue. "This coming from the guy who became a boxer after ending the life of LaMarcus King."

Pike threw his hands into his pockets and kicked at the ground. "I wasn't a boxer."

"Sparring partner. Why?" When Pike didn't respond, she answered for him. "To punish yourself, to offset the guilt. You were hoping to cleanse your soul by hurting yourself. Same as me." She exhibited a sad smile. "We are brother and sister, ya know. We're more alike than you realize."

୯∕୬୯∕୬

"You're welcome to stay with me until you get back on your feet."

Pike barely managed a nod.

"I can line you up with a job at the hotel. Wouldn't be much but it's a start."

"Mm hmm."

"I mean, if things don't work out with Paige."

Paige.

Forty-seven and everything in Pike Graves's life was not what he thought it had been. His memories had deceived him. He felt like some character in a movie who wakes up with amnesia and needs to relearn his own past.

Am I also remembering Paige differently?

How goddamn irrational this entire idea now seemed. Putting his hopes and dreams in the hands of someone he hadn't seen or spoken to in eight years.

But he had nothing else.

Stephanie stopped behind Pike's car. She wanted to say something encouraging, something sisterly. She wanted to apologize for not being there for him when they were younger, for overwhelming him with family secrets, for turning his life topsy-turvy.

But she didn't have a chance. Pike had already transferred his luggage from her backseat to his and had one foot in his Honda when she stopped him. "I need to say something."

"All right."

"Whatever you do, win Paige's heart. Do now what you should've done back then. Tell her what you've kept bottled up your whole life. Get her back." She smiled. "Even if you have to drug her and kidnap her."

Pike's lips turned up.

"But...if she rejects you, walk away. Walk away without regrets, without objections, and without second thoughts. Plead your case and hope for the best."

"Thanks." He pulled his sister close, clung to her, and whispered, "You're too good for Karl."

"Am I?"

As Pike drove away, he watched in the rear view as Stephanie, bawling her eyes out, waved goodbye.

❧❧❧

Pike was in a fog. The man who lived by routine was flying blind. He went from a disciplined, orderly existence to one of impulsiveness to now one of snowballing self-doubt.

He'd felt emboldened when getting on the Penn Turnpike ten days earlier. Ecstatic for breaking out of his shell and embarking on a new life of unpredictability. It was liberating to start anew.

Now he second-guessed his decision.

Was he brave or reckless, courageous or foolish? Would staying put have been wiser? He never would've learned the truth about his mother, his sister, nearly caved to seduction by an underage girl, taken the life of Freddy Marquez. And worst of all, not learned he'd been sexually abused by a pedophile. That last part still hadn't hit him. He hoped it never would.

At a highway overpass, he came upon a red light. He could turn right—east—and return home to what he knew. He could turn left—west—and face his destiny once and for all.

Pike turned left.

Tramping the gas, he prepared for the five hundred mile drive.

His foot nearly pushed the brake through the floorboard. The car fishtailed. Front-end nosed down. The stench of burnt rubber filled the air. He screeched to a stop on the shoulder.

The hitchhiker with the straw hat.

Leaving Philadelphia, he held a sign: *Pacific Time Zone.*

Outside Kansas City: *West Coast.*

In Wickenburg: *California.*

The desired destination narrowing from something general to something specific.

Now he was in Las Vegas, standing at another entrance ramp to another highway holding another sign. *187 Shangri-La Way.*

Paige's address.

PART V

Helping Hand

"We don't meet people by accident.
They are meant to cross our path for a reason."

~ unknown

CHAPTER 23

Pike jumped from his car. "What the fuck?!"

The hitchhiker nodded generically. "Hello."

"Don't 'hello' me. Who the hell are you? And why are you following me?"

A brow went up. "You have a car. I have Reeboks. If anyone's following anyone else—"

Pike dropped to his knees and fanatically ransacked the guy's duffel. "Where is it?"

"Where's what?"

"The sign. The goddamn sign you were holding?"

"Here." Composed, he handed it over.

Pike tore it from his hands. "*California*? Where's the other one?"

"The other one?"

"The one that said One-Eighty-Seven Shangri-La Way."

"One-Eighty-Seven Shangri-La Way?"

"Yes. And stop repeating everything I say."

"I'm repeating everything you say?"

Breathing fire, Pike scanned the guy. For someone loitering alongside interstates from Pennsylvania to Nevada, he looked refreshed and composed, definitely more than Pike. "What's your name?"

"What's yours?"

Pike shook his head. "You're doing it again."

"Doing what again?"

"Repeating—just…what's your name?"

"Jordan."

Pike waited. "Jordan?"

"Now *you're* doing it."

Pike snickered. "Doing what?"

"Repeating what *I* say."

"Jordan. That a first name or last?"

"Moses. Jordan Moses." He offered a hand. "And you?"

Pike ignored the gesture and resumed raiding the man's possessions like a lunatic.

Jordan impatiently tapped his foot. "You're going to put all that back, right?"

Pike was unhinged. Tossing belongings every which way, he came across balled-up socks, underwear, T-shirts, shoes with worn soles, five unopened water bottles, a roadmap, a handful of energy bars, a kit containing personal hygiene items including a straight-edge razor, shampoo and toothbrush, a timeworn Dean Koontz paperback and for some reason, a TV guide. Pike held up the last item. "Why this?"

"Easy crossword puzzles."

Two minutes later, with both of Jordan's duffels emptied, Pike, from his knees, woefully scanned the mess he'd created.

Pacific Time Zone.

West Coast.

California.

187 Shangri-La Way.

Paige's address. Pike's final destination.

A stab through the heart.

Overcome and overwhelmed. Crushed and conquered, beaten and defeated. His memories not his own. His life in tatters. No direction. Lost. Pike's eyes went from rage to tearing up.

On his knees, as if praying for help, for guidance, he pleaded. "*Please*, tell me who you are."

"Jordan Moses."

ოჳთ

Last time someone rode shotgun it hadn't turned out well so Pike paid extra close attention to his new sidekick. Somewhat close in age and height, his clean-shaven passenger looked far less beaten down by life. Dressed in khaki shorts, Reebok hiking boots, and a beige tank top, he resembled someone doing a walkabout through the Australian Outback.

When Jordan undid the chin strap and removed his straw hat, Pike noticed a thick head of cocoa-colored hair.

Jordan claimed he was hitching rides across the country. But following Pike? Impossible. Pike was mistaken. After all, who really pays attention to some guy on the side of a highway? You see him, you pass him, you forget him.

After acting the fool, Pike felt obligated to at least offer him a ride. If nothing else, maybe he'd score some brownie points with the man upstairs.

Jordan, like Roxy, was pleasant, affable, and talkative. Born and raised in Bethlehem, PA, he never had time for a family. Heart disease took his father at a young age. "I never knew my dad."

Pike grinned solemnly. "Me neither."

"Yours also died young?"

"Not really. I just...never knew him."

"Maybe you can remedy that," Jordan suggested.

"I can't. He's...gone."

"Wife? Kids? Siblings?"

"No, no, one sister."

Jordan threw a hand forward. "What happened to your windshield?"

Freddy Marquez. "A rock shattered it."

"Must've been a pretty big rock."

Pike didn't answer.

Jordan explained that his father's death from heart disease was the impetus to become a cardiologist. He got accepted to medical school, but "studying was a killer," so he traded his medical textbooks for a bible and joined the clergy.

"Really?"

"They're parallel," he pointed out. "I could either play God or be closer to God."

"So you're technically Father Jordan Moses?"

"Nah. Gave that up too. Never bought into the whole celibacy thing."

⋅⋅⋅

Jordan sensed a change after crossing into California. "You okay?"

"It's been one hell of a journey but...I made it."

"Not to pry but what's in California?"

"A girl. *The* girl."

"Ah, the one that got away."

"Is it that obvious?"

"Considering you're grinning ear to ear, yes."

Although Jordan didn't ask, Pike offered more. Introverted by nature, he rarely opened up. And never to strangers. He did with Roxy and did it again now. Perhaps Jordan would offer a more adult perspective. When finishing, Pike realized he was hoping someone—anyone—would endorse his brash plan.

"Good for you," Jordan said.

"Thank you."

"So you're on vacation or something?"

"Actually I'm between jobs now."

"And when you're not between jobs?"

"Reporter. Investigative journalist actually."

Jordan stated the obvious. "So you dig until you discover the truth?"

Pike smiled at the irony he hadn't realized. The investigative journalist who discovered truths had lived a life of lies. "What about you?" he asked, passing an Acura.

"I'm a proud slacker. The whole work thing's not my cup of tea." Jordan boasted about living frugally. A penny pincher, as Sam Graves would say. Tiny apartment, no car, standard furniture. He'd collect a paycheck, sock away every nickel, and, when the feeling grabbed him, he'd quit and use his savings to travel. When the money ran out, he'd return home, find a menial dead-end job, and do it all over again.

"Not a nine-to-five guy, huh?"

"Not even a nine-to-nine-fifteen guy." Losing himself in the foreboding desert, he added. "I refuse to believe that's why we're here."

Pike joked, "I'm here to see about a girl."

He smiled. "Not California. *Here*. Life. We're born, we work, we die? Nah, I don't buy it. That's not life, that's going through the motions."

"Okay, Mr. almost-clergyman, then what *is* the meaning of life?"

"Don't ask me. I gave it up to get laid." He winked. "All right, you really want to know my thoughts?"

"Sure."

"We're tourists."

Maintaining a forward look, Pike frowned.

"When you take a vacation, say…Yosemite. You go, you look around, make some memories, enjoy good times. Then, you leave. Life's like that. We're here for a short time. We look around, make some memories, enjoy good times. And then we leave."

Pike conceded there was a simplicity to the statement. He found Jordan's unique perspective and free-wheeling nature inspiring. While he strove to be impulsive Jordan lived it. "Why California?"

"Why not? Never been here."

"So what's next?"

"I'll take it all in, maybe swim in the Pacific, then move on." Jordan read the road sign. "Baker, next exit. I think you owe me a drink. After all, you threw my stuff all over Kingdom Come."

"I apologize. Just been a crazy few days for me."

"Trust me, Pike. I totally understand."

℮ℑℰℑ

Pike nosed in facing the AM/PM mini-mart a minute later. "Coffee?"

Jordan smacked his lips. "Coke."

"One Coke comin' up."

In the store, his sneakers suction-cupped to the sticky overlaid tile as he made his way to the beverage area. A Coke for Jordan, an extra strong Colombian roast for himself. Threading the aisles, he pulled potato chips and other snacks and walked to the front.

The timid young cashier had blonde hair framing a tired face, piercing blue eyes, and an upturned nose. She was skinny to the point of looking emaciated. "Mornin'"

"Good morning," Pike replied pleasantly. Understandably nervous and edgy, working graveyard shift in a tiny town in the middle of nowhere, she likely shuddered every time a stranger came in from the darkness. Eying her nametag, he asked congenially, "How's your night, Natalie?"

"Slow." She lifelessly rang up his order, placed the snacks in a bag and both drinks in a carrier. "Must be thirsty."

Nonplussed, Pike frowned and, after some delay, asked, "You gonna be okay?"

"Yeah."

"You get off soon?"

"Another hour." She retreated a step. "Why?"

"Just making conversation."

"Oh, my God. Are you expecting me to fuck you?"

Pike threw up his hands. "No, no, of course not. I just—"

"What do you think I am? Go away. I have a gun. I'll call the cops."

Pike apologized profusely.

"Go!"

Pike trudged out of the convenience store. Handing Jordan his forty-four-ounce Coke through the window, he trooped around to the driver's side when something in his gut cautioned him. He scanned two other cars in the lot and the nearby street before shaking off his paranoia. Driving to the entrance ramp to I-15, he kept checking the rearview.

"Everything all right?" Jordan asked.

"I'm sure it's nothing."

ᗣᗒᗒ

"Twenty percent!"

"What're you talking about," Cynthia snapped.

"I want twenty percent. Twenty. You said the account Pike listed you as bena...bena...whatever it's called, has one point four million. You offered me ten percent. I want twenty!"

"I don't have time for this now, Dragon." She had just entered the conference room for a critical meeting with five department heads, including Morty. Cynthia intended to plant the seed in her boss's mind that Janice Haas needed to go. She was forgetting things, making stupid mistakes, and losing focus. Cynthia even planned to drop hints that maybe the old hag was showing early signs of dementia.

Janice didn't deserve that office with the killer view, the office Cynthia had been targeting for months. To make sure she'd get her boss's attention, she wore a push-up bra under a low-cut top and skinny jeans. She was about to enter the first volley against senile ol' Janice when her secretary, Gayvin, pranced in with his panties in a bunch. "There's an important call for you," he squealed. Now she was in her office, behind a closed door, losing valuable time discussing this crap with Dragon.

"I did the math. Twice. It comes out to, uh, two, three, carry the one, two hundred forty thousand."

No, two hundred eighty thousand. She kept that to herself. "Why the change of heart?"

"I didn't sign up for this."

"What're you talking about?"

"I go to Vegas, right. Vegas, baby. Sin City. Do I get to gamble?"

Silence.

Cynthia assumed it was a rhetorical question. "Oh. I don't know. Do you?"

"No, not a dime. Do I get to check out any clubs?"

"Uh, no?"

"Do I get laid?"

"I'm guessing not."

"Right. I follow that guy all over the place. Day, night. In this fuckin' heat. I want twenty percent."

"Followed him where?"

"Everywhere. Sam's Town, the Hard Rock. Then some chick's house."

"Stephanie, his sister."

"Yeah, her. She's actually kinda hot, ya know, for being old."

"How about the young girl Pike was with?"

"Her? I dunno. They had a falling out. I think she was a hooker."

Cynthia doubted that. Her ex was a lot of things but she couldn't see sanctimonious Pike Graves lowering himself to the company of a prostitute. "Why do you think that?"

"I saw her go off with a different old dude."

Cynthia cradled the handset against her shoulder, woke her computer, and accessed Pike's credit card, her personalized tracking device where she could keep tabs on him from thousands of miles away. "Go on."

"I think he's going crazy. And I understand why. This fuckin' heat, man."

"What do you mean?"

"After he leaves the Hard Rock with his sister, I stay behind drinkin, right?"

"Okay."

"I'm pretty buzzed and when I'm walking through the garage to leave, I see Pike getting dropped off at his car."

"So he left his sister's early?"

"Yup."

"Why do you think he's going crazy?"

"Okay, so get this. He gets on the highway and all of a sudden, BAM! He pulls over and starts carrying on like a nut."

"Huh?"

"No shit. He's losing it. That's why I want twenty percent. I'm exhausted."

"I never said it'd be easy."

"*Easy*? Fuck easy. I never knew killing someone would bust my balls so much."

Cynthia flinched, hoping no one overheard. "Keep your voice down."

"Twenty percent, Cyn, or do it yourself."

Tempting. Doing quick math, she'd still walk away with over one point one million. She relented. "Fine."

"Yeah?"

"Yes."

"I want more."

"Jesus, what else?"

"A threesome."

Cynthia erupted in laughter. "*What*?"

"Me, you, and that Alex chick you're screwing."

"Oh my God. Are you serious?"

"Hell yes."

"Unbelievable."

Dragon grew angry. "What's unbelievable is this bullshit I agreed to. Either you say yes right now, or you can find someone else to murder your ex."

"Dammit, keep your voice down. I don't need anyone hearing you."

"No one can hear me."

"Where are you?"

"A mile behind him. He just left Baker, California."

"He doesn't know you're tailing him?"

"No, he doesn't know I'm tailing him," Dragon mocked. "Give me some credit. I'm not an idiot."

Cynthia held her tongue.

"And another thing. I want—uh oh."

"What!?"

"He's getting pulled over."

CHAPTER 24

The combination of sitting abnormally in order to see through the cracked windshield brought about by mowing down Freddy Marquez and his passenger almost joining the clergy had Pike asking, "Do you think God forgives our sins?"

"I don't know."

"*You* don't?"

Jordan half-shrugged. "That's like asking a first grader to write a thesis about Einstein's theory of relativity. I didn't get far."

"It's paradoxical," Pike alleged. "On one hand, we're told God loves us no matter what. On the other hand, look at Sodom and Gomorrah."

Jordan now full-shrugged and stared at the lonely gray ribbon snaking the canyons.

"You think He forgives all sins?"

"For what it's worth," Jordan said after giving it some thought, "I think God, or whatever's up there, is practical. We get tested all the time but I believe we're okay if we abide by the basics."

"The basics?"

"The Ten Commandments. Those are pretty standard if you think about it."

Tested? Pike mulled that over. Was his explicit dream about Roxy a test? Was her attempted seduction a test?

Jordan continued. "But even with the Ten Commandments there's wiggle room."

"Oh?"

"Thou shalt not covet thy neighbor's wife?" Jordan chuckled. "We see a hot chick, we don't care if she's married. We covet. On the other hand, 'Thou shalt not kill?' Now *that's* a biggie."

"So what if someone…ya know, does kill?"

Jordan looked at him.

"Accidentally, I mean," Pike quantified.

"I'm not a priest *or* a criminal defense attorney. Accident or not, I'd hate to stand before God and explain why I *accidentally* took a life."

Was he seeking forgiveness? And why in God's name, no pun intended, from a vagabond with a straw hat. "I broke the biggie."

Jordan studied his profile. The green hue from the dashboard made it impossible to see Pike clearly. "Iraq? Afghanistan?"

"Philadelphia."

"*Pennsylvania*?"

"A long time ago."

Jordan made a face. "Well, hey, thanks for the lift. You can let me out at the next exit."

Pike didn't smile. Cracking his neck, he commented, "I've always been surrounded by death. I have fear of dying."

"Thanatophobia?"

Brows shooting up, he faced his passenger. "Yeah. Yes." Then he quickly returned his eyes forward. "My maternal grandmother died when I was young. Mom didn't want me going to the funeral but Dad did. As always, Dad won. And I guess…seeing her lying there just got me." Pike added despondently. "I had a brother born minutes after me, but he didn't live through the night." Thinking about that now, Pike wondered if his mom harbored any guilt. Had she blamed herself? The fact she carried a life for nine months that never got to see one sunrise must've caused anguish and grief. Did she view herself as less of a woman, an unfit mom? Did it lead to depression which, maybe years later, manifested itself in her addiction to valium and the stimulus for the affair with her physician? Pike never considered that until this very moment. He never thought to ask. And now he never could.

"Wanna talk about it?" Jordan offered.

Not the court system, reassurances from family or friends, Jordan Moses, or any boxer pummeling him could ease Pike's remorse. But it felt good to talk. When finished enlightening his passenger about LaMarcus King, Jordan exhaled. "If nothing else, you evened the score. LaMarcus King died but Paige Rhodes, thanks to you, lived."

"But it was a fake gun. Not even real."

"The cops didn't know that. They may have just as easily killed him. So, yes, you unintentionally took a life but you saved one in the process. I think that squares you with Big G."

Crazy logic but Pike hoped his passenger was correct. However, if Paige and LaMarcus cancelled each other out—saving one life in exchange for taking another—then what about Freddy Marquez? If Jordan's rationale was true, Pike would need to save someone else.

When the Honda's interior became floodlit by blinding lights, Pike briefly considered tapping the brake just to piss-off the guy riding his tail.

"Crap. It's a cop." Jordan tilted left and checked the speedometer. "How fast were you going?"

"Eighty-ish."

"It's only sixty-five here."

The cracked windshield. The smashed headlight. The damage to the front fender. Freddy Marquez. Pike switched on his directional, pulled to the side, and tried to prepare himself for what was coming.

The state trooper remained in his cruiser running the plate. Sitting in twilight, Pike grew tense. He grinded his lip, a child again, and chastised himself for heeding Roxy's advice. Had he turned himself in back in Wickenburg, he never would have left the scene of an accident, nor entered California. He never would have gotten *this* close to Paige. Same damn state. And now, only hours away from her, his hope for a better future, for Shangri-La, was getting ripped away.

"Good morning, Officer," he said to the imposing figure filling his window, the trooper's girth augmented by a Kevlar vest. Pike's eyes inadvertently glimpsed the officer's sidearm.

Thanatophobia.

"Where're you off to in such a hurry, son?"

The olive-skinned man boasted a stern jaw, menacing deep-set eyes, and ramrod-straight posture. Right out of a California Highway Patrol recruiting poster and into Pike's line of vision. He also was a good fifteen years younger. *Son*? "Was I speeding, officer?"

"You can say that. I clocked you at eighty-three in a sixty-five. Please turn off the car and withdraw the keys from the ignition. License, registration, proof of insurance."

"Yes, Officer." Leaning forward, Pike moved his hand out of sight.

The cop swiftly backpedaled and moved his hand to his holster.

Pike's eyes went wide in fear. "My wallet's in my back pocket."

"Slowly."

"Yes, sir."

Pike retrieved it, surprised how shaky his hand was. Jordan remained unflinching, staring forward. Only now Pike wondered if his passenger, some hitchhiker he picked up, was a fugitive.

He handed over the requested documents through the open window but they slipped through his trembling fingers and floated to the ground. Going for humor, he joked, "You're not going to get me for littering, are you?"

Remaining stone-faced, the state trooper ordered Pike out of the car.

"Yes, sir." Forgetting about the seatbelt he nearly strangled himself. He chuckled at his clumsiness and, eyes glued to the officer's holstered pistol, freed himself from the seatbelt, and got out. Jordan stayed put.

The trooper, whose name plate read Jesus Higuera, pointed at the scattering papers.

"Yes, sir."

After gathering the documents, Officer Higuera scrutinized Pike then shone a penlight in both eyes. "Have you been drinking?'

"No, sir, not at all."

He redirected the beam into the vehicle. "What's that in the cup holder?"

"Oh, that? Just coffee. But when you said drinking, I thought you meant *drinking*."

Higuera gestured at the windshield. "What happened there?"

"A rock."

"A rock?"

"Yes, Officer."

The highway patrolman wavered and in that moment Pike knew his fate hung in the balance. If the trooper returned to his cruiser, Pike would get off with only a speeding ticket and could continue on. If the trooper went left and saw the front of the vehicle he'd realize no rock could cause that much damage.

Jesus Higuera clucked his tongue, bore his gaze into Pike. And moved left.

Shit.

Steel-toed boots shook the desert. He eyeballed the dented fender, the broken headlight. Then looked at Pike skeptically. "A rock did all of this?"

Pike's throat was sandpaper-dry. "Yes."

Examining the documents, Higuera asked, "Is this your current address, Mr. Graves?"

"Yes. Well, no, not currently"

The trooper arched a skeptical brow. "It's a simple question, Mr. Graves."

Pike ignored the bead of sweat at the tip of nose. He didn't want to spook the officer with sudden movements. "I'm sort of in transition."

"What *is* your current address, Mr. Graves?"

"I…um…don't have one."

Interrogation 101. Silence was the best way to draw out information so Higuera remained quiet.

"I'm on my way to California. Well, I mean, I'm *in* California. But I mean Northern California. San Fran…well, Mill Valley, technically."

Higuera stayed impassive and tightlipped.

"To see an old girlfriend."

"Name?"

"Paige, Paige Rhodes. One-eighty-seven Shangri-La Way."

"She can vouch for you?"

"Uh, well, no. She doesn't know I'm coming."

"And the damage to your vehicle?"

"A…rock. Sir."

"Mr. Graves," Higuera said imperiously, "Kindly turn around and place your hands behind your back."

"Wha…why?"

He whipped a Taser from his utility belt, his voice booming like a deity. "Turn around and place your hands behind your back. Now!"

Pike obeyed, eying Jordan through the window who was church-mouse quiet. Was he actually thinking the highway patrolman wouldn't notice him?

Higuera slapped the cuffs around Pike's wrists and pressed a button on his lapel-mounted walkie-talkie. "Ten-fifteen, prisoner in custody. Request possible backup."

Prisoner in custody?

Static. Higuera repeated his request. The only response was more static. "Higuera to command. Come in."

Nothing.

"Stay here, sir," Higuera harrumphed and returned to the cruiser to communicate with his post.

So this is how it ends. And where it ends. Just hundreds of miles from Paige. What would happen to his car? How could he find a reputable lawyer? What about the felt box he'd been carrying? Who should he call first? Paige would be too dumbfounded. Cynthia would likely hang up on him. Dewayne?

Maybe Pike could ask Jesus Higuera to contact Dewayne. One member of law enforcement helping out another.

On the other hand, Pike deserved whatever fate handed down. Yes, what occurred in Wickenburg was an accident. But leaving the body of Freddy Marquez worsened things. What was that cliché? Something about the cover-up being worse than the crime.

Jordan got out of the car and pointed a finger at Pike. "Don't move." He advanced on the police cruiser.

Pike's stomach clenched. Who was Jordan Moses? A hitchhiker, a slacker, an almost doctor, pseudo-cleric? Or was he a fugitive wanted by law enforcement. "Where're you going?" he yelled.

Jordan waved his arm dismissively and boldly marched toward the cop car.

"Jordan! What are you doing?"

Pike watched in bewilderment as Jordan crouched alongside the cruiser. A huge semi roared past, the backwash rippling Pike's clothes and removing any hope of eavesdropping on the conversation. The hitchhiker appeared to whisper to Higuera through the driver's side window.

What the hell is going on?

Jordan backpedaled, allowing Higuera room to get out. The state trooper pulled on his belt loops as he approached. His expression unreadable. Jordan, a few feet behind, revealed nothing.

"Please turn around, Mr. Graves," Higuera ordered five feet away.

Pike did. And sighed agreeably when the handcuffs came off. He wanted to hug the cop but instead just massaged his raw wrists.

The stoic officer unexpectedly smiled. "I apologize for any inconvenience or delay this may have caused, Mr. Graves."

Pike knitted his brows.

"Kindly repair the damage to your vehicle right away."

"Yes…Officer, sir. I will."

"I'm letting you off with a warning this time, but next time you may not be so lucky."

"Yes, sir, thank you."

Jesus Higuera moved his arm like a gameshow host presenting new appliances. "Be careful, Mr. Graves. There's lot of hazards out there." He returned to his vehicle, brought the engine to life, drove west, and vanished into auburn veins of a new day. Peering across the top of his car, Pike looked at Jordan Moses.

In a tenor that that conjured up memories of being summoned by his father, the hitchhiker declared, "We need to talk."

CHAPTER 25

W hat'd you say to him?"

Ignoring the question, Jordan pointed at the fissure in the windshield. "What caused it?"

"A rock."

"Don't lie to me, goddammit!"

The unforeseen outburst caught Pike by surprise. "It's hard to explain."

"Simplify it."

He emptied his lungs. "I was on my way from Phoenix to Vegas and was coming to this town called Wickenburg." He glanced right. "Was that you outside Burger King?"

"Keep your eyes on the road."

Pike faced forward. "I looked away for just a second and that's…when it happened."

"Continue."

"I didn't mean to kill him. It was an accident."

"Who?"

"This kid, this…fifteen-year-old kid." Pike shook his head. "Why was he out there? Middle of the night, crossing a highway in dark clothes."

"You're blaming *him*?" Jordan derisively snapped.

"No! I *wanted* to come clean. I *wanted* to turn myself in. But Roxy, this girl I picked up, convinced me I shouldn't."

"Now you're blaming *her*?"

"*No*! It's my fault. But I can only carry so much guilt before it becomes too much."

"Then why didn't you turn yourself in?"

"I just didn't, okay."

"Too scared?"

Pike grunted something unintelligible.

"You wouldn't survive in prison."

Angry at his manhood affronted, he wanted to reject Jordan's claim but he knew the accusation was true.

"What's his name?"

"Freddy Marquez."

Jordan rooted around in the backpack between his feet, pulled a cell Pike didn't know he had, and tapped a few keys. "Wickenburg, Arizona. The number for the Marquez family."

"What are you doing?"

"Yes, please connect me," Jordan said. "That's fine. I'll pay the extra charge."

"What're you *doing*?"

He handed it over. "It's ringing."

Pike slanted away from the phone as if it was the vilest thing he'd even seen.

"Take it!" Jordan demanded.

"What do I say? I'm sorry for killing your son?"

Jordan shoved the phone into his hand leaving Pike no choice.

A groggy female answered. "Hola."

Pike checked the dashboard clock. Almost six a.m. in Arizona.

"Someone there?"

"Go ahead, Pike."

"I...can't."

"Someone there? Hola?"

"What do I tell her?"

The frail woman bellowed, "What do you tell me about what? Hay-*lo*!"

Jordan irritably ripped the phone from Pike's quaking hand but held it so they could both listen. "Is Freddy there?"

"Freddy?"

"Yes, ma'am. Freddy Marquez."

"No," the woman drew out. "I haven't seen Freddy in days."

Pike chewed his lips.

"Days?" Jordan asked the sleepy woman. "When did you last see him?"

"Not since he went to Flagstaff for that job."

Pike's brows creased.

"Your husband?"

"Si."

Jordan and Pike exchanged a look. Then Jordan asked, "Do you have a son named Freddy?"

"Oh, you mean Junior."

"Yes. Junior. Is here there?"

"He should be." She lowered her voice as if not wanting to wake the dead. "Now that you mention it, I didn't hear him come in last night."

"Would you mind seeing if he's home?"

"Is there a problem, *senor*?"

"No, ma'am."

"Oh, is this Principal Larrimore?"

Jordan and Pike shrugged at each other. "No."

The woman sounded deflated.

"It's very important, Mrs. Marquez."

Pike and Jordan listened to the woman grouse about her knees as she padded down a hallway and knocked on a door. "Junior, you in there?"

"Ma, go away."

Pike frowned.

An exchange of rapid-fire Spanish followed by a different voice, younger and male. "Yeah?"

Jordan thrust the phone into Pike's hand and leaned away. This was on him now.

"Who the hell's there?"

Pike couldn't make a sound.

"I was sleeping, dickhead." Then lower, "Ma, they say who it was?"

Pike found the strength. "Freddy?"

"Yeah?"

"Freddy Marquez?"

"Yeah, yeah, who's this?"

"You're...alive?"

"Hell, yes, why wouldn't I be?" he shouted. "But *you* won't be for waking me up this early."

"You're really alive?"

Concern replaced rage. "Who the hell is this?"

"But...I saw you."

"*Saw* me?"

Pike's thoughts jumbled. Remembering the student ID Roxy displayed, he asked, "You go to Wickenburg High?"

"Yes, I go to Wickenburg High." Then, "If this is about the stolen basketballs, talk to Tico and Little B. I don't know nothin' about that."

He saw the corpse. Freddy Marquez's corpse. The same Freddy Marquez he was now having a conversation with.

Then again, maybe not.

Pike didn't approach the body. He couldn't. Thanatophobia. Did Roxy check for a pulse? Maybe she was wrong. Maybe he was simply injured. Pike asked hesitantly, "Did you get hit by a car?"

"Fuck off!" And Freddy hung up.

Pike stared at the phone.

Jordan asked, "Dead?"

"No, he's alive."

"I mean the phone, dummy."

"Oh." Pike handed it back to Jordan who promptly concealed it in his backpack. "But how? I don't understand."

Jordan pointed to the speedometer.

So immersed in the conversation, Pike unintentionally slowed to forty. He got the car up to sixty-five and no higher. "I don't get it."

His passenger remained apathetic.

"Maybe that wasn't him."

Jordan looked at him dubiously.

"Marquez? Kinda common name. Maybe that wasn't the right one."

Exasperated, Jordan muttered under his breath, pulled the phone again, and hit resend. "I need a number for Marquez in Wickenburg. I tried one." He recited the number. "But that's not correct. Do you have a different listing?" A second later, he said, "That's what I figured." He put the phone away. "Happy now?"

Pike cogitated aloud. "Maybe...maybe he didn't live in Wickenburg. Maybe he lived in a nearby town."

Jordan asked harshly, "You really wanna play these games all day?"

"I saw him. He wasn't moving."

No response.

"He was dead."

Nothing.

"That was you, wasn't it? Outside Burger King?"

Pike thought he detected a miniscule upturn in Jordan's mouth. But perhaps not. He'd been wrong before. Plenty.

"Was that you, Jordan?" Pike laughed despite himself. "Did you...did you have something to do with...saving him?"

"He's obviously alive, right?"

"Well...yes. I guess."

Jordan snorted. "Just 'cause you're the Son of Sam doesn't mean you're a killer."

The shorthairs on the back of his neck stood on end. His skin prickled when hearing Jordan's remark. It stung now as much as it had decades ago.

When the media dissected the grisly events at Grizzly's several wannabe-journalists scathingly labeled Pike, child of Sam Graves, Son of Sam, an acerbic tongue-in-cheek reference to the .44 killer who terrorized New York City for a year and a half in the 1970s. The moniker hurt then as much as now. Was Jordan's quip simply a coincidence or was he more familiar with Pike's backstory than he was letting on. After all, he claimed to be from Bethlehem which wasn't too far from Philadelphia. Worst of all, Pike never told his passenger his father's name. "How'd you know about that? About the media smearing me?"

Jordan disregarded the question. "All you need to worry about is Paige. The Marquez kid is alive."

"But—"

"No buts!"

"Is Paige in trouble?"

Jordan said nothing.

"Answer me! Is Paige in danger?"

"How would I know?"

"You seem to know a lot."

"You gotta stop looking back all the time."

"That *was* you, wasn't it? Outside Burger King, right after I killed Freddy."

"Obviously you're wrong."

"About killing him or about you being there?"

Jordan remained reticent.

"Answer me, for fuck's sake!"

Jordan prophesized. "There are things in this life people don't understand. Things they're not meant to."

"You're speaking as if you're not people."

"Since the beginning of time," Jordan went on, talking in an omnipotent tone representative of the religious vocation he left, "people have questioned the meaning of life. Why are we here? What's it all mean?"

"You're saying we don't have a choice? That it's all random? There's no master plan?"

"No."

Pike was growing tired of the doublespeak, the riddles. He even regretted picking up this, this…hitchhiker. Learning the truth about his parents and Roxy and Cynthia and Virgil and Stephanie was causing him to lose touch with reality. "What the fuck do you want from me, goddammit?"

"How about some appreciation, you ungrateful prick!"

"Appreciation?" Pike shouted back. "If it wasn't for me, you'd still be standing on the side of the road in Vegas. Or Arizona. Or Kansas. Or Phila-fucking-delphia. Why the hell are you following me?"

"It goes both ways, my friend," Jordan replied calmly.

"Meaning?"

"Meaning," Jordan said after a drawn-out breath, "I can't keep saving your sorry ass. I can't always be there for you."

"Be there for me? For *me*?"

"Yes, for you," Jordan lampooned.

Pike threw his thumb over his shoulder. "You mean with that cop back there, Higuera?"

"Yes. And Kansas City."

"Kansas City?"

Jordan, wanting to end the conversation, leaned forward and turned on the radio.

"The Sounds of Silence." Simon and Garfunkel. *The Graduate.*

Pike turned it off. "What about Kansas City?"

Jordan affirmed, "That so-called mechanic, Emmett, was playing you. He's a crook."

"How do you know about that?"

"He was going to keep your car for a week then charge you four thousand bucks when it was nothing more than a loose wire."

In a whisper, Pike repeated, "How do you know about that?"

"You didn't need to waste time dawdling around Kansas City. Not when you need to get to Paige. She's your destiny."

"Why?"

"Why?" Jordan snorted. "Hello. Newsflash. Mechanics aren't exactly honest people."

"I mean why do I need to get to Paige? Is she in trouble?" Instinctively he pushed down on the gas.

They were having two separate conversations, talking past each other. Jordan stated, "I was the one who left your car keys and the note outside your hotel room door. I was the one who knocked."

Pike thought back. "I looked. Through the peephole. And up and down the hallway." He studied Jordan now, keeping his eyes off the road an unsafe amount of time. "I didn't see anyone."

"Imagine that."

"What are you saying?"

"You were in danger."

"Me?" Pike pointed to himself. "Why am I in danger? Is someone after me?"

"Like I said, I can't keep saving you. I can't always be there for you."

Pike anxiously raked his hair. "I don't under...who *are* you?"

"Told ya. Jordan Moses. Jordan like...the River Jordan the Israelites crossed to get to the Promised Land. Also where John the Baptist baptized Jesus. Ya know, if you believe that stuff. And Moses, well, that's easy." He matter-of-factly hiked his shoulders. "Jordan Moses."

Pike held his churning stomach. "Are you screwing with me?"

"And Philadelphia."

"What are you, like a, I don't know, a guardian angel."

Jordan chortled. "No."

"Is this when you offer to keep protecting me if I give you my credit card number?"

Jordan laughed. "Good one, but no. I don't need money."

The blaring horn startled Pike. He moved right and allowed a convertible to speed by. "What about Philly?"

"LaMarcus King was an all-state running back."

"I know that."

"That kid was destined to have a long career in the NFL had

he not made bad choices along the way."

"If you're trying to cheer me up, it's not working."

"When you saw him outside Grizzly's, you hadn't started boxing yet."

Pike frowned. "I never told you I boxed."

"Correction, sparring. You hadn't killed LaMarcus so you hadn't started sparring to offset the guilt."

"How do you *know* all of this?" Pike asked as he continued crossing the desert, much like the Jews following Moses.

"Tell me something, Pike Graves. How can an all-state running back who made a career avoiding linemen, sidestepping defensive tackles, and evading cornerbacks not simply get out of the way of a scrawny, wiry kid like you?"

"I…caught him by surprise."

"Ah."

"I don't know how it happened, but it did."

"LaMarcus King saw you coming. He easily stepped aside and waved you by like a matador. *You* were the one who went down. *You* were the one who hit the ground. *You* were the one who cracked your skull open. *You* were the one who died."

Pike's hand reflexively went to his skull. "That's not what happened."

"That's *precisely* what happened. Or what would have happened." Jordan inhaled. "Two hands, call it a presence, hold LaMarcus in place. One leg extended behind him. You rush *him*. He stumbles backward over the *leg,* cracks his skull. Game over."

"So…you're the one who killed LaMarcus King?"

"No, I'm the one who saved you."

"You are a Guardian Angel."

Jordan moaned tiredly. "No, Pike. I'm not."

"Then what are you?"

"Most things that happen in life are beyond our control. But sometimes we *can* control them. Sometimes we get a helping hand. Other times, *most* times, we are simply punching at fog."

Pike chilled to the marrow. His skin coated in gooseflesh. He'd never heard anyone use that expression other than his father. "Wh—what—did you just say?"

"You heard me."

His eyes swept Jordan. It was dusk, the time of the day when light and dark are indecipherable.

This hitchhiker knew everything about Pike. But how? Somewhere deep in Pike's soul, in the essence of his very being, he sensed it. He couldn't describe it. Or explain it. He didn't even know where or how or why it came to him. His chin trembled. His entire spirit shivered. "Are you...my dad?"

Jordan stared at him. Cold and hard and rigid. "Do I look like your dad?"

Pike blinked away tears clouding his vision. "It's been years, Jor...I'm forgetting him. His voice, his mannerisms."

Jordan broke contact.

"Are you him? Are you the spirit of my dad?"

Eyes fixed, he replied. "No, Pike, I'm not."

Absurd. Silly. Childish too. Pike wasn't a little kid anymore. He didn't believe in ghosts and wasn't fearful of things going bump in the night. Yet, his heart sank. What he wouldn't give to have a ten minute conversation with his dad. Five minutes. Two. He'd lost his father years ago and in a strange way, felt like he just lost him a second time. Or at least an opportunity to say things he never said because he assumed there'd always be more time.

He heard heavy sobbing and realized it was his own.

"Sorry to disappoint you," Jordan said, "but I'm not Sam Graves."

"I'm sorry, too."

Pike had sunk to a new low. A grown man, actually thinking his deceased father came back to life in the body of a vagabond wearing a straw hat. Trying to regain some normalcy, he asked conversationally, "What'd you say to the cop back there?"

"I didn't *say* anything."

"What'd you do?"

"There are ways to communicate nonverbally. Let's just say I...willed him to let you go."

"Like telepathy?"

Jordan waggled his head. "If you want to call it that."

Recent events shot across his mind with striking rapidity. Jordan Moses marched right up to the side of a police cruiser and *communicated* with a state trooper. He claimed he had knocked on Pike's hotel room door even though Pike saw no one. When he noticed Jordan on the side of the highway in Philadelphia and Las Vegas he was alone; in Kansas City, Roxy was asleep; and, in

Wickenburg, she hadn't noticed him. And most significant of all, the passing comment made by the cashier in Baker after he purchased a coffee for himself and a Coke for his passenger. "You must be thirsty."

Thirsty.

As if two drinks were excessive for one person.

"You're not really here."

"What do you mean?"

Pike repeated. "You're not real."

"You see me. You hear me. We're having a conversation. See-ing is believing, isn't that—*Jesus!*"

Pike yanked the wheel, obliterated a road sign, and rocketed up the exit ramp for Main Street in Barstow.

Jordan slammed his palms against the dash as the car skidded through a red light and stopped in the middle of the intersection.

"Christ, Pike, you trying to kill us?"

Spotting an all-night gas station, he turned a hard right, floored it, and squealed into the parking lot like a bullet fired from a gun. Ripping away the seatbelt, he pointed at Jordan. "Don't you dare move!" He flew from his car, slammed his shoulder against the door, and barged in. The cashier, a grand-motherly-type, filled with terror, started reaching below the counter.

Everyone was on edge.

Pike showed his empty hands. "I'm not here to rob you."

The elderly woman wasn't so sure.

"Turn around please."

"What?" She backpedaled a few steps from the counter.

"I can't reach the register from here. I need a favor. Please. That Honda parked out front is mine. Do you see anyone sitting there?"

The old lady with wildly uncontrolled eyebrows looked at Pike. "Are you some sorta nut?"

He was wondering the same thing. "Please. Do you see any-one in that car? Just answer me, and I'll leave."

The cashier locked the register, gave Pike a vigilant glance, and then peered between a display of cheap sunglasses and a rack of Slim Jims. "Honda, you say?"

"Yes."

She turned around after a moment and faced him. "Sorry. I don't."

"*What*?"

The woman grew frightened again. "Look, you asked, I answered. If you want me to say I see someone, fine, I see someone."

Pike rushed outside.

Jordan Moses was…gone.

☙❧☙

Ten hours later, Pike Graves wearily trudged into his rickety hotel room on the fourteenth floor of the Roosevelt Inn in Larkspur, California. He tossed his suitcases on one of two queens and went to the window. Parting gray drapes, he looked south. Toward Mill Valley. Toward Paige.

It was late afternoon.

The fog was rolling in.

PART VI

Punching at Fog

"Not until we are lost
do we begin to understand ourselves."

~ Henry David Thoreau

CHAPTER 26

The memory as fresh as a springtime rain.

They held hands, fingers intertwined. Both afraid to let go. He remembered her gait—long, confident strides. But as Pike and Paige moved through the airport eight years ago, her confidence ebbed away. Her strides shortened.

Forty-eight hours after Pike shed tears watching a pine box containing his mother lowered into the ground, tears were again clouding his vision. Seeing the plane through massive windows getting fueled for a cross-country flight, he was suffering a different kind of loss. Equally gut-wrenching, equally heartbreaking. But this loss didn't have to be forever.

He'd insisted on taking Paige to the airport. Maybe some words of wisdom would come. Perhaps at the last possible minute she'd have a change of heart, throw all caution to the wind, wrap her arms around Pike, and they could embark on a life together.

What a crock.

That only happened in sappy chick flicks. And as Dewayne reminded him the night before he embarked on this pilgrimage, "Happy endings are Hollywood bullshit."

They chatted about nothing and everything. Pike and Paige doing a two-step, dancing around the issue, each waiting for the other to say something. But when the airport came into view, dialogue stalled and hearts grew heavy.

"You crying?" Paige's voice like silk, her words laced with concern.

"Just thinking of Mom."

Crestfallen, she looked away. She'd seen him at his highest of highs and lowest of lows. And she knew when he was lying.

Fate, as always, was against him. A powerful thunderstorm was rolling in from Canada and the pilot wanted to takeoff ASAP to avoid the coming downpour. Ticket agents hurried to get passengers boarded. Only a few individuals remained in line.

Tightening her hold, Paige noticed his palms were sweaty. Or maybe they were her own. "Hey," she said like in a dream.

Pike blinked once, twice, looked straight ahead, and tried holding his head high.

One inch at a time, they advanced closer to the agent.

"At least you were able to walk me to the gate."

He forced a smile. Pulling strings, he'd dropped the name of his employer, *The Philadelphia Inquirer*, and was allowed to accompany her to where only ticketed passengers were permitted.

Leaning against him, she hooked her arm around his lower waist, rested her head on his bicep and pulled him closer.

"Tickets."

Paige handed over her boarding pass, Pike staring numbly at the plane. How ironic. United, an adjective meaning joined together for a common purpose.

"Sir, your ticket."

Pike looked at Paige. Eyes were theoretically the window to the soul but he believed they were the window to the heart. And looking at her, he saw love. He wondered what she saw looking at him.

"Sir, your ticket?"

He wiped his nose.

Paige held his face. "Pike."

He placed his hand over hers, pressed it against his flesh, kissed her fingers.

"Sir!"

His eyes narrowed. "Paige, I—"

She covered his mouth. "It's okay. I know."

"Please, Paige, don't get—"

"Sir!" the agent hollered. "Are you staying or are you going?"

Paige kissed him on the lips. Nothing passionate. Nothing fervent. Nothing intense. Volumes spoken with just a simple smooch. To the agent, she said, "He's staying."

To Pike, it sounded like a question. Barely able to make a sound, he managed to say "Be good" then turned and, swallowing down tears and with emptiness in his chest, returned to his so-called life.

Seconds later, he heard her cry out, "*No!*"

Heart erupting in hope, he pivoted and reflexively opened his arms.

A wheel had fallen off her carry-on. Embarrassed, she apologized profusely to the ticket agent and struggled righting the suitcase. She moved toward the ramp. She crossed the threshold. Stopped. And looked back.

She looked back.

Pike tentatively took an exhilarated step forward. "Paige?"

She waved good-bye.

And then walked out his life.

CHAPTER 27

Perhaps when it opened in 1912 The Roosevelt Inn had been elegant and glamorous. Or maybe it was dump then too.

Located in a browbeaten area of Larkspur, a stone's throw from Mill Valley, the exterior was designed to conjure up thoughts of the US Capitol. A white dome, severely sun-bleached, was situated on the roof. Marble pillars, now a grimy gray, fronted the hotel. A red carpet welcomed guests.

The foyer was designed to replicate the Capitol Rotunda but more befitted a bordello. Next to a wishing well stood a faux statue of George Washington taking the oath of office outside Federal Hall in lower Manhattan. However, someone placed a Niners helmet on Washington's head and strung a yoyo from his hand placed atop a bible.

The scruffy furnishings had seen better days. Fragmented tile and ratty Oriental throw rugs augmented the despair and melancholy atmosphere. The lobby reeked of smoke and Chinese food. A beggar propped against the wall smoked a cigarette down to the filter. A worn-out woman with fake red hair, platform shoes, fishnet stockings, and a leather skirt gave Pike a come-hither look. The gaps in her blackened teeth didn't help her cause.

At the front desk a fleshy female wore a wide-neck black top, snug pink skirt squeezing round hips, and a disproportionate amount of rosy lipstick. Her squat legs and arms covered in ink. Ears, lips, and nose were jam-packed with studs. The right side of her scalp completely shaved. Busily working on something, she didn't acknowledge Pike.

He cleared his throat.

No response.

He moved his hand toward the bell.

"Don't!" she yowled. "Gimme a sec, boss."

"Take your time," Pike moaned.

A moment later, the young woman leaned back analyzing her work and then displayed it. "Whaddaya think?"

In keeping with the motel's motif, photos of US presidents who supposedly stayed at the Roosevelt lined the walls. Below their portraits, comments proclaimed their so-called fondness. The newest addition had Herbert Hoover declaring "Having a Great Depression? One night at the Roosevelt will cure it."

Pike smiled. "Not bad."

"What'd you need, chief?"

"Graves, fourteen-oh-two. I checked in yesterday and was wondering if I could get some extra towels. There were only two in the room."

"Vinyl."

"Excuse me?"

"Vinyl. My name."

"Oh? Well, Vinyl, I was wondering—"

"There's no need to fear, Vinyl the front desk clerk is here." She bounced out of her chair. "Gotta get some from supplies. Be back in two shakes."

After she merrily skipped away, Pike leaned over and looked at her other creations. Abe Lincoln had written "Four score and seven years ago I stayed at the Roosevelt." Richard Nixon claimed "I am not a crook. But I am a satisfied guest." FDR announced "the only thing we have to fear is staying at a different hotel." Pike also noticed a textbook off to the side: *The Wellington Guide to Bone and Muscle.*

Vinyl bopped to the counter. "They're all locked up, speed racer, but I'll have 'em brought up later if that's cool."

Speed racer? "Thanks. That's room fourteen-oh-two."

"Right, fourteen-oh-two, same year the Tatars defeated the Turkish army in the Battle of Angora."

Pike's chin hit the floor.

"Stanford. Pre-med." Vinyl winked. "Things aren't always what they seem."

He smiled. "True."

"Later 'gator."

⅌È⅌È

Mill Valley, Paige's hometown, was the antithesis to what he left behind in the grungy City of Brotherly Love. Located on the eastern slope of Mount Tamalpais, imposing estates on colossal lots sat far off the street situated among redwoods. Well-manicured lawns resembled putting greens. A banner across Blithedale Avenue, the city's main thoroughfare, boasted Mill Valley was chosen by both CNN and Forbes as one of the top ten places to live in America. There were abundant nature trails, gardens, and lakes. Prodigious sturdy oaks stood sentry on narrow lanes creating a perception of a robust forest.

At a red light, Pike viewed smartly dressed residents sipping wine at a street side café. "What the hell was I thinking?"

He'd spent an exorbitant chunk of time deciding what to wear. Jeans and a T-shirt was too casual. A well-tailored suit, not that he brought one, too extreme. He pulled a sapphire Herringbone, the one dressy shirt he'd packed, but it wrinkled in his suitcase. Hitting a mall outside Larkspur, he purchased an informal yet stylish Carnelian Polo along with tan khakis and comfy tan loafers.

It'd been eight years since Mom's funeral, eight years since Paige looked back before getting on that plane. Some may call it stalking. Dewayne called it infatuation. But Pike knew it was something deeper, something real, something he couldn't explain but rather felt in his soul.

He never had interest in social media, finding Facebook and similar sites nothing more than everyone playing one-upmanship. However, he signed up anyway in hopes of keeping tabs on her. Paige apparently never created an account.

Now, gazing around, awestruck and feeling inconsequential, Pike wanted to chuck it all away. No way in hell she would give all of this up for an unemployed in-transition former boyfriend she hadn't communicated with in nearly a decade. Cold feet? Or slapped in the face by the cold light of reality?

Screw it!

He'd tuck his tail between his legs, return to Vegas and accept Stephanie's handout for a job and a place to stay. He'd learned tragic truths about his parents, his sister, and definitely met interesting people along the way. He freed himself of Cynthia. It wasn't a complete waste, right?

The honking horn snapped Pike back from his reverie. He drove forward, looking for a place to U-turn and get out of here as quick as possible. A gold Rolls Royce Phantom to his left, a red Ferrari riding his tail. His lane veered off but Pike was boxed in and couldn't change lanes. He found himself on meandering narrow streets travelling deeper into the prosperous community.

Up a hill. Down an incline. Around an embankment. Shadowing a reservoir. Bypassing a nature preserve. Trapped in a maze with no exit. Then he saw the street sign.

Shangri-La Way.

As if guided by some unseen power, Pike parked across the street from 187 Shangri-La Way. The home was comparable in size to its neighbors and equally impressive. And for the guy with dead bugs in his grill and a cracked windshield that prevented him from seeing things clearly, intimidating as hell.

The three-story Tudor revival sat off the serene street. A circular cobblestone driveway crossed an opulent meadow containing a creek and a gazebo. The home had timber framing, a gabled steep-pitched roof, parapets, patterned stonework, and diamond-shaped window panes. Large hedges lined the property like a protective sheath.

Pike wanted to throw up. He pulled his wallet, hoping the address he'd gotten from Dewayne was wrong. Unfortunately, for Pike's chances of taking her away, he was at the right place.

Their relationship died when Paige elected to move to the opposite side of the continent and become a tennis instructor to rich kids at Pepperdine University before moving up the coast years ago. The cost of living in California was astronomical and Mill Valley was one of the most affluent communities in the state. The median price of a home was $2.3 million. She'd clearly done well. But *this* well?

Pike knew he failed.

He'd waited too damned long. She had done exceedingly well. As opposed to himself, a guy trying to find himself as if he was some kid out of college, like Ben Braddock in *The Graduate*.

Pike was hoping to start his life. Paige was already entrenched in hers.

Thirty seconds or ten minutes? He didn't know how long he'd been parked when a car passed, turned left, and took the cobblestone driveway toward the front door.

He straightened.

The vehicle stopped at the marbled entryway. He couldn't see the occupant but he knew. In his heart, he knew.

Paige Rhodes got out and scampered up three steps to an impressive mahogany door, entered a security code on a keypad, and hurried inside. Just like that she was gone.

Pike had ached for this moment. Played it out in his mind. Now it was here and he was paralyzed by his own fear.

He'd stood trial for involuntary manslaughter, *the Commonwealth of Pennsylvania vs. Pike Graves.* He once did a ride-along with Dewayne, venturing into the highest crime infested areas in Philadelphia where even well-trained cops feared for their lives. He stepped into countless rings as a sparring partner, literally a human punching bag, getting pummeled and beaten by those perfecting their craft. Pike's job was to stand there and take the hits. Yet he couldn't find the courage to walk forty yards and say hello to the woman he was destined to be with.

He opened the car door then closed it. He got out, eyed the breathtaking mansion, then sat back down, cowering. He gripped the steering wheel. His heart pounded in his chest. The mahogany door opened and Paige floated out angelically. She popped the trunk and pulled a suitcase.

Pike frowned.

She carried the luggage with ease to the front door, moved below the expensive chandelier hanging over the entrance, then abruptly turned.

She looked back.

୧ଉ୧ଉ

Vinyl admired her latest forgery. Across the bottom of President George H.W. Bush's picture she'd written, "Read my lips. I always stay at The Roosevelt." She almost fell out of her chair when someone materialized at the counter. "Dude, you almost gave me a myocardial infarction."

"A *what?*" the man wailed.

"Heart attack."

"Why didn't you just say that?"

"I like big words."

"I have something big for you."

"Your ego?"

"No, my dick."

"Ha." Remembering she was working, she switched to her professional voice. "Welcome to the Roosevelt. Can I help you?"

"You sure can." He displayed what he thought was a flirty smile. To Vinyl he appeared constipated. "I need a room."

She leaned forward and tapped away on an ancient Mac. "We have several available."

"Duh!"

She sneered at the rude guest, regretting not saying they were booked. But looking at him, she realized they shared an appreciation for ink. This guy only had one visible but it was unlike any tatt she'd seen before. Pointing to his left hand, she asked, "That an iguana?"

"No, a dragon."

"Looks like an iguana."

"Dragon on my hand, python in my pants."

Vinyl looked at him like a mother disapproving a child's action then went back the computer. "Single or double?"

"An old friend of mine checked in. And I do mean old. Name 'a Pike Graves." He waited. When she didn't confirm or deny, he pushed. "Right?"

"I can't release that info."

"Because?"

"That's confidential information."

Dragon was deciding how to pry it out of her when lady luck intervened in the form of a housekeeper. "I put those towels in fourteen-oh-two for Graves."

Vinyl slouched.

Dragon smiled. "Fourteen-oh-four available?"

ↄﾟↄﾟↄ

Returning to Larkspur and entering the makeshift parking lot inserted between The Roosevelt and a Chinese restaurant, Pike scolded himself. "Coward."

It was unrealistic thinking he'd find the right words in a week if he hadn't found them in eight years. Part of him wanted to just wing it. Walk up, knock on the door, say "hi" and see how it would play out. After all, he was the new and improved Pike Graves.

But his old self prevailed. He'd plan, strategize, and go back tomorrow. Would one more day really matter? Getting out of his Honda, Pike approached the hotel's entrance.

Something slammed against the back of his head. The cement came up to meet his face. Everything went dark.

ഗ്രഗ

Pike woke in a fog. Vision blurred, cheek to the ground, the first thing coming into focus was a plank of wood split in two. Apparently the weapon that knocked him out cold. Aggressively turned over, he was met by a hideous face.

A bald-headed man crouched over him, sweating profusely and looking around with a panicked gaze. He wore a raggedy oversized suit jacket likely lifted from a dumpster and had a bare, sunken chest. Breath was a mixture of whiskey and diseased gums. A boxer's nose, protruding chin and a faraway look in wild, bloodshot eyes.

"That's it?" The vagrant slapped Pike's face with his own wallet. "Seventy-three fucking dollars?" Spittle flew from his cracked lips.

Pike ineffectively reached for it but the attacker tossed it aside and began rifling through his pockets.

Please, not my car keys. He lifted his head but nausea washed over him and he almost blacked out again. He then realized it wasn't car keys the homeless guy was after. It was worse.

The wild-eyes enlarged as the homeless man stared at the felt box that Pike had kept hidden under the floorboard in his bedroom closet.

"You can't have that." Ignoring the dizziness, he sat up.

A switchblade appeared out of nowhere and pressed against Pike's throat. "It's mine now." The man coldcocked him in the side of his head, laying him flat-out on cold concrete.

Paige.

He'd come too damn far and kept the box too damn long.

"I hit the motherlode!" The deranged man's voice echoed through the alley as he gleefully scampered away.

Pike was in the ring again, on the mat and dazed. This time, however, he was no sparring partner. This time, he'd fight back.

Pivoting on his hip, he overlooked the faintness and the vertigo and got onto all fours. A homeless woman perched on a stoop behind her shopping cart, watching with great interest while eating from a bag of popcorn.

Standing now, Pike skewed left, steadied himself against his car. He took rapid deep breaths. Shook his head as if a fly was buzzing his ear. Squinting, he saw the man getting away and took off running.

The guy was so engrossed doing a happy dance at his good fortune, he didn't hear approaching footfalls and was knocked onto his ass.

"Gimme that!" Pike hissed, prying the box from the man's filthy fingers.

"No!" The mugger's other hand came up, sunlight reflecting off the blade that swiped at Pike's face.

Pike slanted back, narrowly avoiding the knife by inches. He elbowed the guy's arm, sending the switchblade skipping along the asphalt.

An arm hooked around Pike's waist and hoisted him upright. Another man assisted the mugger to his feet and asked in broken English, "You all right?"

Two workers from the neighboring Chinese restaurant saw what was happening and intervened.

The bald-headed attacker spat a clump of blood which landed on Pike's shoe. "We ain't done!" He dashed away, flipping Pike the bird, and disappeared into the sunset.

"You okay?"

Fortifying his hold on the box, he knew it was time to turn the page and get Paige. "I will be."

CHAPTER 28

"Hey."

Eight years. Over three thousand days. Crossing three time zones and eleven states totaling more than thirty-four hundred miles. And all he could come up with was "Hey."

Standing in the entryway, Paige stared into a memory. It looked like him, sounded like him. But it couldn't be him. "Pike?"

He curled his mouth, hiked one shoulder.

"Oh, my…Pike!"

He closed his eyes and allowed his senses to be overcome in her embrace. Clinging to her, promising to never again let her go. It felt good. It felt right. The way it was meant to be. Eight years, three thousand days, eleven states, three time zones. But not a minute had passed.

Paige broke the hug but extended his arms. "Wow, Pike, look at you."

"You haven't changed at all."

Paige rolled her eyes. When Cynthia did that, it grated on his nerves. With Paige, it was charming. "You're silly."

Her blonde hair was in a bob. Face slightly drawn, a few lines around her eyes, still thin. Her indigo eyes, bright and enthralling, hadn't lost their glint and still shone brightly. Outfitted in a scruffy white T-shirt, unbecoming drab running shorts and yellow rubber gloves, Paige ruffled her hair. "You should've called first. I'm all sweaty and stinky from cleaning the bathrooms." She made a show of sniffing her armpits. "Whoo boy."

Not even remotely close to what he anticipated. *Cleaning the bathrooms.* "Nah, you look great."

"Pike Graves. In the flesh." She stepped closer, entering his personal space and tousled the hair at his temples.

His mind journeyed back to the last time he felt her touch. The airport. She was leaving. Their last goodbye. She'd held his face. He turned and kissed her hand. He almost did it again.

"A touch of gray," she noted, "but it looks…debonair."

"Me, debonair? That's a first."

She laughed. "Debonair in a Pike-y way."

Now he laughed too. "Thanks for clarifying."

"You look good." Patting his belly, she added, "A little thin, though. You need a good woman to put some meat on them bones."

Pike blushed. "Yeah, I guess."

"And what? First time you see me in seven years and you don't bring flowers. Jeez-oh-Pete, what's a girl to think?"

"Eight years."

Paige's forehead creased. "Eight, you sure?"

"Positive."

She glimpsed over her shoulder. "Yep, eight. You're right." She turned him to see the name on the back of his authentic Phillies jersey. "Lenny Dykstra, huh?"

She remembers. "Favorite player from the ninety-three league champions."

"I thought it was John Kruk."

"I loved Kruk. But no, Lenny was my guy."

Paige smiled wanly. "I guess I forgot."

Pike swallowed. "It's okay. It's been a long time."

"Eight years."

"Yep, eight years."

Their eyes locked in an uncomfortable silence. "So," she said after a delay, "What're you doing out here? Business or pleasure?" Leaning right, she looked past him. "Did you drive? I thought I saw that same car yesterday. How're things in our old stomping ground? Still living in the same place?"

Pike opened his hands. "What's with all the questions? I thought I was the reporter."

"Huh?"

"The *Inquirer*." He waited. "Where I used to work."

She frowned. "You did?"

He forced a smile. "It was long ago. My most recent job was at fuck."

"*What?*"

"Sorry." He hammily smacked his head. "This rag sheet called the *Franklin Union Chronicle*. People call it F-U-C. Fuck."

"Oh."

"Sorry."

"For what?"

"Cursing."

She waved it away. "It's okay."

"You didn't become a nun or something, did you?"

"Me? I think if I walked into a church it would erupt in flames."

Pike laughed a bit too loud.

"Funny, I don't remember you working for the *Inquirer*."

He nodded.

"Guess I forgot."

"It's okay," he offered. "It's been—"

"Eight years. Right."

Another quietness.

They broke it simultaneously then tripped over each other with the back and forth you-go-no-you-go-no-go-ahead. "I was in Vegas and decided to drive up to see you."

"Vegas?" she whooped. "That's not exactly The East Bay."

Pike didn't know what that meant. "Lots closer than Philly."

"True, true. Stephanie's in Vegas, right? How's she doing?"

She remembered my sister. One small victory. "Doing well," he lied then piggybacked it with another falsehood. "She said to tell you hi."

"Oh? Well, that's nice. Tell her I said hi back." She paused. "Last job, huh."

"Huh?"

"You said your last job was at that *Chronicle* place. Past tense."

"I'm…kinda between jobs."

She shook her head miserably. "Yeah, times are tough all over. That why you went to see your sister? Thinking of starting a new life in Vegas?"

Ouch. "Maybe. Just gonna see how things play out."

Stroppy silence.

Paige broke it, commenting matter-of-factly, "Wow, Pike Graves."

"Wow, Paige Rhodes." His laugh sounded artificial. Filling

the silence, he said, "Speaking of wow, look at this place. It's massive."

"So is the mortgage."

"You must be doing well."

She waggled her head. The gesture drew his eyes to a gold crucifix hanging from her neck. He didn't recall her being religious. But then again it'd been eight years.

"I'm doing okay."

"More than okay, I'd say."

Paige withdrew as if embarrassed by her wealth. "One benefit from my gig at Pepperdine was meeting plenty of rich kids. And rich kids have rich parents. I never knew tennis was such an aristocratic sport."

"Oh?"

"Not like golf but yeah. And those people know investments. Garth can keep his friends in low places. I prefer having friends in high places."

Pike briefly frowned. "Oh, sure, Garth Brooks. So you're into country music now?"

"I always was."

Pike didn't recall that. "Do you still play?"

Paige twisted her mouth. "Music? No, I never did."

"I mean tennis."

"Nah, too old."

"Stop. You're not," he insisted.

"Time eventually catches up to all of us."

"You're never too old to start over," he claimed. *Ironic way of phrasing things.*

"Start *over*?"

"Well, not over. But, ya know, you're only as old as you feel."

"Some days I feel old. I do miss playing but I just…can't anymore. Plus, I'm too set in my ways to start over."

Too set in my ways. His heart skipped a beat.

Paige expounded. Something about mutual funds and stock portfolios and derivatives. Pike nodded vacantly. Her lips moved, words came out, but details were white noise. It was apparent things weren't going as hoped. He was adrift at sea, the water was choppy, the undertow pulling him away from shore, and he was trying to cling to any trivial piece of flotsam to save himself from drowning.

"Are you listening to me?"

"Definitely."

"Then what I'd just say?"

Pike turned red. "Uh, Garth Brooks?"

She chuckled hysterically and punched his shoulder.

"I was, I was," he feebly protested and then steered the conversation to calmer waters. "Mill Valley's a great place to live. Sammy Hagar lives here. Janis Joplin and Jerry Garcia once owned homes here too."

"That's right," she responded slowly.

He rocked on the balls of his feet. "Ta-dah. See, I know stuff."

"How?"

"Huh?"

Paige looked at him "How *do* you know? What're you, stalking me?"

Pike contorted his face. "No, of course…no."

"You never could lie to me."

He grinned. "Busted."

"About stalking or lying?"

Pike opened his mouth but before he could likely put his foot in it again he was saved by a plump middle-aged Hispanic woman surging through the doorway. "Senora Rhodes, Senora—oh, forgive me, *por favor*."

Paige stepped aside. "Pike, this is Estrella. Estrella, this is Pike, someone I knew long ago."

Pike offered his hand which Estrella gripped with a strength that contradicted her size.

"Estrella's my domestic assistant," Paige announced. "*Assistant*? Listen to me. She runs this whole place."

"Nice meeting you, Estrella."

"You as well, Senor Pike."

Paige said, "Estrella's my inspiration."

"Senora Rhodes, *que payaso*."

"I'm not being silly," Paige said to Estrella then faced Pike. "She and her sister, Lucia, crossed over the first time in 'eighty-nine. They left their entire family behind in Sinaloa. They were sent back but tried again two years later. That time they made it up to Bakersfield where they found jobs as migrant workers. They slept eight to a room and worked twelve hour days six days a week. She and her sister earned ninety dollars a week and sent half of that home."

Estrella interjected. "I would've worked seven days but if I didn't go to church Sunday, *mi madre* would be angry." She gnarled her face. "And you don't want to see *mi madre* when she gets angry. *Muy* loco."

Everyone laughed.

"She became a US citizen," Paige bragged, "and is currently enrolled at Contra Costa College."

"That's terrific, Estrella," Pike replied then scolded himself for talking loudly. She was Hispanic, not deaf.

"She knows more about US history than I do."

"*Que payaso*," Estrella good-naturedly giggled.

"You do. She does. Go 'head, Pike. Ask her something."

"Uh, who was our sixteenth president?"

She looked to heaven and shook her head. "*Es muy facil.* Abraham Lincoln."

Pike spiritedly rubbed his hands together. "All righty then, sixteenth amendment?"

"That grants permission to Congress to levy an income tax without apportioning it among the states or basing it on the census."

Paige beamed like a proud parent.

Pike made an *O* face.

Estrella was on a roll. "And since you like *numero dieciseis,* the sixteenth state to join the union was Tennessee. And Georgia and Michigan have sixteen electoral votes."

Paige and Pike shrugged at each other. "I guess."

Estrella clasped Pike's arm. "Would you like to come in, Senor Pike?"

"Good lord," Paige laughed. "Now you see why I'm useless without her. How rude of me." She met Pike's eyes. "Do you have time?"

"All the time in the world."

ↄ◌ↄ

The décor was cheerful and lively, expensive and classy, without being haughty. Porcelain koalas were everywhere. Her interest in the marsupials must've been something new.

While Paige showered, Pike sat in the informal dining room where Estrella brought tea and condiments on a platinum serving tray. Resisting the urge to ask for Grey Poupon. Pike commented, "This is a big house for one person."

Estrella smiled. "I live here also."

"Oh?" Pike thought of Cynthia. And Alexandra. Shuddering, he pushed that from his mind. "Still pretty big for two people."

"It was, how you say, left to her."

"Oh?"

"Her...*la bisabuela*, um, great grandmother, was very, very wealthy."

He smiled. "*Mucho dinero*."

Estrella laughed hoarsely.

Pike knew from the outset he'd be fighting an uphill battle. The prosperity of Mill Valley, sitting in Paige's lavish home surrounded by authentic looking paintings, and being served tea in little cups by a servant, he felt invisible forces aligning against him.

Punching at Fog.

Paige was no fool. Pike, unemployed, and materializing out of thin air on the doorstep of an old girlfriend worth millions because he regretted letting her go? *Yeah, right.*

His reporter instincts kicked in and he created a timeline. Eight years ago, she said nothing about her wealth. Had all of this happened since Cora's funeral? And if she hit the motherlode prior to Pike losing his mom, why had she remained tightlipped? Was she ashamed for some reason? Did she fear coming off snobby to an ex who barely made it to the next payday.

Paige bounded over and lowered herself opposite Pike at the oak dining room table. Opposite, not beside.

She'd applied lipstick and eye liner as well as diamond studded earrings he hadn't noticed before. The body wash she used electrified Pike's senses. What was most noticeable, however, was the baseball cap on her head. "The *Giants*?" he groused. "You're a Philly girl."

"Hard not to get swept up."

He feigned disappointment but, man, she looked adorable.

Daintily using tongs to sophisticatedly lower two sugar cubes into a mug, she announced excitedly, "Guess who I saw? Tony De Luca."

Tony. Pike's stomach tightened. "Who's that?"

"You don't remember Tony?"

"Nope."

"She was in Cohen's World History class our senior year."

"She?"

"Yeah, Toni. Antoinette. You don't remember her?"

Toni was Antoinette. Pike could breathe again. "Nope."

"She sat next to me and you sat behind me." Blushing at the memory, Paige reminisced. "I remember you leaning forward to copy off me but I think you were just peeking down my shirt."

"That wasn't me."

Her face scrunched. "No?"

"I had Coleman for World History."

Paige dismissed the oversight. "Anyway, Toni was out here on business a couple weeks ago and we went to lunch. Had a great time."

Pike nodded blankly as Paige recounted how she and Toni reconnected until he heard her say, "Toni found me on Facebook and—"

"You're on Facebook?"

"Who isn't?"

"Oh. I, uh, looked for you. Ya know, not too often, but occasionally."

"I go by my middle name. Paige Taylor."

Feeling chilled, he gripped his mug tighter. He never knew her middle name.

"Mom loved Liz Taylor." She patted his hand like a mother soothing a wounded child. "It's okay. Can't expect you to remember everything about me."

Pike had no answer.

"So, anyway, where are you staying?"

"Larkspur."

"Nice town."

"Seems okay but the motel sucks." As soon as the words left his mouth, he regretted it. Here he was, out of work and staying in a derelict motel while Paige lived in a huge estate. He hoped he wasn't coming off like a freeloader looking for a place to stay. It was the first time he concerned himself watching every word and concerned how she would take it. Speaking from the head, not the heart. Walking on eggshells.

Paige asked, "You okay?"

"Yep, just thinking."

"You look…pale."

Pike made a gesture with his hands that even he didn't know what it meant.

"Was it hot driving up from Vegas?"

"Very."

"Hit traffic in Fresno? It's always bad down there."

My God, this is what we've become. Weather and traffic. Pike anxiously picked at a scuff on the table that wasn't there. His eyes searched the prodigious interior. Perhaps, somewhere amongst the impressive fireplace, glimmering French tile, spotless granite countertops and Rembrandt's and Van Gogh's, he could find the right words. He brought his eyes back around where they were met by a look of concern.

"Something wrong, Pike?"

He swallowed.

"Are you…sick?"

"Sick?"

"Ya know, dying?"

He laughed glumly. It was the same thing Stephanie asked. He gave Paige the same answer. "Technically we all are."

Paige looked away.

He took a deep breath, laughed nervously, narrowed his eyes, moved his hand toward hers, then drew it back. "Listen, Paige, I…uh, have something I need to say."

She became rigid, her hand moving toward Jesus hanging around her neck.

"I've wanted to say this a long time. I'm…well, I'm not sure how…I mean, I don't want this to…who's that?"

Tilting back in her chair, she looked down the hall toward the front door. The amorous expression was one Pike had never seen.

"That's my family."

CHAPTER 29

Dragon regarded his rap sheet like a code of honor, once suggesting to his parole officer cops should offer a Frequent Arrest punch card. Every nine times you get busted, you get a pass on the tenth. Possession of a controlled substance, possession with intent, assault and battery, public urination, possession of an illegal firearm, and countless moving violations.

Add breaking and entering.

Dive, indeed. No security cameras in the corridor, a musty stench hanging everywhere and a piss puddle in the elevator. No wonder it took him all of twelve seconds to pick the lock. He confidently entered room 1402 as if it was his, not Pike's.

They came from opposite worlds, sharing nothing in common other than they'd both banged Cynthia.

Dragon was thrilled learning she'd finally kicked his pathetic ass to the curb. Anyone with half-a-brain could see she was just using him to better herself. How Pike Graves could go to Villanova and still be so dense was hilarious.

Dragon didn't go to an Ivy League school, nor had he even finished high school. But he was shrewd enough to see Pike and Cynthia would never last. The two of them were like oil and…water? Vinegar? Whichever. Cynthia was restless and always yearning for something better, something new. However, she also wanted to be free and reckless and wild. Deep inside, Dragon doubted he'd ever get her back, but he also knew she'd never sever the ties between them.

She talked down to him like a retard. Gave him shit about his weight. Busted his balls about drugs. Once she commented "Ya know, your dick's kinda small." For the next three hours, he showed her how her how *small* he was. She couldn't walk for days.

In those rare, reflective moments, Dragon accepted he was a shitty father. He never wanted kids and often wondered if Cynthia pricked a minuscule hole in the condom. The fact that his daughter spent her formative years raised and brainwashed by Pike's holier-than-thou bullshit pissed him off. Dragon played no role in Wynter's life. But it infuriated him that Pike did.

When Cynthia proposed the idea of offing the sorry son of a bitch, he enthusiastically agreed. He found it hard to say no to her. Maybe he, too, was on some invisible tether. Pike would be permanently removed from having any role in Wynter's life. The money was damn nice. And hey, homicide could get him another hole in his punch card.

He now looked behind drapes, under the bed, opened accordion closet doors, and drew back the shower curtain but couldn't decide where to hide and wait for Pike.

A ping alerted him of a text. *Call me.* He entered the number. "I was just thinking of ya."

"Oh?" Cynthia sounded pleased.

"Sure. My dick's throbbing."

"You're disgusting," she said, though Dragon knew she liked that kind of talk. "What's up?"

"Just told you. My dick's what's up."

A louder laugh. She told him to write down a number. He looked around, only now realizing his fingerprints were everywhere. *Shit.*

He lifted a notepad and jotted down sixteen numbers. "What's this?"

"Pike's credit card."

❧❧❧

Déjà vu all over again.

Pike refused to consider Roxy was underage, just as he refused to consider Cynthia had played him. The writing was on the wall both times but he chose not to read it. Just like now.

This palatial home was clearly too much for only Paige and Estrella. But his research/stalking revealed nothing about family. Had Dewayne missed something? Pike held out hope. 'Family' could be an uncle or cousin. Nephew, maybe? There was family and then there was *family*.

Out of sight, speedy footfalls echoed down the marble-tiled hall. "Hi, Mommy!"

Pike's heart broke. Paige a mom? A *mom*? He felt like he was at sea again with nothing to cling to. And now he *was* drowning.

Family could be *just* a son, right? No, she would've said son. Family could be two kids, couldn't it? Pike looked around for a family photo. Or better yet, a back door to get the hell out.

"Pike," she called, "I'd like you to meet someone."

Struggling to his feet, the room spun. Shaking off vertigo, he lumbered on unsteady legs to the sound of her voice.

Paige grimaced in discomfort when standing after hugging the small boy. "This is my son. Aiden. Aiden, this man's name is Pike."

Like artillery fire, all of her many smiles boomed through his memory: The one when the Phillies rallied for four in the bottom of the ninth, the one when she and Pike saw the Flyers defeat the Penguins in double overtime, the heartwarming one after they made love the first time, and even the one when he told her he was found innocent in the death of LaMarcus King.

This smile was different. She glowed. She sparkled. Like his mom, Aiden wore a Giants cap. Five, maybe six-years old, jeans he seemed to be growing out of, one shoelace untied and a t-shirt announcing *One boy demolition crew*. "Hi Aiden."

"Hi Pike."

"Go over and say hello."

Aiden slinked behind his mom, suspiciously sizing up the stranger.

"He's shy around people he doesn't know," she explained.

Picking up on the boy's reluctance, Pike took a knee so they'd be eye-level. "Can I shake your hand?"

Aiden's smile revealed he'd recently lost a baby tooth. He accepted the hand.

"You're a strong boy. You shake hands like a grownup."

He beamed.

Pike humorously toppled onto his butt. "Ow, not so hard. I think you broke my fingers."

Aiden giggled.

Pike noticed a strange expression cross Paige's face. One he couldn't identify. Then she told her son, "Estrella made some cookies."

Aiden's chin dropped and his eyes enlarged. "Chocolate chip?"

"I don't know. You should go see."

He started running away then ran back and wrapped his little arms around her waist. "I love you, Mommy."

"Love you too."

The supposedly shy boy tugged on Pike's arm. "Didja want some cookies, too?"

"How about later?"

"Okey dokey." And off he went.

"Seems like a great kid," Pike said.

"He is."

"Kind heart."

Paige shone like the proud parent she was. "Yeah."

"Takes after his mom."

She clucked her tongue and gestured for him to follow.

Pike lagged behind as they went to the door. *Family.* Maybe an uncle or cousin had driven Aiden home, right? Possibly a neighbor who she considered family.

The moment he reached the threshold, Pike witnessed the truth. No uncle, cousin or neighbor would be nuzzling Paige's neck. She giggled bashfully as a man squeezed her ass. It was the same bashful chuckle as decades ago when Pike started smooching at inappropriate times.

Paige guided the man from an Escalade. Her hand around his waist, his remaining on her backside in a proprietary way.

"Howdy," the guy called out.

Pike started chewing his lip. Offering a lackluster half-wave, he sized up his apparent competition. Square-face, thin lips, and long neck, he had slicked-back black hair and gangly arms. Reedy. He wore an open suit jacket and had ghostly-white skin. Probably worked in some career where he stayed inside all day rigging the system in a way to make a fortune while sticking it to the little guy. And worst of all, who the hell says *howdy.* Coming down the stairs, Pike's head tilted up. The guy was a few inches taller.

"Pike, this is Trent Lynch. Trent, Pike Graves."

If the name meant something to him, Trent didn't show it. Self-assuredly, he threw out his arm like parrying with a saber. "Glad to meet you, dude."

Dude? Yeah, I definitely don't like this guy. They pumped hands, Pike adding elbow grease to affirm his manhood. Trent either didn't notice or didn't care. "Good meeting you, Trent."

Trent. What a pussy name.

Still wearing that asinine grin, Trent asked, "So how do you know my fiancée?"

Pike was unsure if the San Andreas Fault ran through Mill Valley, but suddenly the ground was rolling beneath his feet. The rumbling of two tectonic plates pushing against each other was drowned out by the sound of his heart shattering to a million pieces. "Fiancée?" He faced Paige.

She absentmindedly kicked at an unseen pebble while Trent's left hand shot up and rotated a gold band on his ring finger. "Two days now."

"Two days," Pike echoed. That explained why Dewayne's research came up empty. She was engaged, not married. Eight years. Eight fucking years. And he was two goddamn days too late. If only he would've left the night he learned of Cynthia's ongoing affair or not wasted time with Roxy or not gotten stuck in Kansas City or not detoured to Phoenix to settle an old score when there wasn't even a score to settle or not tried reconnecting with his sister in Vegas or…or…or…

Two fucking days. Forty-eight fucking hours.

Sounding small, Paige announced, "Trent didn't want to wait until our big day to start wearing his ring."

"Isn't that sweet?" Pike hissed. "Where's yours?"

"He decided to give me both the engagement ring *and* wedding ring when we exchange our vows."

"Isn't that against tradition?" Pike argued feebly.

"Tradition?" Trent scoffed. "Screw that." Unabashed, he planted a kiss on Paige's lips. "She's a great girl. Why not brag to the whole world, right?"

"That she is," Pike agreed.

Cheerily, Trent punched Pike in the bicep as if they were old college buddies. "How do you know my girl anyway?"

"We go way back. I've known her forever."

Paige's expression hard to place. "Yep."

"I'm in town doing a piece for my employer." Pike puffed out his chest and melodramatically paused. "*The Philadelphia Inquirer*. Thought I'd look her up."

Paige squinted but didn't reveal his lie.

Trent frowned. "What's that, a newspaper?"

"Yes."

Trent took on a look of pity. "I didn't think anyone reads those anymore."

"Those who like staying informed do," he countered.

"Not me. By the time you get it, its old news. And really, who has time to follow what's going on in the world anyway?"

"Newspapers are tradition," Pike reasoned.

"I'm not a traditional type of guy."

"Apparently not."

CHAPTER 30

Pike took an immediate abhorrence to…Trent. Tent. Trench. Whatever his name was. Who the hell names their kid that anyway? But as the day passed into history, he came to terms with a bitter truth. He had no one to blame but himself. The one-time sparring partner had been hit with the most lethal blow of all. He'd lost Paige.

It was foolish to think she'd be single. Preposterous to think he was the only one who saw what a great catch she was. For eight years, he dawdled. For eight years, he hesitated. For eight years, he'd been living in the past while Paige moved into the future.

At least he'd learned the truth. She was engaged, in love, and had a family. He wanted to be happy for her. But it shredded his heart.

It was childish to dislike Trent. Hell, he didn't even know the guy. Sometimes you just have to tip your hat, say "well played" and move on. Or try to.

But how? The heart knows what it knows.

Pike had known Paige since high school. Communication between them diminished when she left for California and became largely non-existent over the past eight years. Still, he knew each her smiles. The way she threw her head back when laughing, the way her brows creased when listening intently, the way she sometimes ended her sentences with an uptick, the way her hand went to her neck when anxious, the way she liked being touched, the passion in her eyes when she wanted intimacy. He knew all of her mannerisms and expressions.

Or thought he did.

Watching her embrace her child was one he'd never seen. And it excruciatingly drove home the most stinging realization of all: Paige cherished being a mom.

And Pike, unable to conceive, could never give her that.

Trent was fit, healthy and looked younger, early-forties. He worked in Silicon Valley for some dot com firm. Pike nodded when he thought he should and threw in a generic comment here and there but was utterly clueless what Trent was talking about. The guy was overly animated and well-caffeinated. His arms gestured wildly when talking. Sometimes his words jumbled together.

But Paige seemed happy. And, in the end, that's what mattered. *At least someone makes her happy.*

They sat in the backyard sipping a chardonnay Pike was unfamiliar with. He was in a quandary. He wanted to leave, yet he had nowhere to go. Seeing Paige this joyful warmed his soul while simultaneously mincing his spirit. He wanted to concoct some excuse to leave but once he walked away, he'd never see her again.

One more final farewell.

Trent was relating a story about a vacation he and Paige took to the Bay of Kotor in Montenegro when Pike came to realize Trent was the better man. If the roles were reversed, he'd never be welcoming to the unexpected reappearance of someone from his fiancé's past. Was Trent that self-assured or was Pike that insecure?

"Daddy, daddy!" Aiden raced from the house and leapt onto Trent's lap. "You know what, you know what, you know what?"

"I know you're getting too big to jump on me."

"My friend Braydon, right? He just got a puppy."

"Uh oh."

"Can we get one, can we, can we?"

"If Braydon got a snake, would you want one?"

"Umm, yeah."

Laughing, Trent looked at Paige.

"Your father and I will talk about it later."

Aiden persisted. "We can get one now and I'll have him potty-trained before school starts."

"That's a lot of work."

"I can do it. *Please.*"

"We'll see, okay?"

"C'mon, please!"

Trent said, "Your mother and I will talk about it later."

Aiden shifted on his father's lap, folded his arms across his chest, contorted his little face, and chewed his lip.

Paige, in a mom voice Pike didn't know she possessed, firmly stated, "There'll be none of that, young man."

"But I wanna puppy!"

"Aiden!"

His lip quivered.

"Aiden, your mom and I will talk about it, okay?"

"I guess." He slipped his hands into his pockets and, head hanging, trudged away like his world was crushed.

Smiling, Trent looked at Pike. "Would you like a child?"

Stab through the heart. "Yeah, I would."

"Last week he wanted rabbits," Trent pointed out.

"And before that a lizard," Paige reminded him.

"Remember last Christmas?"

Paige burst out laughing at the memory. She enlightened Pike. "He was adamant we buy him a reindeer, preferably one with a red nose, so he could fly to the North Pole."

Trent chimed in. "Rather than waiting for Christmas, he wanted to pick up his gifts from Santa himself."

Pike's smile was artificial. Reminiscing about funny memories and sharing family tidbits was unfamiliar territory to him. Unsure what prompted the question, he asked, "So when's the big day?"

"Saturday."

"*This* Saturday?"

"I know, huh." Trent said. "Day after tomorrow."

"Kinda quick, isn't it?"

"Why wait?" He looked at Paige seeking clarification. "Right?"

"No time like the present."

Trent again. "Nothing big. Just family and a few friends. My brother's letting me borrow his Cessna. We'll fly down Saturday morning."

"You're a pilot?"

"Absolutely."

"Down where?"

"Cabrillo National Monument."

Paige enlightened, "That's on the Point Loma peninsula in San Diego."

Pike was grasping at straws. "Are those Cessna's even safe?

Can you get married at a National Monument? And on such short notice?"

Trent's eyebrows danced. "Money talks."

Dancing eyebrows. Pike always hated dancing eyebrows. "Sorry I can't make it."

Trent shot an unsure look at Pike, then Paige. And diffidently smiled. Paige stared hard at Pike, mouthing *what are you doing*?

Pike met her stare.

She broke contact.

Trent patted her knee. "By the way, how's Kristen Chamberlain?"

Paige forlornly shook her head.

Trent matched her somber expression. "Too young."

"Forty-one."

Pike frowned. "Who's Kristen Chamberlain?"

"This really sweet patient at the hospice."

Pike kicked himself. He never thought to ask what type of work she did. "You work at a hospice?"

"Yes. Bereavement counselor."

Thanatophobia. "Isn't that…depressing?"

"Not at all. People are themselves at the end. No games, no ulterior motives. You see them at their most vulnerable and when they are most real."

Trent slanted over and kissed her cheek. "She's their angel. And mine, too."

Paige waved it away. "It's nothing."

"That's why I love her," Trent avowed smugly. "She sees it as nothing, but to others she's everything."

Pike remained quiet.

As if forgetting Pike was there, Paige asked her fiancé, "What's the latest with that IPO and SO-Tek?"

What followed was a cacophony of white noise. Trent and his partner were close to securing a big contract with a firm in San Mateo. The receptionist at Paige's doctor's office was pregnant. The Bryant's were having marital problems. The water heater was going. The Garland's youngest daughter miscarried. Ray Arias was being deployed to Afghanistan. Paige's Volt was rattling. Margaret from the country club got a bad sunburn during her cruise.

For the guy suffering Thanatophobia this was the final nail in his coffin. Paige not only moved on, she moved on with Trent. They shared the same friends, knew the same people. Their lives had become one, intertwined, and woven together. Pike pushed himself to his feet. "I should get going."

Trent stood. "It's been great meeting you."

Paige stayed seated.

"You also." This handshake contained no extra elbow grease.

"Are you out here often?"

"Nope, first time."

Trent said, "Any friend of Paige's is...well, a friend of Paige's." A laugh, followed by another playful punch in the shoulder. "Just kidding. You're always welcome to visit."

"Thanks." Pike's voice broke due to the lump in his throat. "But I won't be coming back."

Paige slowly got out of her chair. She squinted at Pike then looked at her fiancé. A hug, a kiss? What's the appropriate good-bye?

Pike, like always, was in synch and saved her the trouble by offering a hand. "Take care of yourself, Paige."

Ignoring the gesture, she whispered something to Trent.

Listening, his brows came together, his eyes glued on Pike. Then, "Why don't you have dinner with us tomorrow?"

Pike looked at Paige. She met his look but remained expressionless. This was up to him.

"I'd like that."

CHAPTER 31

Pike swung his legs out of the car and found himself mired in quicksand. Using the Honda's fender for support, he righted himself. The quicksand transformed into a viscous river and he found himself walking on water. Ascending a gentle rise, he entered a hospice and somehow intuited to turn left. He gave his name to a wheelchair-bound man at a desk.

Franklin Delano Roosevelt looked up at him. "We've been expecting you, Mr. Graves. You have nothing to fear but fear itself."

"Thank you, Mr. President."

Pike navigated an unremitting labyrinth. Overhead fluorescent lights cast eerie shadows in the corridor while rooms were cloaked in darkness. Except one. Stephanie was on her back, Virgil Holland between her legs, ferociously thrusting. His sister reached for him. "Help…me…Pike."

He ignored her pleas and strolled to the last room dead ahead. From the entryway, he saw Paige seated at a patient's bedside, peacefully stroking a woman's sickly hand. "Come in, Pike," she said without looking back. "It's okay."

But it wasn't okay. "Oh, God." His world went dark. His lungs deflated. The dying woman in the bed was also Paige.

"Graves!"

Pike spun.

Jordan Moses, wearing his customary white straw hat, nodded once and walked away. Pike knew to follow. Instead of the hospice hallway, he was plunged into an impenetrable forest.

Sunlight unable to penetrate the wooded canopy. Fearing he'd lose his way, Pike jogged to keep pace with Jordan. Coming to a clearing, Jordan stepped aside, allowing Pike a closer look.

Cautiously, he skulked forward. A bottomless grave extended into the depths of the earth. Teetering on the lip of the infinite abyss, he noticed a tombstone listing his name and date of birth. His date of death, however, was not there. Jordan handed over a chisel, subconsciously telling Pike to engrave the missing death-date. "I can't always save your ass."

Pike jolted awake. His feet tangled in the sheet, a blanket and two pillows lay discarded on the floor. A third pillow clutched against his chest. He took several deep breaths and wiped perspiration beading the small hairs on the back of his neck.

A splinter of daylight cut through a gap in the gaudy drapes. The nightstand clock read six-oh-nine. Pike tasted dried blood in his mouth, the result of chewing his lips all night. "Forty-seven going on seven," he griped.

He stood, alarmed how shaky he was, rearranged the linens, and plodded to the bathroom. After relieving himself, he used a cloth to dab the blood. Finished, he crossed the motel room and opened the drapes. Morning light hurt his eyes but it was a welcome contradiction to the disconcerting nightmare.

As alertness returned, something clicked. The lurid dream was frighteningly realistic and chilling, but also fortuitous. Just after nine a.m. back east. It was an easy decision. It was the right thing to do. Pulling a frayed business card from his wallet, he punched in a number on his cell.

"Freedom Securities and Investments. Can I help you?"

"Hugh Willhoite, please."

"Who may I say is calling?"

"Pike Graves."

He endured instrumental versions of "Eleanor Rigby," "Thriller," and "Witchcraft" before a voice from the past picked up.

"Pike Graves, as I live and breathe." Hugh never aged. Seventy-five but sharp as a tack, he possessed twice the energy of people half his age. He'd sporadically use a mock British accent to make himself sound erudite and did spot-on impressions of Bob Dylan and Walter Cronkite. More importantly, however, he'd been a family friend since before Pike was born and was a key player in helping Sam Graves accrue his fortune.

"Mornin' Hugh."

They bantered a bit before Hugh asked, "What can I do for you this lovely morning?"

Pike told him.

Hugh was uncertain. "You're sure about this?"

"I'm not sure about anything anymore, Hugh. But this? Yes."

Hugh explained what needed to be done and Pike spent the morning faxing the necessary documents. By noon, everything was in place.

 handbook

Cynthia Grimm was anything but grim.

She woke to Alexandra's face between her legs. That girl's mouth was a gift. Cynthia reciprocated—and then some—when they showered together. On her way out the door, she took a prolonged look at the furniture. Pike's furniture. She'd already gotten rid of boxes of his crap that he'd left behind. The furniture would go next. The new living room set was on the way and should arrive in a few days along with the custom-built F-350 she special ordered. Alex disagreed with her decision to keep the bedroom set.

"I don't like sleeping in the same bed *he* did."

"That's what makes it *so* kinky," Cynthia had responded.

"I know, but still…"

Cynthia held Alex's face. "Every time you make me come, it's like I'm getting back at Pike."

It was a divine day in Philadelphia. Traffic was light, motorists actually yielded, the grumpy security guard in the lobby was atypically friendly. Cynthia, wearing a new power blue business suit, could practically hear birds singing.

Coming around the bend to her office, her male secretary flounced from behind his desk. "Oh. My. God."

"What is it, *Gayvin*?" She never tired of calling him that, the little fruit.

"Janice Haas."

Cynthia's brows rose hearing the name of the geezer in the corner office with the killer view. "Go on."

"She tripped in the parking lot and broke her hip."

"Really?"

"Yes. Can you *believe* that?"

Everything in *Gayvin's* world was always exhilarating. This time, though, she had to agree.

"Rumor going around is she may retire early."

"That's a pity." Cynthia winked and went to her desk, deciding how she'd redecorate that senile old coot's office.

Booting up her computer, she mulled over the best way to take advantage of Janice's mishap. She'd come up with a reason to talk to Morty about something, then cunningly drop hints about Janice's best days being behind her. Assessing her appearance, she pouted. Too bad she looked business-professional today. Something low-cut would have worked better to keep Morty's attention.

She spent the morning dealing with the graphic arts department to formulate an advertising plan for the Wilkins account as well as closing a deal with Mayfield Furniture. She doused a potential fire by agreeing to lunch with Ryan Farrell who was thinking of his taking his account to a competing firm.

And through it all, the smile stayed plastered to her face. The day got even better when she received an incoming text from Alex. Her girlfriend had sidled off to the ladies room while at work, and behind a closed stall, took a topless selfie with the message, *we miss u.*

Miss both of u 2, Cynthia texted back.

At lunchtime, she accessed online menus for nearby restaurants. Since it'd been a couple of days, she decided to access Pike's accounts.

The birds stopped singing.

e/ɔe/ɔ

Bobby Dragovich lay in bed, hands clasped behind his head getting a blow job, thinking about, of all things, September 11, 2001.

He was getting released after serving sixty days on a petty larceny charge when every cop, DA, and lawyer stared at the TV. The more Dragon heard, the more he realized those towelheads were kickass.

No, he didn't comprehend why some *A*-rabs or whatever they were would fly planes into buildings. He didn't know why they hated America. Sure, Dragon wouldn't mind banging fifty virgins but flying a 747 into a skyscraper was extreme, even to get laid. What struck a chord was hearing they'd gone to a titty bar the night before.

He now stared up at the water stained ceiling in room 1404

telling himself *Tonight Pike Graves will die.*

There'd be no repentance. The guy was so self-righteous and pompous. Even the way Pike looked at him. Like Dragon was dog shit. Like Dragon was inferior. Screw that, Mr. Pike stick-up-your-ass Graves. Tonight, I'll show you dog shit.

The kill almost happened this morning.

The Roosevelt was a dump. Paper thin walls. Every time someone closed a door, the entire hallway rattled. Dragon wanted to sleep off his hangover but instead that Graves asshole next door kept going in and out all damned morning. Dragon was tempted to put a bullet in his brain right then and there so he could go back to sleep.

Deciding to wait, he showered, dressed, and followed the trailblazing path of those towelheads. The beer at The Eager Beaver was overpriced and the topless dancers left much to be desired. No wonder they worked early. There were a total of five men present, and that included Dragon, the bouncer, and a bartender tapping away on his phone.

One of Dragon's biggest regrets was never having screwed an Asian chick. He'd heard somewhere they were willing to do anything, so when he saw one polishing a pole with her ass, he decided to end his dry spell.

He hung around until her shift ended, bought her a drink, then another. It took less than ten minutes to close the deal. Riding up in the Roosevelt's creaking elevator, he stated, "I ain't never fucked no Jap chick."

"I'm not Japanese," she said. "I'm Hawaiian. Keilana's my name" She offered a handshake like a CEO.

Dragon noticed her small hands. He liked small hands. They made his pecker look bigger. Missing teeth would make for a better blowjob too. "Jap, Hawaiian? Same shit, right?"

"For an extra fifty, I can act Japanese."

He didn't know what that meant.

Now, lying in bed and formulating a plan to off Pike, Dragon had almost forgotten about her. Unlike those camel jockeys, he wouldn't sacrifice himself, even for a *hundred* virgins. Looking down, he asked, "Are you through yet?"

"Almost."

For a whore with no teeth and little hands, she'd unmistakably failed in dick-sucking class. "I'm giving you five minutes to make me shoot my wad. If not, you ain't getting' that twenty bucks."

At two minutes he was stiffening.

At three minutes he was close to releasing.

At four minutes, his cell buzzed. He shoved Keilana's face away and sprang up without checking the display. "*What*?" he screamed.

"What the hell?"

"Cyn?"

"Yeah."

"I'm kinda busy now. Can this wait?"

"No."

Dragon groaned, whispered to the Japanese-Hawaiian chick, "one minute," then said into the phone, "What now?"

"Are you alone?"

"Yeah, sure."

"Are you?"

He turned to Kilauea, or whatever her name was, put a finger to his puckered lips. *Shhh.* "Yes, I'm alone."

"I don't think you are."

"Jesus Christ, Cyn. *What*?"

She could always see through him. Uncannily, through a phone, too. "Call back in five when you're alone." She hung up.

"Bitch," he said to the dead line.

"Don't call me that," Keilana cooed. "Unless you want to pay more, then you can."

Dragon pulled a twenty from his wallet and tossed it at her face. "Go buy some dentures, whore."

She crawled catlike across the bed. "I can do the whore-thing if you like that."

He thoughtfully rubbed the corners of his mouth. "Yeah?"

"Watch me."

☙❧☙

"What took you so long?" Cynthia roared twenty minutes later.

"I was finishing up something."

She didn't want to know. "Where are you?"

"In my room. And yes, I'm alone."

"It's done."

"Done?"

"It's finished. Done, over, finito."

Dragon, wearing only white socks, was pacing. "What do you mean?"

Cynthia spoke slowly so he'd understand. "I was about to go to lunch and decided to pull up Pike's accounts because it'd been a few days. I'm not listed on them anymore. I even called his financial advisor, an old fart named Hugh Willhoite. He told me he couldn't discuss anything 'cause I'm no longer beneficiary. Something must've happened that reminded Pike and he took my name off."

"Does this mean what I think it means?"

"Yes. Pike dies and I get nothing. Pike gets killed, I get nothing. You see what I'm saying."

Suddenly woozy, Dragon collapsed into a shabby chair. After mulling things over, he said, "Who's the new bena-whatever and I'll kill them too."

"Jesus, Dragon."

"Who is it?"

"I don't know."

"You're lying."

"I'm *not* lying. I don't know. They wouldn't tell me. They *couldn't* tell me. I'm not on the accounts. Don't you get it?"

Dragon was on his feet. "Then I'll call, pretend to be Pike, and put you back as bena-whatever."

"It won't work. They need a form with Pike's signature. Plus, I found out he changed his password. Even if I wanted you pretending to be him, you can't."

This was evidently the reason Dragon heard so much coming and going from Pike's room this morning. "So...what are you saying?"

"I'm saying forget it. Mission aborted. Game over. We tried, we lost. He won."

"Uh huh."

"Not a big deal. Just...just forget the whole damn thing."

Dragon parted the curtains. The entire neighborhood, derelict and downtrodden. Topless bars, pawn shops, hubcap businesses, adult book stores. He had a criminal record, a daughter who wanted nothing to do with him, an ex who was a condescending bitch. And he just pissed away twenty bucks on some toothless slut who barely got him hard. "No."

"No?"

"No, Cyn."

She stammered. "Wh—what do you mean, 'no'?"

"I mean no. Mission's *not* aborted. It's *not* finito."

"Dragon?"

"I'll come home after I kill him. And when I get there I expect that two hundred-forty thousand."

She smirked. "I don't have that kind of money."

"Find a way to get it."

"You think money grows on trees?" Cynthia reprimanded herself. *Sounds like something Pike would say.*

"I don't know where money grows. But I'm a man of my word. When I say I'm—"

"You?" Cynthia crowed. "*You* a man of your word? Oh, *puh-leeze.*"

Patronizing again. It sent Dragon's rage through the roof. Ignoring her sleight, he stayed on point. "Here's what we're going to do. First—"

"There's no 'we're', okay."

"Fine. Here's what *I'm* gonna do. I'm going to kill that fucker like we planned. Then I'll come home and you *will* pay me."

She tried sounding strong but her voice lacked conviction. "You're threatening me?"

"You pay. Or I'll kill Alex."

"*What?*"

"That's right. You pay me after I kill Pike. You *don't* pay me and Alex will be next."

"You're lying."

"Two hundred forty thousand, Cyn." And he terminated the call.

CHAPTER 32

Pike looked up and down the street, then at his watch. Six p.m. and no sign of Paige and Trent. With the altercation involving the vagrant fresh in his mind, he debated waiting inside. Then again, seeing the Roosevelt's clientele, that wasn't much safer.

Pike had played tourist all day. He partook of the various shops and sights at Pier 39, enjoyed a scrumptious lunch at Fisherman's Wharf, walked around historic Haight-Ashbury, and drove to the summit of Twin Peaks. Under different circumstances, it would have been enjoyable. But the best moments in life are those that are shared. He merely went through the motions, killing time, until tonight when he'd say goodbye.

A black Escalade with opaque windows pulled curbside at six-thirty. "Sorry we're late," Paige said through the powered-down window.

"No worries." Looking past her, he curbed disappointment. He knew her fiancé would come, but he'd hoped that maybe…"Hey Trent."

"Yo. Isn't that what they say in Philly?"

Pike offered a crooked smile, buckled himself in the backseat behind Paige and ruffled Aiden's hair. "Hey, buddy."

Completely engrossed in a game on his phone, he ignored the greeting.

"Aiden," Paige said over her shoulder. "Pike said hello."

Pike joked, "Technically, I just said 'hey, buddy.'"

"That's not the point."

He decided to leave parenting to parents.

Pulling into traffic, Trent asked, "How come you're staying at a shithole like that?"

"Trent!" Paige howled, cocking her head toward Aiden.

He amended his question. "A *place* like that?"

"I saw billboards advertising it coming into town."

Trent met Pike's eyes in the rearview. "You *drove*?"

"Yep."

"I thought the *Inquirer* sent you here."

Oops. He noticed Paige shift nervously. Pike was a journalist, not a novelist. Fiction wasn't his forte. "To Los Angeles actually."

Trent nodded to himself. "How long did it take to drive up?"

It was a role reversal, the investigative reporter getting grilled. With no idea of driving time from Los Angeles to San Francisco, he replied noncommittally. "Not too long."

"How'd you come?"

"By car."

Trent sneered. "I mean which freeway?"

Blocking for Pike, Paige interjected. "Why's that matter?"

Trent glared at her. "Doesn't matter one bit."

A few moments later, she broke the edgy quietness. "What'd you do today?"

Pike answered but obviously no one cared. Trent stared straight ahead, Paige inattentively bobbed her head, and Aiden butchered zombies. When Pike stopped talking mid-sentence, no one even noticed.

Pike was in a navy blue dress shirt hanging loose over black jeans and sneakers. Paige outfitted in a gray top, form-fitting white pants and sandals. Trent was dressed to the hilt in a leather bomber jacket over a starched white shirt and perfectly creased black slacks. "You come straight from work?" Pike asked conversationally.

"No." Nothing more.

After more obdurate silence passed, Pike leaned closer to Aiden. "Are you winning?"

"These zombie asshole are everywhere!"

"*Aiden*!" Paige squealed.

"Well, Mommy, they are!"

"Where'd you learn that word?"

"Asshole?" He shrugged. "I dunno."

"*Aiden*!"

Pike managed not to laugh while Trent smiled. Paige looked at the three of them. "Boys will be boys."

కావం

"Where're we eating?" Pike asked casually.

Trent replied, "A pizza place in Corte Madera that the kid likes."

"The kid has a name," Paige snapped.

Pike pretended not to notice the palpable tension between Paige and Trent.

Mouth tight, Trent revised his statement. "*Aiden* likes it. It's one of those places where they have carnival games but the food tastes like shit."

Paige gave her *mom* look to her fiancé. "And I wonder where *the kid* learns bad words from."

Trent looked at her, pushed his tongue into his cheek, and tightened his hands around the steering wheel as if strangling it.

కావం

The south end of the sprawling shopping center was ringed with restaurants, sports bars, and local fast food joints unfamiliar to a Philadelphian. Growing frustrated at the inability to find a parking space, Trent reminded everyone, "I didn't want to come here."

Pike noticed Paige, either consciously or subconsciously, angle away from her fiancé.

"Screw this." Trent squealed into a handicap spot, slammed the SUV into park, and showed Paige his hand. "Don't! I've got the thing, all right?" Hostilely, he retrieved a handicapped permit from a pouch and threw it on the dash. "Happy?"

"It doesn't even look real," she sighed. "And what if someone who really is handicapped needs this spot?"

Trent looked back. "*You* wanna spend twenty minutes drivin' around?"

Caught in the middle, Pike mumbled something to avoid taking sides.

"Exactly!" Trent barked and bolted out of the Escalade.

"C'mon, sweetie," Paige said. "Let's go."

C'mon, sweetie. Let's go. Pike knew it was meant for Aiden, but still…

It seemed bad business to name a restaurant after someone

who murdered twenty-one men but Billy the Kid Pizza was packed.

Bringing up the rear, Pike winced hearing the joyful screams of wound-up children mixed in with resounding bells, shrill whistles and droning buzzers. He felt a migraine coming on. Paige, however, was immune to the ruckus. Apparently parents tune it out.

The top two levels served as a dining area where the adults could watch the activity on the lower level. The bottom tier served as the arcade, housing video games, car racing contraptions, skee ball, target shooting games, whiffle ball tic tac toe, basketball hoops, and so on.

They sat at a red and green picnic-like table. Trent, Paige, and Aiden on one side, Pike alone on his. Various mascots—a dog with floppy ears, an octopus, a gorilla, and old-time gunfighters—milled around. "Pretty loud in here," Pike noted.

Trent turned this way and that. "Where's the damn waitress?"

Paige inhaled. "Give her a minute. They're busy."

Animated as always, Trent channeled his inner Keith Moon and began drumming on the table. A family nearby gave him a look. Trent drummed louder. Paige folded in on herself. A moment later, she said, "Honey?"

Trent looked at her. So did Pike.

Contriving an upbeat tone, she suggested to Trent, "How 'bout you get tokens for Aiden and I'll order when the waitress comes by."

Trent's head swiveled between Paige and Pike, deciding how he felt leaving his fiancé alone with someone from her past. Could he sense Pike still held her in high regard? That he still cared for her. "How 'bout I wait outside instead." With a flourish, he indignantly marched off. Aiden didn't react, the boy immune to his father's temper.

The waitress showed up seconds later and Paige ordered for the four of them. When Aiden asked for a root beer float, Paige said, "No," then relented. "Oh, okay. Extra cherries please."

"Yay!"

Pike looked around. No sign of Trent. If there was one last chance to confess his feelings it was now. Leaning forward, he clasped his hands and realized impulsiveness wasn't his strong suit. For eight years the appropriate words never came. Not while crossing the rust belt, the prairies, the mountains, and the desert had he figured out how to tell Paige what was in his heart. It was irrational to think that now, being granted only a few minutes, he'd find the right words. But he needed to. Time was running out.

"Paige, I—"

"He's got a lot on his plate right now."

"Trent?"

"Yes. This IPO thing is stressing him out."

"Sure."

"He is a good man."

"Of course."

"He's got a good heart."

"Understood."

"He just, well, stresses sometimes."

"You don't need to explain anything to me."

"Don't I?"

Pike narrowed his eyes. After a strained silence, he said softly, "I don't know, do you?"

Her hands went to her neck, something she did when troubled. "Would you do me a favor?"

Pike smiled. "For you? Anything."

She rifled through her purse, pulled a ten from her wallet. "If you wouldn't mind, can you get tokens for Aiden?"

He waved away the bill. "I got ya covered." Standing, he patted the boy on his shoulder. "C'mon, kiddo."

Aiden, beaming wide, took Pike's hand and pulled him toward the arcade. As they walked away, Pike looked back.

Paige was dabbing the corners of her eyes.

∾∾∾

Pike was surprised enjoying the boy's company. He'd forgotten what it was like to derive pleasure from simple things. He and Aiden shot some hoops, played two games of skee ball and three games of whiffle tac toe. Pike lost every time.

"You're letting me win."

"No way. You're really good."

"Bullshit!" Aiden giggled.

Pike looked toward where Paige had been, didn't see her, and dropped to a knee. "You really are winning. No bullshit."

Aiden giggled louder.

Moments later, after Pike knocked over six plastic bottles with two lobs of a ball, he waved his arm at dozens of suspended stuffed animals. "Which one do you want?"

Aiden's eyes bulged. "I can pick *any*?"

"Yep."

"Cool!" Aiden wrinkled his face. "Umm…that one. No, that one on the end."

The attendant handed over a plush Grim Reaper. *Thanatophobia*. Not what Pike would've gone with.

"Having fun boys?"

Pike jumped. The touch, the warmth, the energy. He looked down. Paige's hand was in his.

Surprised by what seemed natural, she turned beet-red and quickly pulled free. "Pizza's on the table. We're waiting for you. Me and uh…"

"Trent."

"Yeah, Trent."

☙❦❧

Fresh air apparently did wonders for his sour disposition. Had Pike imagined the other Trent Lynch? Had he wandered into *The Twilight Zone*? Pizza and bread sticks were divvied up, conversation lively, and smiles abundant.

Paige, sitting at an angle and no longer having a problem remembering her fiancé's name, played doting mom, making sure her son was well tended to. Seeing her in action and hearing passing comments about how cute other kids were left no doubt she was cut out for motherhood. And in twenty-four hours, she'd be Trent's wife. The probability they'd give Aiden a brother or sister hurt Pike's heart. Unable to conceive and feeling like less of a man because of it drove home the point he had no place in her future.

Aiden pointed. "Mommy, mommy. Look!"

"Don't talk with your mouth full." She turned peculiarly to look back. "Oh, no."

Trent echoed her lack of enthusiasm.

Aiden was bouncing in his seat. "It's him, it's him!"

Spotting a character in head-to-toe black like an old-time gun-slinger, Pike asked, "Who's he supposed to be?"

Aiden yelled, "Wyatt Burp."

"Wyatt *Burp*?" Pike laughed.

Paige lamented. "Kids love him, but parents? That's another story. He's the most popular character here."

"Why Wyatt *Burp*?"

Trent explained. "Eight silver buttons on his duster, each one makes a different burping sound."

"I didn't think there were that many."

"See for yourself. Here he comes."

"Howdy, folks," Wyatt said, fingering the brim of his Stetson.

"Howdy, Marshal," everyone said in unison except for Pike.

Wyatt winked at Paige. "Hello to you, little lady."

Playing along, she batted her eyelashes and extended her hand which Wyatt promptly kissed.

"No tongue this time," Trent warned jokingly.

"You're an ace-high lady."

"Thanks…I guess."

The waitress threaded her way around Wyatt and dropped off the check. Trent reached for it but Pike was quicker on the draw. "I got it."

"Thanks, dude."

"No problem."

Wyatt again. "You folks enjoyin' your time here in my town?"

"Absolutely."

Wyatt's gaze swept the table. Twirling the end of his mustache, he scrutinized Pike. "You're not from 'round these parts, I reckon. Just come in off the stage?"

Pike thought he looked more like a guy playing Kurt Russell playing Wyatt Earp. Or maybe he'd watched *Tombstone* too many times. "Nope, not from 'round here."

"Dodge City?"

"Philadelphia."

"Ah, the old states. My friend Doc went to school there. Pennsylvania College of Dental Surgery."

As a dozen youngsters gathered around and parents recorded the entertainment on their phones, Wyatt continued. "Scuttlebutt has it that those Clanton scoundrels are shootin' their mouths off again. Would you fine folks know anything 'bout that?"

"No, Marshal."

"Ike, that blowhard, he's gonna be pushin' up daisies in the bone orchard if he doesn't simmer down some."

"Can I push a button?"

Wyatt backpedaled, pretending to only now notice Aiden. "Who do we have here?"

"Aiden."

"Pleased to make your acquaintance, Aiden." They shook hands.

"Can I push a button? I wanna hear you burp."

"I don't know 'bout that. I'm plum tuckered out from ridin' the range."

"Oh, please."

He addressed Paige. "Ma'am, has he been good or has he been a rascal?"

"He's been good."

"Sir?"

"He's always good," Trent confirmed.

"We have to strike a deal, young man."

"A deal?"

"I'll burp for you on a few conditions."

"All right."

"You're gonna listen to mommy and daddy ev'ry day, okay?"

"Yes."

Wyatt shook his head. "That's not the right answer. When I say okay, you say corral. Okay?"

"Corral."

"Gonna listen to mommy and daddy ev'ry day, okay?"

"Corral."

"Gonna stay in school and mind your teachers, okay?"

"Corral!"

"Gonna brush your teeth ev'ry night before bed and wash behind those ears, okay?"

"Corral!"

"You're not gonna play with guns, okay?"

"*Corral*!"

"Not gonna gamble, okay?"

"*Corral*!"

"Not gonna visit a house of ill repute, okay?"

Aiden knotted his little face. "What's a house of—"

Paige jumped in. "Corral, Corral, Corral."

"All right then, *podner*. Push away."

For the next several moments, Wyatt Burp burped, belched, eructed, hiccupped, gulped, posseted, and made a few noises that sounded more like farts. Aiden couldn't stop laughing. Pike, Paige, and Trent tried acting like mature grownups but got caught up in the hilarity.

At the conclusion of the burp-fest, Wyatt tipped his hat to his adoring fans before taking on a serious tone. "I read in our local newspaper, the *Tombstone Epitaph*, someone's having a birthday." Over his shoulder, he shouted, "Morg, Virg. Skedaddle on over 'ere." Seconds later, Wyatt was joined by two identically dressed hombres. One of them, either Morgan or Virgil, presented a plate with a birthday cake and three lit candles.

"Which one of you fine folks is Pike Graves?"

Paige pointed. "He is!"

Pike had been so wrapped in everyone else—Roxy, Virgil, Stephanie, Jordan, Paige—he'd lost track of the date. Checking his watch, he now realized it was his birthday, July nineteenth. He feigned an angry look at Paige for embarrassing him.

She winked. "I remembered."

She remembered. "I'm gonna get you back for this."

She laughed and stuck out her tongue. "Take your best shot."

"Happy birthday, old man," Trent said.

"Thanks."

With the Earp's gone, Paige sliced up the cake. The waitress who'd been lingering apprehensively crouched beside Pike.

"That's impossible," he insisted.

"What's wrong?" Paige asked.

"They're telling me my card was declined." To the waitress, "Can you run it again?"

"I did, sir. Three times."

"That can't be. I used it this afternoon."

Trent came to the rescue. "It's all good. I got it."

Pike grew warm. Accepting he had no place in Paige's future was bad enough.

Having his credit card rejected in front of her and her fiancé was downright humiliating. It was a hell of a birthday.

"Must be a mistake," Paige claimed gently.

"I guess."

"It can happen to anyone."

"Never happened to me," Trent asserted.

"I don't know how—oh, yes, I do." *Cynthia*. She was the likely culprit. But why? There was nothing left between them. She'd stolen from him, taken advantage of his trusting nature, and openly cheated on him. But this? It showed how vindictive she could be. Pike wondered what else she was capable of.

The waitress returned.

"No problem, right?" Trent asked arrogantly.

"None at all. Thank you."

Maybe it was Pike's imagination but the waitress seemed to give him a pitiful look before going off to tell her co-workers about the deadbeat birthday guy in her section.

"Let's get some air," Trent demanded, getting to his feet, cracking his knuckles, and throwing his chin at the door.

"Uh, sure."

Paige frowned at her fiancé then shrugged at Pike. *I don't know.*

Pike went wide-eyed. Something erupted in his gut. Something he never felt before. Never. Riding over, he sat behind Paige. He brought up the rear when they entered the pizza joint. When she came to the arcade to retrieve him and Aiden, she kept her head down. During the meal, she straddled the bench seat. When turning to see Wyatt, she turned peculiarly.

It wasn't until this moment, seeing a full frontal for the first time all evening, that he noticed a bruise on her right cheek the size of a fist.

Pike Graves had taken the lives of LaMarcus King and Freddy Marquez. Those, however, had been unintentional. Seeing the shiner on her face, he knew for the first time he was capable of killing someone. And this time, it would be no accident.

CHAPTER 33

The weather had turned melancholy and overcast. Gale force winds sent debris skittering along the sidewalk. White bands of lightning streaked across the moonless sky. The gods were angry.

"Buckle up," Trent ordered, slipping behind the wheel of his Escalade. As Pike did, Trent pulled a snuff box from a compartment on the door, opened it, snorted two lines of cocaine, pinched the bridge of his nose, and brought the SUV to life.

"I hope you don't do that with Paige and Aiden in the car."

"Your concern's noted." And he tramped on the gas.

Pike sensed what was coming but decided to play it cool. For now. "This is a nice ride," he commented conversationally.

"So is Paige."

Pike decided to hold his tongue. "Where're we going?"

"Just takin' a drive."

The outside world was obscured from behind tinted windows. Unfamiliar businesses, unknown streets. Pike was far from home.

"Why are you here?" Trent asked.

"You wanted to talk."

"I mean in my city."

My city? Perhaps he got too wrapped up in the whole Earp-Clanton dust-up. "What're you, the town sheriff?"

"And talking to *my* wife."

"She's not your wife."

Trent glowered. "She will be soon."

Despite being a stranger in a strange land, Pike's anger was on the upswing. "What happened to her face?"

Trent snickered.

"I asked—"

"I heard what you asked." Trent jerked the wheel right, flipped off a slow-moving motorist, and floored it.

"Then tell me."

"Aiden."

"Aiden hit his mom?"

"She tripped over his fucking bike. And since they're not here, I *can* say fucking. Now, answer me. Why're you here?"

Zooming past newspaper vending machines, Pike recalled one of the first stories he covered for the *Inquirer*. It took a lot for Philadelphians to be shocked but the case of Rick and Lara Wheaton riveted the city. It was one of the most brutal cases of physical, emotional, and sexual abuse anyone could recall. The DA had Rick dead-to-rights, but Lara downplayed the allegations and refused to press charges against her husband. The DA had no choice. Five weeks later, Lara Wheaton's limbs began turning up in dumpsters all over the city.

"I asked you something, *Pike*."

He had a decision to make. Were Paige and Lara alike? The girl he knew was strong-willed, independent, tough. He'd never known her to back down. She wasn't weak. But that was a long time ago in what seemed like another life.

Trent's backhand to his sternum snapped him back to the present. "Answer me!"

Fuck it. "I came for Paige."

"I see."

"I didn't know she was with you."

"She's not *with* me. She's *engaged* to me."

"I know that now."

Trent turned left down a snaking residential road and accelerated to fifty in a thirty.

"We're getting married tomorrow."

"I know."

"You're leaving tonight."

"That a question, Trent?"

"Man to man?" He theatrically paused. "It's an order."

"I see."

"No, I don't think you do."

"Enlighten me."

"You don't know me, you don't know the kid, and you sure as hell don't know Paige. Not anymore."

Pike ceded his point. "Fair enough."

"You can't make her happy. I can. I *do*."

"How'd she get that bruise?"

"But I know all about you, Pike."

"Oh?"

"I know you have no job, no money, and no one in your life. And I don't need a loser like you around my family. You're yesterday's news."

Pike persisted. "How'd she get that bruise?"

"I'm not an idiot. I see the way you look at her. And the way she *can't* look at you for fear I'll see it in her eyes. You think you're in love with her. But you're not."

"No?"

"No. You're in love with the memory of her. And maybe, shit, maybe she feels the same. But you're not kids anymore. She's moved on. You need to do the same."

"Thanks for the psychological evaluation, *Doctor* Lynch. How'd she get that bruise?"

Trent snubbed him. "There's plenty you don't know about her, my friend, plenty."

"I'm not your friend, Trent." Pike knew it was a futile comeback. But the passing comment sent his mind spinning. *Plenty you don't know about her.* Since beginning this journey only one thing remained true: Everything Pike knew, or thought he knew, was null and void. But this time it felt different. For once, his heart and his head were on the same page. "How'd she get that bruise, Trent?"

He nearly T-boned a Peugeot. "Told you. Aiden's bike."

"Sure."

"I want your word."

"My word about what?"

"That you're gonna pack your shit and leave. Run back to Philly, kiss your sister's ass in Vegas. I don't care. I want you gone. Tonight. You're bad luck." Trent squealed to the curb, slammed the car into park, leaned across Pike's chest and threw open the door. They were back at the Roosevelt. "Get out of my car, get out of my city and get away from my fiancé."

Pike extended one leg, then turned and bore his eyes into Trent. "How'd she get that bruise?"

Trent rolled his eyes. *Like Cynthia.* "Give it up. You had her, you lost her. Live with it."

"I'll leave. But, as you said, man to man?"

Trent sighed, bored and disinterested. "I can hardly wait."

Pike threw his finger at him. "You hurt her, you lay one finger on her. I don't care if I'm in Vegas, Philly, or the other side of the planet. I promise you, *friend.* I'll hunt you down and fucking bury you."

"Get outta my car. You're embarrassing yourself."

ৎৠৎ

From the fourteenth floor the entire city seemed shrouded in a surreal, netherworld aura.

Pike didn't like being a sparring partner any more than he liked being Trent's verbal punching bag. But in three hours since being kicked to the curb, he came to admit the guy was correct.

Tomorrow they'd become Mr. and Mrs. Lynch. Trent was her future. Pike was her past. And the past should remain buried in the past.

She had moved on. Now Pike would try to do the same. The ache in his chest came from not being able to say good-bye.

When first returning to his room, he paced for a good hour before swallowing what remained of his pride and made a call. "Hey, Steph."

"Pike?"

"Yep. How are you?"

"Um, okay. What's up?"

Pike listened for Karl in the background. "So, about that job and a place to stay?"

"Yeah?"

"I think, uh, I'll take you up on the offer."

A delay. "Oh?"

"Yeah."

A longer delay. "Sure, sure, all right."

"It *is* okay, right? You did offer, remember?"

Stephanie laughed anxiously. "Of course I remember. It's just that, well, the economy's tough and we're not hiring now but…things always pick up around New Year's."

Pike's throat went dry. "It's July."

The longest pause yet. "You wanted something *sooner*?"

Eyes closed, he chewed his lips. It was clear her proposal was a baseless gesture that carried no weight. "I was hoping."

"Oh? Well...I know a couple people I can call. May not be glamourous at first but...shit."

"What?"

"That extra bedroom? I was gonna turn it into a home office for Karl but...I can try and make it work."

Changing gears, Pike reminded her, "Today's July nineteenth."

"So?"

Paige remembered his birthday. His sister didn't. "Never mind."

He intended on leaving tomorrow morning rather than tonight as Trent ordered. At least he'd keep some semblance of self-worth leaving on his own terms. But observing the city seized by an eerie deathlike grip, he decided it was time to go. Being close to Paige knowing things were over was too agonizing.

ோைக

Dragon nursed his shitty beer looking around the shitty bar at all the down-on-their luck shitty people listening to shitty music from the shitty jukebox, incensed at the shit he'd gotten into and how shitty his life was.

He loved Cynthia. After all, she was the mother of his kid so he kinda had to. The fact she sucked dick like a porn star also helped.

He didn't hate Pike Graves. Not really. Truth be told, he didn't feel anything for the guy. He was just one of those dudes who got under Dragon's skin. When Cynthia first suggested the idea, it was a twofer. Get rid of Pike *and* get a big payday out of it.

But then Cynthia recanted and the plan turned to shit. *When Bobby Dragovich sets out to do something, he does it.* He sensed Cyn was jerking his chain. That line about Pike removing her as bena-whatever was a load of crap. He knew her longer than Pike, longer than that dike chick she was screwing. He knew she'd simply gotten a change of heart, cold feet, appealed to her better angels, and all that shit.

Incarcerated or on the streets, when someone gives you their word they better damn well deliver. Dragon would send Pike Graves to his grave. No compunction and no regret. With Pike out of the way, he knew she'd relent and pay him that money she promised. If she continued the line about not being bena-whatever, Alexandra would follow Pike into the ground.

"Want another one, bro?" asked the smelly bartender.

Dragon nodded. One more shitty beer, then off to room 1402 to put a bullet in Pike's skull and end this.

⸱ↄ⸱ↄ⸱

Paige told herself it was because Trent was overworked and jittery. And when he got like that, sex between them was forceful. Adding to Trent's understandable anxiety was the reemergence of Pike.

After coming home and sending Aiden to his room, Trent was rougher than he'd ever been. Never before had she been sore after intimacy.

He swiftly got out of bed and showered. That was something he constantly did after sex, as if cleansing himself of her. She never thought much of it. Tonight, it peeved her.

Why?

"Almost your big day," he said when returning. Within seconds, he was asleep. Even his snoring now vexed her.

She turned but couldn't see him clearly in the shadows swathing their bedroom. *Your big day.* Not ours. He'd made that remark before too. Weren't they both getting married? The wedding would be small but the following weekend they'd host a full-scale reception for friends, extended family, and co-workers. Paige had taken charge of ironing out all the details. Insight and feedback, even a little, from the groom would've been appreciated. Instead, he watched from the sidelines.

Vacantly staring at the ceiling, his snoring louder than usual, she admonished herself. *I'm about to marry this man! I intend to be with him, 'til death do us part and all that. Aiden needs an adult male in his life.*

Dammit, what's wrong with me?

Was she overthinking? Was it buyer's remorse? Paige once saw a Julia Roberts movie where she repeatedly leaves men at the altar and thought it was silly. Not anymore.

Paige was a middle-aged woman who'd never married. Was she too set in her ways to change? She and Trent lived together for years but something about making it official was tantamount to locking a dead bolt.

Was Trent the right one or just here at the right time?

Was it fate that brought her and Trent together?

Was it destiny that brought Pike to her doorstep days before her wedding?

And what was up with Pike leaving so suddenly? Trent claimed that while they were outside the pizza joint, he received a call from someone in Vegas that his sister had been in a bad car accident. Couldn't he have waited two minutes to say goodbye? In her heart, she felt Trent was lying. And lying to your fiancé hours before tying the knot is a bad omen.

Equally unforeseen was the way Aiden bonded with Pike. Her son was always cautious and timid around people he didn't know, something she blamed herself for. You raise your children to be respectable and friendly. In the next breath you warn them not to trust strangers. Although friends and neighbors told her repeatedly she was a wonderful mom, Paige made it up as she went along. She had no clue what she was doing.

Or what she was about to do.

ೞೞೞ

Thirty minutes later, wearing no makeup, gray sweatpants, a loose-fitting pink top, light blue Asics and hair tapping her shoulders, Paige crossed the lobby of the Roosevelt. She ignored the gawking of a man seated in a worn-out chair, the appraising look from a hooker sitting on some guy's lap, the stale air laced with cigarette smoke and Chinese food, and strode to the front desk. It took some cajoling but eventually a young girl named Vinyl broke motel policy. "He's in fourteen-oh-two."

"Thanks."

Paige impatiently tapped her foot watching the indicator light as the elevator took forever to come down four lousy floors. Once inside, she pressed *14*.

"Hold it!" The door was inches from closing when a hand slipped through activating the sensor. The door reversed and a man entered. On his hand, Paige noticed a tattoo resembling a dragon.

CHAPTER 34

Pike checked his room one final time verifying he was leaving nothing behind. *Leaving nothing behind.* Like the Tony Bennett song, he was leaving his heart in San Francisco. Lifting his suitcases, he opened the front door and was greeted by a raised fist.

"I was about to knock."

"Paige?" He looked around her. "Where's Aiden?"

Her bewitching eyes exposed love. An earnest heartfelt smile crossed her lovely face. A simple question speaking volumes. Arriving unannounced, his first concern was of her child. "He's home. We should talk."

He smiled falteringly. "I'd like that."

She entered, immediately noticing the duffels in his hands. "You're leaving?"

"Yes."

"For good?"

"Yes."

"Why didn't you say goodbye?"

Pike stalled. Closing the door, he lowered his gear and made a conscious effort staying outside her personal space. After all, she was almost a married woman. Unable to read her, he didn't know how to answer.

Her fiancé had likely concocted some story and Pike wasn't sure if he should throw Trent under the bus. Yet.

"It's best that I go."

As always, she saw through him. "If I have to ask everything twice, it's going to be a long night. Why didn't you say goodbye?"

"It would hurt too much."

Paige was stunned, both by the authenticity in his words and the void in her chest. "In the middle of the night?"

"Couldn't sleep."

"Seems to be plenty of that going around."

Nodding, he went for humor. "I'd offer you a drink but there's no mini-bar. Imagine that?"

She swept the substandard room then locked on him like a heat-seeking missile. "You don't think you deserve something better?"

Are we talking about the motel or something else? "Do I?"

"Why'd you come for me, Pike? Why now?"

Like a blind man without a seeing-eye dog, he was feeling his way. "Just seemed like a good time."

"Did you know Trent and I were engaged?"

"No."

"Had you known we were would you still have showed up?"

Pike took a deep breath. "Excuse me." He needed to sit.

Her hands went to her hips. "Would you have?"

"I don't know."

"And you were expecting me to…what, throw away my future for my past, throw away everything I know for something I don't? You're the regimented one, Pike. I'm the impulsive one."

"Why are you raising your voice?"

"I'm not," she yelled. Then smiled. "I should probably sit too." She lowered herself into a ragged chair, a disfigured wobbly table between them. "Why didn't you call and at least give me a heads-up?"

"Would you have told me not to come?"

She stroked her neck. "Maybe."

"Everything's not black and white, Paige."

"I love Trent."

Not since being pummeled in the ring had he felt such pain. "How'd you get that bruise?"

She pointed to her cheek. "This one?"

His stomach clamped. *How many bruises do you have?* "Yes."

"Aiden's fault."

"Oh?"

"I'm always telling him to put his stuff away but you know how kids can be."

"Actually, I don't."

Paige smiled despondently. "I tripped over his bike in the backyard."

Pike thought of Lara Wheaton who defended her husband until it was too late. "Right."

"I did," she maintained.

"Okay."

"Then why are you making a fist?"

Unaware, Pike unclenched.

"You think I'm lying? You think Trent beats me?"

Hands up like a traffic cop. "I'm not saying that."

"You're thinking it. I can tell."

Elbows on the table, he rested his chin in his thumbs and stared into Paige's soul. "Then tell me what I'm thinking right now."

Paige met his eyes then broke contact. "I'm not psychic."

"Never said you were."

"How would I know what's in your head?"

"Then what's in my heart?"

"I'm not a cardiologist either."

"Why are you avoiding my question?"

"I'm not."

"Yes, Paige, you are."

"Why'd you come, Pike? Why now, dammit?" Raking her hair, she continued. "Look at it from my point of view. You lose your job, your girlfriend's cheating on you, and poof, you show up on my doorstep."

"I know how it looks."

"I won't be anyone's rebound."

He almost took her hand then thought better of it. "You're not."

"Then what am I?"

Pike Graves's final stand. All this time, all these years, all the miles between them. And suddenly there was no time at all. The moment was at hand. The former sparring partner would pull no punches. "You're the one I should be with. The one I let get away. The one I lost. I fucked up, Paige. I admit that. I never should've let you leave." Breathing deep, he added, "The one…the one I'm in love with. The one I've never stopped loving. And never stop thinking about."

Arms folded across her chest, she leaned back. Instead of being moved, her eyes flared. "And you didn't realize that until Cynthia left?"

"I left her."

"Semantics."

"If I said yes, would you believe me?"

Paige stood, parted the curtains, and spoke to the fog choking the Bay Area. "I don't know what I believe anymore."

"Maybe things didn't work out with Cynthia, or anyone else, because it wasn't meant to be. Maybe you and I *are* meant to be."

"Maybe you're not thinking clearly."

"This time I am. In a life filled with mistakes, this is one thing I'm certain of."

Paige sat back down and bore her eyes into him. "I'm getting married tomorrow."

He grinned. "That's your problem, not mine."

Paige scowled. "Not funny."

He shrugged.

"Trent's a good man."

"I'm sure he is."

"But you don't think I should be with him?"

"You really want me answering?"

Paige curled her mouth. "No, probably not."

"What's in here?" he asked, pointing toward her heart.

"I'm not sure anymore."

This time he didn't pull back when reaching for her. Her fingers trembled. "Look me in the eye, Paige. Look me in the eye and tell me we shouldn't be together. Say it and I'm gone."

"I don't believe in soul mates."

"Tell me to go and I'll go."

She jerked her hand free. "Goddamn you, Pike Graves. Why'd you show up *now*?"

He offered a weak smile. "Better late than never."

"It's already late."

He grew rigid. "Meaning?"

"It's too late. *You're* too late."

"Paige, I—"

She cut him off. "You had your chance. I'm sorry but it's...no, this can't happen."

"It's not too late." His words weak, his voice cracking. Pleading.

"You should've stopped me back then."

"When?"

"At the airport. Why didn't you say something then? Why didn't you stop me from getting on that plane eight years ago?"

"God help me, I ask myself that every day."

"You stop me then and we're not having this conversation now." She brought her hands to her neck and shook her head forcefully as if willing everything to be different. "Goddammit, why'd you let me leave?"

Pike blinked away a tear. "I don't know. But I've never stopped beating myself up. If I could go back in time, I would."

"Isn't that what you're trying to do now? Go back in time? You had your chance. *We* had our chance. Now you want a second one?"

"I don't deserve one, but yes."

"I love Trent."

"You don't want to be with him."

Paige's brows went up. "Okay, Dr. Phil, why don't I?"

"You're too opposite. He drives an SUV, you drive a Volt. What more proof is there?"

She grinned. "Asshole."

"Things are looking up. We agree on something."

Paige stood, paced, sat back down. She massaged the back of her neck, pulled her chin, looked at her ring finger which was barren. Until tomorrow. "This isn't fair," she whispered softly.

"Life isn't fair."

Paige mirthlessly laughed. "Life isn't fair. Don't I know it?"

Pike creased his brows.

"We're not in high school. We've grown up and grown apart." Her eyebrows knitted in sadness. "There's an entire continent between us."

"And I crossed the continent to be here." He cleared his throat and sang a line from "Ain't No Mountain High Enough."

Paige shook her head and giggled like a high school kid again. They gave each other a sideways glance.

"I've changed," she said. "You don't know me. And…well, I don't know you."

"So?"

"You know what kind of food I like? What music I listen to or movies I enjoy? Do I prefer vacationing at the beach or the mountains? Were you there when I had my car accident? Do you know what my typical day consists of? Can you name even one of my friends? Where were you when I cried the first time I dropped Aiden off at Kindergarten?"

Pike had no answer.

She got up. "And you expect me to throw away everything because of something we once had? That's not fair to me. To *me*."

"Paige, please, sit down."

"It's late…in more ways than one."

"What do you want me to say?"

"I want you to wish me good luck and let me be with Trent. This…*shit,* you're killing me." Her shoulders were rising and sinking, her face flushing.

Pike rose and reached out to wipe away her tears.

She pivoted and went toward the door.

"Paige!"

He thought she was leaving but instead she went to the bathroom, blew her nose, returned, and sloped her head back. "Do I have boogers?"

Pike laughed. "And you're the one saying we're not kids anymore?"

Her smile was desolate. "Pike, I don't know how—"

"*The Graduate.*"

"Huh?"

"The theater in Conshohocken that played old movies. It was a Dustin Hoffman marathon. *Midnight Cowboy* and *Papillion* but *The Graduate* was first. That was the first movie we saw together. You wore a white sweater with light blue piping, white boots, and black jeans. The Green Whale down the shore was the first hotel we stayed at together. You got a bad sunburn because we forgot to bring lotion. Our first slow dance? 'Maybe I'm Amazed.' The front seat of my car was the first time we kissed. Your father's aboveground pool was the first time we made love."

Paige smiled, her lips quivered.

He continued. "You had a crappy rebuilt Plymouth Duster. Brown exterior, red interior, a sunroof that leaked and a tape deck that ate cassettes. By the way, you owe me *Slippery When Wet.* And speaking of Bon Jovi that was our first concert. At the Spectrum on the New Jersey tour. They opened with "Bad Medicine." We double-dated with Kaye Beckley and Al Foster to see Springsteen at the Meadowlands."

Paige twisted her face. "And I suppose you remember what I wore then too?"

"*Darkness of the Edge of Town* T-shirt and little white shorts. You had a sign that read, 'Dance with me, Bruce.'"

Her eyes watered.

"I bought you a heart-shaped pendant after you lost yours at a Phillies game. You always ordered the Fried Calamari at Luigi's, the sweet and sour pork at Ho-Wan's. We once spent two hours debating how they get the fortune inside the fortune cookie. You like vanilla ice cream, not chocolate, prefer Dr. Pepper to Coke, had a crush on Ralph Macchio, and hated James Spader."

"Well, he was mean to Ducky in *Pretty in Pink*."

"Tell me, Paige, tell me I don't know you."

She gave him a faraway look. "Now I like chocolate and hate Dr. Pepper."

His throat constricted.

"People change, Pike. I'm not the same person I was. I'm not a teenage girl or a college kid. I'm a grown woman."

Pike's heart misfired.

"You're trapped in the past. You're living with a memory of someone who no longer exists."

"Then we have plenty to catch up on." His smile was transitory, his words heavy, his tone beseeching. "Don't we?"

"I'm sorry." She turned away.

"Don't we?"

She half-heartedly waved without looking back.

"Paige, please."

When she turned, tears were flowing. "I'm sorry."

He wanted to hold her, feel their hearts beating in unison, to not let her leave again. But the truth was inescapable. She'd already left. Their time had passed.

He entered her personal space. She didn't retreat. When he held her shoulders, she didn't flinch. When he cupped her beautiful face in his hands, she closed her eyes. When he kissed away her tears, more tears came. "I'll always love you," he whispered.

She kissed his fingers, the way he did at the airport eight years ago. "I'll always love you too."

It was Pike who broke the embrace. "Go. I want you to be happy and…if it's with Trent, so be it."

"Thanks." The tears lessened.

"One thing?"

"Sure."

He inhaled deep. "I—have an account back home with Freedom Investments and Securities. There's—a good amount in there."

She frowned. "Oh—kay?"

"Earlier today I made Aiden my beneficiary."

The lines in her forehead deepened. Before she could say something coherent, Pike continued. "One point four million. I didn't come for your money, Paige. I came for you."

"But—"

"But nothing. Look," he said soberly, "I'm forty-seven. Well, forty-eight. I've got no one to leave it to. I missed out on your life but, I don't know, in a way, maybe I can be part of his." He shrugged.

"But—how'd you know?"

"Know what?"

"About Aiden?"

Pike frowned. "What are you talking about?"

Paige turned white. Like she said something she shouldn't have.

He chewed his lips. "I'm confused."

"Is that why you're leaving Aiden your money?"

The one-time journalist couldn't find the words. His mind swimming, his heart about to explode through his chest, his knees weakened. When Trent was driving back to the hotel, he told Pike, *'You don't know me, you don't know the kid, and you don't know Paige anymore.'* Why those words? Not *my* kid, not *our* kid. *The* kid. When Pike first showed up at Paige's door, she thought it'd been seven years. He reminded her it'd been eight. She looked over her shoulder, into the house before realizing he was right. What was she looking at? *Who* was she looking at? She mentioned it was unusual the way Aiden bonded with Pike because her son was typically shy around strangers. Unless…they weren't strangers. Not exactly. Finding the courage, he asked tentatively, "How old is Aiden?"

"Seven."

A lump rose in his throat. "Seven?"

"I thought you knew. I thought you could tell."

"I thought he was five or six."

"He's seven, Pike."

Pike never had kids. He couldn't conceive and wouldn't know the difference between a five-year old and a seven-year-old. "You're saying Aiden…Aiden is…"

"I flew home for your mom's funeral eight years ago. The night before I left we were together." She smiled demurely.

"That was our last time. I remember."

"You'd just buried your mom. You were hurting. I loved you. We missed each other. It seemed natural."

"But how?" He dropped his head shamefully and made a joke of it. "My soldiers don't march, remember? We went to that fertility doctor way back when. They said I had a one in a million chance of impregnating a woman."

"I guess Aiden's the one in a million."

"I have a son?"

"Yes."

"I really have a son?"

"You do."

"Does Trent know?"

"Aiden was two when I met Trent at support. I told him I didn't know who the father was. I even left that section out on his birth certificate."

Pike's heart crumbled knowing he hadn't been listed.

"Trent legally adopted him. He's the only father Aiden's ever known."

"Why didn't you tell me?"

"Why didn't you stop me from getting on that plane?"

"I don't know."

"I don't know either. Guess we're even." Paige wandered in a circle. "I figured you didn't want to be with me. I thought if you wanted to, you never would've let me leave eight years ago."

The silence was deafening. Just like that, in the wink of an eye, everything changed. If Paige had reservations about Pike coming for her money, she learned that wasn't the case. Yes, he was old-fashioned. Cynthia teased him about that repeatedly. Wynter too. His sister chided him about his archaic thinking. But he wore it like a badge of honor. Pike Graves always did the right thing. "Paige?"

"Yeah?"

He reached into his pocket.

Her eyes followed his hand. "Pike?"

He withdrew a black felt box.

"Pike?"

He dropped to a knee.

"Pike? What…"

He looked up at her.

"Pike, get up. *Please…*" Her words trailed away into the ether, her eyes closed.

Looking at her, he opened the felt box. "Marry me, Paige." There was limited light in the room as Pike presented the Tacori diamond engagement ring he bought decades ago. Waiting, just waiting for the right time. And that time was now.

She opened her eyes, shifting her glance between Pike and the box. She blinked, tried to focus through the tears. "Pike—"

"I know this isn't overly romantic. I never imagined it playing out this way."

"Pike, stand up."

"Everything's changed. Aiden's *our* child. Ours. Yours *and* mine. We're a family. Us. Not Trent."

"Pike, please get up."

"I've had this ring for thirty years. I've been keeping it. For you."

"It's empty."

Pike wrinkled his brows. "Empty?"

She gave him a sad look. "The box. It's empty. There's nothing in there."

Pike turned his wrist. His eyes went wide in shock. He'd moved on from Cynthia. He put three thousand miles between them. An entire continent. Yet, she was still affecting his life, still screwing with him. Would it ever end?

When he'd pulled the box from beneath the floorboard in the bedroom closet, he didn't bother opening it. He assumed Cynthia didn't know. He was wrong. When that vagrant mugged him and started running away, he, too, never looked inside. The box was empty, worthless. No ring. Trying to shove aside the anger, Pike continued pleading his case.

Paige said, "It's not that easy anymore."

Pike remained on his knees. Proposing? Begging? "Cancel the wedding. Call it off. Marry me, Paige. Make everything right."

She was unable to look at the empty felt box, nor the expression of desperation in Pike's suppliant eyes. "You don't understand."

"Then explain it."

Her eyes drifted to the parted curtains. It was easier confessing to the fog outside. "I'm dying."

CHAPTER 35

I can't believe this!"
Dragon stormed around his dilapidated room, punching the mattress, flinging pillows everywhere, ripping sheets from the bed, and slamming his fist through the drywall. "And I can't believe I'm talking to an empty fucking room!"

He was ready, psyched up, put on his game face. All that stuff. He'd gotten a blowjob like those towelheads on September 10, 2001, and a good buzz from the shitty bar down the street. He returned to the Roosevelt to retrieve his Glock, finally kill Graves, leave town, and get his money.

But everything changed when he saw the middle-aged broad in the elevator. Sure, she was dressed down, kinda homely, and not his type. She probably could be do-able with some makeup and hot clothes. As they rode up, he made a pointless remark. "Ain't this fog somethin'?"

She didn't even have the courtesy of answering, like she was preoccupied with something. What a bitch! No wonder she went into Pike's room. She didn't look like a hooker but nowadays, who could tell?

Killing Pike? Easy. Killing someone he didn't know? Not the same. Adding a homicide, if he got caught, would get another hole in his imaginary punch card. But *two* homicides?

When he wasn't pressing his ear to the wall eavesdropping on Pike next door, he plodded in a circle. If Pike was leaving with that chick, he'd blow his chance. And his money.

Dammit!

He kicked things around in his drunken mind. No time like the present. Isn't that what they say? The early bird gets the worm, right? Dragon slammed a fully-loaded clip into the Glock and steeled himself. He'd never taken a life before. But he valued having the power in his hand. God-like.

For a brief moment, he considered unloading a volley of gun-fire through the wall. That'd be kickass. But he'd deprive himself of actually seeing the fear on Graves's face. Maybe the guy would piss himself. Dragon laughed at that possibility. "Who's the better man now, you dumb shit?"

The knock at the door startled him. He hesitated, cautiously approached, and looked through the peephole.

He saw no one.

∽∾∽

"What do you mean you're dying?" Pike, still on his knees, his proposal having morphed into prayer.

She hiked her shoulders. "I'm dying."

Resorting to his old standby, he remarked, "We're all dying."

She smiled woefully.

He struggled to his feet then collapsed on the edge of the bed. He patted the area next to him.

Paige remained standing. "I have MS."

He closed his eyes.

"Multiple Sclerosis."

"I know what MS is. How?"

"How?" She laughed. "If I only knew."

"I mean how long have you known?"

"Aiden was two when I found out. That's where I met Trent. In a support group. His mom battled it for years." She lowered her voice. "There's no cure."

"I *know* there's no cure."

"Trent's been there for me. He's wiped my tears, encouraged me when I'm at my lowest, and puts up with my mood swings. He knows what to expect and he's preparing me for what's coming. It's not pretty."

She described how the disease attacks the nerve cells in the brain and spinal cord and, in turn, destroys the ability to communicate with the rest of the body. Trouble with coordination, sensation, double-vision or blindness, probable confinement to a wheelchair. Lesions would cover her body. "There's not only physical problems but mental ones as well. And this?" she said pointing to the bruise, "*was* Aiden's bike. I was moving it out of the way and blacked out."

Pike couldn't think of one damn thing to say.

"As your dad used to say, 'punching at fog,'"

He was beginning to loathe that term.

"Funny." She fingered the gold crucifix around her neck. "When I was young, my parents always wanted me to go to church. It took something like this to get me there."

Pike remained silent.

"When I'm...not here, Aiden needs to be with the only father he's known. That's Trent."

"How long?"

"Do I have?"

Pike managed a trifling nod.

She pursed her lips. "It won't be tomorrow. The life expectancy for someone with MS is five to ten years less than a healthy person. But it's the quality of life. Ironically, many people diagnosed don't actually die from the disease itself."

A trace of hope. "Oh?"

"Suicide. They take their own lives. Too much pain, no dignity. And so they go out on their own terms."

"I know you. You'd never do something that extreme."

"I don't know how much I'll be able to take."

"Oh, c'mon, that's crazy talk."

She looked away.

"Aiden doesn't know?"

"No."

Pike squinted then dropped to his knees again. "Marry me, Paige."

"Pike—"

"I'd rather live a short time *with* you than the rest of my life *without* you."

"I love you, Pike—"

"And I love you."

"—and that's why I don't want you to see me that way."

"I'll make that decision, thank you very much."

"No, it's *my* decision. Allow me my dignity. Let me go. Remember me the way I was. Remember me being young and healthy and pretty. Do that for me, Pike. That way the illness doesn't win. Keep me in your memory and I can live forever." Paige walked over, placed her fingertips under his trembling chin, and angled his face so their eyes would meet. "In some odd way, it's like we can be together forever if you hold me in your heart."

CHAPTER 36

Since his first breath, he sensed the icy grip of death clawing at his back.

A fraternal brother born minutes after him didn't see one sunrise. Parents. Grandparents. LaMarcus King. Maybe or maybe not Freddy Marquez. And soon, Paige Rhodes.

No wonder he battled thanatophobia.

After Paige walked out of his life, Pike rested his forehead against the back of the motel room door, fingernails clawing at whittled paint. "Come back," he beseeched of the tomblike hush. Legs turning to rubber, he slithered to the floor, curled like a frightened child, sobbing, and drawing blood from his own lips.

It was at this moment Pike learned a hard truth. All these years combatting thanatophobia and fearing the inevitability of death. And now he realized, for the first time, living could be as bad as dying. Maybe worse.

His heart pumped, his lungs inflated and deflated, his brain functioned. But for all intents and purposes Pike Graves was dead on the inside. Where it counted the most.

To punish himself for taking the life of LaMarcus King, he became a sparring partner. Challengers on their way up, dreaming of a title shot and a big payday, perfected their craft and honed their skills at the expense of Pike's physical and emotional well-being. He got injured, he got beaten, he got knocked down. But he always got back up to endure more abuse.

That pain, that hurt, that aching, paled in comparison to how he felt now. The most painful blows in life aren't the physical ones.

As if guided by an unseen entity, he found the grit to stand and slogged to the bathroom. Splashing frigid water on his face, he refused to acknowledge the broken-down conquered reflection staring back.

Well-organized Pike Graves reviled gray areas. He preferred black and white, no in-between. But since leaving Philly he realized life was nothing but one big gray area.

Sam Graves wasn't a verbally abusive workaholic father. Instead he simply could not bear the despair of an unfaithful wife. Cora Graves, his sainted mother, had sinned. His sister Stephanie was not a rape victim but rather someone who, like Pike, elected to punish herself and reached out to Erik Casella. Virgil Holland, the man he spent his life abhorring, had never laid a hand on Stephanie. He did, however, lay hands on Pike. Roxy was not the victim of an abusive relationship but rather an underage girl who wanted to have fun at Pike's expense. And now Paige. The one he revered, the anchor in his turbulent life, the one he assumed somehow, someway, he'd grow old with, was dying.

Nothing was what Pike believed, nothing was black and white. His entire existence shrouded in gray fog.

I gotta get the hell outta here.

Heaving his suitcases, Pike checked the room one last time. He paused spotting the empty black felt box on the table. Pike didn't need it. Didn't want it. It only served as another heartbreaking reminder. He crossed the room, foolishly lifted the box. It was empty but at one time it contained a reason to live, a reason to keep going.

His eyes intuitively gazed through the window.

His heart fluttered.

Through the murky fog, fourteen floors below, she was motionless in the steely vaporous streetlight. Standing there, pondering a profound life-altering decision. "Paige?"

The distance, combined with the gray mist, made it hard to see. But she appeared to be crying.

"Paige?" Pike's moist palms pressed against the windowpane.

She took one step forward then another. And another. Her Chevy Volt ten feet away. Then stopped.

Like at the airport eight years ago, she looked back.

She looked back.

"Paige!" He banged his hands against the glass.

She was counting floors, searching for his room.

"Paige!" He laughed at the absurdity. The walls were paper thin but the windows were like Fort Knox.

Their eyes found each other through the haze. She smiled.

She smiled.

Pike excitedly threw up a finger, yelled "One minute," even though she couldn't hear. He raced across the room, stumbled over his suitcases, jerked open the door, and dashed down the hallway.

His soul teeming with happiness, elation and unmatched joy gushing through his bloodstream. Pike never grasped the concept of tears of happiness until now. Thirty yards ahead, the elevator arrived and a hotel guest stepped in.

"Hold it!" he called out, relieved he wouldn't be racing down fourteen flights. "Thanks," he panted when entering.

"You're welcome."

He blinked, blinked again. Unsure what to think. What the hell was going on? Was it really him? Was he even real? "You?"

Jordan Moses asked, "Going down?"

"Why…why are you here?"

Jordan, as always, exhibited a flair for the dramatic. He rocked on his feet and watched the display.

Fourteen.

Twelve.

Eleven.

Pike grabbed him by the shirt collar—the same shirt he wore when Pike picked him up in Vegas—and slammed him against the wall. "I asked you a question. What are you doing here?"

Unfazed by the outburst, Jordan replied calmly. "I told you. I can't keep saving your sorry ass."

Pike's brows furrowed. "What do you mean?"

"I can't always be here for you."

"Be here for me?" Pike clipped. "I don't even know if you're real."

"What do *you* think?"

"I…don't know. Is this about Paige? Are you here for Paige?" His chin grew taut. He frowned noticing blood on Jordan's hands.

"Paige Rhodes isn't my concern."

"What the hell does *that* mean?"

"She's on her own."

Pike tightened his grip on Jordan's collar. "What the *fuck* are you saying? Is she in danger?"

"I have enough on my plate saving you all the time."

Ping.

They reached the ground floor. Pike peered across the lobby at the motel's entrance. Paige just beyond. He gave Jordan the evil eye. "You wait right here. Don't move."

Jordan snorted. Pike didn't have time. He took off running.

He'd only covered a few steps when out of nowhere someone grabbed his arm. "Are you okay?"

He stopped, shooting an impatient glance at the door, trying to free himself from the woman's hold.

"Are you okay?" Vinyl asked again.

"Why wouldn't I be?" He cocked his head.

"Did you hear anything?"

"Hear anything?" Pike repeated, pulling her across the lobby as she clung to his arm.

"The cops are on their way. They're probably gonna ask you some questions."

Pike froze. "Cops?"

She nodded.

"*Me*? Why?"

Frazzled, Vinyl spoke hastily. "I was sitting right there at the front desk." She pointed. "Working on this." She held up her latest creation. Under the portrait of President Jimmy Carter were the words, *you'd have to be (pea) nuts to stay anywhere else.* "I didn't hear a thing. But when I looked up, I saw a white straw hat on the counter. I don't know how it got there. It just…appeared."

White straw hat. Pike looked at the elevator. Unoccupied. No Jordan Moses. "Go on," he implored Vinyl.

"There was a note next to the hat. It said fourteen-oh-four. That's the room next to yours."

"Right."

"So I went up and knocked but the door wasn't locked. I went in." The blood drained from her face. "It was awful."

"What was?"

She hugged herself and almost dry-heaved at the vivid recollection.

"What did you see?" Pike asked, looking around in vain for Jordan.

"The guest's body was in the bathtub but…his head? His head was in the sink." She was ashen. "Like his head had been ripped right off his neck. Who could do that? It would require like, supernatural strength or something."

Jordan.

"You didn't hear anything, Pike?"

"No, I was…I had a guest. She's waiting for me. I need to go."

"You were next door. The cops will want your statement."

"That's fine. I'll be right outside." He eased himself free and took one quick step forward when Vinyl murmured, "Poor Mr. Dragovich."

Pike stopped dead in his tracks. "What'd you say?"

"The guy in fourteen-oh-four. Mr. Dragovich."

He gulped. "Bobby Dragovich?"

"You know him?"

"Here? What's he doing out here?"

"How do you know him?"

"Did he have a tattoo on his hand? A dragon tattoo?"

"Yeah, though it looked more like an iguana." Vinyl moved closer. "That dude was bad news."

Pike's mind was on overdrive.

"Crazy, huh?"

He'd put the pieces together later. Paige was waiting. "I need to go." Taking off, he threw his shoulder against the door and darted outside where he was promptly enveloped in gloomy miasma. The fog was heavy tonight. Sprinting to the lot on the motel's south side, his heart bursting with pride. The smile on his face would remain there forever. For once, everything in his life would turn out all right. *And Dewayne told me happy endings are Hollywood bullshit. Ha!*

Paige, forty yards away, waved.

Even through the vapor, her infectious eyes warmed his spirit. He could read it on her face. *I don't know why I'm doing this but I'm doing it.* "I love you, Pike," she cried through the mist.

"I love—"

"Don't move, motherfucker!" The man surged forward from Pike's periphery. "I told you I'd come back."

The deranged knife-wielding vagrant from two days ago traded up for a handgun. A handgun that was now pointed between Pike's eyes. His bald head glistened with sweat, eyes were glossy, distant and soulless. His body twitched. Whatever this guy was on was potent. No awareness of what he was doing.

"Take it easy, buddy."

"I'm not your fuckin' buddy."

Paige, twenty yards behind, was a terrified girl again just like she'd been at Grizzly's when Pike saved her life. Now the tables were turned. She may need to save him. He stammered, "P—put - put the gun down. No one has to get hurt."

"No one has to get hurt? No one has to get hurt? I've got the gun, motherfucker. It ain't gonna be me gettin' hurt."

"You want money, fine. You want my wallet, it's yours."

"You know what I want."

Paige, confused and helpless, was trying to tell Pike something without speaking. Communicating nonverbally.

But he couldn't get a read on it because he was unfamiliar with her mannerisms, her gestures, her facial expressions. He didn't know her that well.

"Hand it over."

"Fine, take it." Pike reached into his back pocket.

The butt of the handgun slamming his head jarred his teeth. "Not your wallet, asshole."

Starbursts exploded in his eyes like fireworks. Fireworks. July Fourth, the day he decided to leave Cynthia. "Then what?"

"That box, that fuckin' box."

"Okay, okay, just relax."

A second powerful blow, this one against his ear, rattled Pike's brain.

"I'll relax when you hand me that ring box."

"All right." Pike raised one hand in supplication, reached into his pocket with the other.

Nothing.

It was upstairs. In the room. Left behind on the table when he'd barged out to meet Paige downstairs.

"Where's the fucking ring!?" The homeless man was losing control.

"There's no ring," Pike said. *How ironic. An altercation taking place over an empty goddamn ring box.*

"You expect me to believe that?"

Pike had been a piece of meat for professional boxers. Pugilism was an art form, a ballet of sorts. It was choreography and formulaic. But this was different. This guy was irrational and unrestrained. And unlike any adversary he'd ever opposed.

Pike was weighing his limited options when the decision was made for him.

Paige, still unseen by the mugger, removed her cell, probably to call the cops. Silly, really. Blood would be spilled long before they arrived. Petrified, shaking. And as a result, the phone slipped through her trembling fingers and crashed to the pavement.

Alarmed, the vagrant spun and carelessly squeezed off a round.

She screamed.

Pike dived forward, wrapped his arms around the guy's waist, and attempted to bring him down.

The vagrant fell to a knee but drove his elbow into Pike's gut. Again and again, with herculean strength brought on by whatever substance coursed through his blood. He wiggled free from Pike's bear hug, emitted a guttural wail, and drove a steel-toed boot into the side of Pike's head.

The impact sent Pike toppling against the side of a sedan. The car's alarm stabbed the night.

The vagrant was on him again, releasing a bone-breaking kick into Pike's side. Pike knew a rib, possibly several, had been broken.

"Stop!" Paige scurried closer holding something. *Mace*?

The thug recklessly released two rounds over his shoulder.

Pike heard a cry followed by a body falling to the pavement. "Paige!" His frantic cries sliced through the fog.

He started running toward where she'd been standing but got clotheslined and went down.

Sirens drew nearer. Cops responding to the corpse in 1404. Bobby Dragovich, courtesy of Jordan Moses. '*I can't keep saving your sorry ass.*'

"Hurry, please," Pike gurgled in desperation.

"Come out come out wherever you are," the vagrant cackled and shuffled his feet to the location Paige was last seen.

Pike had been knocked onto his ass plenty, both in the ring and in life. He had cracked ribs, couldn't get air into his lungs, tasted blood in his mouth. He came too far and suffered too damn much. "I won't lose you, Paige. Not again. Not ever." He put a level palm on the saturated asphalt for support. His elbow buckled.

"Want some candy, little girl?" Chortling, the vagrant sauntered purposefully, peering up and down rows of parked cars.

"Not gonna lose you," Pike vowed.

On his knees.

On his feet.

Standing up.

The attacker reached the row where Paige went down. She wasn't there.

Instead, she double backed, sprang up from behind a dumpster on the attacker's right side, and sprayed the mace.

The guy shrieked and erratically squeezed off more salvoes, peppering the area with a torrent of bullets. Windows shattered. More car alarms perforated the darkness. Smoke billowed from an engine. A punctured tire hissed like a cobra.

Pike rushed at the disturbed man.

Hearing rapidly approaching footfalls, he spun. His eyes, as result of the mace, discharged a gooey substance. Deprived of sight made him more desperate, more frantic and therefore, more dangerous.

Pike, like he'd done at Grizzly's thirty years ago, transformed himself into a human battering ram. Tucking his head into his shoulders, he crouched and charged at the man's gut. Bullets whizzed inches above his head. Both men fell to the ground. The gun remained clutched in the thief's hand.

"I want that fucking ring!"

Pike locked his hands around the guy's wrist and, amped up on adrenaline, smashed the wrist against the cement, trying to dislodge the weapon. Again and again. "Drop the weapon!"

But the guy wasn't weakening.

Pike started unpeeling the guy's grimy fingers from the hand-cannon.

"Give me that box!"

"I'll break your fucking arm."

The knee to Pike's scrotum caused him to see stars. He was knocked aside. Paige frantically bounced in place five feet away. Mace at the ready but she couldn't get an unimpeded shot.

They tussled on the dew-covered cement. Piercing sirens cutting through the night. Two blocks away, maybe less.

Two warriors battling for possession of the firearm, fingers vying for control, tormented screams, throaty cries as two men fought to stay alive.

"Pike!" Paige howled, her voice chockful of fear.

"Let go!"

"That's my gun, motherfucker!"

Hands intertwined, bodies brawling, two combatants engaging.

A spark of fire emitted from the barrel. A bullet discharged.

Everything went quiet.

CHAPTER 37

James Hilton's timeless classic, *Lost Horizon*, published in 1933, introduced the world to Shangri-La, an enchanted, magical place set in China's Kunlun Mountains. Over the past century, the fictitious locale became synonymous with paradise. Utopia. A flawless nirvana where all people lived harmoniously.

Heaven on earth.

Pike proceeded along Shangri-La Way, pulled curbside, killed the engine, and ruminated. Unlike the street's namesake, his life was Hell on earth.

The dazzling sun was high and bright. Clouds absent against an azure backdrop that pushed to the ends of the world. A calm breeze wafted from the Pacific. It was, well, utopian. But Pike knew, tonight fog would return. It always did.

Three days had passed. Pike knew this only because the date on his watch changed. For him, time stopped. He was caged in an everlasting existence he'd never move forward from. He hadn't slept, eaten, or shaved. He didn't care anymore.

The paramedic treating him after the confrontation, whose face Pike hadn't bothered noticing, insisted he be kept overnight for observation, stating prophetically, "You're not all right."

Pike laughed at the candor in that simple observation. He definitely wasn't all right.

While recovering in the hospital, he was interrogated by a detective with a bad toupee and overpowering halitosis. The investigator's interest became piqued when learning of Pike's connection to Bobby Dragovich. A fully loaded Glock had been found in Dragovich's room.

"Do you think he meant to harm you, Mr. Graves?"

Pike shrugged.

"When did you last have contact with Mr. Dragovich?"

"The day before I left home."

"Had he made any kind of threat?"

"No."

"Have you ever feared for your life?"

Pike smirked. *Thanatophobia.* "Every day."

"You claim you were in your room at the time of Mr. Drago-vich's murder?"

"Yes."

"Can anyone corroborate that?"

"Paige Rhodes."

"Oh." Defeat in his voice. "Any idea who may have killed Mr. Dragovich?"

Jordan Moses. "None."

"If you're holding out on me, I'll find out. Better to come clean now."

"You'll never find the guy."

"How do you know it was a guy?"

"Can I rest now?"

The cop leaned in so there'd be no misunderstanding. "Trust me, Graves. I'll find the *guy*." He gave Pike a knowing look. "Even if he's right under my nose."

A different investigator, clearly going through the motions, questioned Pike about the assault. Homeless guy in San Francisco? Sure, no problem.

Pike knew the vagrant who attacked him would never be found.

Just like Jordan Moses.

Both men had vanished as if ghosts.

Heavy heart and heavier gait Pike vacuously trekked along Shangri-La. With bloodshot eyes he scanned the property. Several dozen mourners, all dressed in black wearing forlorn expressions, lingered on the front lawn. Pike hovered, an outsider looking in. The distance prevented him from hearing their muffled conversations. No one knew him but they definitely knew of him. He sensed their contempt.

At the lip of the driveway he spotted a makeshift shrine: cards, candles, depictions of Christ, and stuffed koala bears Paige had adored.

He knew he should cry. He wanted to. But he'd run out of tears and became numb to everything. He had nothing left inside.

His heart cold, his soul empty, his spirit crushed. Anaesthetized.

He noticed Aiden.

My son.

Our son.

The seven-year-old was in a little powder-blue suit, probably what he wore to church. He sat cross-legged on the grass, feet away from the memorial to his mom. Close enough to the loving tribute but too timid to move nearer. In the age of unheralded and ever-changing technological advancements, Aiden was abstractedly digging a hole with a stick. A lost little boy.

"What are you doing here?" Trent, black suit jacket, black slacks, black polished shoes and loosened black tie over a white shirt, stomped closer, shoulders squared. "You son of a bitch, what do you want?" He bellicosely yanked Aiden to his feet, nearly wrenching the kid's arm from his socket. "Go inside, Aiden."

"But, Daddy—"

Daddy.

"Go inside!" Trent growled.

Pike didn't like the way he manhandled the boy, *his* boy. But he had no right to say anything.

Don't be a hero, Pike Graves.

The mourners watched the scene unfold. Husband's shielded their wives, others filming with their phones.

"Call the cops," Trent yelled to the gathering.

"I'm not looking for trouble," Pike heard himself say.

Trent was five feet away, nostrils flaring. "There's an irony if I ever heard one. You're nothing *but* trouble."

Pike detected alcohol on his breath.

"Why are you here?"

Why am I where? In Shangri-La or in this life? The answer was the same for both. "I don't know."

"You murdered Paige."

Pike knew the unbalanced vagrant squeezed the trigger. Or maybe not. They were both struggling for control of the weapon. A round discharged, ricocheted off a car, and tore through Paige's skull. The fact it was quick, that she didn't suffer, that she didn't realize what happened, was no consolation. "I know," he agreed.

"Look at you." Trent flicked Pike's generic T-shirt that hadn't been changed in three days. "Pathetic."

Too stricken to meet his gaze, Pike hung his head.

Trent stepped closer. "I should be on my honeymoon now. But instead of laying on a beach in Maui, I buried my fiancée. Instead of starting our lives together, I watched her casket lowered into the ground." He spit in Pike's face.

Pike didn't wipe it away. He deserved it. And much more. "Sorry."

"What?"

"I'm sorry."

"For what exactly? Sorry for killing my wife, for destroying my future, for fucking up my life, for having the kid grow up without his mother? Sorry for what? Sorry for being born?"

Biting his lip, Pike drew his own blood. "Yes. All of it."

The blow to his face knocked Pike onto his ass. Trent danced over him, a victorious boxer knocking down his opponent. He ripped off his suit jacket. "Get up."

Pike acquiesced, rose to his feet.

The next blow shattered his nose. Cartilage snapped like a twig. Pike buckled, splayed across the ground like a beaten animal. He slid his hand across his lip. More blood. His eyes watered from his broken nose. From everything.

"Get up!"

Pike nodded, struggled to his feet again. He wasn't fully standing before Trent pummeled him with a powerful jab to his belly, causing Pike to double over. The uppercut to his jaw sent him airborne.

"Get the fuck up!" But Trent didn't wait. He pulled Pike's limp body to an upright position, and coldcocked him in the side of the head. He tilted left but a powerful jab flung him the opposite way.

Face down on the ground.

He was a sparring partner again, taking the hits, punishing himself for what he had done.

A violent kick to his bandaged ribs had Pike rolling right. A kick on the opposite side sent him rolling the other way. Three broken ribs from the vagrant, another three or four from Trent.

"Get up, you worthless piece of shit."

On his knees, Pike shook off the pain, the unclear vision. He emitted a clump of blood containing two teeth. He stood, tottered, gained his bearings. He met Trent's incensed glare and opened his palms. Begging? Surrendering? Sacrificing himself?

"Put your hands up! Defend yourself."

Pike shook his head.

"I said put your hands up. Be a man. Defend yourself, god-dammit!"

Like a blistering combination of rights and lefts, faces shot across his mind. His mom. His dad. Stephanie. Virgil. Roxy. La-Marcus King Freddy Marquez. Paige Rhodes.

Paige.

"Fight. Put your fucking hands up!"

"I've got no fight left in me, Trent."

The homeless guy who beat Pike to a pulp was hopped up on an illegal substance resulting in superhuman strength. Trent was hopped up on something more potent than any narcotic. Anger, hatred, revenge. And the age old desire for blood.

Fists flew. His face, his head, his gut, his kidneys, Blood spewed from Pike's mouth and his left ear. He wasn't shielding himself. He wasn't even trying. Choked in a headlock, subjected to an endless barrage of fierce bone-crushing blows. His retina detached.

The physical pain was nothing compared to emotional pain.

Trent whirled him around like a human discus and propelled him headfirst through the window of a parked vehicle. The car alarm activated.

Pike heard it in only one ear as he dissolved to a knee. Trent drew his leg back and launched a barrage of powerful kicks into Pike's ribcage.

Pike, gasping, unable to breathe and lying in a pool of his own blood, peered up at Trent with his one good eye. "Kill me."

Infuriated beyond reason, Trent heaved him up, placed a beefy hand around Pike's neck, and began tightening like a vise.

"Kill me. Please," Pike crowed.

Trent released a thunderous uppercut that pitched Pike across the hood of a car, his head cracking the windshield the same way Freddy Marquez had.

A shrill siren wailed in the distance. "Kill me," Pike begged. "Before the cops get here. Tell 'em I deserved it."

Trent dragged Pike off the hood and propped him against the side of the car evaluating his next move.

The siren louder.

"Before they come."

"No." Trent, drained from exertion, clipped through gritted teeth. "You live with the pain like I'll have to."

"Daddy!"

Both men turned simultaneously.

Does he know? Pike wondered. *Does Aiden know I'm his father?*

"*Daddy!*"

Aiden's face flushed. His all-out bawling so deep, he was hyperventilating. He jumped off the curb and ran to his father.

Pike?

Trent?

Trent became stock still, shooting glances between the boy and his fiancé's ex, and for the first time considered the possibility that Pike was Aiden's dad. His back was to the street, unmindful of a police cruiser barreling around a blind curve and speeding closer.

The young boy darted from between two parked cars. And froze. The police cruiser hurtling like a rocket down the peaceful street. Chaos had come to Shangri-La.

Trent shouted "No!"

Mourners across the street screamed.

With no concern for his own safety and with agility belying his battered debilitated state, Pike ran forward.

The police car braked. But not soon enough.

Pike extended his arm, reached for Aiden, and, with what little strength he had remaining, shoved his son out of the way. He saw Aiden somersault safely onto the sidewalk.

A devastating, blistering impact took Pike's legs out from under him. The sky was below him. The ground above him. He pinwheeled through the air. End over end. Headfirst on top of the cruiser. His neck snapped. He rolled off the back and dropped to the street. His skull crashed against the asphalt with a thud reminiscent of LaMarcus King at Grizzly's.

☙❧

Pike stared into a peaceful cerulean sky. Into his sightline, Trent's face appeared. His ire replaced by worry. His eyes exhibiting fear, not venomous hatred. Filling the other half of Pike's vision was someone he didn't know.

Trent stuttered. "Off—Officer I'm—it was an accident."

"Give him room to breathe," the cop roared, shouldering Trent aside.

"I'm okay," Pike claimed.

"Officer, I swear, I just got…carried away."

"I said get back!" the cop demanded.

"I'm okay," Pike repeated.

"Paramedics are seven minutes out," claimed the cop's partner a few feet away.

The cop beheld Pike then shook his head. "Tell 'em never mind."

Pike frowned. Despite the thrashing, he saw clearly through both eyes.

And oddly, felt no pain.

Beyond the cop's shoulder, Pike saw an angelic face gradually reveal itself and come into focus, slowly taking form as if emerging through fog. A welcoming yet sad smile.

"Paige?" Eyes glued to her, he sat up.

But the cop hadn't moved. He still had his head down, seemingly unaware that Pike sat up. "Gutierrez," the cop called to his partner. "Grab that blanket outta the trunk and get this guy covered up."

Sitting up, Pike looked back and saw himself on the street. Not moving. Inert. Eyes fixated on nothing.

Turning back around, his brows wrinkled.

Paige nodded once, unveiling her pure, wholesome smile and extending her arm. *It's time.*

Pike understood.

The emerald trees were joyfully cheerful and vibrant. The immaculate lawns sparkled. A sky so blue and beautiful it seemed too faultless, too perfect. Everything dazzling, colorful. And alive.

Utopian.

In Paige's eyes, he could see forever. He felt her take his hand. It wasn't physical but rather a sensation, an awareness.

He looked at her, into her soul. And he understood.

She guided him forward, his steps effortless and light, but he couldn't draw his eyes away from her. Her face hung but the corners of her mouth turned up in a small smile.

Something inside Pike persuaded him to look forward. On the

sidewalk, there but not really there, an unearthly spectral vision.

The man was exactly how Pike remembered him. *I'm sorry, Dad.*

Sam Graves smiled. *It's okay, son.*

I was so hard on you all those years. I was so unfair to you.

I know.

All those stupid arguments. All those ridiculous fights.

That doesn't matter anymore.

All the things I've wanted to ask you. All the times I wished we could talk again. Just for five minutes. All the things I wished I could have said.

Now we have the time.

Pike's eyes shifted to Sam's right. He apologized silently.

I wasn't perfect, Cora Graves inferred. *Far from it.*

Neither was I, Mom. I'm sorry for not being a better son.

You tried, Pike. You tried. That's all any of us can do.

Pike shook his head sadly, looking back and forth between his parents. *All those times I avoided answering the phone when I knew it was you calling. All the times I made some excuse not to see you, thinking I had something more important to do. I always thought there'd be more time.*

We all think that, Cora said wordlessly.

Recalling the LaMarcus King trial that played a part in destroying his family, he insinuated, *All the heartache I caused. And the embarrassment.*

Sam Graves may be a spirit, but he still had the same commanding presence. *I won't stand for that kind of talk from you. Stop that right now. That's no longer necessary. Guilt has no place here.*

But—

But nothing. You gave your own life to save your son. To save Aiden. You've made us proud.

Cora added, *We're glad you're our child.*

And I'm lucky to have you as my parents.

Pike was so absorbed and transfixed in the exchange, he was oblivious to the silhouetted form loitering behind his parents. The entity floated forward.

Pike blinked. *Jordan?*

Jordan Moses nodded.

As Jordan drifted closer, everything made sense. Jordan Moses wasn't his real name. He had no name, never had been given one because he hadn't lived to see one sunrise.

Pike shook hands with the fraternal brother he never knew, the fraternal brother who died minutes after he was born.

I told you I can't always save your ass.

I know.

I didn't need to this time. You wanted to die.

Pike nodded. *I know.*

"Dammit, Gutierrez, where's the blanket?"

Pike smiled at Paige.

She reciprocated. *We'll be together. Forever. For all eternity.* She gracefully turned around, her smile dipping seeing her son.

As if perceiving something, Aiden peeked around Trent and regarded the nothingness across the street. He eagerly pulled on Trent's arm, pointed at the hollowness.

Trent turned, frowned, shook his head, and held the boy against him. "It's your imagination. Mommy's not there."

Paige waved goodbye to her child. *You'll see me again someday. Until then, I'll keep an eye on you. I'll look out for you.*

Pike looked around one final time and took it all in. Despite a life of tears and torment, heartache and heartbreak, regret and remorse, bad decisions and bad judgements, he sure would miss it.

His parents simultaneously offered a helping hand as if Pike was a small boy again. *Let's go.*

Thanatophobia.

Pike was no longer afraid of death.

And like the last wisp of a dying flickering flame, he was gone.

EPILOGUE

L ife sucks!"
Cynthia Grimm lifted herself from the substandard chair she'd picked up at a thrift store and crossed the studio apartment she rented by the week. She weakened, crumbled to a knee, and laughed drunkenly as the beer bottle rolled away. On all fours, she crawled over and fervently drained the last few sips of Sam Adams. Using a lopsided end table for leverage, she righted herself, burped, and tottered to the kitchenette.

Placing the empty bottle beside three others and the Jack Daniels she'd polished off by noon, she opened the fridge. Empty, except for another six pack, string cheese, and a packet of baloney. She pulled one slice from the pack, hungrily downed the sliver of processed meat in two hulking bites, and washed it down with cloudy tap water.

Late September but summer was already a fading memory. The days were growing shorter, the darkness coming earlier. And soon the harsh reality of winter would make its presence known.

The temperature was only in the mid-fifties but Cynthia felt cold. Stumbling to the thermostat, she turned on the heat. Nothing. "Life sucks!"

She slid down the wall, ass on the floor, and chortled grimly at how far she'd fallen and how fast everything fell apart.

When first learning Janice Haas, that senile old coot with the corner office and killer view had retired early, she was like a kid Christmas morning. They had a going-away pot luck for the old fart. Cynthia baked a pie and made sure to give Janice the slice she'd spiked with dog food.

One day.
Two days.
Cynthia heard nothing.
On day three, wearing extra snug jeans and two buttons un-

done on her blouse, she walked into Morty's office. Leaning over his desk and offering a view of cleavage, she reminded her boss how she'd done a bang-up job with the Mayfield account.

Morty thanked her for her dedication before abruptly ending the conversation. "I have to make an important call."

The following day when she was summoned to HR, she bounded down the hall on a natural high with a pep in her step. But her shoulders slouched the instant she walked in.

In the office sat Morty, the head of Human Resources, and *Gayvin*. And two suits from the legal department.

She heard them talking but nothing penetrated the fog clouding her mind. *Gayvin* had filed a sexual harassment suit, claiming Cynthia mocked his homosexuality. She attempted to downplay it, arguing he misunderstood. It was a slip-up. Hell, she was a lesbian. She offered to attend that sensitivity training horseshit employees are forced to sit through.

Cynthia was terminated with no severance package. Salt in the wound was that *Gayvin,* the little fruit, ended up with her job and Janice's corner office with the killer view.

Three days after losing her job, she lost Alex. Her lesbian lover announced the lifestyle wasn't for her. She'd always been curious, decided to try it for a while, but, nah, it wasn't her thing. She moved back in with her ex-boyfriend.

"So…you used me?" Cynthia screamed in her face.

Alex shrugged. "Yeah, I guess so. Well, see ya around."

Wynter discovered she got knocked up by Brock. Cynthia wasn't upset that her sixteen-year-old daughter was boinking her thirtysomething married boss, didn't care that her reckless kid had been stupid enough not to use protection, and didn't even care that Wynter decided to abort the bastard child. What truly chapped her ass was her daughter's decision to use this as a wake-up call. Wynter moved to New York and enrolled in some lame fashion design school.

"Why not stay here? With me? We can hang out and get drunk together."

Wynter gave the same eye roll her mom perfected. "Uh, *no*. I want to make something of myself. Duh!"

Life sucks.

Anticipating a big payday, she'd overextended herself by pawning off all of Pike's shit and refurnishing the home they had shared. Her custom-made, specially ordered F-350 arrived. Then it was repo'd when Cynthia couldn't make the first payment. Dragon screwed up everything. She not only lost out on the financial bonanza she deserved but lost the furniture, the car, and now her credit score was back in the shitter.

Fuckin' Dragon! How hard could it have been? People were killed all the time. Yet, he couldn't even do that right. What a loser. She didn't care that his murder remained unsolved. Fuck him. Let him rot in that Potters Field way out in California. The asshole.

No furniture, no car, no job, no Alex, no Wynter, no Dragon. And now no heat. She polished off her fifth beer in three hours. Everything that was so good had turned to hell in two months. It was as if invisible forces were plotting against her. Like Pike used to say, "punching at fog."

It took three attempts but finally she managed to get to her feet. She'd take a piss—hopefully the toilet would flush this time—and then see if the guy a few doors down would give her forty again for another blow job. The knock at the door hindered her plan.

She traversed the frayed sullied carpet and looked through the peephole but saw no one. "Who the hell's there?"

"Cynthia, it's Dewayne."

It took a moment. Oh, yeah, Pike's friend she'd always found hot. The black dude with a white wife. Why was he here? She'd never been with a black guy so she patted down her wrinkled, food-stained shirt, combed her hair with her fingers, and opened the door. "Hey."

Dewayne said, "This is Detective Dina Locatelli. Can we come in?"

Cynthia sized them up. Locatelli was on the young side but cute. A threesome with a black dude *and* a white chick would be kinky. "Sure." She stepped back.

"How've you been, Cynthia?"

"Livin' the dream." She smiled. "This is just temporary. I'll be back on my feet soon."

Dewayne nodded.

"Would you like anything?" she asked suggestively, sticking out her tits.

Dewayne looked away. Despite his best efforts, he'd never

bonded with Cynthia, always found her promiscuous and never grasped the connection Pike had for her. He suppressed the urge to gloat at what she'd become.

She looked pitiful, like a used-up prostitute well beyond her prime but still believing she possessed a high level of sexuality. Her limited possessions and barren existence was cause to smile.

"Nah, I'm good."

Cynthia faced Locatelli. "How 'bout you? See anything *you* like?" She winked.

Dina Locatelli stepped back to avoid the fog of alcohol surrounding Cynthia.

Cynthia turned back to Dewayne. "So what's crack-a-lackin?"

"Missed you at the funeral."

"Funeral?" Cynthia contorted her face. "Oh, yeah, right. Pike's."

"Thought you'd be there."

"I was busy that day."

"Mm hmm. Been to his grave yet?"

Cynthia guffawed. "No."

"He did love you."

The patented eye roll. "Whatever."

"I've been talking with a Detective Farnsworth in Mill Valley."

"Okay."

Dewayne gave her a sideways glance, paused dramatically. He'd played out this scenario countless times in his mind, trying to come up with something poignant and clever. Instead, he simply blurted out, "Bobby Dragovich had recording capability on his phone."

"So?"

"All your conversations were recorded. All your texts were saved."

Even through her inebriation, Cynthia knew this wasn't good. She failed at sounding disinterested. "Good for him."

"Conspiracy to commit murder carries a term of anywhere from five to life."

Cynthia's face twisted like she bit into a lemon. "Conspiracy to—you're crazy."

"I'd like you to meet a friend of mine." Keeping his eyes on Cynthia, Dewayne said, "Detective Locatelli, will you kindly introduce this young woman to Miranda."

"You're under arrest for conspiring with one Robert Drago-vich to commit murder. You have the right to remain…"

Cynthia was in a fog. She looked at Dewayne in shock, looked at Locatelli in disbelief. She wouldn't do a threesome with them if they paid her. She saw Dewayne step behind her, felt handcuffs locked around her wrists.

Outside, neighbors peering through drawn curtains, gawked as Cynthia did her perp walk down the stairs, across a courtyard, and toward a waiting police cruiser. Winds had picked up causing the day to grow prematurely sad and dark. Humidity laced the air, an uncharacteristic fog rolled across the Delaware Valley.

"Watch your head," Dewayne said, helping her into the back seat.

Cynthia stepped off the curb, stumbled on a sewer grate, and fell against Dewayne.

He gave her a look.

"I tripped on *that*," she said, looking down at a black felt box in the gutter.

The detectives saw nothing.

In the backseat, Cynthia felt confined. Wrists cuffed behind her back, she had difficulty getting comfortable.

Dewayne positioned himself behind the wheel while Locatelli called in some code.

It was surreal. Cynthia had never been in a police car before, much less arrested. It was cleaner than she expected. She looked through the rear window, giving a departing glance at where she'd been holed up for the last six weeks.

And frowned.

Forehead to the window, she wondered if it was the alcohol. Perhaps everything was weighing her down and causing hallucinations. Losing her health insurance forced her to go without her Prozac. There had to be some reason for the vision.

She could swear Pike was standing at the entrance to her apartment. He appeared to be smiling at her. Then he leisurely lifted his arm and waved good-bye.

About the Author

From his earliest memories, Rob Silverman had two dreams. One was to play Right Field in the majors, the other was to become a published author. Well, he ended up batting .500.

His first foray into writing came in 2008 when he started blogging for a popular website. An avid reader, he spends his spare time yelling at the TV during the baseball season, listening to Bruce Springsteen and classic rock from the '80s, re-watching all six seasons of *LOST*, or waiting for one of his two spoiled dogs to get out of his favorite chair so he can sit down.

Feel free to check out his website
http://www.robsilvermanbooks.com/

And to follow him on Facebook.
https://www.facebook.com/Rob-Silverman-author-377042895829631/